ACCLAIM FOR JEREMY BATES

"Will remind readers what chattering teeth sound like."
—*Kirkus Reviews*

"Voracious readers of horror will delightfully consume the contents of Bates's World's Scariest Places books."
—*Publishers Weekly*

"Creatively creepy and sure to scare." —*The Japan Times*

"Jeremy Bates writes like a deviant angel I'm glad doesn't live on my shoulder."
—Christian Galacar, author of GILCHRIST

"Thriller fans and readers of Stephen King, Joe Lansdale, and other masters of the art will find much to love."
—*Midwest Book Review*

"An ice-cold thriller full of mystery, suspense, fear."
—David Moody, author of HATER and AUTUMN

"A page-turner in the true sense of the word."
—*HorrorAddicts*

"Will make your skin crawl." —*Scream Magazine*

"Told with an authoritative voice full of heart and insight."
—Richard Thomas, Bram Stoker nominated author

"Grabs and doesn't let go until the end." —*Writer's Digest*

I

BY JEREMY BATES

SUICIDE FOREST

World's Scariest Places 1

Jeremy Bates

ISBN-13: 978-0993764622
ISBN-10: 0993764622

SUICIDE FOREST

PROLOGUE

Suicide Forest is real. The Japanese call it Aokigahara Jukai (Ah-oh-kee-gah-hah-rah Ju-kii), which means "Sea of Trees." Each year local authorities remove from it more than one hundred bodies, most found hanging from tree branches and in various states of decay. Abandoned tents, moldy sleeping bags, dirty daypacks, and miles of ribbon litter the forest floor. It is said the area is haunted by the ghosts of the suicides, and locals often report hearing unexplained screams during the night. Signs warn visitors not to leave the hiking trails. These are routinely ignored by thrill seekers hoping to catch a glimpse of the macabre. Most find their way out again. Some never do.

JAPAN

2004

1

WE took two cars from Tokyo to Yamanashi Prefecture, where Fujisan, better known in the West as Mt. Fuji, is located. The first car was directly in front of ours. It was a Toyota minivan, smaller and boxier than the ones you see back in the States. It belonged to a salary man named Honda. I guess you could make a joke about Honda driving a Toyota, but that was his name: Katsuichi Honda. Also in his car was Neil Rodgers, a fifty-five-year-old English teacher from New Zealand, and a guy named John Scott. I didn't know anything about John Scott except that he was an American soldier stationed in Okinawa, and he knew my girlfriend Melinda Clement because they went to high school together.

Driving our car was Tomo Ishiwara, a twenty-two-year-old university student studying psychiatry, which was a rare major in Japan. Generally speaking, people over here didn't speak about their problems; they drank them away. One of the first expressions I learned fresh off the plane four and a half years ago was *nomehodai*, which basically means all-you-can-drink shōchū, sake, and beer. For some people in over-stressed Tokyo, this was a nightly occurrence, and in many cases it was better therapy than weekly sessions with a shrink.

I sat shotgun. Mel was curled up on the backseat in a fetal position. We went to a bar the night before for a friend's birthday party. She got silly drunk. It wasn't the smartest thing to do on the eve before you climbed a mountain, and I hoped she was going to be okay on the way up. Nevertheless, a potentially more serious concern than her hangover was the weather. When we left Tokyo this morning at ten o'clock, the sky was a dismal felt gray. That was typical, and it hardly meant it was going to rain. But it should have lightened when we got out of the sprawling metropolis. Instead it darkened, the light grays becoming thunderhead grays. In fact, the entire sky had seemed to swell, pressing fatter and lower over the landscape of rice fields and woodlands. For the last two hours I'd been waiting in vain for the clouds to blow away, for a crack to form, filled with blue and sunshine, because I didn't think you could climb Fuji in the rain. The flanks of the mountain were covered in volcanic rubble, which would be slick and treacherous. Your jacket and clothes would get wet, which would freeze when the sun went down and the temperature plummeted. Not to mention at some point you'd be walking *through* the clouds. What if lightning decided to strike? I had no idea what it would be like to be inside a cloud where lightning was birthed, but it didn't sound very safe at all.

Staring out the windshield now, at the iconic Mt. Fuji towering in the distance, I shook my head, an almost imperceptible gesture. I'd planned for everything—everything except the fucking weather.

WE continued west along the Chuo Expressway for another ten minutes before entering Kawaguchiko, a touristy town around the eponymous lake at the base of Mt. Fuji. The town seemed dead, nobody out and about, perhaps because of the foul weather. I thought I heard music and wound down the window. I was right. Playing over loudspeakers lining the street was some nostalgic eight-bit Nintendo music. It reminded me of the cheesy stuff that played when your videogame character enters a new town in *Pokémon* or *Final Fantasy*.

Only in Japan, I mused. And it was true. Japan was a different world for me, completely foreign but seductive, and I rarely went a day without marveling over some aspect of the country's culture or technology.

Mel and I—and Neil, for that matter—all worked together at the same private English teaching company called HTE, aka Happy Time English. It was by far the largest company of this type in Japan, with some four thousand schools across the country. Although it was a notorious teacher-farm, it was a good choice to go with if you'd never been to Japan before because they did everything for you, from sponsoring your visa to getting you a fully furnished apartment. They even gave you an advance on your salary, if you needed it. Most did because the majority of teachers they shipped over were broke college graduates with no savings, and Japan could get pricey.

Mel and I have both been with HTE for close to four years now, though this was likely our last year. Mel had her mind set on heading back to the States when our contracts expired in three months' time. This was the reason I'd organized the trip to Fuji. Living in Japan and not climbing the mountain would be equivalent to living in France and never visiting the Eiffel Tower, or living in Egypt and never exploring the Pyramids.

Honda put on his blinker and turned off the main street.

"Where's Honda going?" I said. Katsuichi Honda preferred to be addressed by his surname, as was common practice among older Japanese.

"Don't know," Tomo replied. "I follow."

We tailed Honda's van through several side streets before ending up at the town's train station, a stucco and half-timbered building with a brown shingled roof, something that would look more at home in the Swiss Alps rather than in rural Japan. The parking lot was as deserted as the rest of the town. Honda pulled up in front of the main entrance. We stopped behind him.

"Why do you think he's stopping here?" I asked.

Tomo shook his head. "Beat me," he said. His English was pretty fluent, but he consistently butchered his articles, prepositions, and plural forms.

I turned in the seat. Mel remained fast asleep.

"Wait with her," I told Tomo. "I'll find out what's going on."

I got out of the car. The air was crisp and smelled of autumn, which was my favorite season. It always evoked childhood memories of trick-or-treating and hoarding candy and making ghosts from tissue paper and cotton, and spiders from fuzzy pipe cleaners.

I stopped at Honda's van, where the others were already out and stretching. Honda wore a red jacket and khaki pants with pleats and cuffs. He had a full head of thick black hair, graying at the temples. His wire-rim eyeglasses sat perkily on the flat bridge of his nose. He worked for a Japanese construction company, and he claimed to have met Donald Trump in Trump Tower during a business trip to New York City. He said Trump's daughter personally escorted his sales team to Trump's office. On first sight, before any introductions were made, the chubby Queens native with the bad hair stood up from his desk and announced, "You guys want a picture with me, right? Come on over here." Stereotyping the flash-happy Asian? Or pure megalomania?

Neil's hedgehog hair was light brown, and he disliked shaving, so his jaw was usually covered in stubble, as it was now. Like Honda, he also wore eyeglasses, though his sported trendy black frames. He's lived in Japan for something like twenty years, teaching English as a second language the entire time. He doesn't open up much, and we've never sat down for a heart-to-heart, but from what I've gathered from coworkers, he came here with his first wife, a fellow Kiwi, to save up for a down-deposit on a house in Wellington. This was back during Japan's "bubble economy" when the yen was ridiculously strong and the New Zealand dollar equally weak. At some point he began to have an affair with a student a dozen years his junior, which would have put her at about twenty-two then. The missus found out, returned to New Zealand, and divorced him, taking all of their savings in the process. He remained here, living from paycheck to paycheck like most overseas teachers regardless of age, and enjoying his life.

I didn't know what to make of John Scott, the army guy. He was several inches shorter than me, standing at about five foot ten, and stockier. Beneath short-cropped hair with a ruler-straight hairline he had an everyman face, cornflower blue eyes, and a strong jaw and nose. Maybe it was his leather jacket I couldn't get past. It was thin, three-quarter length, and more stylish than functional. Who wore a jacket like that while climbing a mountain? Or maybe it was his boorish confidence. When we picked him up out front a Tully's Coffee, and everyone made introductions, he was backslapping and acting as if he'd known us all for months, not minutes.

"Ethos!" John Scott greeted. I could only assume he'd forgotten my name, which is Ethan, or this was some sort of buddy-buddy nickname.

"Why did you pull in here?" I asked Honda.

"It's going to storm," he said, looking up at the sky. I looked up too—a mimicking instinct. Unsurprising, the clouds were as dark and low as they had been when I'd looked up two minutes ago.

"It might blow over," I said, turning to Neil. "What do you think?"

He shook his head. "I wouldn't hold my breath."

"We can wait it out."

"For how long? I thought the plan was to start climbing right away?"

Mt. Fuji was divided into ten stations, with the first station located at the foot of the mountain and the tenth being the summit. Paved roads went as far as the fifth. Our original plan was to drive to Kawaguchiko Fifth Station and begin climbing at approximately 4 p.m. Then, after a three-hour trek, we would stop in one of the mountain huts that dotted the trail to get something to eat and rest before starting off again at midnight, ideally passing through the Shinto gate at the top at around 4 a.m., right before sunrise.

"We could hang around town until ten or so," I said. "Start the climb then."

"One continuous hike through the night?" Neil said.

I nodded.

"What are we going to do all day?" John Scott said. "Sit around and talk?" He made it sound as though talking were a punishment.

"How about Fuji-Q Highland?" Honda suggested.

"The amusement park?" I said.

"I'm not spending the day in an amusement park, thanks," John Scott said.

"What do you recommend?" I asked him.

"I don't know yet. But let's think this through."

"There are many hot springs here," Honda said. "We can go to one, then take lunch afterward."

"Have lunch," I corrected him vacantly. I didn't usually do this outside the classroom, but "take lunch" always irked me, one of those expressions the Japanese favored that just sounded wrong. You teach for long enough, you'll hear some pretty odd stuff. Once I asked an attractive female student what she had for dinner, and she told me a cock. I asked her where she got the cock, to puzzle out the mispronunciation, and she said the machine at the front of the school. It took me a second before I realized she'd meant "Coke."

"Ah, have lunch," Honda said. "I'm sorry. I always forget."

"I don't think hanging around naked with a couple dudes all afternoon is really my thing," John Scott said.

Bluntly stated, but it's what I was thinking too.

"We can head up to the fifth level," Neil said. "Look around."

"And do what?" John Scott persisted. "There's a tourist store where you can buy a hiking stick. That's about it."

"You've climbed Mt. Fuji before?" I said, surprised.

He nodded. "Went with a couple buddies last year."

"Why do it again?"

"Why not?"

I frowned. Climbing Mt. Fuji was hard work. I didn't know anyone who'd done it twice, especially in consecutive years. An old Japanese proverb put it best: "You are wise to climb Fuji once, but a fool to climb it twice."

"We can always cut our losses and head back," John Scott added. "It's Saturday. Tokyo will be hopping."

I looked at him evenly. He didn't know anyone here except Mel, he was a last minute tag-along, and suddenly he was calling the shots for all of us?

The main doors of the train station opened, and a young Mediterranean-looking couple emerged. Their hiking boots and backpacks suggested they were here to climb Mt. Fuji, though I would have guessed that even had they been dressed in tennis whites and runners. Why else did foreigners come out this way? They walked past us, heads down, in conversation with one another.

"Excuse me," I said to get their attention.

They stopped and looked at me, then at the rest of our small group. They were quite attractive, both with dark, wavy hair, dark eyes, and smooth, olive-colored skin. The girl was petite, the guy average height and springy in an athletic way. They couldn't have been any older than me, twenty-five or twenty-six, tops.

"Yes?" the guy said. He was smiling and seemed like a good-natured sort.

"Are you two climbing Mt. Fuji?" I asked.

"That is why we came here. But the woman at the ticket booth told us we cannot climb." He shrugged. "She said wait until tomorrow."

"Did she say the trail's closed, or it's just not recommended to climb?"

"I do not know. Her English was worse than ours, you know."

He found this funny and laughed. Based on his gentle accent and cadence, I guessed he was Israeli. While in Thailand by myself the year before during the Christmas break—Mel had gone back to California to visit her mother—I'd met an Israeli named Moshe on the ferry from Ko Samui to Ko Phangan. He was a chatty, friendly guy, and to save cash we agreed to share a room on top of a restaurant which, judging by the mops and buckets in one corner, might have doubled as the janitor's closet when unoccupied. That same afternoon he invited me to a party to meet his friends, who were already on the island. They were all Israeli, and I quickly became something of a celebrity-oddity. Israelis were notoriously close-knit when traveling together, and an Irish American infiltrating their group was apparently a hoot. I left a couple hours later drunk and stoned and glad to be on my own again.

"I am Benjamin—call me Ben," the Israeli added. "This is Nina."

I introduced myself and everyone else.

"So what are you two going to do now?" John Scott asked them, though it seemed the question was more directed at Nina.

"We are going camping." Ben pointed west. "We were going to climb Fujisan today, then camp in Aokigahara tomorrow. But now we will switch the order. Camp then climb."

"*Honto?*" Honda said, with a rising intonation on the *to*. His eyebrows shot up above the rims of his glasses. He mumbled something more in Japanese, shaking his head.

"You're talking about the suicide forest or whatever it's called?" John Scott said.

I saw Neil nodding.

"Yes, that is right," Ben said. "Every year many people go there to kill themselves."

"Seriously?" I said, surprised I'd never heard of the place before. "Why there? What's special about it?"

"There are many stories about Aokigahara," Honda said. He was frowning, clearly uncomfortable to be talking about the subject. "According to our myths, it was once the site of *ubasute*. Families would abandon their young or elderly there during periods of famine, so there would be less mouths to feed.

Because of this, many Japanese think the forest is now haunted by *yūrei*, or the souls of the dead."

I tried to imagine the psychology behind the decision to doom a loved one to the slow and agonizing death of dehydration, starvation, or exposure. It sounded like the folklore of Hansel and Gretel, only in reverse, with the young abandoning the old. "But what does that have to do with people going there to kill themselves?"

"It has always been a place known for death," Honda said simply, "so it attracts death."

"And there are those books," Ben said.

"What books?" I asked.

"Many years ago there was a bestselling novel about a couple who kill themselves together in Aokigahara. This made the idea very romantic and popular. Then there was another book called *The Complete Manual of Suicide*. It described the forest as beautiful and peaceful and the perfect place to die."

That last bit struck an awkward note with me.

The perfect place to die.

Silence ensued. I looked at Neil, then John Scott. Neil's brow was furrowed, as if he were perturbed by the dark turn the conversation had taken. John Scott, too, seemed preoccupied with his thoughts. Ben said something to Nina in Hebrew. She said something back. She saw me watching them and smiled.

Ben said, "We will take a bus to Aokigahara now." He pointed to a nearby bus stop. There was no bus there yet. "You know, you and your friends should come with us. It will be an adventure, what do you think? We do not mind the company."

I was about to decline when John Scott said, "I'm up for that." He shot a cigarette from a pack of Marlboro Reds that had appeared in his hand. "Beats an amusement park." He lit up and blew the smoke out of his mouth in a long, relaxed stream.

I'd quit smoking a year ago because Mel had wanted me to.

She'd said she was concerned about my health, though I suspected she simply didn't like the smell of the smoke on my clothes and in my hair. Still, to this day, a freshly lit cigarette always unleashed a craving inside me I had to forcibly ignore.

John Scott took another long drag, blowing the smoke around his words while he spoke: "So how about it? We wanted to kill some time? Camping in a haunted forest sounds sick."

Neil was gazing at nothing in the distance, which I interpreted as noncommittal. Honda had started shaking his head again. He was definitely not cool with the idea.

"Neil?" John Scott pressed. "What do you say, big guy?"

Neil wasn't a big guy, and considering he was about twice as old as John Scott, I thought "big guy" sounded disrespectful.

Neil shrugged. "I like camping, and I've heard of the forest. It could be interesting. But it's going to rain. The last thing I want to do is spend the night cold and wet."

"Aokigahara, it is special," Ben said. "The trees, you know, are very dense. The canopy keeps most of the rain out."

I found that hard to believe, but I didn't say anything—because I was warming to the whole camping idea. It was a long weekend, which meant we could still climb Fuji on Sunday and return to Tokyo on Monday without anyone missing work. "We're pretty well prepared to camp," I said tepidly. "Food, tents, warm clothes..."

"Dude, let's do it," John Scott said.

Honda made an X with his arms and bowed apologetically. "I'm sorry, I cannot go, not there. But you go. I think you are crazy. But you go. No problem."

Ben shifted his weight from one foot to the other, as if impatient for us to make up our minds.

"Give me a sec while I run this by my girlfriend," I said.

I climbed in the front seat of Tomo's souped-up Subaru WRX. Mel, I noticed, was still sleeping. I said to Tomo, "What do you know about Suicide Forest?"

"Ah! Is that what you talk so fucking long? Leave me here?"

"You could have come over."

"You say watch Mel."

"What do you know?"

"It's famous for Japanese. Guys go there to suicide."

"So that's true?"

"Crazy, right?"

"What would you think about camping there tonight?"

"Are you fucking kidding, man?" Tomo was a hip guy, and it was hip for young people in Japan to use swear words when speaking English. It showed off their fluency. But some used four-letter words too much. They didn't grow up with them, weren't lectured against their use as children, they were just words. Tomo was one of those guys. "You want camp there?"

"We can't climb Fuji because it's supposed to rain. So we either go back to Tokyo or do something here. Honda doesn't want to camp. But Neil and John Scott are okay with the idea. Those two there"—I pointed to the Israelis—"are going."

"She's so hot."

I think Tomo currently had two or three girls chasing after him. He was handsome, with the shaggy hair popular with Japanese guys, almond eyes, and a sharp nose and cheekbones. He could use a visit to the dentist, however, because his teeth were crooked every which way. But that was only my opinion; *yaeba*, or snaggletooth, was commonplace in Japan and considered attractive. I've even heard of people paying for a dental procedure to get their own fake *yaeba*.

A newsboy cap with a stiff peak sat atop his head while a cashmere scarf was looped around his neck, the tails dangling down over a vintage motorcycle jacket. It was leather, like John Scott's, but somehow it seemed less pretentious.

"Who's hot?" It was Mel. I turned and saw her stirring. She sat up, blinked, and rubbed her eyes, which were a sparkling blue. Her blonde hair was messy and all over the place. She had the same makeup on from the night before. The right side of her face was red, from where it had been pressed against one of her arms.

"Hey," I said, leaning between the seats and kissing her on her cheek.

"Thanks," she said, brightening up. She was always thanking me when I kissed her. You might think she was being sarcastic, or bitchy even, but she didn't have a sarcastic or bitchy bone in her. I believe she simply enjoyed it when I showed affection. I was flattered she felt this way. I've known couples who can't stand each other after six months of steady dating. The fact Mel and I still got along so well was a good sign of our compatibility, I thought.

"Are we here?" she asked.

"Almost," I said. "We're in the town at the bottom of Fuji. There's a bit of a problem."

"Of course there is."

"It's supposed to rain. It doesn't look like we can climb today."

"Good, I can keep sleeping." She flopped back down on the seat and closed her eyes. "Wake me up when we get back to Tokyo."

"Actually, we just met a couple who were supposed to climb Fuji today too. They're going camping in a forest nearby. We're deciding whether we should join them."

She opened one eye and peered up at me, pirate-like. "How far is it?"

"I don't know. Right around here somewhere."

She considered this for a moment. "Okay."

"Really?"

"Why not? We're already here."

"There's a catch."

"What?"

"It's called Aoki—?" I looked at Tomo.

"Aokigahara."

"So?" Mel said.

"It's also called Suicide Forest," I told her, "because Japanese apparently go there to kill themselves."

She frowned.

"I'm sure it's more hype than anything," I added quickly. "A few people have probably killed themselves there over the years, and it's gotten a bad reputation—"

"No, I've heard of it," she said, sitting up again. She pulled her hair back over her shoulders, revealing her slender neck. She slipped an elastic band off her wrist and used it to tie her hair into a ponytail. The pair of emerald studs I'd given her for her birthday back in June glittered in her ears. "My students told me about it. And it's not hype. I think a lot of people kill themselves there every year."

"We don't have to go far in—"

"You don't have to baby me, Ethan. I'm not scared. I'd like to see it for myself."

I nodded, pleased with how easy that had been.

I turned to Tomo. "So how about it, T-man? You up for this?" I waited expectantly for his answer. With Honda out, he had the only car.

"Yeah, okay," he said, flashing those savage chicklets of his. "Let's go see some fucking ghost, right?"

2

BEFORE we left for Aokigahara we visited the restrooms in the train station and bought some extra snacks from a Mini Stop, given that weight was no longer much of a problem. I stopped by the ticket booth to get a map of the area. A uniformed woman greeted me pleasantly. As soon as I mentioned "Aokigahara," however, her eyes narrowed and her cheery smile vanished. She studied me, perhaps trying to piece together my intentions. All she knew was that I was here by myself, asking how to get to a place where people went to kill themselves. I didn't know how to explain I was with my friends, and we just wanted to check the forest out, so I adopted a guileless expression to alleviate any concerns she might have. Apparently it worked, because she gave me the map, though I felt her eyes follow me as I walked away.

Back outside I found everyone already packed into the vehicles. I climbed into the Subaru, then we were on our way.

Tomo cranked the stereo and rapped along with some Japanese-English hip hop band. He knew all of the Japanese, but when it came to the English he would keep the beat by tapping the steering wheel and only belt out the words he could catch such as "nigger" and "fucking hoe" and "my bitch."

When I'd first met Tomo over eight months ago, I'd had him pegged as a sex, music, and party type of guy. But after I spent a day with him and his younger sister, who was autistic, I discovered he had a surprisingly caring and nurturing side as well, though this was something he would never admit and, of course, something I often teased him about.

He changed CDs now, crowed "This nigger is shit, man!" and began rapping to some misogynist song.

Doing my best to ignore him—I was pretty sure he'd meant *the* shit—I opened the map the ticket-booth woman had given me. Mt. Fuji was represented by a triangle. There were railway, bus routes, and expressways, each marked in different colors. The five nearby lakes and other tourist attractions were labeled in both English and Japanese. Off to the side was a magnified inset of the area surrounding Lake Saiko, which was pronounced "Lake Psycho." It showed a number of walking trails that connected certain lava caves that had formed when Fuji last erupted.

Aokigahara, which should have been in the vicinity, was notably absent.

I tossed the map on the gaudily carpeted dashboard and tried to imagine what lay ahead of us. How many people killed themselves in Suicide Forest every year? A dozen? Two dozen? Would we stumble across a skull half buried in leaf litter? A corpse hanging from a tree branch? That last thought gave me pause. Not bones. A corpse. Was I prepared to experience something like that, something so dark?

Abruptly, against my will, I saw my older brother Gary in his shiny beige casket, his hair washed and brushed, his ears and nose stuffed with cotton, his lips waxed over, his eyes glued closed, the makeup on his face thick and caked, the red tie perfectly knotted around his throat.

Blinking away these last images, I shifted uncomfortably in my seat and focused on the trees passing by outside the window.

SOME twenty minutes later Honda's minivan pulled off the highway onto a back road, and we followed. Dense forest crowded us on both sides. Honda turned into a nearly empty parking lot. We parked two spots down from him. I got out and closed the door, which echoed loudly in the stillness. More doors banged closed as everyone else got out.

"So here we are!" Ben announced. His delicate features almost gave him an effeminate appearance. He pulled Nina against him and kissed her on the forehead. Then he hooked an arm around Tomo, who was standing next to him, and kissed him too.

"Hey, man, I'm not gay, right?" Tomo said, pushing himself away.

But Ben's enthusiasm was infectious, causing everyone to smile or chuckle. It was a welcomed diversion from the overcast sky and stark, somber parking lot.

Tomo, blushing, popped the Subaru's trunk. I retrieved Mel's fern-green Osprey backpack, which sat on top of a jack and lug wrench, and helped her shrug into it. I tossed Tomo his bag, looped mine over one shoulder, then shut the trunk lid.

"You're sure you don't want to come, Honda?" I said.

"This forest, it is not for me." His eyes flicked nervously to the trees. "Daytime maybe. But nighttime?" He shook his head.

The seven of us said goodbye to him, shaking or bowing awkwardly—foreigners rarely master the bow—and started toward the sole path that led into the trees. Parked next to it was a late-model Mitsubishi Outlander. The white paint job was patchy with dust or grime. Numerous dead leaves protruded from the groove where the windshield met the hood.

"Does that car look abandoned to any of you?" Mel asked.

"Shit, you're right," John Scott said. He peered through a window. "Hey, check it out."

The rest of us squeezed in for a peek. The backseats were folded down. On them rested a tire pump, a first-aid kit, and a spare bicycle tire. A black sheet covered most of the available cargo space. Beneath it were two humps, one beside the other.

John Scott opened the back door, which unsurprisingly was unlocked. Theft was virtually nonexistent in Japan.

"What are you doing?" I said.

"I want to see what's under the sheet."

"You can't break into his car."

"I think we know he's not coming back."

"Maybe he's camping."

"He'd have to be camping for a hell of a long time. Look at all those leaves."

"I want to see," Ben said.

"Me too," Tomo agreed.

John Scott pulled the sheet clear, revealing a dark blue suit, a pair of black dress shoes, and a rectangular leather briefcase.

We stared at the belongings for a long moment, nobody speaking. The sight was quietly disturbing, and I don't think any of us knew what to make of it.

"Let's go," Mel said, and her voice had changed. It was sharper than before.

John Scott made to close the door.

"Put the sheet back," I said.

"Why?"

"Because he covered that stuff for a reason. That's what he wanted."

"And he might still be coming back," Mel added.

I knew she didn't believe that, no one standing there did, but we didn't say anything to the contrary. John Scott replaced the sheet, closed the door, and we continued toward the path. I glanced back over my shoulder and was surprised to see Honda still standing by his van, watching us. I raised my hand in farewell. He did the same.

Then I followed the others into Suicide Forest.

3

Suicide Forest, or Aokigahara Jukai, was unlike any other forest I had visited before. The variety of evergreen conifers and broadleaf deciduous trees grew too close together, bleeding into one another, confusing your eyes and creating the illusion of impassable vegetation. Their branches formed a tightly weaved canopy overhead, blocking out much of the sunlight so it was darker than it had been only minutes before in the parking lot. And everything inside this shadowed, sepia-toned world seemed twisted and primordial and...wrong. That's the best way I can describe it. Nature gone wrong. The spruce and hemlocks and pine couldn't root deep, because beneath the thin layer of windswept ash and topsoil the forest floor was an uneven layer of solidified magma left behind from when Mt. Fuji last erupted roughly three hundred years before. Instead, many of their roots grew aboveground, a tangle of gnarled, woody tentacles crawling over the protruding bluish-black volcanic rock in a desperate struggle to gain a foothold in life and survive. Consequently, several trees seemed to be a victim of their own success, toppled by their inability to properly anchor their massive weight, so they either leaned at angles, caught in the indifferent embrace of their neighbors, or lay flat on the ground, among all the other crooked branches and rotting deadfall. In fact, it wouldn't have been hard to imagine the forest was sick and dying had it not been for the profusion of bright green leaves and mosses and lichen and liverworts, which painted everything with a much needed coat of color.

"Sort of like Middle Earth, I reckon," Neil said, breaking the silence that had stolen over us. "The Ents. Treebeard."

Eyeing a nearby nest of tree roots, I could almost imagine one of these trees coming to life and walking away.

"An enchanted forest," Mel said. "That's what I think. It's so *green*. Like from a fairytale."

The conversation continued for a bit. It was trite, talk for the sake of talk, noise to fill silence. It petered out quickly. Over the next twenty minutes we passed several rusted, grime-covered signs. Some urged potential suicides to reconsider their actions and think about those who loved them, while others asked hikers to report to the local authorities anyone who was alone or seemed depressed or angry. One warned that camping was not permitted. This gave us pause, but Tomo insisted it was meant only as a suicide deterrent, because many Japanese would come here under the pretext of camping while they worked up the courage to kill themselves.

The farther we went, the more apprehensive I became. The forest was too still, too quiet. In fact, I had yet to hear a single animal. No bird calls, no insects. Nothing. How could a place so lush with vegetation be so devoid of life? And why? Animals certainly wouldn't care that the forest was a suicide hot zone.

Mel, who was walking beside me, took my hand and squeezed it. I squeezed back. I wasn't sure if she was being affectionate or wanted to talk about something.

When she didn't say anything, I assumed she was being affectionate.

"You're in a good mood," I said.

"I feel good."

"You're not hungover?"

"Not anymore. I guess I slept it off."

"You're not weirded out or anything being in this forest?"

"I think it's amazing. I mean, not in a good way. It's just such a special place. It's so different than Tokyo, you know?"

19

I thought about that for a moment and wasn't sure I agreed completely. Tokyo was a forest of glass and steel while Aokigahara was a forest of trees and rocks, but both were graveyards of sorts. Because, if you knew anything of the merciless corporate culture in Japan, the shiny skyscrapers that dominated Tokyo's skyline were really nothing more than impersonal tombstones, the people who worked within them slaves in an endless sojourn to get through to the next day, to reach the "golden years" of retirement. Ironically, many died spiritually long before that. Just ask that poor guy who'd left his suit and briefcase and dress shoes in his car.

I was about to mention this but didn't know how to convey it intelligibly in words. Instead I said, "Yeah, it's a crazy place."

"It's these types of trips I'm going to miss when we leave Japan. We should have done them more. Why didn't we do them more?"

I shrugged. "We're always working."

"Because we've stayed at STD. We could have had way more holidays somewhere else."

She always called HTE that—STD. It was her joke. Something we caught and couldn't get rid of.

"You know," she went on, "my friend Francine got a job with a university. She gets six months off. *Six months*. Half the year. And she still gets paid more than we do."

"We can apply at a university, if you want?"

"It's too late, Ethan. We've been here too long."

I didn't say anything.

She glanced at me, apparently thought I was angry, which I wasn't, not really, and ballet-toed to plant a kiss on my cheek.

"Thanks," I said.

"Don't make fun of me."

"I'm not. I enjoyed it."

Smiling, she said, "I'm going to go talk to John."

I glanced ahead at John Scott, who was telling Tomo some story.

"Okay."

She hurried to catch up. I watched as she squeezed in between John Scott and Tomo. John Scott hooked his arm around her shoulder, said something that made her laugh, then, after what I considered to be an inappropriately long amount of time, withdrew his arm again.

Neil took Mel's spot next to me. He was whistling that popular American Civil War song—the one everyone calls "The Ants Go Marching" nowadays—though I couldn't recall the original title.

I glanced sidelong at him. Neil Rodgers. More affectionately referred to as "Neilbo" or "Mr. Rodgers" or sometimes "That Fucking Kiwi" when spoken about in jest by the people we worked with. A Canadian coworker named Derek Miller went after him the most for being what he called "an oddball serial rapist." That was going overboard, of course, but Neil was admittedly a bit of an oddball. I think Neil would even admit it himself if you asked him. He didn't have tape holding his glasses together or anything like that, but he did have a handful of idiosyncrasies. He only owned one suit, for example, which he wore every day. I knew this because there was a small hole in the seat, next to the left pocket. He kept his cell phone in a pouch attached to his belt, like he was Captain Kirk and it was his phaser. And he would always eat the same thing for each meal. Rice, fermented beans, some nuts, and a salad if he had a day shift. Rice, a piece of chicken, and three or four pork dim sum if he worked evenings. His wife prepared the dishes for him, packing them in a Tupperware container that had his name written on the lid in black marker.

Nevertheless, of the twenty or so full-time teachers at our school, I'd say he was the most popular among the students —at least, he was the most requested for private lessons. We taught everyone from kids to the elderly, either one on one or in small groups. The majority were sleepy salary men forced by their companies to learn English, or bored housewives wanting someone to talk to. After years of delivering the same lessons over and over, I sometimes dreaded certain classes with certain students in which I would be going over past participles for the thousandth time.

Not Neil.

He had a zany, manic energy. He was like that kid's television presenter Mr. Rogers, hence the moniker "Mr. Rodgers." This was why the students liked him so much. They knew he was always giving one hundred percent.

"Do you think this is a good idea?" I asked him now, mostly to shut him up. The nostalgic tune was out of place in the forest, almost creepy.

He blinked at me. "Camping here?"

"Yeah."

"It was your idea."

"It was the Israelis."

"But you and John Scott were keen for it."

"I thought it would be interesting."

"And now?"

My eyes scanned the trees. "It's still interesting."

"You want to back out?"

"It's not like we're the first people who've come here to check it out. They have trails."

"But how many people camp overnight?"

"Who's going to know?"

"Do you think we'll see a body?"

"I don't know." I shrugged. "Maybe."

"Do you want to?"

"I'm not sure. Well, I guess. If we see one, we see one."

As I contemplated how honest I was being with myself, I realized there had been another option to pass the time until the weather cleared up. We could have stayed at a Japanese inn with those tatami-matted floors and screen doors. I was sure Mel and Tomo would have been up for this option. But I didn't know about Neil; he was notoriously cheap and had likely agreed to camp only because it was free.

I glanced ahead again. Mel was still next to John Scott. She was dressed in a violet K2 jacket and jeans. I had on an identical jacket, only mine was black. We didn't buy them to be cute. They had been fifty percent off in some store in Shinjuku, and neither of us had brought warm jackets with us to Japan. That was the thing with teaching overseas: your worldly possessions were limited to what you could pack into a suitcase or two.

Mel kept turning her head to look at John Scott, making me wonder what they were talking about. I caught a couple words, but that was all.

Neil resumed whistling. I asked him, "How's Kaori?"

"She's taking the kid to Disneyland this weekend."

"How old is Ai now?"

"Four."

"She's going to school?"

"She's in kindy." He nodded at Mel and John Scott. "How do they know each other?"

John Scott said something to Mel. She punched him playfully on the shoulder.

"They went to high school together."

"You don't like him, do you?"

It was a good question. Did I like John Scott? I had a bad habit of judging people quickly and sticking by those judgments even when they were proven to be completely wrong. In the case of John Scott, however, I didn't think my initial impression was off. He was a mouthy jock.

"What does it matter?" I shrugged. "I don't know him."

Neil nodded, as if I'd made a salient point, and began to whistle once more. I couldn't be bothered to tell him to stop.

THREE Japanese hikers were coming down the trail toward us. Two men, one woman, all attired in hiking clothes and armed with clear plastic umbrellas.

"*Konichiwa!*" Ben called amicably. "*Konichiwa!*"

His pronunciation was worse than mine. The Japanese returned the greeting, smiling and bowing.

"How is your hike?" Ben asked.

They appeared confused.

"Walk?" I intervened. "Good?"

Several hesitant nods.

"Hey—*sumimasen*?" John Scott said. He struggled express-ing what he wanted to say in Japanese, gave it up, and switched to English. "We're looking for some other trails. Not the main ones. You understand?"

They did not. In fact, they seemed eager to move on.

John Scott held them at bay with: "Yo, whoa, wait, wait, wait." He turned to Tomo. "Translate for me."

"Translate what?"

"What I just said. Secondary trails, off this main one?"

Tomo seemed reluctant.

"Dude," John Scott said. "Just ask."

Tomo asked.

The eldest of the three Japanese—full head of white hair, matching mustache, gold-rimmed glasses—frowned. He shot something back. Tomo replied, holding up his hands, but was promptly cut off. The man began shouting. I saw spittle fly from his mouth. Every time Tomo tried to appease him, he shook his head and his arms and raised his voice louder. I watched, dumbstruck. I've rarely seen Japanese people lose their temper. They had a saying: the nail that stands out gets hammered down—hard. This could mean anything during a typical day. Don't leave work before your coworkers. Don't make business decisions on your own. Don't ever, ever be late.

Don't show your emotions.

So what was going on here? White Hair had totally lost it. Tomo realized the futility of arguing and gave up. I put my hand on his back and led him away. The others followed.

John Scott said, "What the hell's his problem?"

Tomo shook his head. "He says we don't be here."

"Why's he here?"

"He go lava caves, ice caves."

"What's the big deal?"

"He thinks we look body."

White Hair continued to yell at us.

"What's he saying now?" I asked.

"He report us."

"Is it illegal to go off the path?"

"Don't think. He's fucking crazy guy. Who cares?"

"Fuck you, kemo sabe!" John Scott yelled back, flicking the finger.

"Hey," I told him, "cool it."

"What's your problem?"

"You're being a prick."

"Listen to the spaz."

"He has a point," I said. "Maybe we shouldn't be camping out here."

"Don't give me that shit. This is all about us not being Japanese. Being *gaijin*. If we weren't foreigners, he wouldn't have gone off on us like that. They've got to get over their racism."

"You're just feeding into their stereotype of the loud, obnoxious American."

"Yeah? And he's feeding mine. Xenophobic asshole."

"This isn't your country," I said.

"That gives him a right to spaz out?"

"You know 'kemo sabe' isn't Japanese, right?"

"What is it?"

Shaking my head, I walked on in silence.

NOT long after I'd first arrived in Japan I was at a restaurant with a bunch of friends. The deal of the day was all-you-can-drink shōchū, beer, cocktails, and high balls at a self-serve counter for three hundred yen. The catch was you only had thirty minutes to imbibe before you had to pay again. Being unapologetic boozehounds we were good-heartedly smashed within the hour. While taking the train home with my Scottish roommate, I was on my cell phone, speaking loudly to my ex, Shelly, back in the States, who'd just happened to call.

The Scot sat across from me, staring silently at the glass in his hand, which he'd taken, full of rum, from the restaurant so he could keep drinking. I was oblivious to the old man who'd stalked over until he began railing me out in Japanese. I had no idea then how big a faux pas it was to speak on your phone on the train, and I argued back. The Scot stared up bleary eyed, said something, then puked all over himself. To his credit he managed to catch a fair bit of vomit in the stolen glass. The man, red-faced, stormed off the train at the next station.

At the time I thought the guy was being an asshole for not minding his own business. In retrospect, I realized I was being the asshole by not conforming to Japanese societal norms. True, he probably thought of me as a typical *gaijin*, but that's exactly what I was. So was he being racist? I don't think so. Japanese have a complex set of sensitive rules to dictate social situations. They know those rules. Foreigners often don't. Hence foreigners are perceived—and treated—differently. That's simply Japan. You either get used to it, or you go elsewhere.

WE must have walked for another ten minutes before we found what we were looking for. To the left of the main trail a rope was strung horizontally between two trees. A placard hung from the middle of it and read "DO NOT ENTER" in English. Beyond, a narrow, lightly trodden path snaked away deeper into the forest. The spindly saplings lining the margins leaned inward, their branches interlocking overhead like bony fingers, forming a forbidding tunnel.

The uneasiness I'd felt earlier was back, more persistent, and I began second-guessing the wisdom of our camping out here.

Mel was apparently on the same page. She folded her arms across her chest, as if she was suddenly cold, and said, "Don't tell me we're going down there?"

"Yes, of course," Ben said.

"Why don't we camp right here?"

"Here is no adventure."

"I've had a pretty good adventure so far."

"People will see us."

"Who? We've only passed those three hikers."

"We walk down the path," Ben said, "find a good spot to make camp."

"That Japanese guy threatened to report us," Neil said. "What if he does just that and the local police come? I don't fancy getting arrested."

"Arrested? For what?" John Scott said. "Straying off the path?"

"Trespassing. They saw all our camping gear. They can put two and two together."

"This is public land."

"That sign specifically says not to enter."

"There's no threat of punishment."

"What does that bit say there?" Mel said. She pointed to a placard next to the English one. It was smaller, the words written in kanji.

"Don't go in woods," Tomo translated. "You get lost."

"That's all?" I said.

"See?" John Scott said.

I glanced about, searching for other warning signs—and spotted a surveillance camera ten feet away, atop a black metal pole. It was partly hidden behind a tree.

"What the hell's that?" I said, pointing to it.

Everyone looked. There were a few exclamations of surprise.

"Who put that there?" Neil asked. "The police?"

"Must be," Ben said. "But it is no big deal."

"What do you mean?" Mel said. "They could be watching us right now."

"Even if they watch," Tomo said, "they don't care."

"Why not?" I asked.

"They worry the suicide guys. You? Foreigners? They know

you don't suicide, right? They don't care."

"So are we agreed?" Ben said. "We go in?"

I looked at Mel. She shrugged resignedly, and that made up my mind too. Ben, grinning broadly, stepped over the line, then helped Nina. As she stepped over it her shorts rode up her legs. John Scott went next, scissor-style, then Tomo, then Neil, who caught a foot and almost tripped. I lifted the line, and Mel and I ducked beneath.

Leaving the main trail behind, we ventured into the unknown.

4

We walked in silence. The time for chatting and gaiety was over. What had begun as a novel idea, something to pass the time, had become serious business. We might not be technically trespassing, but we were definitely somewhere we were not supposed to be. Aokigahara was a place where people came to die. It was home to the dead, not the living. I think the reality of this was beginning to sink in for all of us as we proceeded down the stick-tunnel, which was both claustrophobic and menacing.

Nevertheless, nobody made any mention of turning back. We were drawn forward, I suppose, by morbid curiosity. It was human nature to want to know what was around the next corner, regardless of what might await you.

My heart was beating faster than normal, my senses heightened, as if I had just downed a large energy drink. My eyes scanned the snarl of forest that bordered us on both sides, though I wasn't sure what I was expecting to find. A dangling noose? A body? A white-faced ghost flitting through the trees toward us? I couldn't hear anything besides the crackle of our footsteps and my excited breathing. I wondered again about the peculiar silence of the forest and said, "Hey, Tomo. Where are all the animals?"

He glanced back over his shoulder. "What you mean?"

"There're no animals. No birds or anything."

"It fucking haunted forest, man. Birds scared shitless. They go other forest."

"What about the wind?" Ben said. "There is no wind either."

"I reckon that's because of the trees," Neil replied. "They grow too thick for any wind to blow through."

"If this trail is off limits, Tomo," Mel said, "then why is it here? Who made it?"

"The police. They use to find body."

"How many do they usually find each year?"

"One hundred. Two hundred."

Mel stopped. "What?"

We all stopped too.

Tomo shrugged. "Sometime more, sometime less."

"I had no idea the number was so large." Mel had blanched. "I figured—I don't know—like a handful of people every year."

That was closer to the dozen or two I'd estimated the number to be.

"Japan has the highest suicide rate in the developed world," Neil said matter of factly.

"Are we really going to see a body?" Mel asked.

"It's a big forest," I told her noncommittally.

"And probably if you do," Ben said, "it will only be an old skeleton or something."

"Much better," she said.

"Do you want to go back?" I asked her.

She looked at me. "Do you?"

"Don't be a cheesedick, dude," John Scott said. "We've decided. We're here."

"Do you want to go back?" I asked her again.

"Pussssieeee," John Scott said.

"Stay out of this," I told him.

"I'm just saying—"

"It's not your business."

"It's okay, guys," Mel said. "I'm fine."

Snorting like he'd just won some bucking challenge, John Scott took the lead with Ben, and we continued on. I glanced ahead at the guy a few times, continuing different conversations in my head. Some scenarios had me telling him nobody wanted him here. Others deteriorated into a fistfight in which I handily defeated him.

Gradually my irritation diminished, and my attention returned to the forest. It was getting creepier the farther we went. The saplings seemed to be pressing ever closer together, their trunks lining up as tight as prison bars, while some of the lower branches reached toward us, like skeletal hands.

Suddenly Ben cried out. Then everyone was crowding over something on the ground, just off the path. I leaned over Mel and saw a pile of relatively new equipment. There was a silver flashlight, batteries still in the package, a hacksaw with an orange handle, black rubber gloves, scissors, tape, and a clear bag filled with numerous cans of chemicals.

"This must belong to the police or volunteers who search for the bodies," Ben said. "See the scissors and the saw?"

"But what are the chemicals used for?" Neil said.

Nobody had an answer to that.

John Scott grabbed the flashlight and batteries.

"John!" Mel reprimanded. "What are you doing?"

"It will come in handy."

"You can't take it."

"Why not? Someone obviously left it here."

"They might be coming back for it."

"I'll return it on the way out tomorrow."

"I think you should leave it."

"Do you have a flashlight?"

"Yes, I do."

"Anyone else?"

"I have one," Neil said.

"That's it? Two for seven people?" John Scott glanced at each of us in turn. "Is anyone else against a third flashlight? It's going to be pitch black out here later."

Put that way, nobody objected.

SOMEHOW a pebble had snuck into my left shoe, annoying me to no end. I wasn't wearing hiking boots like the others. My feet were size thirteen—a size that was nearly impossible to find in Japan, even in a city as large as Tokyo. Consequently, I hadn't been able to buy proper boots for this trip and instead wore the pair of tattered Reebok trainers I'd brought with me from the States.

John Scott, now chatting up Nina ten feet ahead of me, lit a cigarette. He blew the smoke back over his shoulder.

I noticed his shoes for the first time: eighteen-hole Doc Martins, black leather, yellow laces. Like his leather jacket, I didn't know what to make of them.

Had he planned on wearing them to climb Fuji? Or did he have something else in his big military-issued rucksack?

"What were you guys talking about earlier?" I asked Mel.

"Who?"

I didn't reply. She knew who.

She said, "He was telling me stories about Okinawa. He said it's a great place. We should visit there sometime."

"Where's he staying in Tokyo?"

"A love hotel actually."

"Ha. Whereabouts?" Love hotels were neon-garish places where you rent a room either for a three-hour rest or for the entire night. You select the room from a panel of buttons and settle the bill via a pneumatic tube or pair of mysterious hands behind a pane of frosted glass. Mel and I had stayed in a bunch of them over the years for kicks, and the rooms had featured rotating beds, ceiling mirrors, karaoke systems, hot tubs, and vending machines selling everything from beer to S&M gear to women's panties, previously worn.

"That one in Shibuya we stayed in. Remember, on that small, windy street?"

"Yeah, I remember." I think the area was called Love Hotel Hill. Our room had no windows for the same reason casinos don't. "There are a bunch of hotels there. He stayed in the same one we did?"

"I recommended it."

I frowned. "How long have you known he was coming to Tokyo?"

"A couple days before he arrived."

"Is that when you invited him to climb Fuji?"

"I told him we were climbing it, yes. He said he'd climbed it before and had other plans. But then he texted me last night and said his plans had fallen through."

I stared ahead. John Scott took another drag of his cigarette, blew the smoke back at us.

"What do you think about his jacket?" I asked.

"What about it?"

"A leather jacket like that? To climb a mountain?"

"He wasn't planning on climbing. I just said that. I guess it's the only jacket he brought with him."

Fair enough, I thought. But I still wanted to get a dig in. I didn't like this relationship Mel had with him. Maybe I was overreacting. I don't know. Something just didn't sit right.

"Where's he from?" I asked.

"Why all this interest?"

"I'm jealous."

"St. Helena. I told you we went to school together."

"What's his last name?"

Mel gave me a look.

"What?" I said.

"Scott, duh."

I raised my eyebrows. "Are you kidding me?" I'd thought John Scott was a double name or something, like Billy Bob.

"No, it's his last name."

I couldn't help but laugh. It felt good—partly because the forest was so damn gloomy, but more so, I think, because I was laughing at John Scott.

"Why's that funny?" she asked.

"Who introduces themselves with their full name?"

"A lot of people."

"In a business meeting maybe. Do you call him John Scott?"

"I call him John."

"What about other people?"

"Back in high school people called him Scotty. I don't know now."

"That's like people calling me Ethan Childs."

"He didn't tell you to call him John Scott. That was your decision."

"Yeah, well, if people kept calling me Ethan Childs, I'd tell them it was just Ethan. Who does he think he is? A celebrity?"

"What's your problem with him?"

"I don't have a problem with him—"

"Hey, look there!" Ben shouted.

For an instant a rush of dread washed through me. We'd found someone. He would be hanging from a noose. Dead and cold and—

It was a shoe. That's it. A lone white shoe.

It sat about ten feet to the left of the path, next to a mossy rock.

Ben and John Scott were already making their way toward it.

"It's a Nike," Ben said.

The rest of us ventured closer. It was a men's. Size eight or nine. The laces were missing.

I surveyed the area, but didn't see any other sign of human intrusion.

"Looks like it's been here for a while," Neil said.

"You think it's from…you know?" Mel said. "Someone who killed themselves?"

"Whose else could it be?" John Scott said. I considered thinking of him as just John from now on, but I stuck with John Scott. It still amused me that he allowed himself to be thought of as a two-name guy, like Tom Cruise. "A hiker would notice if his shoe fell off."

"So would someone planning on killing themselves," I said.

"We're talking about a person here, not a zombie."

"Where are the laces?" Mel asked.

"Maybe he needed them to do the deed," Neil said.

"With shoelaces?" I said.

"You know what I think?" Tomo said. "I think the animal eat the guy."

Ben shook his head. "There would be a skeleton, clothes."

"Maybe it drag him away. The shoe fall off."

"I don't like this," Mel stated.

"Are there bears in these parts, Tomo?" I asked.

"Yeah, man," he said. "So many."

"I'm serious."

"Yes, there are," Neil said. "I've read about people seeing bears while climbing Mt. Fuji. But they rarely attack humans unless you get between them and their cubs."

"I don't say the bear eat the live guy," Tomo said. "I say he eat the dead guy."

"Who cares what got him?" John Scott shrugged impatiently. "All we're doing is guessing. And all that's doing is wasting time. I want to see a *body*." He returned to the footpath, heading deeper into the forest.

After a beat, the rest of us followed.

5

I T became noticeably darker, quickly. Earlier, pieces of
the granite-gray sky had been visible through the patch-
work of overhead branches. Now little if any gray penetrated the thickening canopy, turning midday into a prema-
ture dusk. I usually enjoyed the twilight that bridged late
afternoon and early evening. There was a sereneness associated with it. But not here in Aokigahara. Here, the trees took
on a sinister, emaciated appearance. Their green leaves lost
their vibrancy, as if drained of life. Elastic shadows thickened
and pooled. My mind and eyes began to play tricks on me to
the extent I'd see a tortured face in a twisted tree trunk, or
a blackened skull in a mound of volcanic rubble. Moreover,
I had the uncomfortable sensation of being watched. Several
times I sensed movement in the corner of my field of vision.

And still there were no animals, no wind, just the trees and
us in this...crypt.

I wasn't the only one getting spooked by the forest. We
were all acting like animals sniffing out a trap, sneaking
glances at the canopy or the suffocating trees, as if searching
for some lurking threat.

A crackling of vegetation sounded off to the right. Ben
and Nina, who were both ahead of me, jumped a foot off the
ground. Tomo dropped into a squat, his hands framing his face
like the guy in *The Scream*. Mel grabbed my forearm so hard it
hurt. Then, from behind us, John Scott howled with laughter.

I knew what he'd done before he tossed another rock into the trees.

"Gosh, John!" Mel cried. "That wasn't funny!"

He continued to laugh. Neil, who was beside him, and who I could imagine John Scott elbowing conspiratorially when he'd picked up the rock, appeared guiltily amused.

"You fuck-ass!" Tomo said, though he was smiling witlessly. "I almost shit my brains."

This caused John Scott to crack up harder. Ben and Nina joined in, then everyone was having a good chuckle. We needed it. A release from the pressure that had evidently been building inside all of us.

It was a brief reprieve, however, and after the laughter died down, and we were on the move once again, the silence inevitably returned, just as disquieting as before.

I glanced beside me at Mel. She was chewing her bottom lip, her eyes downcast, watching where she stepped. I could almost feel the tightness in her body. She looked over, smiled. It was a hesitant smile, a hospital smile, how the nurses smiled at me while I was with Gary in his final hours. A reassuring smile.

I felt suddenly bad for springing this camping trip on her. She wasn't cut out for stuff like this. She often refused to watch horror movies because they were too scary, and she rarely, if ever, did anything that was dangerous or illegal.

I took her hand in mine and said, "Still feeling like this is an enchanted forest?"

"A little," she said. "But I feel like we've just walked into the wicked witch's domain."

"I know what you mean."

"What were you thinking about? You haven't said anything for the last five minutes."

"Our Spain trip," I said, which was true. I'd been compiling a mental list of some of the dumbest things I've done or attempted to do in my life. Making the top three was my decision last summer to cross Spain's Camino del Ray, a three-foot-wide decrepit walkway pinned against a sheer cliff face three hundred thirty feet above a river. I'm afraid of heights, and I'd believed conquering the walkway might help me overcome the fear. But when I got to a section where the concrete had collapsed, leaving a large open gap bridged only by narrow steel beams, I returned the way I'd come, meeting up again with Mel, who'd had the sense to wait behind.

"Blue skies, warm weather," Mel said. "That was such a nice vacation. I wish you didn't mention it."

"You'd rather be there?"

"You mean rather there than Japan? Or rather there than a haunted forest?"

I'd meant a haunted forest. But now that she'd brought it up I said, "Than Japan. We don't have to go back to the States. We could teach in Spain. They need English teachers."

"It's not that easy. They'd rather hire someone from the UK who already has a EU passport."

"What about Thailand, or the Czech Republic? We could even go to Turkey. They're always hiring. That's the best perk with teaching. We can go anywhere, travel anywhere."

"And what about the future, Ethan? We can't keep hopping around the world until we're sixty. We need to—"

"Grow up," I finished for her.

"It's true."

"We're only twenty-six."

"That's closer to thirty than twenty."

"It's closer to twenty-five than thirty."

"Whatever."

"It's still young."

"We're getting older. And what do we have to show for it? We have no house, no savings. No—" She trailed off. "What about children?"

I swallowed. Kids again. She'd been talking about them more and more lately. I would like to have one or two...eventually. Thirty always sounded like a good age to me, though I don't know why I chose this number aside from the fact it's the beginning of a new decade. I suppose I figure I would have matured the necessary amount to be a father by then.

"You really want to have kids now?" I said.

"Soon."

"We're too young."

"Young, young, young!"

"You know how expensive they are?"

"Exactly. It's why we're leaving Japan—and why we can't simply keep country hopping for however long you want. Not on the salaries we're making. We're okay now because we're just supporting ourselves. But if we had a child? There's schooling, clothes, food, medical bills. In the States I could get a job with the Board of Education. I'd have maternity leave, benefits."

"And you'd be in California. You know how far that is from Wisconsin? I may as well be in Japan."

"You could come to St. Helena with me."

St. Helena? I was gob-smacked. St. Helena was a small town in the Napa Valley whose only claim to fame was that Robert Louis Stevenson had walked down the throughway with his bride more than a century before. This was the first I'd heard of the idea of relocating there, and it surprised the hell out of me.

I've come to believe there are four types of ESL teachers in Asia. The first are young people looking to travel for a year or two and save a bit of money before returning home and starting the careers they would sink into for the rest of their lives. The second are those who end up marrying an Asian and living the rest of their lives as expatriates, maybe flying home every so often for a wedding or a funeral or Christmas with their ageing parents. The third are the more adventurous who are willing to give up the better salaries and standards of living in Japan and South Korea for a more laissez faire lifestyle in a tropical environment in Southeast Asia. These are predominantly male and have little interest in getting hitched in the near future, if ever. In fact, many of them have dreams of retiring early, buying a hut on a white-sand beach, and spending their twilight years with a constant supply of fifty-cent beers and a revolving door of girlfriends half their age.

The final type are the Runners, and their label is self-explanatory: they're running from something.

This was where Mel and I fit in. I was running from Gary's death, while Mel was running from her family's reputation.

Her parents divorced when she was in her senior year at UCLA, and her mother soon began seeing another man. When her father found out, he broke into the new beau's house and suffocated him to death with a plastic bag. He was tracked down by the San Diego Regional Fugitive Task Force and was now serving life in Corcoran State Prison, the same shithole where Charles Manson was spending his remaining years.

After Mel graduated she returned to St. Helena to be with her mother, where the population was something like five thousand, and where the murder remained the talk of the town. She was harassed constantly, and a month later she flew to Japan to get away.

You can't run forever, however, and although she's made it clear she wanted to return to the States, I never imagined to her hometown.

Mel was looking at me expectantly, as if waiting for my reply.

"We can't go back there," I said.

Anger darkened her eyes. "Why not?"

"You know why."

"That was a long time ago. People forget."

"Not in small towns."

"I didn't do anything."

"That doesn't matter."

"It's a nice place."

"There are a lot of nice places, Mel. Why St. Helena?"

"My mom's lonely," she said after a few seconds deliberation. "I think she'd like me back there."

Panic gripped me. "You want us to live with your mother?"

"Of course not. But we'd be close. I could visit with her a

few times a week."

"Are there even schools in St. Helena where we could work?" I asked diplomatically.

"You think I was home taught? The high school has about five hundred students."

"What are the chances they'd have a teaching position available, let alone two?"

"It couldn't hurt to check, could it?"

I opened my mouth to reply, then closed it. I didn't want to fight with Mel, not here, not now. So I merely shrugged non-committally.

She gave me an unreadable look, then picked up her pace, leaving me behind to ponder the next five years in St. Helena surrounded by lilacs and grandmothers and perhaps an angry mob keen on a lynching.

WE'D been walking for over an hour and a half now, and I was just beginning to get used to the brooding strangeness of Aokigahara when the path ended abruptly at two grotesquely fused trees that instilled in me both fascination and revulsion. They wound serpentine-like around one another, fighting, grappling, spiraling up and up in a decades-long struggle to reach the spot of sky that must have opened when another tree had fallen. They were the perfect embodiment of the vicious survive-at-any-costs ruthlessness that had taken root everywhere in the forest, reinforcing my perception that this was a cruel, primeval, unforgiving place, a slice of hell on earth, even for plant life.

Someone had painted what looked to be a white arrow about ten feet up on each trunk. They pointed in opposite directions.

"Are those arrows?" Mel said, frowning.

"I reckon the police made them," Neil said, "to find their way to other trails."

"Or bodies," I said.

Everyone looked at me.

"You really think they lead to bodies?" Mel said.

"Maybe not anymore," I admitted. "The police would have removed them already."

"So which way do we go?" John Scott said, lighting up a cigarette.

"I don't think we should leave this path," Mel said.

"We won't go far," he assured her.

Ben nodded. "We will split up. Half of us will go left for an hour, the other half go right. If either group sees something, we will call the other."

Mel and I checked our phones. We both had reception.

"What happens if neither of us find anything?" Mel asked.

Ben shrugged. "Then we meet back here in two hours."

"So we good?" John Scott said.

"Yeah, man," Tomo said.

John Scott nodded at Neil. "What do you say, big guy?"

Neil was gazing off into the forest. "I don't know," he said. "I have a bad feeling about this place."

"Of course you do. It's fucking freaky as hell. We're all freaked. But we've already come all this way. We're so close to finding something."

"Mate, that's the thing. I don't reckon I *want* to find any-thing."

"You don't want to see a body?"

"We don't belong here. It's wrong what we're doing, disres-pectful."

Mel was nodding.

"Anyone else want to chicken out?" John Scott said.

This pissed Neil off. "I'm not chickening out."

"Then come with us."

"Yeah, man," Tomo said. "Don't be chicken guy."

Neil threw up his hands. "I'm not a chicken! And if it will shut you two up, fine, I'll come."

"Hooah!" John Scott cawed idiotically. He looked at Mel and me.

Although I'd begun to rethink the wisdom of what we were doing out here, the arrows had admittedly piqued my sense of adventure. And John Scott was right. We'd already come all this way. Why stop now? It was just a little farther to see what was behind that final corner. Then we could make camp, eat, relax, and leave here tomorrow with a sense of accomplishment.

Mel saw my decision in my eyes, and she relented. "One more hour," she said. "And that's it."

"One more hour," Ben agreed, smiling. "Okay—Nina and me, we will go left. Who would like to join us?"

"I'm down," John Scott said. He ground his cigarette under his heel, told us, "Peace out," then started into the trees like a dutiful Boy Scout eager to earn his next merit badge.

The Israelis waved goodbye to us and fell into line behind him.

"And then there were four..." Neil said quietly.

6

THE terrain off the footpath was challenging and slow going. This had less to do with the obstacles of trees than with the ground itself. Every few yards we were stepping over rotting logs and dead branches and volcanic rocks. I tried to grab hold of saplings for support, but they would often tear free from the thin soil as easily as a decaying limb from its socket. Most hazardous of all, it turned out, was the fact a massive network of lava tubes extended beneath our feet. Twice we passed areas where the solidified magma had collapsed beneath the weight of a tree into one of these underground tubes, creating jagged craters twenty feet wide. We circumnavigated the moss-covered and scree-filled depressions with caution. If you stumbled into one and the fall didn't kill you, the sharp rock would shred your flesh and you would likely bleed to death before help could arrive.

The only positive to the difficult landscape, I thought, was that I was so focused on the topography and keeping a straight line I had little time to reflect on hanging bodies and rapidly approaching night.

When we stopped for a much-needed rest, I took out my water bottle from my backpack and passed it around. It came back to me almost empty. I finished it off, knowing Mel still had half a liter in her bag, which would get us by until tomorrow.

Tomo went to pee behind a tree. I decided to go as well.

While standing on a log with my back to the others, staring out into the trees, I was struck by a sobering notion. If we got disorientated out here, we could become hopelessly lost. The signs had already warned us of this, of course, and Mel had mentioned it, but I had never taken the idea seriously until now.

Lost in Suicide Forest.

Tomo and I returned to the others at the same time. He was fastening his belt buckle, boasting that his dick had grown since the last time he'd taken a leak. Neil told him it must have been pretty small to start off with.

"How do you guys feel?" I asked.

"Tired," Mel said.

"Hungry," Tomo said.

"Hungry and tired," Neil said.

I nodded. "Another thirty minutes or so. Then we'll head back and eat."

Mel looked the way we'd come. "We sure we know *how* to get back?"

"I know the way," I said.

"Because if we get turned around…"

"I know the way," I repeated.

"I guess we could always yell."

It was true. If we began yelling, John Scott and the Israelis would likely be able to hear us and find us. Or if Mel called John Scott's phone, and told him to yell, we could make our way to them. Yet this would be embarrassingly desperate for all of us, and I was sure it wouldn't be necessary.

We continued in the direction the arrow had pointed.

After only a few minutes I was once more breathing hard, and I was glad I had quit smoking. In the back of my mind I heard Mel tell me, "See? I told you that you should quit." She was always saying things like this. If we went to a restaurant, and it turned out to be good, she would say, "See? I told you we should come here." Same if we watched a particularly entertaining movie: "See? I told you we should see this one."

Tomo picked up a long vine that continued for as far as I could see ahead of us. "We follow this," he said. "We don't get lost."

Less than five yards later he shrieked and tossed the vine aside.

"What happened?" I asked, thinking something had bitten him.

He was sniffing his hands. "It pee on me!"

"What?"

"Feel!"

I picked up the vine hesitantly. It was coarse and dry.

"There!" Tomo said, pointing to a spot further down the stem.

"Yeah, I see it," I said, noticing a six-inch section that seemed to be covered in some kind of liquid. It appeared to be the only wet spot.

"Smell it!" Tomo said.

I did so and detected a faint ammonia odor.

"It does smell like urine," I told Mel and Neil, who were staring at Tomo and me like we were talking apes.

"So what?" Mel said. "An animal—"

"You see animal?" Tomo said. "Where? I don't see none."

"Where else would it come from?"

"I piss on forest, it piss on me."

Neil harrumphed. "Please, Tomo."

"It's true! Go smell!"

"Forget it."

Tomo turned to me. "Taste it."

Rolling my eyes, I started off again.

A vine peeing back on us. Fuck.

I flirted with thoughts of the paranormal for a while. A sentient forest that lures people and animals deep into its heart with the illusion of green tranquility, then, when they become hopelessly lost and expire, it feeds on their carcasses. If

I ever wrote a book, I could call this story *The Venus Forest*, or perhaps *The Flytrap Forest*. There would have to be a large cast of characters so the forest could pick them off one by one. And the protagonist would have to somehow survive and defeat the forest. This stumped me for a while, because how could you defeat an entire forest apart from burning it to the ground? Then again, I decided eventually, if the genre was horror, it didn't need a happy ending, did it?

When I tired of amusing—and frightening—myself, I purposely blanked my mind and focused on keeping in a straight line. Unexpectedly, I began to think of Gary. That's when it always happened. When I least expected to think of him. Of course, in the months following his death, I thought about him incessantly. But time had a way of dulling the pain, distancing the memories. You never forget something like your brother dying, you never accept it either, but at some point, for good or bad, you learn to live with it.

Gary was shot early in the morning on December 12, 1999, while heading to practice at the Giant Center in Hershey, Pennsylvania. He'd played for the Hershey Bears of the American Hockey League. Although he went undrafted by the NHL in '96, he was signed as a free agent by the Washington Capitals the following year and spent the next three seasons bouncing between the Capitals and the minors. Most sport pundits agreed he could become a permanent fixture in the pros if he could recover from a knee injury, which had required reconstructive surgery. The injury should have ended his career, but Gary had a determination like no one else I've ever met. He must have trained twice as hard as anyone on his team to get back into playing condition, and the last I spoke to him, about a month before his death when I called him on his birthday, he said he was as good as new.

The guy who shot him was an eighteen-year-old heroin addict who'd been in and out of juvie his entire adolescence. He didn't know Gary. They'd never met. Gary had simply been at the wrong place at the wrong time.

Gary used to jog every day along North Hockersville Road, which cut through secluded woodland. On the day he died he'd left the road to offer assistance to someone slumped against the trunk of a tree. The person, Jerome Tyler, pulled a gun and demanded Gary's wallet. Gary refused and was shot with a .22 caliber gun. Tyler took Gary's wallet and fled. Gary managed to get back to the road before collapsing. He was taken to the hospital where it was learned the small bullets did a huge amount of damage, piercing his liver and aorta.

I was a senior at the University of Wisconsin-Madison and had been sleeping off a mild hangover when my mother called me in hysterics and told me Gary had been shot. I flew to Pennsylvania and arrived at the hospital that evening. My parents were there with Gary's wife, Cheryl, and their infant daughter, Lisa. My father took me aside and explained Gary's condition. His eyes were red, an indication he had been crying, something I had never seen him do. Walking into Gary's hospital room was the hardest thing I have ever done. He was lying on his back in a mechanical bed, hooked up to a life-support machine. He was pale, his skin oily, an oxygen mask taped over his mouth. I didn't know it at the time, but he wasn't getting circulation to his feet and brain. I remained at his bedside for as long as I was allowed, not speaking, not doing anything except holding his hand.

I fell asleep on a sofa in the visitor area and was woken in the morning by my parents and Cheryl. It was written all over their faces: bad news. Doctors had told them that Gary would likely never wake from his coma, and even if he did, he would be brain dead. The decision had been made to pull the plug.

I flew back to Wisconsin in a daze. I don't remember the flight. Don't remember anything about the days that followed. I vaguely recall the funeral. Most of the people present were family. The rest were Gary's teammates. It was an open casket service. Gary looked remarkably lifelike, and I half expected him to open his eyes and say it was all one big joke. I brushed his cheek with the back of my fingers. His skin was gravestone cold, almost rubbery. The knowledge that this would be the last time I ever saw him was like a physical blow, I found it hard to breathe, and I went outside for some air. Three of Gary's teammates were there, smoking cigarettes. One of them was smiling as he told a joke, like this was just another day in the locker room. I walked over and asked the joker what he was saying. He had the sense to appear suitably ashamed. I didn't care. I punched him in the face, pushed him to the ground, then dropped on top of him, raining down more blows until I was pulled off.

Jerome Tyler, who'd been arrested by the police the day after Gary died, was convicted of first-degree murder. The trial lasted one week. The jury took an hour to return a unanimous verdict. The sentence was life imprisonment with the possibility of parole after ten years.

It wasn't fair, I'd thought at the time. Jerome was a cold-blooded murderer. He didn't deserve parole. He deserved death, an eye for an eye. I used to have fantasies about killing him myself; it helped me get to sleep at night. In each of these scenarios I would kill him a different way. Never instantly. It would always be a long, drawn-out process. I would talk to him during this time, mock him, celebrate my life in the face of his death, paint a clear picture of the nothingness he was headed for.

I don't have these fantasies anymore. It's not that I've forgiven Jerome. There's simply no reason to continue to hold ill will toward him. After seven months in prison he was found in a bathroom, his head in a toilet bowl, seven stab wounds in his back. Official cause of death was drowning.

Not one of the ways I'd imagined it, but good enough for me.

WE came to a white ribbon twenty minutes later. It was tied loosely around the trunk of a small tree and continued perpendicular to us deep into the forest. We stared at it, each of us coming to our own conclusions.

"Did the police leave this too?" Mel asked.

"Police or suicide guy," Tomo said.

"Why would a suicidal person leave ribbon behind?"

"So his body could be recovered?" Neil suggested.

Tomo shook his head. "So he go back out."

I was confused. "If he came here to kill himself, Tomo, it would be a one-way trip."

"Some guys, they don't decide. They still thinking."

"So they spool out this ribbon behind them in case they change their mind about killing themselves?"

"Yeah, man," he said, then started along the ribbon.

"Wait!" Mel said. "Where are you going?"

He looked back. "We follow, right?"

"You know what might be at the end of it?" Neil said.

"Don't be chicken guy again."

Neil scowled. "Don't call me that."

"What? Chicken guy?"

As we started along the ribbon, I tried to get into the mindset of the person who came to this forest, alone, spooling out a lifeline behind them in case they changed their mind and wanted to return to civilization. They would have been suffering for some time. Suicide wasn't something you did spur of the moment. So what had happened to them that they'd want to end their own life? The death of a spouse or child? Financial ruin? Poor health?

Or just some really bad luck?

I pictured the person sitting at their computer late at night, perhaps smoking a cigarette in the dark, researching different ways to kill themselves, researching this forest, at least how to get here, where to park. Goosebumps broke out on my arms.

Researching your own death.

Man almighty.

I became aware I had begun to move faster. At first I imagined this was due to the fact I wanted to cover as much ground as possible in the time we had allotted to us before turning around. But I realized there was more to it than that, for it almost seemed as though the forest, like the sentient one I had imagined, was *pulling* me deeper into its embrace.

I didn't realize I had left the others behind until Mel cried out.

She was twenty feet back, submerged in the ground to her neck. Her elbows were hooked over a twisting root, which was likely the only thing preventing her from sinking deeper.

From what I could tell when I reached her, she had stepped into one of those volcanic craters, only this one had been obscured by a latticework of roots and debris. I guessed the mouth was almost six feet wide, but it was difficult to be certain because I wasn't sure what was true ground and what wasn't. My first thought was of a trapping pit used by hunters and camouflaged with branches and leaves—though this one was made by the forest, not man.

"Are you okay?" I asked, my mind racing for a way to help her.

"I don't know," she said, her eyes wide with panic. She swiveled her head from side to side, searching for something else aside from the root to grab hold of.

I knelt at what I determined to be the lip of the hole. She was too far to reach. "How deep is it?"

"I don't know." She was trying to keep panic from her voice and failing. "I can't touch the bottom."

"Can you try to climb out?"

She struggled for a moment, twisting this way and that, until the root she was dangling from shifted, dropping several inches.

She yelped.

I dove forward and grabbed her wrists. It was a stupid move. Instinctual. Because I was now on my stomach, my upper body cantilevered over the crevice, and I had no leverage to pull her out, no way to move back on my own.

Beneath us, through gaps in the dead leaves and branches

and roots, all I could see was darkness.

How deep was it?

"Don't let go of me," she said in a frightened whisper.

"I won't."

I heard Neil and Tomo coming toward us.

"Careful!" I warned them.

"Oh boy," Neil said.

"Oh shit!" Tomo said. "The forest fucking eat her."

"Grab my legs," I told them, "so I don't fall in."

A moment later I felt hands around my ankles.

"Don't let go."

"I don't, man," Tomo said.

"Mel," I said, doing my best to affect calm, even though I felt like a man on very thin ice. "Put your arms around my neck. I'll put my arms around you. Then Tomo and Neil will pull us free."

"I can't let go."

"Yeah, you can. The hole's probably not very deep anyway. Don't think about it."

"You saw how big those craters were."

"This is just a small one. Come on. You can do it."

She looked so scared I thought she might cry. She shifted, so her right armpit was hooked firmly over the branch, then she reached for me with her other arm and snagged the collar of my jacket. I slipped my arm beneath hers.

"Good," I encouraged her. "Do the same with the other."

She followed my instruction and now had both arms around me, her hands locked together behind my neck, while my arms encircled her torso.

We had become one big Barrel of Monkeys chain: Mel, me, Tomo, Neil.

"Tomo, you got me?" I called back to him.

"Yeah, man."

"Neil, you have Tomo?"

"We're good, mate. Tell us when."

"Now."

They began to pull.

"Wait!" Mel cried. "My hands are slipping!"

"I got you," I told her.

The rearward movement caused my shirt to ride up my stomach. Sharp sticks scraped my bare flesh. Slowly, however, Mel emerged from the hole, the root she'd been dangling by now beneath her navel. Then I was back on solid ground. I rose to a kneeling position, pulling her toward me. Tomo released my ankles and squatted beside me—

Suddenly the roots Mel had moved onto gave with a wicked crack. She screamed and plunged into the darkness below, her hands clawing at the rocky wall as she disappeared.

I pitched forward in a futile effort to grab her. I likely would have fallen in as well had Neil and Tomo not restrained me.

"Mel!" I shouted.

I listened with sick anticipation for her to strike the ground. I heard nothing.

"Mel!"

Tomo and Neil were yelling also.

"Ethan!" Mel's voice floated up, high-pitched and uncertain.

I couldn't tell how far down she was.

Had she broken an ankle on impact? A leg?

At least she was alive.

"Mel, what happened?"

"Help me—Oh God!"

"What's wrong?" I demanded. "What happened?"

"I'm on a ledge or something. There's—there's nothing below me."

For a moment I had an image of a massive subterranean cavern opening below her, filled with the bones of all the animals—and perhaps suicides—that had fallen down the crevice in the past.

I swallowed my fear and said, "Don't move, Mel. Don't do anything. We're going to get you out." I turned to Neil. "Get your flashlight."

He scavenged it from his backpack and aimed it into the yawning hole. Mel had taken most of the roots and deadfall that covered the opening with her when she fell, and we had a clear view down. The shaft didn't follow a straight line but corkscrewed around the vertical axis, resembling the cardboard core of a paper towel roll that had been twisted and untwisted. Mel was fifteen to twenty feet down, standing on a narrow, debris-covered ledge. Her stomach was pressed against the rock face, her arms spread eagle.

Beyond her the shaft continued into blackness.

"Good Lord," Neil said.

I clenched my jaw.

"How deep is it?" Mel called, unwilling to move at all to look down.

I pretended not to hear her. "Go find a long vine!" I told Neil and Tomo. I turned back to Mel. "We're getting a vine, Mel. We're going to get you out."

"Hurry, Ethan."

"Don't move. Don't do anything until we get the vine—hold on."

I joined Neil and Tomo, who were two dozen feet away, tugging at a tangle of lianas, trying to pull them free from the tree trunks and branches that their shoots had latched onto.

I shrugged off my backpack and dug through the top pocket for the Swiss Army knife I had brought. I popped the small blade and began sawing at the woody stem of one liana a few inches above where it was rooted in the ground. The diameter was about twice that of a garden hose. It took me close to a minute to cut through it.

I stood and looked up. The severed liana dangled from a mess of branches and other lianas above. Both Tomo and I tugged at it with all our strength, but we couldn't free it.

"Shit," I said, wiping sweat from my forehead with the back of my hand.

Then I saw Neil behind me. He was dumping his tent from

its nylon sack. Out fell a polyester flysheet, metal poles, several stakes, and guy ropes.

Guy ropes!

There were four of them, each five or six feet in lengths.

"Yes, Neil!" I said.

"We tie them together," he said, "I reckon we can reach her easy."

"Mel! We have rope!" I shouted. "We'll toss it down in a minute!"

Neil was laying the ends of two ropes parallel to each other.

"The knot has to be strong," I said, wishing I knew something about knot tying.

"I know what I'm bloody doing."

I watched as he coiled the working end of one rope twice around the second rope, passing it through the inside of the coils. He repeated this with the second rope in the opposite direction. Then he pulled the free ends to tighten the knots.

"That's it?" I said skeptically. It looked secure, but it seemed too simple.

"A double fisherman's. It's the best way to tie two ropes together."

He attached the third and fourth segments, stood, and held up the finished length proudly.

"Can you tie the end of it in a loop?" I asked.

"Is there enough rope?"

"I think so. If not, we'll untie it."

Neil secured the end in a large bowline knot, then we returned to the hole.

Tomo was kneeling at the edge. He glanced at the rope and said, "Neil, man, you fucking James Bond."

"Mel!" I called. "We're going to toss down a rope. You ready?"

"Yes!"

Neil passed me the rope. "There's nothing close enough to anchor it to."

I nodded and fed out the slack.

"Can you reach it, Mel?"

"I have it!"

"Slide the loop over your head and under your arms."

"Is this going to work?"

"One hundred percent."

The best method would be for her to lean back until she was perpendicular with the wall and rappel upward like a rock climber. But I knew she would never attempt this. Also, if she fell, she would tumble head over heels past the ledge all the way to the bottom, however deep that was.

On the other hand, if Tomo, Neil, and I simply pulled her up hand over hand like you pull a fish out of a hole in the ice, and something catastrophic happened such as the rope breaking, she would hopefully slide back down the wall and land on the ledge again.

This was my thinking anyway.

"You ready, Mel?" I said.

"I don't think I can do this!"

"You have to. It's the only way out. Look up at the light. It's not far. It's only fifteen feet or so."

"I can't do this!"

"Yes, you can. We'll be pulling you, so you just have to hold on."

"What if I fall?"

"You won't. Just hold on tight."

"What if it snaps?"

"It won't. It's strong. I promise you. Don't think about that. You ready?"

She didn't answer.

"Mel?"

"Yeah."

"You ready?"

"Yeah."

"Don't let go, no matter what."

"Okay!"

I looked over my shoulder at Neil and Tomo. Like me, they

both had their right arm twisted around the length of rope for extra traction.

We heaved while stepping backward. One step, then another, then another. Mel was incredibly heavy. The polyethylene rope dug into my palms, but I ignored the pain.

It was working.

I pictured Mel, peering at the circle of light overhead, her body swinging back and forth as she inched upward, bouncing against the rock face.

If the rope snapped, or the knots came loose...

I didn't let myself think of that.

Then, what seemed like a very short time later, Mel's arms appeared over the lip of the crevice, then her head. Her face was a mask of agony and grit. She was so focused she didn't glance at us. She was squirming, kicking with her legs.

Then she flopped forward on solid ground. She scrambled the rest of the way to us, as if she feared something was about to leap from the hole and drag her back down. She collided into me, gripping me in a fierce hug, and we collapsed together, panting with exertion.

WE remained locked in an embrace for several minutes as our heartbeats returned to normal and our nerves settled down. I enjoyed the warmth of Mel's body against mine, the softness of it. I breathed in the fresh, lemon-scent of her hair.

"Thank you," she whispered into my neck.

"It's okay," I said, stroking her back reassuringly.

"I was so scared."

"It's okay."

When I couldn't ignore the stinging in my hands any longer, I kissed Mel on the forehead, shifted out from beneath her, and sat up. The rope had left angry red furrows across both palms. Thankfully, the skin hadn't torn, but I wouldn't be surprised if it began to blister at some point. I lifted my shirt. There were a couple thin cuts, but that was all. I barely felt them.

I turned my attention to Mel, who was still lying down, eyes closed.

"You good?" I said, squeezing her thigh.

She opened her eyes and nodded.

"You didn't twist your ankle or anything?"

"I don't think so." She glanced at the crevice. "I didn't even see it."

"I didn't either," I said. "I must have walked straight past it."

"You were going so fast. I was just trying to keep up."

"I know, I…" I shrugged, recalling the pull I'd felt.

"How deep do you think it is?"

"Not that deep," I lied.

"I dropped my phone."

"Down the hole?"

"When you were pulling me out. It fell from my pocket. I think I heard it land on the ledge below me."

"You want to go get it?" I said lightly.

"Funny."

"We'll get you a new one in Tokyo. It's about time you updated anyway."

Neil cleared his throat. "So what do you reckon we do now?" he asked, as he cleaned the lenses of his glasses with his shirt. "Keep going or head back."

"Keep going, man," Tomo said, jumping to his feet. "Why not?"

"Because Mel just went through a bit of an ordeal, Tomo. Perhaps she doesn't want to continue."

We all looked at her.

"Let's keep going," she said. "I actually feel pretty good."

In a strange way I did too. Alive and invigorated. Maybe it was adrenaline, but I thought it was more than that. We had been challenged, and we not only triumphed, we did so with a cool head and as a team. Really, with Mel now safe, I felt more proud than anything of our accomplishment.

Suicide Forest zero; Team Tokyo one.

"You heard her," I said. "Let's move."

MEL and I walked side by side holding hands, keeping a careful eye on the ground for anymore crevices. Less than five minutes later we spotted a second ribbon. It was blue and continued parallel to the white one for a bit before gradually angling off to the left. I wondered which had been laid down first and whether the person who'd come second would have been comforted by the sight of another ribbon. To know you were in a place where others killed themselves as well. Where it was somewhat acceptable to kill yourself. Where you could disappear and not burden family and friends, who otherwise would have to identify your body at the morgue, arrange a funeral, attend the funeral.

The perfect place to die.

The longer I was in Aokigahara, the more I believed this statement to be true. Despite the pervasive atmosphere of death and struggle and sadness, you felt cocooned here, isolated from the outside world. And wasn't this exactly what someone contemplating suicide would want? It certainly seemed like a more suitable place to spend your last time on earth than, say, the Golden Gate Bridge, with motorists screaming past, some stopping to stare, some to play hero, as you scaled the suicide barrier.

I was by no means an expert on suicide, but I could relate to the state of mind of someone contemplating it because I had contemplated it myself in the days after Gary died. That had been a shitty time, the worst in my life, and often I would wonder how I was going to get through the next day, or the next week. I couldn't stop thinking about everything that Gary had forfeited: his family, his career, his future. He'd had everything to look forward to. Perhaps this, in some way, was why I felt it should have been me instead. Gary was the star; I was the understudy. I was the disposable of the two of us. Sometimes I wondered if my parents felt this way as well. Parents will always tell you they don't have a favorite child, but I don't know if I believe that. How could they not have favored Gary over me? How could anyone not have? He was—Gary.

I'd say the worst of the depression—the suicide-thinking depression—lasted one month, maybe two. During this time I rarely left the apartment except to attend my classes. I had wanted to be by myself. I had wanted nothing to do with the outside world.

I had wanted a place like Aokigahara, a place where I could be left alone and forgotten.

Nevertheless, I've always been a pragmatist, and I also understood that my death wouldn't bring Gary back and, just as those signs we'd passed earlier had insinuated, it would only cause my family and friends more pain.

Unfortunately, I had witnessed this domino effect first-hand. It occurred back when I was in high school. On a Saturday afternoon during summer break six guys I knew had crammed into a car with five seatbelts and were driving to see a Pearl Jam concert. Barry "Weasel" Mitchell was behind the wheel. He was speeding. My close friend Chris, who was in the car, told me he'd wanted him to slow down, but he'd been too timid to say anything. Everyone else was fine with the speed, he figured he could be too. They were passing around a two-foot-tall bong, hot-boxing the car. When the bong came to Weasel, he told his little brother Stevie, who was in shotgun, to hold the steering wheel straight while he took a hit. At this point Chris no longer wanted them to slow down, he wanted them to stop, so he could get out, and he was just working himself up to say something when the car drifted onto the gravel shoulder of the road. Weasel shoved the bong aside and yanked the steering wheel to the left. He overcompensated. The car knifed across the two-lane blacktop. He swung the wheel back the other way. Again he overcompensated. Suddenly the vehicle took on a life of its own, swerving back and forth, back and forth, out of control. Inevitably it launched off the highway, nosed into the shallow culvert, shot back out, and crashed headlong into a tree a little past Blackhawk Airfield.

This was as much as Chris remembered because he was knocked unconscious. Newspapers and the gossip that filtered through our school filled in the gaps for me. A passing motorist called in the accident. The guy who didn't have his seatbelt on—the sixth passenger, Anthony Mainardi—was launched through the windshield, but miraculously he was the least injured, suffering only lacerations to his face and some bruising. The other injuries ranged from Kenny Baker needing facial reconstruction surgery to Tom Reynolds suffering several broken ribs and swallowing half his teeth. Stevie, who was two years younger than everyone else, was the sole fatality. The collision with the tree shoved the engine block back several feet, crushing him in his seat. Apparently his guts were squeezed out of him, similar to what happens to roadkill. He was pronounced dead at the scene.

Two weeks after Weasel was charged with vehicular homicide by intoxication, he stuffed some socks in the exhaust pipe of his parents' remaining vehicle, climbed in behind the wheel, started the engine, and got fatally high on carbon monoxide poisoning. His mother had a nervous breakdown shortly after and was checked into Badger Prairie Health Care Center (which in the nineteenth century had been called the Dane County Asylum for the Criminally Insane), where she failed to kill herself by slitting her wrists but succeeded by jumping from an eighth-floor window. The day after she was buried Weasel's father, a police detective, took his service revolver and blew his brains out—

"Ah, shit," I heard Tomo say, tugging me back to the present.

Some two dozen feet ahead of us was a glade created when a large tree fell over and knocked down several smaller ones. The white ribbon ended there.

"It's a dead end," I stated.

"Looks like it," Neil said.

As the meaning of this sank in, disappointment welled inside me. We wouldn't be calling John Scott and the Israelis to come meet us. We would have to walk all the way back to the intertwined trees. And if the others hadn't found anything either, then this entire excursion would be a bust.

A white ribbon, that was all.

When we stepped into the clearing, I looked up. It was the first time I had seen the sky clearly since we'd started down the secondary trail. It was low and gray and foreboding. I continued forward, my eyes still raised, my hands out, feeling for raindrops, when Mel hissed at me to stop.

I froze, thinking that maybe I was about to step into an unseen hole. But, no, I was on solid ground. Frowning, I turned toward her, my eyes sweeping the forest floor, and I saw what she had seen. My heart locked up in my chest, and I went cold all over.

I was standing in the middle of a gravesite.

7

T O the right of me, strewn on the ground, were a number of innocuous items that wouldn't have been out of place in anyone's home. But here, in the middle of the forest—*this* forest—they were a ghastly sight. There was an old, torn umbrella. A ruined handbag, covered with dirt and dead leaves. A pack of Seven Stars cigarettes. An empty bottle of Smirnoff vodka. A broken mirror, a toothbrush, a hairbrush, a tube of lipstick.

And, perhaps most disturbing of all, an upside-down doll nailed into the trunk of an adjacent tree.

I couldn't move, couldn't look away from the eclectic arrangement of items as my mind raced, trying to make sense of what lay before me. The lipstick indicated that the person who had apparently died here had been a woman. That made this gravesite even more tragic to me. I don't know why. Women kill themselves too. I guess I just expected if we found someone, it would be a man. A woman dying in this way—in the wilderness, alone—it didn't seem right.

I wrenched my eyes from the sad remnants of a life and looked up. No body hanging in the trees. No broken noose. I scanned the surrounding forest. No bones, no clothes.

A darkness rose within me, mirroring the darkness that permeated the forest, and I wondered about the woman herself. Who was she? A secretary? A housewife? A flight attendant? I've taught housewives and secretaries, dozens of them, and I realized this woman might once have been a student at my school. I tried to imagine one of my students taking their own life. I couldn't. They were all so happy, so bubbly, eager to learn English, curious about the world.

Neil was moving. The sound of his feet crunching leaves startled me out of my trance. I blinked and looked at him. He scavenged an old stick from the forest floor, returned, and poked the bag. It was as stiff as a board.

I wanted to tell Neil to leave the bag as it was. Viewing a dead person's belongings was intrusive enough; rifling through them seemed sacrilegious. But I said nothing while he worked the end of the stick into the large pocket and dragged out something white.

"Underwear?" Tomo said. He'd crept up next to me. "This kinky shit."

Neil kept digging and extracted a purple T-shirt, a pair of socks, a small-cup bra, a pair of scissors, and a paperback book. The book was partially obscured by another shirt, but I could see some kanji and the English letters IDE.

"Flip the book over," I said.

"Why?"

"I want to see the cover."

"That is the cover."

I forgot that in Japan books were read right to left. "Move the shirt then."

Neil did so. The cover image was a two-dimensional coffin in which rested what looked like some sort of crash test dummy. The title read: *The Complete Manuel of Suicide.*

"Holy shit," I said. "That's the book Ben mentioned."

Neil nodded. "The one that describes this forest as the perfect place to die."

It's one thing when someone tells you something; it's another thing entirely to witness it with your own eyes.

Seeing this book was like being slapped in the face with cold, cruel reality.

"Hey, look there," Tomo said, pointing at the forest floor. I didn't see anything but leafy mulch. He dropped to his knees, brushed away some dead leaves, and snatched up a small piece of plastic. He uncovered five or six pieces in total.

"Is that an ID?" Mel asked.

"Driver license," Tomo said, examining the snippets of plastic he cupped in his hands. "Yumi Akido. January 18, 1983. Damn, she young. Where picture?"

He spread out his search, brushing aside leaves and twigs. He unearthed more of the driver's license, as well as a destroyed VISA credit card and a Softbank debit card.

"She's hot," he said, examining one piece. "Why would hot girl suicide?"

"Let me see," I said.

He passed me the small section of ID. I held it so Mel and Neil could view it as well. The woman's hair was dyed a reddish blonde and cut in a layered shag. She had a small mouth and a perky nose. Her black eyes were heavily lashed—those fake ones you could buy from a 7-Eleven that all young Japanese girls seemed to favor. Her face was a little too round, but Tomo was right. She was attractive.

I visualized her dead, her head flopped sideways, her neck broken, the color drained from her over-blushed cheeks, the sight gone from her eyes, her skin shriveled like an orange peel left in the sun.

"Why did she cut them up like that?" Mel asked.

"I reckon for the same reason she nailed that doll to the tree," Neil said. "They represented a society to which she no longer felt she belonged. This was her way of saying screw you to everyone and everything she left behind."

As we stood there, silent, each of us thinking our own thoughts, I tried to piece together the bizarre ritual this woman performed before she killed herself. Judging by her scattered personal belongings she—and in no particular order —put on clean undergarments, got drunk, destroyed her identification, nailed the doll to the tree, applied lipstick, brushed her teeth and hair, smoked a few cigarettes, then ended herself.

"Let's go," Mel said, taking my hand.

"Okay," I mumbled, but I didn't move.

The woman—Yumi—would have arrived here during the daytime; she couldn't navigate the forest in the night. Given that she had brought the book about suicide, she was likely one of the hesitaters that Tomo had described. She was still contemplating killing herself, trying to convince herself it was a necessary evil. So what had she been thinking about while she sat here on her own? Whether to turn back, head home, and go to work on Monday morning? Her parents and siblings? The problems that drove her here? And what could those be? She was only twenty-fucking-one.

The underwear and bra.

Why?

Because, like I'd theorized, she wasn't completely sure she wanted to kill herself, and she wanted to remain hygienic until she decided? I didn't know about that. It seemed a little like worrying about a fever when you were standing before a firing squad. And what about the toothpaste and hairbrush and lipstick? Hygiene again? Keeping up appearances? Or was I not thinking symbolically enough? Brushing her teeth, combing her hair, applying lipstick, these were actions she'd performed every day of her life. Perhaps she'd wanted to go through the motions in an effort to experience humanity one last time. And if that was the case, did she have tears in her eyes while she brushed her teeth? Anger as she smeared lipstick over her lips? Regret as she combed her hair, one hundred strokes?

Or was she smiling, relieved her pain was finally coming to an end?

I knew I was oversimplifying all of this. But rationalizing, whether correctly or not, was my way of coping with death.

I turned away from the belongings. I couldn't recall whether I'd been looking at them for thirty seconds or two minutes.

Mel, I noticed, was faced away, staring into the trees. I thought she was having her own moment of reflection when she said, "Can you hear that?"

Those words put me immediately on edge. They weren't the words you wanted to hear in the woods, standing on a gravesite.

"What?" I said softly.

"I thought I heard something."

I listened. I didn't hear anything.

"We should call the others," Neil said.

"It's not a body," I said.

"No, but it's good enough, I reckon."

"Okay. Mel?"

She turned, frowning. "Yeah?"

"Can you call John Scott? Tell him to come here?"

"Come here?"

"To see the grave."

"To see the grave?"

"He and Ben and Nina, they'll want to see it."

"Oh. Right. Wait—I don't have my phone. But I know his number. Give me your phone."

I frowned at her. She had John Scott's number memorized?

What the fuck?

Still, I passed her my phone.

She took it and dialed his number.

8

"JOHN? It's me. Can you hear me?" Mel asked him how they'd fared with their path, listened for a bit, asked a few questions—asked him to repeat himself several times, indicating a bad reception—then explained that we found a gravesite. She told him how to reach us and to watch out for the crevice she fell into. She recounted everything that happened to her, getting more and more worked up in the process. Then she ended the call.

"Did they come across anything?" I asked.

She nodded. "He said they found a metal dog kennel."

"What?"

"Those carrying things you take your dog to the vet in."

"Was there a dog in it?"

"I didn't ask. I doubt it. John would have said so."

"Why someone bring dog?" Tomo asked.

"Because they didn't want to die alone?" Neil suggested.

"Like a murder-suicide, only with your pet?" Mel said.

I wondered about that. Did the person kill the dog before they killed themselves? Or did they just want its company in their last hour? Was there a wild canine running around the forest now, surviving off of small rodents—and perhaps human bodies?

I pushed aside the thoughts and said, "So what do we do? It's going to be an hour or more until they get here."

"I still want to see dead fucker," Tomo said.

I raised an eyebrow. "A grave's not good enough?"

"No, man."

"Then go look. I'm going to rest here."

"Me too," Mel said.

"Neil?" Tomo said. "You wanna come?"

"I don't think so, mate."

"Come on, man. I don't go alone. Maybe I get lost, die. Then you blame."

Neil shook his head.

"Please, man?" Tomo said. "Just little."

"I told you, no."

"Don't be chicken guy."

"I swear, Tomo—"

"Okay, okay. But come. Please?"

"No."

"Please?"

"No."

"Please?"

"Oh, for heaven's sake, Tomo!"

"Please?"

Neil sighed.

"So you come?" Tomo said.

"Will it shut you up?"

"I don't say nothing."

Neil told me to keep an eye on his backpack, then he joined Tomo, and they wandered off deeper into the forest together.

"Let's go that way a bit," I said to Mel, nodding past her.

We moved a respectable distance from the gravesite and flopped down on a flat patch of ground at the base of a large cedar, our heads on our packs, staring at the canopy overhead.

We didn't say anything for a while. I wanted to talk about the woman named Yumi, but I didn't know how to break the ice or what to say. Specifically, I didn't want to trivialize what we'd experienced. Finding the grave the way we had, raw, untouched, the personal belongings spread bare on the ground, it seemed as though there should be some moral weight behind my words.

Mel said, "Do you remember when we first met?"

That caught me off guard. "Yeah, of course. At work."

"Remember Elise?"

"Yeah."

"She was in your group."

"My group?"

"You know what I mean."

I suppose I did. Like in any working or social environment, there were cliques at our school. One "group," to use Mel's terminology, consisted of the older, married teachers, like Neil, who for the most part kept to themselves. Another group was the guys in their early thirties. There were four of them. Every day they swapped stories about their late-night debauchery: Russian prostitutes, transvestite bars, street fights with other expats. They were funny, friendly to everyone, and I got along with them well enough. My group was made up of those in their twenties, recent college graduates, traveling for a year or two to see the world. Lumped in there with me were the Canadian Derek Miller and three girls, Jennifer, Karen, and Elise. Mel was half in, half out. Derek liked her; the girls didn't.

The last group to speak of, if you could even call it a group because it comprised notorious loners, would be the freaks and geeks. I don't like either of those labels, but I don't know a better way to describe some of the fringe characters we work with. An example would be Brendan Christoffson, aka Blade. That's what he changed his name to halfway through the year: Blade, as in Wesley Snipe's Blade the Vampire Killer. Outside of work he often wore barrettes or colorful headbands in his long black hair, platform boots, and more chains than Keith Richards. He spoke effeminately and regularly stunk up the teacher's room with his black nail polish.

There's an ill-proportionally high percentage of Brendans teaching English in Japan, likely due to the fact the country is so quirky you can let your freak flag fly with pride, and the myth that if you're Caucasian you're some sort of Viking god in the eyes of the Japanese. A popular comic strip that contributes to the latter perception stars a scrawny, introverted Canadian who, once he moves to Japan, instantly morphs into Charisma Man, a Rock Hudson type with a bevy of girls hanging off his arms.

"What about Elise?" I asked, curious to see where Mel was going with this trip down memory lane.

"She had a thing for you."

"I know."

"Why didn't you date her?"

Coming from your girlfriend, that was an odd question, and I struggled with how to answer it. "Because," I said.

"Because what?"

"I don't know. I wasn't attracted to her."

"Why not? She was pretty."

"She was loud." Elise was Australian, from some country town in western Queensland, and she didn't have a volume switch. She pretty much shouted everything at a nasally one hundred decibels, her vowels pinched and drawn out to excruciating lengths.

"She was so loud," Mel agreed.

"And," I said.

"And?"

"I met you."

Although I couldn't see Mel's face—we were still side by side, looking up at the canopy—I could sense her smiling. This was the right answer. Even so, I wasn't blowing smoke. A couple weeks into my contract I arrived at work one Monday afternoon and found Mel in the teacher's room, keeping to herself, poring over a textbook she had to teach. I remember Derek pulling me aside that same day and making a cock-sucking face, which seems surreal now, given he's become one of my better friends and she my girlfriend.

Over the next few days I struck up conversation with Mel whenever an opportunity presented itself, though this proved difficult because as a new teacher she was busy learning the textbooks, the system, and so forth. Elise could see the effort I was making, and two things happened. First, she stopped flirting with me, which had been going on pretty much nonstop since we met. Second, she became frosty toward Mel, so much so they rarely talked in the two years before Elise eventually returned to Australia—which was the reason Mel never quite fit into our group.

"She was a bitch," Mel said.

"You were a bitch," I said.

"Me?"

"Remember the first time I asked you out for a drink? When we were taking the train home from work?"

"So?"

"Do you recall what you said?"

"I didn't have an umbrella."

"What the hell did that mean?"

"It was raining."

"I wasn't going to take you on a picnic."

"I don't know. I panicked. It was my first week at work. I didn't want to seem like...that kind of girl."

"I thought you had a boyfriend."

"I did. Sort of. Like you."

"Me?"

"You had a girlfriend. Shelly MacDonald."

I was surprised Mel knew Shelly's surname. I didn't think I'd ever told her. "We were broken up," I said.

"Hmmm."

"What does that mean?"

"Nothing."

We fell silent again. I played over what we'd just spoken of, that first year in Japan when the country was still new to me. I imagined myself reminiscing about stuff like this—Japan stuff —at a dinner party in Madison in twenty years' time. Would my friends back home care? Would they be able to relate? If Mel and I ever broke up, would all these memories cease to mean anything, cease to be? If a tree falls in the forest...

"Do you remember Degawa?" Mel asked abruptly.

"Degawa...?" I said, as if speaking the name would elicit a memory.

"He was one of the first students I taught. I used to tell you about him. He bought me the stereo system."

Before we moved into the guesthouse near Shinagawa together, Mel's apartment building had been adjacent to a used electronics store called Hard Off. She'd been searching for a cheap stereo system there one day when she bumped into Degawa. He helped her pick out a Panasonic setup with massive speakers and insisted he pay for it. She objected, of course, but he wouldn't take no for an answer. Then, during one of their classes later in the week, he asked her to join him for dinner. He assured her he only wanted to practice his English.

I cautioned Mel against taking up his offer. He was a fifty-year-old man. He was divorced. She was a young blonde American girl. Nevertheless, she always takes people at face value. She looks for the good, not the bad. This was likely why she told him she'd join him—with the provision her roommate, an Irish girl, come as well.

Apparently Degawa had been the perfect gentleman, genuinely interested in improving his English. Come to think of it, I didn't hear much about him after that dinner.

"What about him?" I asked idly.

Mel hesitated. Then she said, "He killed himself."

I propped myself up on my elbow, stared at her. "When?"

"Couple years ago."

"Why didn't you ever tell me this?"

"You never liked him—"

"That's not true."

"You thought he was an old pervert."

"I didn't—"

"You did."

"Who told you he killed himself?"

"One of the other students. They all knew."

"No one informed me."

She shrugged. "I knew him better."

"How did he do it?"

"He hanged himself."

I stiffened. "Don't tell me he did it here?"

Mel shook her head. "In his apartment. He wasn't discovered for a week. Nobody bothered to check on him."

"Why...?"

"I don't know. He was lonely probably. Anyway, seeing the grave, it made me think of him."

I wanted to say something about Yumi right then, about the ritual she'd performed before killing herself. Instead I said, "Are you okay being here?"

"Camping in the forest?"

I nodded.

"It's just one night."

"But you're okay?"

"Yes." She paused, then asked, "Are you?"

I was about to tell her I was fine, but there was something in her question, a subtext, and it took me a moment to realize what it was. "You mean because of Gary?"

"Seeing the grave..."

"It's not the same."

"It's depressing here."

"It doesn't bother me."

"You're sure?"

I didn't know. But I didn't want to talk about Gary. I never talked about Gary to anyone. At least, not in any real depth. Even after spending four years with me, all Mel knew was that he was my older brother, he was a hockey player, and he was shot. That's how I wanted to keep it.

"Yeah, Mel," I said. "I'm sure."

"Okay."

I lay back down and tried to picture Degawa's face, but it stubbornly refused to reveal itself. All I could remember about him was his van. It was compact, like Honda's, a Mitsubishi maybe, with curtains covering the side and back windows. He'd honked at Mel and me one day while we were walking home from work together. Mel had said, "That's Degawa." And I had replied, "The pervert?"

A loud peal of thunder sounded overhead, followed by another, both still distant but closer than I would have liked.

"Guess it might rain after all," I said.

Mel sighed. "And I was having such a lovely day."

9

I didn't know who instigated it—Mel rolling against me, me placing a hand on her backside—but soon we were half naked, making love in Suicide Forest. It was risky, considering Tomo and Neil could have come back at any moment, but I didn't care, and I guess Mel didn't either. Given the dismal environment, and the hard ground, I was surprised the sex had gone off without a hitch. Well, almost. Halfway through Mel complained about a piece of bark rubbing against her back. We moved, but then it was a stick. Then something else. Regardless, I didn't have any regrets, and I didn't think Mel did either.

I began to drift into a light afternoon siesta when Mel, lying next to me, jerked into a sitting position, crying out.

I sat up immediately. "What's wrong?" I asked.

She was taking deep breaths, her hand against her chest.

"Mel?" I pressed, getting worried.

She shook her head. "It's nothing. A dream."

"More like a nightmare. You're wired. What was it about?"

"I fell down that crater again. Actually, you pushed me."

"What?"

"It doesn't mean anything. Just a dream thing. I don't think you meant to. But I didn't land on the ledge this time. I kept falling and falling and splashed into a huge, cold lake. It was completely dark. And for some reason I couldn't swim. I started sinking. There was something in the water with me."

She shivered. "I was so scared. I didn't know what it was. It kept brushing against my legs."

"Did you get out?"

"I was drowning. I could see you and John looking down into the hole. I was trying to yell, but water filled my mouth. You guys didn't do anything. You were just watching. Then I sank to the bottom of the lake—and woke up." She pulled her knees to her chest and wrapped her arms around them. She turned her face away from me.

"Hey," I said, "it was just a dream."

She looked at me again, and I saw tears in her eyes.

"What if back then, for real, I missed that ledge?"

"I told you...it wasn't that deep."

"I could have died."

"You wouldn't have died."

"I could have. It was a matter of inches."

"Yeah, and you could have walked straight past the hole without stepping in it. Everything in life is a matter of inches. Jaywalking across the street is a matter of inches. Don't think about it." I wiped away one of her tears with my finger. "Okay?"

She nodded.

In the distance I heard John Scott's voice. A few moments later I saw him and Ben and Nina moving through the vegetation, following the ribbon, toward the gravesite. Ben noticed the scattered belongings first and cried out excitedly. They began whispering in hushed, reverent tones. I couldn't hear what they were saying.

Mel rubbed her eyes and called to them.

"Mel!" John Scott said. He came over and crouched in front of her. "Holy shit, Mel. We passed that hole you fell in. It went to fucking China." He took her hands and examined them. "You don't have any cuts or anything?"

I almost told him to stop touching my girlfriend, but I held my tongue.

"Ethan said it wasn't very deep—"

John Scott stared at me like I was insane. "Do you need glasses, dude? There was no bottom."

Mel frowned. "No bottom?"

I willed him to shut up.

"Even with the flashlight," he went on, "we saw zip. It just kept going and going. I dropped a rock but didn't hear it land."

Mel turned on me. "You said—"

"I didn't want to worry you."

"Hey, it doesn't matter," John Scott told her. "Neil saved your ass. You're all good now."

I glared at him. Neil? Just Neil? I recalled Mel explaining to him over the phone how we'd used Neil's guy ropes, but he obviously knew Tomo and I were there as well. Was he purposely trying to piss me off?

"Ethan and Tomo helped too," Mel said.

John Scott nodded, but it didn't seem like he was listening. He hooked his thumb toward the grave. "How cool is this shit? And it was a chick. Where's Tomo and Neil?"

"They went for a walk," Mel said.

"Looking for the body?"

"They're right over there."

She pointed past us to where Tomo and Neil were emerging from the trees. John Scott strode over to them and began back-slapping and congratulating and high fiving.

I gritted my teeth.

Why did I care?

Then I heard him asking about a body, saw them shaking their heads. Nevertheless, Tomo started talking excitedly about something. From what I could make out it sounded as if he'd found several more ribbons. Ben and Nina went to them.

"Come on," Mel said to me, getting up and going over.

"Coming," I said.

Tomo went on about his discovery, then John Scott started talking about the dog kennel, holding everyone's interest. Deciding I had brooded long enough, I got up and joined them.

"Tomo and Neil found another ribbon," Mel said, filling me

in.

"Ribbon *and* string," Tomo said.

"Did you follow them?"

"We followed the ribbon to the string," Neil said, "then we came back."

John Scott asked, "So who's up for checking them out?"

"Nina and I will continue," Ben said. "Definitely."

"I've had my adventure," Neil said. "I reckon I'll wait here."

"But I forget way," Tomo said.

"Bugger off, Tomo," Neil retorted.

"It's true."

"We need you, dude," John Scott told Neil, giving him a shit-eating grin and patting him heartily on the shoulder. "Mel?"

"We agreed only one more hour," she stated. "I—I think I want to leave."

"The forest?" John Scott said, surprised. "You can't. You'll never make it all the way out before it gets dark."

"Why don't we just stay here then?"

"Beside that gravesite? You want to sleep next to that?"

Mel frowned.

"Listen," John Scott added, seeing he'd scored a point, "it's not like we can get lost. We simply stick to the ribbon and the string."

"We need to find firewood if we want a fire."

"We'll collect it on the way."

Mel shook her head, biting her lower lip. She was clearly distressed. The buzz from escaping the crevice had long since dissipated, and it seemed the experience had shaken her more than I'd suspected. Once again, I regretted bringing her out here. It had been selfish of me. I'd been focused only on what I'd wanted.

"I'll head back with you, Mel," I said, taking her hand. "We'll get a room somewhere—"

"Didn't you hear me?" John Scott said. "You're not getting out before dark."

"We'll manage."

"And fall in another fucking hole—"

"Why don't you fuck off—"

"Stop it!" Mel shouted. "You two—stop fighting!" She exhaled loudly. "We're not leaving. Not in the dark. And we're not staying here either. Not by that grave. So we'll go a little farther. Then we'll make camp. We'll make a fire, it will be fine."

John Scott issued another one of those stupid army hooahs.

And that, it seemed, was that.

CONVENIENCE stores in Japan offered much healthier and fresher food choices in comparison to their counterparts in other countries, especially the US. I thought this once again as I watched everyone chow down on what they'd bought earlier at the train station. Mel had a bowl of thick wheat noodles; Neil, a rectangular tray of chilled buckwheat noodles served in a soy-based broth; John Scott, sushi and a salad. Tomo, Ben, and Nina each had a bento box. And I'd opted for a single *onigiri*, a triangle-shaped rice ball wrapped in seaweed. I was hoping I'd chosen one filled with tuna fish or salmon, but because I couldn't read the kanji on the plastic packaging, I'd inadvertently ended up with *umeboshi*, a type of pickled plum. It wasn't very appetizing.

"I don't get it," John Scott said with a philosophical look on his face as he poked at his salad. "Suicide, you know."

"What do you mean?" Ben asked.

"Why people kill themselves. Can life really get that bad you want to blow your brains out? I mean, someone is always going to have it worse than you. You think you have it bad because you can't pay your mortgage? Well, a pal of mine lost both his legs in a training accident, and he's one of the most go-happy motherfuckers I know."

Ben shrugged. "I think it depends on the person. Everyone reacts to circumstances differently. It is in your...how do you say...constitution."

John Scott nodded and said, "You just got to deal with what your problems are. Move on. There was this guy, true story, I shit you not. Growing up, he was always the shortest kid in his class. Like tiny. He also had this whiney, womanly voice, and he used all these effeminate gestures. You would have sworn he was gay, but he wasn't. And you'd laugh if you knew what his name was. Insult to injury, you know? But I can't tell you that yet. Anyway, you wouldn't think it could get much worse for the poor sucker, right? A weak dick who could never get any chicks? Well, get this. On top of everything else he was a black dude in some white hick town in Minnesota. So when the guy wasn't getting the shit kicked out of him by the homophobes, the racists were doing it. Bottom line is, he knew he wasn't going to get any taller or whiter or less gay, so if anyone's going to kill themselves, it's going to be this guy, right? You know what he did?"

We looked at him blankly.

"He buys a guitar and practices the shit out of it. Then, when he's seventeen or eighteen, he signs his first record contract. A few years later he releases *Purple Rain*."

There was a moment of silence.

"The guy was Prince?" Mel said.

"Symbol Man?" Tomo said.

"Is this story for real?" Ben asked.

John Scott grinned. "Real as rain, brother. That's my point. You never know what life's going to throw at you. So why take yourself out of the game early before you know how it ends?"

AS soon as everyone had finished eating we set out. I thought the rest and the food would have dispelled some of the heaviness that had settled inside me after discovering Yumi's gravesite. It didn't. In fact, I felt grimmer than ever, and again I began to worry about the possibility of getting lost in Aokigahara. If we couldn't find this new ribbon, and we couldn't find our way back to the white one, we would be in serious trouble. We had limited food and water. If we failed to make it back to the main trail, and it didn't rain, we likely wouldn't survive more than a few days. I believed we were heading south, but that was a guess at best, because the forest never seemed to change. Just more malformed trees and zigzagging roots and teeth-like rocks. The white ribbon could have meandered southeast or southwest. Hell, for all I knew, it could have looped back upon itself, taking us north. The forest was that disorienting, that deceptive.

Sometime later, just as I was beginning to believe we had indeed gotten lost, we spotted the ribbon. It was red and fifty feet to the right and continued in the same direction we'd been heading.

"Looks like we strayed a little," Neil said, scratching the stubble on his chin. "No matter. We're not far now."

He marched toward the ribbon. The rest of us fell into line behind him. For his age Neil was in good shape, showing little signs of fatigue. Nina, Ben, and Tomo also seemed to be doing okay, and the four of them gradually pulled away, so soon there was a thirty-foot gap between them and Mel, John Scott, and me.

Mel was thin and sprightly looking. You would think she went to the gym several times a week, but the most exercise she got was her once-a-week salsa lessons. Her muscles would be rusty for this kind of continuous exertion. It was part of the reason I'd originally planned to climb Mt. Fuji in two stages; I knew it would be difficult for her to climb the mountain in one continuous trek.

Like most soldiers, John Scott was fit and muscular. You could see this in his gait, the roll of his shoulders, his bullish neck. But he was a smoker. I could hear his labored breathing. It was wheezy, and every so often he would cough, hawking up a large amount of phlegm.

And me? What was my excuse for lagging behind? I was simply a big guy. I had a lot of weight to move. At six foot four I weighed two hundred ten pounds, which put me roughly twenty pounds overweight. Fortunately, because of my large frame, this was not very noticeable, though Mel often cautioned me about something called invisible fat.

When had I begun to put on the weight? I wondered. Growing up, Gary and I had been equally athletic. We both played center for top-tier hockey teams in our respective age groups. We both scored similar numbers of goals, had similar numbers of assists. Gary won the MVP trophy while in Bantam AAA; I won it in Peewee AAA. Then sometime in high school, grade ten I believe, I began slowing down, losing my edge. Soon I was no longer the fastest skater or the best stick handler. In Midget Minor I was moved to left wing. In Midget Major my coach suggested I try defense. Still big and strong, I performed adequately in the new position, but I had become a mediocre player at best.

Gary, on the other hand, continued to excel, continued to score, continued to attract all the attention of the scouts. Then he was signed by the Capitals. He met Cheryl the same year. She was the friend of a teammates' girlfriend. They got married six months later at the church that Gary and I had attended since we were kids. I was his best man. Cheryl fell pregnant almost immediately, and Lisa was born.

Cheryl called me late one evening a few weeks after Gary's funeral. This was during my suicide stage when I rarely left my apartment. I had classes the next day, but I wasn't sleeping. I never went to sleep early then. People say when you get depressed all you want to do is sleep, but that wasn't true for me. Sleep was the last thing I wanted, largely because of the nightmares. Instead I would watch TV or movies until I couldn't keep my eyes open any longer.

I checked the call display, saw Cheryl's number, and didn't answer. I didn't want to talk to her. I didn't want to talk to anyone. There was nothing to say. I didn't want to console or be consoled. I wanted to feel my grief. I wanted it to be mine.

Nevertheless, Cheryl called back ten minutes later, then

ten minutes after that. Realizing something bad might have happened, I picked up. As soon as Cheryl greeted me I knew I had made a mistake. Although she sounded somber, unsure, there was no panic in her voice. She spent the first several minutes asking me questions about college, my classes, campus, like we were friends, but we had never been friends. She had been my brother's wife. I saw her at birthdays and on other special occasions. I didn't feel comfortable talking to her like we were friends. I didn't even know why she was calling. Comfort, I imagined. She was lonely. I was too. Gary connected our lonelinesses.

I interrupted her and told her I had to go. She didn't ask me why, didn't protest, didn't start talking about Gary, for which I was grateful.

We hung up and have never spoken again.

She was seeing someone else now. My parents told me this. Initially the revelation made me angry, which was unjustified. Gary was gone. Cheryl had to move on with her life. Still, it felt like a betrayal. If things worked out with this guy, this stranger, he would one day become Cheryl's husband, Lisa's father.

Lisa had just started grade three. She sent me a Christmas card every year I've been in Japan. I wondered how long this would continue for, how long Cheryl would feel obligated to help Lisa to write them—

"Hey," Mel said, poking me in the side to get my attention. "We're here."

THE string bisected the red ribbon at perhaps a sixty-degree angle, heading southwest, or at least what I believed to be southwest.

"This is where Tomo and I stopped," Neil said.

"So which way should we go?" Ben asked.

"I say the string," John Scott said. "Something a little different, you know?"

"That is okay with me."

John Scott and Tomo stepped forward at the same time, eager to go, and they almost bumped into each other. John Scott waved. "Gentlemen first."

Tomo said, "More like pimp daddy first."

"You've been watching too much MTV, dude."

"Fa shizzle dizzle it's the big Neptizzle with the Snoopy D-O-Double Gizzle!"

Tomo spitting out Snoop Dogg lyrics in his off-kilter English accent was both bizarre and comical, though John Scott was the only person to laugh.

Tomo took the lead, followed by John Scott, Ben, Nina, and Mel.

Neil, it seemed, was finally feeling his age. He waited until everyone passed him by, then fell into step beside me, at the rear.

"Hope you're keeping track of the way we've come," I said to him.

"I thought you were."

"We're getting pretty far in."

"We just retrace our steps."

"Easier said than done."

"We follow the white ribbon to its beginning, make a left. That's it."

"If we can find the white ribbon again."

"How could we not? It's ten minutes that way." He gestured the way we'd come.

"More like twenty," I said. "And if we miss it, even by a little, we might never find it."

"We won't miss it."

I didn't reply. Not because I agreed or disagreed. There was merely nothing more to add. We either found the white ribbon again or we didn't. If we did, we were fine. If we didn't, we'd have to put our heads together and figure out what to do.

"What do you think happened to that girl's body?" Neil said.

"The police must have taken it out."

He nodded.

"What?" I said. "You don't agree?"

"I nodded, didn't I?"

"But...?" He appeared to be holding something back.

"Why would they leave her stuff behind?"

"Maybe their hands were full."

"Maybe."

"Or maybe she changed her mind and left on her own accord."

"After cutting up her ID and bank cards?"

I shrugged. "She could always get them replaced."

"Same question then. Why not take her stuff with her? The bag, the umbrella."

"What are you getting at, Neil? She either walked out of here, or the police carried her body out. What other alternatives are there? You think one of those *yūrei* came for her?"

"Now there's something to think about."

I glanced at him. He was watching the ground, his face expressionless. "You don't believe in ghosts, do you, Neil?" I asked.

"I never used to," he said. "It's not a Western thing, is it? But Kaori does. Her belief has rubbed off on me."

"She's seen a ghost?"

"Says she has. One night she woke up and says she saw the face of a little girl at the end of her bed. Earlier that day a little girl—she swears it was the same one she'd seen—was killed crossing the street outside our apartment. Kaori didn't learn about the girl's death until the next day."

My first impulse was to laugh. I didn't. I've met several people who've claimed to have seen a ghost, and they took their supernatural encounters quite seriously.

As a teenager I worked as a bellhop at a small family-run hotel in downtown Madison. The owner was a woman named Bella Grayson. She had no siblings and took over the business from her father a decade earlier when he became ill in his old age. She'd started working at the hotel when she was a child and had moved her way up through every position: dishwasher, housekeeper, line cook, office administration, etcetera. She'd seemed proud of this, getting to the top not via a handout from her father but through years of grunt work. She came across as a smart, down-to-earth woman—until halfway through my job interview when she cautioned me that the hotel was haunted, or at least had been in the past.

The story, as I remember it, went like this: six or seven years previously, around midnight, after most of the other staff had gone home, Bella Grayson had been in the office, placing the day's revenue in the wall safe, when she heard a loud noise from the adjacent saloon. She went to check it out and found a little girl in a red dress and shiny black shoes walking away from her, disappearing down the far hallway. Bella chased after her. She swore she was only a few seconds behind, but when she reached the hallway it was deserted. Back in the saloon she noticed all the ashtrays were aligned along the edges of the tables.

She called to the barmaid, a twenty-three-year-old girl named Grace who'd been in the kitchen changing into street clothes. Grace denied seeing anyone since the last customer left, the man who ran the hardware store across the street, and she was adamant she'd set the ashtrays in the middle of the table, alongside the cardboard coasters, where they belonged.

Nothing else unusual happened until a month later, when a bachelor staying in a room on the second floor complained about a little girl in a red dress running up and down the hallway all night.

A few weeks after this, when Bella arrived at work, she found the safe in her office wide open, though no money was missing.

She told her ailing father about the mysterious happenings, and he confessed that he'd seen the girl himself, and that a girl had died at the hotel in the early 1900s.

I recalled the way Bella had watched me after this revelation, intently, almost as if she were daring me to contradict the claim in some way. I assured her I believed every word and got the job. I ended up working at the hotel for three consecutive summers, often remaining late into the evenings.

I never heard so much as a boo.

Although I don't believe Bella was having me on, I remain convinced there must be a rational explanation to her tale, even though it eludes me.

Regarding Kaori's ghost, I can only assume it was nothing but a collection of shadows at the foot of her bed. The fact a girl died the same day was a coincidence. Either that, or Kaori unknowingly heard about the death not long after it happened, perhaps as a passing comment between two mothers in the apartment's lobby, something her conscious mind missed but her subconscious registered and manifested when she was half asleep and more susceptible to suggestion.

"Did you see it too?" I asked.

"The ghost?" Neil said.

I nodded.

"No, I didn't."

"You think Kaori really saw it?"

"I don't think she would make up something like that."

"She might have been...confused."

"It's possible."

"But you don't think so."

"When she woke me up she was scared white and in a near fit. She wouldn't go back to sleep and made me stay awake with her until morning." He shrugged. "You would do well to remember that while no one has been able to prove whether ghosts exist or not, no one has been able to disprove whether they do either."

"You can say the same thing about the tooth fairy."

"I don't want to argue this point, Ethan. I'm not a full-blown believer, but neither am I a skeptic. There are simply some things we cannot understand. Let's leave it at that."

And we did.

A couple hundred yards along the string we came to yet another ribbon, this one yellow. Like the original white one, it ran north-south, meandering into the forest. You could only see its length for twenty or thirty yards in either direction before the dense bracken swallowed it from sight.

"What should we do?" Ben asked. "Continue along the string, or down this new ribbon?"

"I say the ribbon," John Scott said.

"We did what you wanted, John," Mel said, and it was almost an accusation. "We came to see the ribbon and the string. If you want to keep going, fine, go ahead. I'm making camp."

"I'm with you, Mel," I told her, and she brightened immediately. "But the ground here is warped and rocky. I suggest we continue a bit further along the string until we find a better spot."

She nodded quickly, apparently happy for any compromise.

"You guys do what you want then," John Scott said. "Ben, you're cool?"

"Yes, Nina and I will keep exploring with you. That is why we are here."

"Since my services are no longer needed," Neil said, "I'm going to bow out, thanks."

John Scott said, "Tomo?"

"I'm bush, man."

"You're a bushman?"

"I'm tired. So much walking."

"Whatever." John Scott shrugged. "You pansies go find a good spot to make camp. We won't be too long behind. Just don't leave the string."

He, Ben, and Nina left without further discussion. The rest of us carried on along the string.

"What's pansy?" Tomo asked me.

"A flower," I told him.

"He call us flower?"

"He's an idiot."

"Ethan, be nice," Mel said from behind us.

A dozen paces onward I walked straight into a spider's web. "Ugh," I said, wiping the silky strands from my face, spitting them from my mouth.

"What is it?" Mel asked, catching up to me.

"Spider web."

"Wonder what it's eating out here," Neil said. "There're no bugs."

"Maybe they come out at night."

The string didn't follow a straight line. Instead it weaved left and right, almost as if the person who'd left it had been drunk. I wondered at this and decided it wasn't unlikely. After all, Yumi had brought a bottle of vodka with her. Wasn't that how most people killed themselves? A lethal cocktail of booze and sleeping pills?

I pictured the person forging the same path we were on, their shirttail untucked, their hair a mess, a spool of string in one hand, a bottle of vodka or whiskey in the other. Stumbling as they walked toward their death, drifting drunkenly back and forth between the trees, tears streaming down their cheeks, cursing their boss or their spouse or the world in general, knowing they wouldn't miss it one bit.

We came to a fallen tree. It was decaying and covered in moss and fungi. The string passed over the thick midsection. It was too large to clear in a single step. I had to straddle it and swing my legs over one at a time. As I pushed myself clear my left hand punched through the rotten bark to the hollow cavity beneath. A sharp pain ripped across my wrist and I cried out.

"Ethan!" Mel exclaimed.

Little pill bugs swarmed around the hole I'd made. I jerked my hand free in disgust. There was a bright red line across the inside of my wrist.

Mel appeared beside me. "Gosh, you're cut." She examined

the thin wound. "We don't have Neosporin or Band-Aids or anything."

"Ewwww!" Tomo exclaimed. "Look this one!"

"Gross," Neil agreed.

They were hunched over the hole. The oval pill bugs were scurrying everywhere. Two centipedes were trying to squirm back beneath the bark. Tomo was poking a fat black millipede with a twig. It had curled its segmented body into a protective spiral.

"Careful," Neil said. "They spray acid."

I checked my wrist again. The blood had begun to flow freely.

"Shit, man!" Tomo said to me. "You look like suicide guy."

"You need to put pressure on it," Mel said. She shrugged off her backpack and scrambled through the main pocket. She pulled out a white sock and handed it to me.

I pressed it against the wound.

"You have to hold it there until the blood clots," she instructed. "Are you sure you're okay?"

"Yeah," I said. "It's not deep."

"The ground's a bit better here. We'll make camp and boil some water to wash it out. You don't want it getting infected."

I glanced at the surrounding forest. It was already getting dark, the greenery losing its vibrancy, the shadows gathering and lengthening.

"Sounds good to me," I said.

I shrugged off my backpack and unbuckled the tent I had brought. Unlike Neil's traditional tent—a flysheet held up by poles and guy ropes and anchored to the ground with stakes —mine was a small dome design, made for one person, but it would be fine for both Mel and me. I'd suggested everyone bring a tent in case the huts lining the trail up Mt. Fuji were not open. I'd read online that many shut down in September. John Scott, I'd noticed when we'd first met this morning, hadn't brought a tent. That was his problem though. He could sleep under the stars or, if it started raining, squeeze in with Neil or Tomo or the Israelis. All I knew was that he wasn't cuddling up next to me—or Mel for that matter.

When I'd finished erecting the tent, Mel was still determined to boil water and rinse my wound thoroughly. Neil, however, brandished a bottle of whiskey he'd brought and poured a tiny bit over the cut. The alcohol didn't sting as much as I'd thought it might. Mel gave me a fresh sock, which I tied around my wrist.

"Anyone fancy a nip?" Neil asked, holding up the bottle.

"Yeah, man," Tomo said. "Let's get drunk."

"I said a nip," Neil said. "Get drunk on your own booze."

"I don't bring none."

"Guess you're not getting drunk."

Neil retrieved some paper cups from his backpack and poured a finger for both Tomo and me. He offered Mel some, but she declined.

"*Kampai*," Tomo said, raising his cup.

"To nature," Neil said.

I thought about the gravesite, the young woman who had likely perished there, and said, "To life."

"To life," Neil repeated thoughtfully.

We sipped.

"Hey," I said to Neil, "where did you learn to tie two strings together like that?"

"I used to kayak now and then in New Zealand. It's how we tied grab handles to the boat."

"You don't kayak anymore?"

"In Japan? Nah."

"By the way," I added offhandedly, "what did John Scott say to you guys when we met up back there?"

"What do you mean?" Neil asked.

"I saw him congratulating you and stuff."

"He said we did a good job at the hole."

"Did he tell you that if he were there, he would have saved

Mel single-handedly?"

"He never said that, Ethan," Mel intervened. She was sitting behind me, on a rock.

"It's what he was thinking. I could tell."

"You're just angry he didn't give you any credit."

"I couldn't care less what he thinks. The guy's a joker."

"Give him a break, Ethan."

I turned to look at her. "Why do you keep defending him?"

"He's my friend."

"From high school. You know how long ago that was? Did you keep in touch with him afterward?"

"A little bit."

"Did you see him during college?"

She frowned. "What are you getting at?"

"What was up with him touching you and all that shit?"

"What are you talking about?"

"Checking your hands for wounds and everything."

"Ethan, stop this."

"Stop what? You know, I still don't know why he's on this trip with us."

She sighed. "Can we not get into this again?"

"Did you guys used to date or something?"

She stood abruptly and went to our tent.

I turned back around.

Tomo and Neil were trying not to act awkward.

"What?" I said. "Do you guys like him?"

They didn't say anything. Shaking my head, I leaned against the rock Mel had vacated and sipped the whiskey.

I regretted mentioning John Scott. I should have left things as they were. Mel was already on edge and stressed. The last thing she needed was me accusing her of sleeping with John Scott. And what if she did? It would have been before I met her. She was perfectly within her rights to do that.

But if that was the case, why wouldn't she simply tell me?

Because it never happened?

Or because something else was going on...?

Neil and Tomo began debating the best science fiction movie of all time, and I was happy to distract myself by listening to them. Neil said *2001: A Space Odyssey*, hands down. Tomo said *Jaws*. This set Neil off because, according to him, *Jaws* wasn't science fiction.

"Yeah, it is, man," Tomo said. "You see shark so big? Never."

"It's a horror film," Neil said. "Thriller at best."

"Science fiction fake shit, right? Jaws, he fake."

"Science fiction has to be set in the future."

"Not necessarily," I said.

Neil gave me a look. "Don't tell me you think *Jaws* is science fiction?"

I didn't, but I enjoyed seeing Neil get worked up over trivial things. I shook my head. "I'm not getting involved."

"You're being a fool, Tomo," Neil said testily. "Choose another film."

"I told you. *Jaws*."

"I told you, it's not science fiction."

"Okay, okay, let me think."

Neil watched him, his face pinched. Tomo kept thinking.

"Well?" Neil demanded impatiently.

"Okay. I got it. *Jaws 2*."

Neil made a disgusted sound and stood. He took a step toward his tent, turned back, and grabbed the bottle of whiskey.

"Wait!" Tomo said. "Wait! *Star Wars*. Best movie. *Star Wars*. Come back!"

Neil disappeared inside his tent.

"Stupid guy," Tomo mumbled.

"You shouldn't have pissed him off," I said.

"I was joking, right? He don't like joke?"

I was pretty sure Neil could hear us, and I didn't want to get into his bad books, so I merely shrugged. I looked for Mel, to see if she'd calmed down, but didn't see her anywhere.

I sat up straighter. Glanced at our tent.

"Mel?"

No reply.

I scanned the forest. It was ghostly in the near dusk. She was nowhere in sight.

I stood.

"Mel?"

Nothing.

"Mel?" I shouted.

"I'm here," she replied. She sounded far away.

"Where?"

No answer.

"What are you doing?"

"I'm going to the bathroom!"

"Oh—sorry."

"I'm hungry," Tomo said.

"I have peanuts in my bag—" I stopped midsentence, mentally slapping myself on the forehead. "Shit."

"What, man?" Tomo asked.

I was shaking my head. "My Swiss Army knife. I think I forgot it back at the crevice, where I cut the vine." I set the whiskey aside and went to my backpack, knowing the knife wouldn't be there but wanting to check nonetheless. I stuck my hand in the main pocket and felt around.

"Ow!" I bellowed, jerking my hand free.

For a moment I thought the knife had pricked me. But the pain consumed my entire hand, as if I had stuck it in a hot flame.

Tomo was asking me what was wrong, but I barely heard him. I was staring at my hand in horror. It was covered with dozens of ants—and they were still stinging me.

"Fuck!" I shouted, shaking my hand madly. "Fuck! Fuck! Fuck!"

The pain was incredible. I tried smacking the ants away, but the little fuckers had sunk their mandibles in and wouldn't let go.

I felt a sting on my ankle. Then another. More.

I looked at my feet.

The ants were crawling all over them.

I kicked off my Reeboks, launching them ten feet away. Then I stripped out of my jeans, all the while suffering more bites on my ankles and calves.

I brushed at the ants frantically, my mind reeling.

Where were they coming from? How many were there?

What if I went into anaphylactic shock?

Tomo and Neil, who had been quick from his tent upon hearing the commotion, charged past me, taking the offensive, shouting and stomping, looking like a pair of Native American rain dancers.

Tomo nudged my backpack tentatively with the toe of his shoe, then sprang back. "Ah!" he shrieked. "So many!"

Neil yelled, slapping his ankle.

In the poor light I made out an undulating mass of ants beneath where my backpack had been sitting.

I had set it right on top of their bloody colony.

"Ethan!" Mel said, reaching me. "What's going on?"

"Ants! Get back! They're everywhere! Pack up the tent. We have to move."

She was scanning the ground at our feet.

"I don't see—"

"Go!"

She ran back to the tent.

I jumped atop a rock and told Neil to get my shoes. He collected them, banged them against a tree, then tossed them to me. I slapped them against the rock for good measure, then slipped them on. My right hand was thrumming with heat. I shoved it under my left armpit.

We spent the next few minutes dismantling our tents and packing our bags while at the same time keeping well clear of the agitated colony. My backpack was squarely in enemy territory, covered by the angry little things, and I decided to leave it. I would pick it up on the way back tomorrow.

Then, with a last glance at the swarm, we got the hell out of there.

WE followed the white string for another ten minutes, to make sure we were well out of the ant colony's territory, stopping at an area padded with spongy pine needles at the base of a one-hundred-foot spruce.

I put my jeans back on and examined my hand. It continued to throb and had developed dozens of tiny bumps. Neil had a few bites on his ankles, while Tomo and Mel had gotten away scot-free.

After we set up our tents again, Mel rubbed some face moisturizer on my bites, though this did little to soothe the pain and irritation. Then Neil offered me more whiskey, which I accepted gratefully.

"What kind of ants do you think they were?" Mel asked.

"I couldn't really see the color," I said. "They might have been red, or ginger."

"Killer ants," Tomo said.

"Fire ants," Neil said knowingly. "And I reckon we're lucky we escaped with only a few bites. They're responsible for more human deaths than any other predatory animal on the planet. Vicious little buggers, they are."

I didn't want to talk about ants—I was in too much discomfort—so I lay back down with my head on Mel's backpack and found myself thinking about our ubiquitous companion Mt. Fuji out there somewhere. We would have been halfway up it by now. We'd either be in one of the seventh- or eighth-level huts, or outside them in our tents, trying to catch a few hours' sleep before we completed the final leg to the summit.

Would any of us have the energy or desire to still climb it tomorrow? I wondered. I was pretty sure Neil and Mel felt similar to how I did: spent, both physically and emotionally. This had been no stroll through the park. We'd gone a lot farther into Aokigahara, experienced a lot more, than I'd imagined we would. Then again, what *had* I imagined? An hour or two hike, a campfire, marshmallows, ghost stories?

The truth of the matter was that I wanted this whole week-end to be over already. I was cold and hungry and in pain and... empty. There was no longer any sense of adventure left inside me, no curiosity, no excitement. There was nothing. I was numb.

If Mel's scare in the hole in the ground had started me down this track, Yumi's gravesite, I was convinced, had been the turning point. Up until then this had still been a game of will of sorts, like fasting for two days, or swimming across a small lake. You did it to see if you could. After witnessing Yumi's scattered belongings, however, so pathetic, so desperate, it hit home that this was as real as it got. People did indeed kill themselves here. They flocked here like lemmings, hundreds if not thousands over the years, each of them tortured in their own private way.

And in our ignorance and selfishness we had come to rubberneck, drawn by the morbidity of the spectacle, just as motorists slow as they pass a roadside accident in the hopes of glimpsing something gruesome.

Clearing these thoughts from my mind, I imagined I was someplace far, far away.

"YOU *in the jungle, baby,*" a tinny voice trilled. "*Wake up. Time to dieeeee!*"

I must have dozed off for some time, because when I opened my eyes it was fully dark and John Scott and the Israelis had returned. Everyone was sitting at a fire they had gotten going. My phone continued to ring—or, more precisely, Axl Rose continued to sing—which was what had awakened me.

"Ethan?" Mel called over to me. "Your phone."

"Yeah, I'm up." My right hand, I noticed, had swelled and begun to itch. Ignoring the temptation to scratch it, I fumbled inside my jacket pocket, flipped open my yellow KDDI phone, and checked the display. It was Derek Miller, the Canadian coworker who'd labeled Neil an oddball serial rapist.

Derek and I had an almost nightly ritual. After we got off work at 9 p.m., we would stop by the Family Mart down the street from the school, buy a couple cans of beer, Kirin or Asahi, find a spot off to the side of the stream of suits and skirts flowing in and out of Shinagawa station, and hang out there while admittedly looking conspicuous. Regardless, it was affordable. A beer at a bar, even at a dive, cost about seven hundred yen, or roughly seven bucks, and it wasn't uncommon to pay ten.

In fact, it was during one of these budget evenings when we'd first met Tomo, who had been doing the very same thing.

Although it was legal to drink alcohol in public spaces in Japan, the only people who really did it—outside of the national cherry blossom festival/drinking party in April—were foreigners. Japanese tend to worry too much about what other Japanese think of them. So when I caught Tomo's eye as he merrily gulped back a tallboy, I tipped my can to him. He tipped his back, flashing me his toothy smile for the first time. Then he did something else that was very un-Japanese: he came over and started chatting with us. He was funny, Derek and I were having a good time, and we all bought another round. About thirty minutes later a girl showed up in hooker boots and a miniskirt. Tomo introduced her as Minami and invited us to join them at a nearby bar. It turned out to be packed with other hot university-aged girls. Some of the guys there thought it was cool to be hanging out with foreigners and bought Derek and me tequila shots over the next two hours. All I remember after that was ending up in a dungeon-themed karaoke room and somehow stumbling back to the guesthouse at two or so in the morning, to a suitably unimpressed Mel.

"Miller Time!" I said into the phone now. "What's up?"

"Mr. Childs!" Derek said. "I didn't know if you'd get reception up there. You guys reach the top yet?"

"We postponed the climb. It was supposed to rain."

"It's not raining here."

"It's not here either. Not yet. False alarm, I guess."

Derek laughed. "You morons. So what are you doing now?"

"We're camping in Aokigahara Jukai."

"Aokigahara what—? Hold on a sec. Sumiko's going nuts."

While Derek and his Starbucks-employed, barely legal girl-friend yabbered back and forth, I examined my right hand again. The pain had dulled, and the little bumps had turned into white pustules. I touched one with a finger experimentally. It was hard and uncomfortable. Then Sumiko came on the line and said, "Ethan? What are you doing in Aokigahara Jukai?"

"Camping."

"You shouldn't be doing that. You should leave now."

"We can't. It's already dark."

"It's not safe."

"Ghosts, right?"

"You must be careful there. And don't bring anything back from there. Okay?"

"Why not?"

"Just don't. I really don't think you should be there."

She was beginning to freak me out, and I said, "Can I speak to Derek again."

Static interference sounded as the phone changed hands.

"Suicide Forest!" Derek crowed gleefully. "Awesome. How is it? Have you found any bodies?"

"Listen, I gotta go. I'll tell you about it when I get back."

"If you get back. Kidding, man. Okay, later."

I hung up, frowning. What was up with Sumiko? I got it that this place was taboo for most Japanese, but she'd sounded downright terrified for us. Did she really believe the legends associated with the forest? And what was that stuff about not taking anything from here? Was that part of the folklore too? Did you get cursed or something?

I stuffed the phone away and went to the fire.

"Who was that?" Mel asked.

"Derek. His girlfriend thinks we're crazy for being here."

"We are."

John Scott said, "Heard you were attacked by some ants, buddy. How you feeling?"

"I'm fine."

"Good to see you got your pants back on."

Nina, I noticed, was staring intently at the ground, doing a bad job of trying to hide her smile. I was glad it was dark, because it masked the blush that had risen to my cheeks.

"You know," John Scott went on, "I've heard the expression 'ants in my pants' before, but I've never known anyone who's actually experienced it."

He was grinning broadly, while chuckles spilled out of everyone else.

"Find anything down the ribbon?" I said, to change the topic. I felt stupid standing there, the butt of the joke. I was also pissed they'd been talking about me behind my back.

John Scott shook his head. "It ended at nothing. Maybe there was a connecting one at one point. Who knows?"

I sat down next to Mel, who suggested it was time for dinner, and everyone took out whatever food we had either brought from Tokyo or bought at Kawaguchiko station, which was similar fare to what we had at lunch. John Scott passed several cans of beer around, apologizing that they were warm. I waved aside his offer. I would have liked one, but I felt I would owe him somehow if I accepted.

The fire was comforting, keeping the night—and the forest—at bay. We fed it with the sticks we had collected during the trek here and talked about the day: the ribbons, the solo shoe, the gravesite. John Scott, apparently in his element with a beer in one hand and a cigarette in the other, invented an entire backstory for Yumi. She was a journalist, he said. She came here to do a story on all the suicides and the *yūrei*. She planned to spend a couple nights. That's why she had the change of undergarments, the toiletries. But then she ran into a man who came here to kill himself. A hesitater. She tried to interview him and he got angry and killed her—no, better, John Scott amended—he decided he wanted to fuck her. Nobody was going to know. Even if they found out, he was going to kill himself, so what did it matter? So he raped her over and over, hanged her from a tree branch, then hanged himself next to her. "Bam! It explains everything," John Scott concluded proudly. "The underwear. The missing body."

"What about the cut-up ID?" I said.

"What ID?"

"Oh shit," Tomo said. "I don't show you."

He took the small pieces of plastic he'd collected from his pocket and passed them to John Scott. Ben and Nina crowded close.

John Scott whistled. "She's fit."

"I know, right?" Tomo said. "Why hot girl suicide?"

Ben said, "Maybe, you know, that is an old photo. Maybe she was in a fire and was disfigured."

Nina nodded. "Or she had a brain tumor."

I glanced at Nina. She'd been reticent all day, and I believed this was the first time she'd spoken English. She had aristocratic features, with arched eyebrows, an aquiline nose, and a neatly composed mouth. She'd pulled her hair back into a ponytail, and a single strand hung down in front of her face. She caught me looking. Her eyes were large, brown, almost reflective in the poor light, like a cat's—and there was something else in them.

A mischievousness? A seductiveness? Or was I imagining that?

Ben said, "I wonder what would be the best method for suicide?"

"Slitting your wrists," Nina replied immediately. "In a hot bath."

"No way," John Scott said. "One, it's pussy. Two, it takes a while to bleed out like that. If you kill yourself, you want it to be instant. You don't want to sit there waiting for yourself to die. It could take hours. I say sucking on the barrel of a Glock and pulling the trigger."

I shook my head. "Most people who try that end up permanently maiming themselves and spend the rest of their lives in a wheelchair missing a chunk of their brain."

John Scott cocked an eye at me. "So what do you say, boss?"

I gestured vaguely around us. "Hanging probably."

"Yeah, and if you don't do it right, or the rope breaks, you're left a paraplegic."

"I know," Tomo said. "Jump in front the train. Splat, you dead."

"That would be fine for you, Tomo," Neil said. "But then you're forcing your death on someone else, forcing them to live with the memory of your splattered guts because you couldn't kill yourself by yourself. Not to mention the train company, in Japan at least, will likely sue your surviving kin for disrupting their service."

"Well?" I said, wanting to hear Neil's theory.

"Jumping off a building."

"That's so nineties," John Scott said. "You know why no one does that shit anymore?"

"Tell me," Neil said dryly.

"Because it's been proven that most people change their minds about killing themselves halfway down. Imagine that."

"How could that possibly be proven?" I said.

"It has, dude. Check it out."

"What about an overdose?" Mel said. "That's painless, right?"

"Not reliable," John Scott said. "You pass out, then vomit all the pills back up. This leaves you alive and in a puddle of your puke, probably next to your suicide note, which, given the fact you're not dead, looks plain gay."

The flames of the fire had shrunk to less than a foot tall. I glanced around the circle we had formed but didn't see any more wood.

"Is that all the firewood?" I said.

"That went fast," Ben said.

"We need campfire," Tomo stated.

"Indeed we do," Neil said. "It's going to get colder."

I cursed myself for falling asleep and not scavenging more wood earlier. I grabbed a flashlight and stood. "I'll go get some."

"I will join you," Ben said, pushing himself to his feet.

"Me too," Nina said.

"Wait, in the dark?" Mel said. "You might get lost."

I shook my head. "We won't leave the string."

I could see her deliberating, weighing the pros and cons. Apparently heat and light won out over potential hazards because she handed a flashlight to Ben.

"Fine, but don't go far," she told us. "And watch out for those holes."

10

IF Aokigahara was unsettling during the daylight, it was ten times worse at night and away from the perceived safety of the fire. The blackness of the forest pressed against us like a physical force. Ben and I fought it with our flashlight beams but succeeded only in revealing patches of the chaos that surrounded us: vines dangling like nooses, craggy trees bent at demonic angles, roots bubbling out of the ground, as if ready to snare unsuspecting prey. And everything remained shrouded in that maddening silence. In contrast, our footsteps crunched and crackled, seemingly loud enough to wake the dead and bring all the *yūrei* within a mile radius screaming toward us.

I was in the lead, on edge and jumpy, with Nina behind me and Ben bringing up the rear. We were following the string in what I thought was a westerly direction, passing through undiscovered territory. We had each brought backpacks to fill with deadfall—I was using Mel's—and so far I had collected several sticks and a large branch I had broken into thirds with my foot.

The ground began to angle upward. I lowered myself to all fours as I climbed, careful not to trip or cut my hands on the volcanic rock. At the top I shone the light down on Nina and Ben so they could see better.

Then, off in the trees, I heard something. I snapped the light left.

"What is it?" Nina whispered, moving close to me.

I played the beam back and forth, but saw nothing but ghostly tree trunks. "I thought I heard something."

Ben joined us. "Was it an animal?"

"I don't know."

"What kind of animal?" Nina asked.

I shook my head. "A fox?"

"Should we go back?"

"We have not found enough wood yet," Ben said.

"It was probably just a rodent or something," I said. "And Ben's right. We need more wood."

We began walking again, only now I kept up conversation. It was reassuring, normalizing, to hear our voices. Also, I wanted to scare off whatever had been out there.

Ben seemed happy to talk. He told me he was born in Haifa to French-Algerian Jewish parents and moved to Tel Aviv when he was eight. He was the third of five children, graduated from university with a degree in economics, and spent the last few years in the Israeli Defense Forces. Somehow we got onto World War II, and he explained that his grandfather was killed in a concentration camp while his grandmother survived by hiding in a convent in Czechoslovakia.

"What are you going to do when your time's done in the military?" I asked.

"I will move to New York City," he said.

"He wants to be an actor," Nina said.

"Is that true?" I asked him.

He nodded. "Many Israelis, you know, are Hollywood actors. But they always change their nationality to American. I will remain an Israeli."

"Maybe you should move to Los Angeles then, not New York."

"You think that would be better?"

"New York is more Broadway acting. Stage stuff. If you want to be in the movies, you should be in Los Angeles."

"Thank you, Ethan. I mean, for not saying 'Why do you

want to be an actor?' or 'You cannot be an actor.' That is what everyone tells me."

He seemed upset by this and went silent.

"Tell him why you want to be an actor," Nina said.

"For the fame, of course," Ben said, "and the money. I could move my parents to Los Angeles with me. Away from the rockets, the fighting."

"He wants to marry a beautiful American wife," Nina said. "He told me that once."

"I did not!"

"He did. He says he will keep his Israeli citizenship, but he wants to marry an American. I do not know what to make of him. He is a madman, I think."

"I will marry you," he said.

Nina huffed.

"How about you, Ethan?" Ben asked. "You are a teacher, yes?"

"How did you know?"

"John Scott told me."

I frowned. "What else did he say?"

"Nothing else. Only that you teach kids."

"Kids?"

"You do not?"

"I teach adults." Then, for whatever reason, I added: "A lot of business executives, in fact."

Kids, I thought. What the fuck? Why would John Scott say that? He had no idea.

"Sometimes," I continued, feeling I had something to prove, "I give seminars to large groups at their corporate head-quarters. Sony. Rakuten. Roche."

"I see," Ben said.

I stopped talking. I was making a fool of myself.

"How long will you live in Japan?" Nina asked me.

"This is probably my last year."

"Where will you go?"

"Maybe back to the US."

"Will you continue to teach there?"

"I think so. I like teaching."

"Your family is there?"

"My parents."

"You do not have any brothers or sisters?"

I hesitated. "No."

"An only child. How is that?"

"You get used to it."

I picked up another stick, snapped it in half, and stuck it in my bag.

Ben said, "John Scott, I like him. How long have you been friends?"

"We're not friends," I said. "I just met him today."

"I thought you were friends. I think he said you were."

"We're not."

Nina said, "But Melissa? She is your girlfriend?"

"Melinda, yeah—"

"Stop!" Ben hissed.

"What?" I said, freezing mid step.

Nina bumped into the back of me.

"Did you hear that?" His eyes were wide and white in the darkness. "It sounded like...I do not know. Another animal?"

We stood perfectly still for ten long seconds, but we heard nothing more.

"Are you sure you heard something?" I asked.

"Maybe it was just the wind."

The wind? I thought. There was no wind.

The forest was a friggin' vacuum.

Tense with adrenaline, I continued forward. No one spoke for a little, and I began to wonder what was wrong with Ben. There was something about the way he was speaking. It was different than before. More intense yet...spacy. Like he was asking questions for the sake of asking them, not really listening to my answers.

Because he was scared?

Nina, at least, was still being Nina.

Still being Nina? I could have laughed at that. I'd met her all of five or six hours ago, and this was the first time we'd conversed. Suddenly I realized how little I knew about the Israelis. They were strangers. And here I was walking in a dark, sprawling forest with them, alone. What if they were psychotic? What if they jumped me, bashed my head in with a rock, and left me here to die?

Ben, I'd noticed back at the hill, hadn't picked up any firewood except a four-foot stick, which he was using to bat vegetation out of the way or slap against tree trunks.

"How did you guys meet?" I asked them.

"We met in Thailand," Ben said. "At a full-moon party last month. I was with my friends. We met on the beach one night."

"But we lost each other," Nina added.

"That is right. I did not see her for a week. Then I was looking for a restaurant one morning and I heard my name called. She is there."

"He left his friends and stayed with me," Nina said.

"We got a hut. We surfed, we ate food, and we watched movies."

"So how long have you been in Japan?" I asked.

"Just a couple days," Ben said.

"I have a world ticket," Nina explained. "Japan was my next stop after Thailand. You have to keep going in the same direction around the world, yes? Ben wanted to join me."

"How long have you been traveling?"

"Four months or so now," she said.

"Isn't that getting expensive?"

"I couch surf. Do you know what that is?"

"You stay at people's homes?"

"Yes, you sign up for an account on the website, say when you will be in a town or city, and people usually respond and invite you to stay. It is very easy to get a host when you are a female by yourself. But when you are with someone, it is much more difficult."

"So far in Japan we have stayed in hostels," Ben said. "It is okay."

"Isn't it dangerous for a girl to couch surf?" I asked.

"Ninety-nine percent of people are wonderful," Nina said.

"You had a bad experience?"

"Yes, one."

Something in her voice made me glance over my shoulder at her. I couldn't read her expression in the dark. I wanted to ask what happened, but didn't feel it was my place.

"Four months," I said instead. "Aren't you tired of traveling yet?"

"Sometimes. But I meditate. I can sit for hours on my own. It is very relaxing. I would like to find some special place to stay for my final month. No TV. No tourists. Just meditate. I have not found it yet."

"Have you guys noticed the trees?" Ben said, his voice taking on a strange timbre. He skipped his flashlight back and forth among them. "See how close they are?"

It was true. They had become smaller, thinner, denser.

"I think it is time to go back," Nina said.

I checked my wristwatch and was surprised to note we had only been gone from camp for fifteen minutes. If we returned after half an hour without enough firewood to last through the night, I'd never hear the end of it from John Scott, even though he hadn't volunteered to help gather any. I said, "Another five minutes."

We pressed on. I batted branches from my face. There was a lot of deadfall here, which I gathered greedily. I was just standing up, having collected yet another stick, when I spotted the blood. It was splashed on the trunk of a tree cater-corner to me, at chest level.

I froze. My skin tightened with a ticklish fever.

Had someone stuck a pistol in their mouth and blown their brains out against the tree?

But where was the body?

I saw my hand reach out and touch the blood, even though a voice inside my head was shouting at me to get the hell out of there. A flake broke off from the bark. I rubbed it between my index finger and thumb, grinding it down to a powder. I smelled it.

"Paint," I said torpidly. "It's paint."

Who had splashed the tree with red paint? And why?

Operating in some sort of bubble, aware of little happening around me, I turned in a circle, the flashlight beam crisscrossing the trees. Nothing. Just trees and more trees and—*what the hell?*

Twenty feet ahead, hanging from a branch by red suicide ribbon, was a crucifix made with two small sticks and string. Then I spotted another. Then another beyond that. They were everywhere. At least a dozen.

Each of them was swinging slightly in the wind—

There is no wind.

I closed my eyes, waited a beat, and opened them again.

The crucifixes were still swinging.

I tried to turn and flee, but my legs weren't working correctly, and I stumbled backward, pin-wheeling my arms for balance.

Something smacked me from behind.

WITH the exception of insects, fish, and perhaps small birds, the sight of a rotting carcass will almost always give you a jolt. We don't see death every day, we're not programmed to take it in stride. Only a week ago I was walking along a backstreet in Tokyo, trying to find a ramen shop Tomo had recommended. You could find ramen shops on pretty much any corner in the city, but the best ones aren't advertised. Lacking signs, and located in rundown, nondescript buildings, the only way to identify such establishments is the long line of businessmen waiting out front between 11 a.m. and 2 p.m.

The particular ramen shop I was looking for was somewhere in the maze of streets behind Omatchi Station, just off the Yamanote Line. Tomo had said it had a really good cheese curry ramen. I'd been walking for twenty minutes, fearing I was getting hopelessly lost, when I spotted out of the corner of my eye a dead dog on the side of the road. It was a jet-black baby Labrador retriever. The lips were curled back, revealing pink gums and bone-white canines. It was less than two feet away from me.

The sight of it made me jump. I wasn't scared—just startled to see something dead. The startle quickly left me, and I studied it more closely.

It appeared as though it had been run over because the middle section was split open, spilling forth a tangle of guts. The hind legs were almost completely flat. Flies buzzed around it, eager to lay their eggs in the spoiled meat.

Death, I'd thought at the time. It stirs within you so many different emotions.

Fascination.

Disgust.

Sadness.

Relief—at least, relief in the sense that what you're seeing isn't you.

I felt none of this, however, only mind-numbing fright, when I turned around and saw the body dangling from a rope behind me.

I noticed the hair first. It was black, thin, combed over from the left side of the tan skull to the right. From the brow down, the face was unrecognizable. It almost appeared as if it had melted away. The eyeballs were gone, likely eaten by animals, leaving behind empty black holes, the left one larger than the right. Encircling the orbits was a clumping gray matter that had once been skin. Where the nose had been was a small gaping triangle. The mouth and jawbone appeared to be missing, though it was difficult to tell for certain because that gray matter stretched down from the cheekbones in long strands, masking the mouth and chin and neck, collecting at the top of the chest.

The man had chosen to wear a golf shirt on the day he killed himself, a light color, with horizontal stripes. This, along with his degree of dissolution, suggested he had probably hanged himself several months ago during spring or summer. Clipped inside the shirt's front pocket was a ballpoint pen. The arms poking out from the short sleeves were little more than skin over bones. Somehow the beige pants remained in place, not slipping off the shrunken waist.

Time seemed to have slowed down while I took this all in, though in reality only a couple seconds had passed. I spun away from the ghastly sight and vomited what was in my stomach. It required three goes to get everything out.

While I was doubled over, my hands on my thighs, my throat stinging, my eyes watering, I became aware of the commotion around me.

"Ben!" Nina cried. "Stop!" She grabbed my arm. "Ethan, come!"

"Where's he—?"

"Come!"

She took off.

I didn't move. I was confused. What was happening? Why were they running? Then I remembered the crucifixes—*they were swinging*—and I began floundering back the way we'd come.

BEN and Nina were far ahead. I could see Ben's flashlight beam jerking wildly as he ran. I was charging through the dense thicket of spindly trees. An errant branch got past my upraised arms and sliced my cheek. The pain was hot, quick, then forgotten as I plowed forward. I tripped, scrambled on my knees, got back to my feet, kept going.

I heard my pants and grunts of exertion. I saw my feet appearing below me, the left then the right, one after the other. Eventually, as the trees began to open up, I slowed to a jog.

The Israelis were too far ahead to catch. I glanced behind me, knowing nothing would be there, but doing it all the same.

My heart was beating rabbit-fast, and I took deep breaths to slow it down.

The bloody crucifixes had been blowing in a non-existent wind.

Was I sure there was no wind?

There hasn't been any wind all day.

Was I sure?

Pretty damn sure.

Then what had caused the crucifixes to blow? Ghosts? *Yūrei?* There had to be a wind. I was just freaked out. I let my imagination run wild. Had to be a wind.

I looked over my shoulder again.

"Had to be a wind," I mumbled to myself.

LIGHT ahead. It blinked in and out between the trees.

"Hey!" I called.

"Ethan?" Mel.

"Yeah, it's me."

When we found each other, I discovered she was with Tomo. She wrapped me in a tight hug. I thought she would ask me about the body, but she only said, "We have to get back to the camp. Quickly."

"Why? What happened?"

"It's Ben. He's tripping out big time."

11

I had expected the camp to be in turmoil. Maybe Ben kicking stuff around, or shouting gibberish, or howling at the moon. But all was calm when we emerged from the trees. Neil and John Scott were standing by the dying fire. Farther away, in the trees, I made out the silhouettes of Ben and Nina. Their heads were close together, indicating they were likely speaking to one another.

On the way back Mel had given me a brief rundown of what had happened. When Ben and Nina had returned, Nina was okay, but Ben started pacing and saying stuff in Hebrew no one understood. When Tomo tried to get him to calm down, he shoved Tomo backward, knocking him over. Nina told them I was fine, I was coming. Still, Mel enlisted Tomo's help and came looking for me.

"What the hell did you guys see?" John Scott demanded when I approached the fire.

"A body," I said.

"That's it?"

"What do you mean 'that's it?'" I quipped, annoyed at his apathy. He'd been sitting here on his ass the entire time. He had no idea how terrifying discovering a body in Aokigahara at night could be.

"Ben's having a bloody meltdown," Neil said.

"Yeah, Mel told me." I paused, trying to figure out how to word what I was going to add. "There were these...these little crucifixes hanging from the trees."

"Crucifixes?" Mel said.

"Made from sticks."

"So is that what set Ben off?" Neil said. "These crucifixes?"

I shook my head. "I don't know what happened. We saw this paint on the tree—"

"An arrow?" John Scott asked.

"No, just…red paint. Then I saw the crucifixes. The guy who killed himself must have made them."

"How big?" Tomo asked.

"The crucifixes? I don't know. A few inches tall. Then Ben was shouting, and he took off. I mean, it was scary. But his reaction was over the top. He was also acting a little strange before that…"

"What do you mean?" Mel asked.

"The way he was talking. I don't know. He just didn't seem like himself."

"Because the guy eat mushrooms," Tomo said.

John Scott elbowed Tomo in the side.

"Mushrooms?" I said. "Magic mushrooms?"

"Just a little," John Scott said breezily.

I'd heard you could legally purchase psychedelic mushrooms in mail-order shops and head shops across Japan as recently as a few years ago (as long as you promised not to eat them), but they were now illegal and impossible to find. So where had Ben gotten his from? And what was he thinking eating them in this forest at nighttime?

"How do you know he's on mushrooms?" I asked.

John Scott shot a Marlboro from his pack and lit up. "I gave them to him."

I frowned. "*You* did?"

"Sure."

"Where did you get them from?"

"I found them."

For a moment I imagined him finding a bag of mushrooms on the street. Then some brain cells kicked in. "You mean you picked them?"

"Yeah."

"Here? In the forest?"

He exhaled smoke, nodded.

"What do you know about picking mushrooms?"

"We do it all the time off-base."

"Did you take them too?"

"Sure."

I was watching him closely. "And you're fine?"

"Perfectly."

"Anyone else take them?"

Neil, Tomo, and Mel all shook their heads in the negative.

"Nina?" I asked.

"Nah," John Scott said.

I looked in the direction of the Israelis. Ben appeared to be rocking back and forth. Nina's arm was around his shoulder.

"There's always one guy who has a bad trip," John Scott said indifferently. "Like I said, he just needs some space, some time to mellow out."

"Like eight hours," I said.

"I can't control how other people are going to react."

"Then don't give out fucking mushrooms. What are you, a drug dealer?"

"Dude, chill out."

I was getting angrier by the second. I was no saint when it came to experimenting a little with drugs, but the idea of John Scott handing out wild mushrooms in Aokigahara Jukai was beyond stupid.

"You still have some?" I asked.

"Yeah."

"Anyone else want to do 'shrooms in this forest?"

Nobody replied.

"What happens if he has a serious reaction? How would we get him help?"

John Scott waved his hand. "Dude, you're killing my buzz."

"I don't give a shit about your buzz! Doing mushrooms in

a controlled environment is risky enough. But stuff you pick? And here in the middle of nowhere? He could go into a coma —"

"Don't give me that shit—"

"It's true!"

"Fuck off. I don't want to talk about this."

"Ethan—" Neil began.

"No, it's irresponsible and it's fucking stupid."

"Ethan, John, stop it!" Mel shouted. "Just stop it."

There was a long, tense silence.

Biting back my words, I shrugged my backpack off, dumped the wood I'd collected onto the ground, and began building the fire.

12

I got a roaring blaze going with little trouble or help from anyone else. Neil opened his bottle of whiskey again, this time sharing it freely. He and Tomo and John Scott drank silently, passing the bottle back and forth. Mel attempted small talk, trying to lighten the mood. Tomo got drunk quickly and talked everyone except me into a game that involved naming actors who had won an Academy Award. This helped to alleviate the negative atmosphere that had settled over the camp. It was still far from cheerful, but it was no longer gloomy.

For someone on mushrooms John Scott was acting amazingly normal. He either didn't eat as much as Ben, or he was one of those guys who could function well on drugs. He was playing the games Tomo kept coming up with and chatting to the others and ignoring me, which I was more than fine with. Nina and Ben remained off by themselves. Mel and I sat next to each other with our feet warming by the fire, our backs against a rock. The flames popped and jumped in front of us. I watched them in an almost hypnotic state, trying to block everyone else out. Every so often a tiny spark would zip away on its own into the night, then blink out of existence. I wondered if that's what happened to Yumi and the comb-over guy and the others who decided to end themselves here.

Blink out of existence.

Because what was the alternative? Ghosts and spirits and

an afterlife? I wish I could believe in all that stuff. It was comforting to think you're part of something bigger than yourself, that life goes on in some form after your death. But I simply couldn't convince myself of this. I've thought about death too much. I've lived with it for too long. I've come to know it too well.

It was the end, and telling yourself otherwise wasn't going to change that fact.

MY Guns 'N Roses ringtone snapped me out of my morbid reflection. I took my phone out of my pocket, thinking it was Derek again. I glanced at the display and swore to myself.

"Aren't you going to answer it?" Neil said.

"I don't feel like talking much now."

"Maybe it's Honda. He might be checking up on us."

"It's not Honda."

The ringtone continued to play, Axl's screechy voice seeming all the louder and insistent because of my refusal to acknowledge it.

"What the fuck?" Tomo said. "I answer."

He reached for the phone, but I shooed him away.

Finally, an impossibly long time later, the goddamn thing shut up.

"Was it Derek?" Mel asked.

"No."

"Who?"

"What does it matter?"

"Why are you getting defensive?"

"I'm not."

"Maybe ex-girlfriend," Tomo said.

"Well?" Mel said, looking at me expectantly.

I blinked at her. "Well what?"

"Was it an ex?"

"Come on."

"What's the big deal?"

"It was just an old friend."

"Shelly?"

"No," I said, and instantly regretted the lie.

Mel studied me.

I tried to ignore her.

"Let me see your phone," she said.

"Are you kidding?"

"I don't believe you."

"Have you gone mad?" I was doing the suitably outraged act, and probably coming across guilty as hell. "So I didn't want to answer my phone. What is this?"

"Let me see the phone."

I considered denying her request, but that would be as good as admitting it had been Shelly. I shrugged and handed the phone to her.

"Mac," she said, reading the name in the call log. "Who's Mac?"

I almost told her it was a guy I'd gone to school with, but there was something in her eyes. She *knew*. She was luring me into a trap.

"You know," I said.

"Shelly MacDonald?"

I didn't reply.

"Why didn't you input 'Shelly' into your phonebook? Why 'Mac?'"

What the hell was this interrogation about? "Because if you saw her name," I said evenly, controlling my temper, "I knew you would flip out, like you're doing now."

"I'm not flipping out."

"Yeah, you are."

"Because you lied to me, Ethan."

"Give me a break."

"If you'd simply told me it was Shelly when I'd asked, that would have been that."

I shook my head. "What's this all about?"

"Really, Ethan? I have to tell you? Okay. Your ex-girlfriend calls—the second time in a month—someone you once told me wanted to marry you. You don't answer the phone and lie about who it is. I think I deserve some answers."

"What did you want me to do? Answer it here? What am I supposed to say? 'Hey, Shell! What's up?' You and I would be doing exactly what we're doing as soon as I hung up, which is what I wanted to avoid."

"I wouldn't have gotten mad."

That was a load of crock. Mel had been insanely jealous of Shelly ever since she'd found provocative photographs of Shelly on my computer. It had been on the day Mel and I celebrated our six-month anniversary. She'd been going through my photos, looking for a good one of us to print and make into a card, when she came across the pictures. I had completely forgotten I had them, and when Mel asked me to delete them, I did so gladly. But after that she would always bristle at not only any mention of Shelly but any mention of my college days in general, for it represented a world to which she had not belonged and knew little about.

Then, last month, Mel and I had been at dinner for my birthday when my phone rang. I didn't recognize the unlisted number and answered it, thinking it might have been my parents. It turned out to be Shelly, calling me out of the blue. I hadn't spoken to her for years, so I excused myself and was gone for ten minutes. I admitted to Mel who it was when I came back. Mel went into a mood, and the rest of the evening was ruined.

"Can we drop this?" I asked tiredly.

"No."

"You think I'm having some trans-Pacific affair?"

"I want to know why she's calling again."

"How am I supposed to know? I didn't answer."

"Tell me the truth, Ethan!"

"She called me on my birthday. And she called me tonight. Twice. That's it."

"Has she messaged you?"

I glared at Mel. What did she know? Obviously more than she was letting on.

"Have you been going through my phone?"

"It buzzed last week," she said. "You were in the shower getting ready for work. You were late because of Becky's party the night before. I thought it might have been Mr. Kurosawa wanting to know where you were. So I checked to write back for you. Do you want me to tell you what I read?"

I knew what she would have read.

"You don't understand," I said simply.

"Yes, I think I do."

"You don't know anything!" I shook my head. "I can't believe you went through my phone. Do you go through my emails too?"

"I told you why I checked it. And don't try to turn this on me."

Neil cleared his throat. "Perhaps we should go for a walk."

"No, stay," I said. "I'm going."

I got up, grabbed a flashlight, and left.

No one tried to stop me.

13

I didn't bother following the string. I simply walked off in a random direction, my anger trumping my delusory fear of the forest. Ghosts and bears were the last thing on my mind right then. I was playing over everything that had just transpired and cursing myself for how I'd handled it. Eventually I found a large rock and sat down on it. I could see the campfire in the distance, a small orange glow.

Shelly.

Christ.

ALTHOUGH my parents' farm was only a twenty minute drive from UW Madison, I had chosen to live in residence during my freshman year to gain the campus experience and to meet people. I joined Kap Sig the following year and lived in a small room on the third floor of the sprawling frat house. Nevertheless, the nonstop drinking and partying had left my grade point average in danger of going negative, so during the summer before my senior year I moved into a two-bedroom apartment with a non-frat friend.

On the day I'd met Shelly I'd been in the convenience store across the street from my building. Shelly entered not long after me, wearing dark sunglasses, a breezy summer dress that revealed ample cleavage and long legs, and two-inch-tall clogs. She passed behind me in a cloud of perfume. I watched her for a moment while she went to the freezer and contemplated ice cream.

Suddenly George, the store-owner, blurted, "Ethan, come here! Come quick!"

I joined him at the cash. A mother duck had entered through the store's front door, which was always propped open in the summer months, followed by four golden chicks. They were zigzagging all over the place, seemingly with no purpose or care.

"They must be from the river," George said excitedly. "Somehow they got lost and came here."

I opened the bag of potato chips I had selected earlier and tossed a few chips on the floor. It was a feeding frenzy.

"Good idea, Ethan! Grab some bread too!"

George knew publicity when he saw it and called *The Capital Times*. A reporter and a photographer arrived ten minutes later and took pictures of the event. Shelly and I got talking and exchanged phone numbers. Later that evening we met for a drink. Two days after this we went to another bar. Over the weekend, dinner, and on the following Monday, a small festival in a park. Within a week of meeting her it became clear to me that we were dating. I didn't know how I felt about this. Shelly was a lot of fun, but come the new semester in September I wasn't sure I wanted to be the boyfriend of another sorority girl. I'd dated a few in the past and knew what it entailed: parties, cheese-and-wine soirées, parties, formal balls, parties, semi-formal balls, more parties. Basically everything I was trying to distance myself from.

Nevertheless, I became comfortable in the relationship, and after Gary died in December, Shelly was supportive and helped me through the next few months. We graduated, got jobs in Chicago, and moved in together. Everyone thought we were the perfect couple—everyone except for me. I felt trapped. Restless. I felt like I was playing at being somebody I wasn't. The air kisses, the expensive fashion, the cocaine that went around as freely as grass did in college—none of this was me. I wasn't ready for any of it. Then Shelly began talking about getting married. That's what made up my mind. I had this image of working at the same company, socializing with the same people, doing the same silly stuff in ten years' time—only then with kids—and I decided I needed to get away.

I had a few thousand dollars saved, enough for a decent holiday somewhere, but I wasn't looking for a couple weeks in the Caribbean. I wanted a reboot. For whatever reason India had sounded like a good place to start. It was cheap and huge and I could easily lose myself there for a year. Problem was, I would need some kind of work, and the only jobs available for Westerners were call center managers, which I was neither interested in nor qualified for. I switched my focus to Asia and found that English teachers were in high demand.

It was the best move in retrospect, considering I never would have met Mel otherwise. After only a couple months in Japan, the pain of Gary's death faded, I was in a much better place mentally, and with each passing day, with each passing year, my old life ceased to exist.

But, of course, the past always has a way of catching up with you.

TO say I was surprised when Shelly called me on my birthday a couple weeks ago would be a gross understatement. We hadn't communicated once since I'd left Chicago. So when she said, "Hey, Ethan! It's me! How are you?" I had no idea who it was. I went along with the conversation until her voice clicked. She asked me how Japan was. The food, the culture. Had I met any Japanese girls? To that last question I answered no. I should have mentioned Mel. If I had, that would likely have been the first and last call I received from Shelly, and I wouldn't be in the dilemma I was in tonight. Regardless, I didn't. It hadn't seemed like any of Shelly's business.

I remained on the phone as long as I did because I kept expecting her to drop some sort of bomb. Like a friend had died.

Or she was pregnant. But ten minutes later she said, "Good talking, Ethan! I have to run. Stay safe." And just like that the surreal conversation was over.

A few days later she sent me an email, a rambling three or four paragraphs in which she explained she was thinking about me a lot lately, our time together, and some of the things we had done. She never came out and said she wanted to get back together, but the implication was there, which I found bizarre considering I was half a world away. Did she think I was going to fly home—or she fly here? She ended with, "Missing you. Love, Shell."

I cringed, because this was the message Mel would have read. What would she have thought? And why hadn't she said anything to me before now? Had she given me the benefit of the doubt? Had she been waiting to see if I got another message? Obviously she had been keeping watch on me. Perhaps waiting to catch me in the act, just as she had done tonight...

With these thoughts in my head, I started back toward camp to sort things out.

14

I was so focused on avoiding the trees and branches and holes in the dark I didn't see the red glow of a cigarette ember until I was less than ten feet from it. The person was sitting at the base of a tree. I couldn't make out any more than an inky silhouette, but who else smoked aside from John Scott? I was preparing to give him a wide berth when Nina said, "Ethan?"

I went over to her. She had her knees pulled up against her chest. And it wasn't a cigarette in her hand. The smell was green and skunk-like.

"Hey," I said.

She held the joint out for me without a word. I considered for all of one second before accepting. I hadn't smoked pot for years; it was almost as hard to get in Japan as mushrooms. Nevertheless, I decided it was exactly what I needed right then to unwind.

I sat down across from Nina and took a long drag. She hadn't mixed the marijuana with tobacco, for which I was grateful. I held the smoke in my lungs until a tickling in my throat told me a coughing fit was about to commence, then I exhaled, slowly, evenly.

"Where's Ben?" I asked.

"He went to the tent to lie down."

"How is he?" I passed the joint back.

"He is okay."

"Is he still…?"

"Tripping out? It is his own fault. I told him not to eat too much. He is greedy."

"You were there when they ate them?"

She nodded.

"Where did John Scott find them?"

"By a tree trunk. Ben, this happened before, you know."

"Recently?"

"At the full-moon party in Thailand, there was this mushroom bar. We went there with some friends, had mushroom milkshakes. But you have to go down this very steep and narrow staircase to leave. There are no railings. It is dangerous actually. Ben got scared and could not do it. We joked we were going to leave him in the bar. He started to trip out."

"Why would he do them again?"

"John Scott said the mushrooms were mellow. He would be okay." She took another toke and passed the joint back.

I inhaled deeply. "Can I ask you something, Nina?" I said.

"You can ask me anything you want, Ethan."

"Why did you and Ben want to come to Suicide Forest? It's not exactly a tourist destination."

She seemed to contemplate this. "Ben wanted to."

"But why? Just for the hell of it?"

"Ben…he knew someone who committed suicide. The person was very close to him." She shrugged. "He became obsessed with suicide after this. He watches movies about it, reads books, everything. I think he wants to understand it better, understand why people choose such a fate. So when he heard about this forest, he wanted to see it for himself. See if it would…help him to understand. Does that make sense?"

"Yeah, I think so."

"What about you, Ethan? Why are you here?"

"Because you and Ben invited us."

"You do not have any secret obsession with suicide?"

I hesitated. "No," I said. "No obsession."

"I see. So—what are you doing out here?"

"You mean in the woods?"

"Yes, by yourself."

I forgot that Nina had been away during the phone incident.

"I had a fight with Mel."

"When?"

"Forty-five minutes ago or so."

"Do you always walk alone in the forest after a fight?"

"There weren't too many other places to go."

"You have been with your girlfriend for a long time?"

I found it odd how she referred to Mel as "my girlfriend." She knew her name. I wasn't calling Ben "her boyfriend"...or was I? I couldn't recall. My thoughts had become foggy.

I offered her what was left of the joint. She shook her head so I stubbed it out.

"Well?" she prodded.

"What was the question again?"

"How long have you been with your girlfriend?"

"About four years."

"You are American?"

"Yup."

"I have never dated an American."

I blinked.

"I have dated a German, Italian... Hmmm, and a Greek. No Americans."

I started giggling—quietly. I didn't want the others back at camp to hear.

"What is so funny?"

"I don't know."

"Maybe you are high."

"I think so."

"How about you?"

"How about me what?"

"Have you dated an American?"

"Yeah, I've dated an American. Mel's American."

"Oh, I see. Who else? What other country?"

"None," I said.

It was Nina's turn to giggle.

"What?" I said.

"You are a world virgin, Ethan."

"A world virgin?"

She nodded.

I guess I was.

"Hey," I said. "I was wondering. You mentioned you had a bad experience couch surfing. What happened? I mean, if it's personal or whatever, you don't have to tell me…"

"No, I can tell you, Ethan. It is in the past." She appeared thoughtful, as if she was working the story out in her head, or at least how to begin. She said, "I was in Pakistan, going to India. A couch surfer in New Delhi said I could stay at her place. I thought it was a single woman, but it turned out to be an entire family. Her husband and their four children. The place was small, but they were very nice people. They cooked for me every day."

"Curry?" The thought of vindaloo beef or butter chicken made me realize how hungry I was. I could have done with a large pizza right about then.

"Yes. I ate so much. It was all vegetarian. Very healthy. I was only planning on spending a couple days in Delhi. I wanted to go to Agra, and if I had time, Jaipur. But I was having such a good time with them I ended up staying an entire week."

"You never went to the Taj Mahal?"

She shook her head.

"You know there was supposed to be a black one made too?"

"What happened to it?"

"I guess the shah changed his mind."

"I think that is a myth."

"It's not a myth."

"Do you have any more interesting facts to tell me?"

"Are you patronizing me?"

"Are you done interrupting me?"

"Go ahead."

"*So*," Nina said with emphasis, feigning annoyance with me —or at least I thought she was only feigning, "my next destination was China. The day before my flight the woman's brother came by for dinner. He got drunk and stayed there overnight."

"Hindus can drink alcohol?"

"Of course, Ethan. Hinduism does not forbid anything. There is no bad karma if drinking is done in moderation. You are thinking of Islam."

"No, I'm not. I know the difference between Hinduism and Islam."

"Are you sure?"

"Of course."

"Because Muslims ruled India for a long time. Perhaps that is why you have gotten confused with the different religions."

"I'm not confused. I just thought—" I shook my head. "Whatever." I was too damn high to know whether she was messing with me, though I suspected she was. "So did you get to China?" I asked, to move on.

"You keep distracting me."

"I'm sorry."

"You said you would not do it anymore."

"I won't."

"I hope not." She crossed her legs in front of her. "What? What is wrong?"

"Huh?"

"You are looking at my legs."

"Oh." I felt my cheeks redden. "You're still wearing shorts. I —I was wondering if your legs were cold."

"They are fine, Ethan."

I took a deep breath and tried to act normal. "So what happened with your family?"

"After dinner that evening, the evening I was telling you about before you wanted to know if my legs were cold, I went to bed early because I had an early flight the next morning. The brother who stayed the night was a taxi driver. He offered to drive me to the airport. His taxi was parked right out front. It seemed perfectly safe." She gave me a look, as if I would challenge this.

"Yeah?"

"New Delhi is a big city. I had no idea where the airport was. Everything looked the same to me. But the longer we drove, the more I got the feeling we were not going in the right direction."

"How long did you drive around for?"

"By this time, twenty, thirty minutes. Traffic in that city is so bad. But it was early. Not so many cars. So we should have been to the airport already. Fifteen minutes later I was sure we were nowhere near the airport and I told him to stop. He pulled down an alleyway. I was very scared now. But I had this huge backpack. I could not run away. When I got out he grabbed me and..." She paused for a long moment. "He pinned me against the car and lifted up my dress. I tried to scream, but my chest was so tight I could not make a noise. While he was working to get his pants off, I pushed him away—and I am not kidding, Ethan—I karate chopped him in the throat. That is the best way to stop an attacker. The groin, the neck, or the eyes. I karate chopped him like this"—she demonstrated on me, only pulling the chop short before she bruised my Adam's apple—"and he released me."

"Holy shit. Did you tell the police?"

She shook her head.

"The guy tried to rape you!"

"If I told the police, I would be stuck in New Delhi for a long time. Right then, I just wanted to leave. Besides, it was my word against his."

I could sort of understand. She didn't want to get stuck in red tape in a developing nation. And India was India, a patriarchal society. The authorities might have dismissed her story out of hand. Still, it seemed incomprehensible that this guy could simply walk free.

"What about his sister—the one hosting you? Did you tell

her what happened?"

"I considered that. But by the time I landed in China and was with my next host, it seemed like it happened a long time ago, in a different world. After how nice she was, I did not think I could tell her what her brother tried to do."

"What if he attacks someone else?"

"I know, Ethan. I am not happy with how things turned out. Sometimes that is life." She shrugged. "Anyway, that is my bad experience couch surfing."

"I don't know what to say. I'm—I'm happy you were okay."

"Thank you, Ethan."

I nodded lamely. I didn't know what else to do. I'm not good with condolences. This is because ever since Gary's death I'm usually on the receiving end of them, and I'm well aware of how awkward and trivial they sound.

"Hey," I said, remembering something. "Back when we were collecting wood, and we found that body—"

"You were sick."

"I bumped right into it. I touched it. The smell…"

"I understand."

"Did you and Ben see the crucifixes hanging from the trees?"

"Crucifixes? No."

"None of them?"

"We saw the paint on the tree. We were examining it when we heard you yell. We saw you pushing away from the body." She snickered.

"You think that was funny?"

"It looked like you were dancing with it. That is what I thought. That you were dancing with it. Then you turned around and vomited."

"So Ben freaked out because of the body?"

"Have you ever done mushrooms?"

"Yeah."

"Imagine being on them here and seeing a dead body—especially one that looked like the one we saw. I think I would have reacted the same. So what about these crucifixes?"

"They were made from sticks. There were at least a dozen of them, hanging from branches." I hesitated. "And they were moving."

"Moving?"

"Swinging back and forth. Like there was a wind. But I don't think there was a wind."

Nina frowned. "Are you trying to scare me, Ethan?"

"No—"

"Is this a ghost story?"

"It's what I saw." I shrugged. "I don't know. There must have been a wind."

"Strong enough to blow the crucifixes? You would have felt it."

"There's no other explanation."

"Yes, there is. You just do not want to acknowledge what it might be." She took her camera out of her pocket and passed it to me. "There is a photograph I want to show you."

I powered the device on and pressed the Play button. A photograph of Tomo, Neil, John Scott, and Mel appeared. They were sitting at the campfire.

"The one of everyone by the fire?" I asked.

"Yes, that one."

"When did you take this?"

"A little earlier when you were gone."

"What about it?"

"You will see."

I studied the picture more closely. Smoke billowed up from the fire before them, masking much of the right side of the photo—and in it was something that...wasn't smoke. The edges were too hard, too defined, and it was a slightly different color, lighter, almost white.

"You see it, yes?" Nina said.

"You think it's a ghost?"

"I do not know what it is. How about you?"

A shiver had shot down my spine, as if a cold finger had

touched me at the base of my neck. Swinging crucifixes—and now this?

"I don't believe in ghosts," I said.

"Then what is it?"

I had no answer. I used the zoom function to magnify the image. The longer I looked, the more I thought I could almost see the vague formation of a face.

"A light reflection?" I said.

"It is nighttime, Ethan."

"A dirty lens?"

"I took more pictures. Look. That mark is only on that one."

I pressed the button to scroll right. There were a number of shots of the forest, including one of the dog kennel and several of the signs we passed on the way into the forest. There was one of Mt. Fuji through what appeared to be a train window. The bronze statue of the famous dog Hachioji, which was a popular meeting spot at Shibuya station.

Nina naked.

She stood in a room facing a wall mirror. A white towel was wrapped around her head. Her back and the upper half of her buttocks were visible.

I should have turned off the camera. Instead I clicked right. Nina again, this time reaching for the camera, as if to stop the shot from being taken. This one left nothing to the imagination.

The next was of Nina in a bra and panties, brushing her hair. The one after that of a large airplane docked at an airport boarding gate.

I returned to the photograph of the campfire and the supposed ghost. I cleared my throat. "Yeah, I don't know what to make of it."

"You see, it was not a dirty lens."

I handed the camera back to her. "No…"

"But you think there must be a rational explanation."

"Don't you?"

"Maybe. Maybe not. I am too high to think of rational explanations right now."

I recalled how I'd felt earlier in the day when we'd started down the secondary trail. The shapes I'd thought I could see in the twisted tree trunks and clumps of roots.

"We're projecting," I said.

"Huh?"

"Like when you see a giraffe or an elephant in the clouds. They're not really there. But you want to see them, so you project."

"Were you projecting when you saw the crucifixes swinging?"

"I don't know." I shrugged. "I guess I probably was."

"You know, Ethan," Nina said with a discerning smile, "you are an awful liar."

I spent another half hour or so talking to Nina. I didn't mention the naked photos of her, and she didn't either, if she even knew they were on the camera. Then my phone rang.

I fumbled it out of my pocket, cursing myself for not powering it off. The last thing I needed was Mel thinking I was chatting it up with Shelly in the woods. I glanced at the screen and hesitated. It was a blocked number.

I pressed the Talk button. "Hello?"

Silence.

"Hello?"

A scratchy voice: "Why you in my forest?"

For a moment I couldn't breathe let alone reply—until I realized it was Derek, had to be Derek, trying to scare me. "Fuck you, Miller," I said. "I know it's you."

"Why you in my foressssssst?"

It's not Derek, it doesn't sound anything like him.

"Who is this?" I demanded.

A dial tone.

I stared at my phone, iced to the bone.

"Who was that?" Nina asked, concerned.

"A...friend."

"You asked who it was."

"He was trying to scare me."

"What did he say?"

"He asked why I was in his forest."

"My goodness, Ethan! Are you sure it was your friend?"

"Who else could it be?"

"Check the number."

"It was blocked."

"Did you recognize his voice?"

"No—yeah. He was disguising it."

"What did it sound like?"

"Like—like a Japanese person."

"Scary?"

"Yeah."

"Like a Japanese ghost?"

"What does a Japanese ghost sound like?"

"This is not funny."

"I know. I'm going to kick his ass when I see him."

"This is wrong, Ethan. It is very wrong."

"Nina, it's okay—calm down."

"Are you sure it was your friend?"

"Yes...positive."

"Call him back."

"You can't call blocked numbers."

"Call his real number."

Nodding, I dialed it. After seven unanswered rings I hung up.

"See?" I told her. "He knows I know. He's not picking up."

"I hope you are right."

"Who else could it be?"

"Maybe it really was—"

"No, it wasn't, Nina."

MY eyes had become dry and my eyelids droopy from the pot, and Derek's prank phone call had scared me sober, so I told Nina I was going to crash. Back at the camp the fire was mostly smoldering charcoal. Everyone had retired to their tents. I glanced around for John Scott, wondering where he had chosen to sleep. I didn't see him anywhere.

I slipped my phone into Mel's backpack, so I wouldn't roll onto it while I slept, then crept into our tent, hoping Mel wouldn't smell the marijuana on me. She was against the far wall beneath one of those emergency space-age blankets. I've never used one, and I was curious to discover whether they actually provided any warmth or not. I slipped off my shoes, lifted the blanket, and slid in beside her, mindful not to get too close.

"Hey," I said softly.

She didn't reply.

"Are you awake?"

"No."

"I want to explain about Shelly—"

"Don't mention her name."

"I want to explain about *her*—"

"Not now."

"It's important."

"I don't want to hear it."

"When?"

No answer.

"Mel?"

"Goodnight."

I almost explained anyway, but I didn't want to risk getting kicked out of the tent. I shifted to get more comfortable. The ground was hard. So far I detected no heat benefit from the blanket.

Laying there in the dark, still wide awake, I contemplated Mel, and our relationship, and wondered how things had gotten so fucked up so quickly. After replaying our earlier argument, I pushed the matter from my mind, telling myself it would work itself out in the morning.

My thoughts turned to Nina. I couldn't shake the feeling that she had known those photographs of her were on her camera, she hadn't forgotten about them, and she had wanted me to see them.

But why?

A fantasy played out in my head. Nina and me back where we'd smoked the joint. She hands me the camera and I see the pictures of her. This time, however, I mention them.

"What do you think, Ethan?" she asks.

"You have a nice body."

"Do you like my breasts?"

"They're nice."

"Do you want to see them for real?"

At this point she stands up and leads me deeper into the trees, where we begin undressing each other. Only when I take off her clothes I find a dry, rotting body, nothing but bones jutting through saggy, grayish skin...

I snapped open my eyes. I had been drifting off to sleep, passing through that murky world where you're awake but not awake. Although I was staring into darkness, I was seeing the body of the hanging man. A cold, clammy, almost paralyzing sensation overwhelmed me, as if death had followed me into the tent. I wanted to hold Mel, feel her body, her warmth, her presence. But I couldn't. We were in a stupid fight about nonexistent infidelity.

I closed my eyes again and rolled onto my side.

Morning couldn't come quickly enough.

15

WE were in the communal kitchen of the Shinagawa guesthouse. I was at the stove, cooking breakfast for Gary and me. The eggs in the frying pan were scrambled, how Gary liked them, the bacon extra crispy. Gary was seated at the table: dark curls, straight nose, gold-flecked green eyes. He was dressed in his white-and-maroon Hershey Bears hockey uniform, a captain "C" on the front of his jersey, his number 14 on the back. He even had his skates on, rubber guards protecting the blades. Getting dressed at home before a game or practice was something we had done as kids. It had given our father, who was regularly hungover on weekend mornings, some extra time to sleep in.

"Why are you already dressed, Gare?" I asked him. "You haven't done that since house league."

"I have practice this morning, bud."

"But why not dress at the arena?"

He frowned. "Because I'm late."

"Who cares? It's just practice."

"No, bud. I'm late for something else."

"For what?"

"I have an appointment to keep."

"What appointment?"

His frown deepened: sadness or fear, I couldn't tell. "I can't talk about it." He stood. "Thanks for breakfast. I have to get going."

A terminal dread filled me, because I knew wherever he was going he wasn't coming back. "Wait! Gare! You haven't eaten your breakfast yet. At least stay for breakfast."

"Don't burn the eggs, bud."

Then he was gone. I stared at where he had been, willing him to come back. Nina appeared instead, from the hallway, and made her way to the shower stall that was off the kitchen, near the coin-operated washing machines. A navy T-shirt fluttered loosely over her body, ending halfway down her thighs.

"Good morning, Ethan," she greeted.

"Hey, Nina," I said, cheering up. "You missed my brother, Gary." I wished she could have met Gary.

"Oh, that is too bad."

"Do you want breakfast? I have extra."

"Toast is okay. Where is your girlfriend?"

"I don't know." And I didn't. Mel didn't sleep in our room. I should have been more concerned—she never went somewhere overnight without telling me—but I wasn't. I knew she was still angry at the whole Shelly thing, and I didn't want to deal with any of that right then.

"You should marry her, Ethan."

"I know."

"Are you ready?"

"I'm not sure."

Nina disappeared into the shower cubicle. The water rumbled through the building's old pipes. I was alone once more.

I stirred the eggs and turned the bacon. Then I stuck two pieces of white bread in the toaster. Whole-wheat bread was about as hard to find in Japan as real mayonnaise, or toothpaste with fluoride.

Nina began calling me. She needed a towel.

I fetched one from my room and rapped on the shower door with my knuckles.

"It is unlocked."

I opened it. There was a small vestibule where you can change and the shower stall itself. Nina stood beneath the needle spray in a white bikini. I hung the towel on the clothes hook.

"Are you surprised?" she asked me.

"About what?"

"That I have a swimming costume on."

"No," I said, though I was—and disappointed.

"Do you want me to take it off?"

Steam billowed around her. I could feel the humidity.

"Your toast should be ready."

"Goodbye, Ethan."

I remained there for a moment, not wanting to leave, but she was ignoring me. I closed the door and went back to the stove. I topped one plate with bacon and eggs, the other with two slices of toast.

Nina emerged from the shower. The towel I'd given her was wrapped around her body. When she sat down at the table, it slipped down her torso and bunched at her waist. She was no longer wearing the bikini. She didn't seem to notice or care that her breasts were exposed, and I felt a sense of déjà vu. Once again, however, I chose not to say anything. As we ate, she told me about the time in India when she was almost raped. Halfway into her story I heard something on the other side of the sliding glass door that opened onto a balcony. The drapes were drawn and I couldn't see out. The noise continued. It sounded like footsteps. Like someone walking on dry leaves.

"Are you going to see who is there?" Nina asked me.

I was frozen with indecision. What if it was Mel? If she saw Nina sitting half naked at the table with me, she would surely lose it. Still, I felt compelled to check.

I stood and opened the door—

I snapped awake again, reliving the last moments of the dream. The guesthouse kitchen. Gary. Nina. Mel—had she been at the door? I never had a chance to see. As the immediacy of the dream faded I remembered where I was.

I had rolled against Mel during the night, so we were spooning, my right arm draped over her side. Either she was too deep asleep and wasn't aware of my transgression, or she'd noticed at some point but didn't care. I hoped it was the latter.

I heard a noise outside the tent and stiffened with alarm.

Was that what had woken me?

I remained perfectly still, listening.

Footsteps.

The alarm ballooned into full-out fear.

I sat up. The emergency blanket fell away from me, the vaporized aluminum crackling and making a lot of noise.

Mel didn't stir. I listened once more, but didn't hear anything else.

I was about to open the tent flap, though I couldn't bring myself to do it.

What if it was...what?

A *yūrei*?

I berated myself for being a twenty-six year old six year old. It was just someone going to urinate. They'd be in the trees now. They'd be returning any minute. I'd hear them as they climbed into their tent.

I lay back down, wickedly alert.

"What are you doing?" Mel asked sleepily.

"I heard something outside."

"What was it?"

"Someone going to the bathroom, I think."

She didn't reply.

One minute slugged toward two, then three, then four.

Perhaps it was not a bladder but a bowel call?

When ten minutes passed, and all remained quiet outside the tent, I began to wonder if I had imagined the sound.

No—I was sure I hadn't.

Had it been an animal then?

It would have to have been something large.

A bear? A deer?

Maybe. But I wasn't convinced. I had the impression the steps had been taken slowly, with the intention of not making much noise.

Really? You were half asleep. Stop spooking yourself.

I closed my eyes and took my own advice.

16

THROUGH the haze of sleep I heard Nina calling Ben's name. I don't recall how many times she called it, or at what intervals, only that I kept hearing it repeated over and over. For a while I thought I might be dreaming, but reality slowly penetrated my slumber, telling me I should probably get up, something might have happened. Reluctantly I propped myself into a sitting position. It was light out. Not sunny-day bright. The gray, filtered light of another overcast morning.

Mel was not in the tent. I never heard her get up, which meant I must have been pretty out of it. I was surprised by that, because after hearing the footsteps in the middle of the night, I rested only fitfully, kept semi-awake by the conundrum of the footsteps, the hard ground, and the frosty weather. Also, Mel had been tossing and turning and sleep-talking, something she never did. It made me wonder if she'd been having more of those crevice-related nightmares.

I pushed aside the emergency blanket, rubbed my arms for warmth—and noticed that my right hand had swollen even more overnight. The pustules had turned into clear blisters filled with cloudy fluid. They continued to itch terribly, especially the ones along the creases in my palm and between my fingers. Again, however, I refused the temptation to scratch them. If I broke any open, there was a good chance they would become infected out here.

I crawled outside and stood. The forest appeared as bleak and desperately hellish as it had the day before, but I was not so bothered by it. We had gotten through the night, and we were leaving. Hallelujah.

I could see my breath puff before me. The fire was going, and the smoky smell made me feel semi-human. Tomo and Neil sat next to each other. Neil was reading a book—he always had some non-fiction book or another—while Tomo was thumbing through one of his manga comics. He says the stories are sci-fi or horror, but every time I've glimpsed a page over his shoulder there's something traumatizing happening to a busty woman in skimpy clothing.

John Scott was curled up at the base of a nearby tree. He looked bulky, as if he had put on extra clothes beneath his leather jacket. He was using his rucksack as a pillow. I must have walked right past him the night before after leaving Nina.

Mel was twenty yards away, sitting on a rock, her back to us.

"Hey." I cleared my parched throat. "Morning."

"Morning, Ethan," Neil said. "Fancy a cuppa coffee? I'll put the pot on again."

I noticed they each had paper cups next to them, filled with black coffee. This kicked my olfactory sense into gear, and suddenly I could smell the rich, strong aroma.

"Would love some."

Neil set the pot directly on the flames, maneuvering it to keep the black plastic handle from melting. "This is the last of the water unfortunately."

"We're not sticking around."

Tomo pulled his ear buds free. "Hey, man. You sleep so late."

I checked my wristwatch. "It's only half past seven." I glanced at Mel again. Could she hear me? Why wasn't she turning around?

"You two lovebirds still fighting?" Neil asked, shaking instant coffee into a cup.

"Think so."

"Because you pussy guy," Tomo said.

"Because Mel and I got in an argument?"

"Yeah, and you run to trees and cry like girl. You gotta be man, right? Tell her you talk any bitch you want."

"Thanks for the advice, Snoop."

"You know it."

Nina called Ben's name again from somewhere in the trees.

"What's going on with Ben?" I asked.

Neil shrugged. "He hasn't been around since we woke up."

I frowned. Where did he go? For a walk—without telling Nina or anyone else?

"You think we should help Nina look?" I said.

"No need to panic," Neil said. "We'll sort out what's going on when she comes back." He poured boiling water into the cup and handed it to me, which I accepted, pinching it by the rim so as not to scald my fingers. "Meanwhile," he added, nodding past me toward Mel, "you have your own problems to suss out, don't you think?"

MEL didn't say anything as I sat on a rock close to hers. I set my coffee beside me.

"Hey," I said with false normalcy.

"Hey," she said.

"What time did you get up?"

"Fifteen minutes ago maybe."

"Have you eaten anything?"

"Tea."

"That's not eating."

"I'm not hungry."

"I think there's some nuts—"

"I'm not hungry, Ethan."

We sat in silence. The morning air was not only frosty but damp as well. The fragrant smell of dead leaves perfumed the air.

"Listen, Mel, this Shelly stuff, it's such a dumb thing to get upset over."

She looked at me. "Are you calling me dumb?"

"What?"

"I think lying about calls from an ex-girlfriend is a big thing. You think lying about calls from an ex-girlfriend is a dumb thing. So are you calling me dumb for thinking it's a big thing?"

I clenched my jaw. "No."

"Well?"

"It's been blown out of proportion, that's all."

"Benjamin!" It was Nina again. She sounded closer than before.

"Look," I said. "It's not helping us any putting this off—"

"John and I slept together," she said abruptly.

I blinked, not thinking I'd heard her correctly. But that passed in a flash, and a wave of red-hot jealousy swept through me. "When?" I asked quietly.

"In college. He was on leave from the Army, visiting friends at UCLA. I ran into him at a bar."

"And you took him home?"

She didn't say anything.

"And after that?" I said. "Did you see him again?"

"No. He went back to the base he was stationed at. It was my senior year. I returned to St. Helena a couple months later. Then I came here."

I let this revelation sink in. It was infuriating to hear, and I had to tell myself she hadn't done anything wrong. It happened before I knew her. If I hadn't met John Scott on this trip, I wouldn't have cared less. Then again, I *had* met John Scott. He *was* on this trip. What the fuck was that all about?

"Have you seen him since you've been in Japan?" I asked.

"No."

"Never?"

"No."

"Don't you think you should have at least said something

to me about this history between you two?"

"Please, Ethan, like you ever told me anything about Shelly and you."

"There's nothing going on!" I snapped. "Nothing!"

"And there's nothing going on between John and I."

"He's here now, Mel. He's fucking camping with us. Do you see Shelly anywhere?"

"I can't be friends with my ex's?"

"You could have told me we were going to be spending the weekend with one of them."

"Well, now you know." She stood. "I'm going to get more tea."

"Wait—I want to talk about this."

"I don't, Ethan. I need time to think things over."

My chest tightened. *Think things over?* I didn't like the sound of that. It sounded like something you say when you're contemplating breaking up.

"Think what over?" I asked.

"Things, Ethan. Things."

She left.

I remained where I was, trying to make sense of what Mel had told me. So she and John Scott had gotten together. I didn't like it, but whatever. It happened in the past. But why had she invited him to climb Mt. Fuji? And why hadn't she told me about her history with him? Why the secrecy? Was this her way of getting back at me? She had known about Shelly's messages for a while now. She'd suspected, albeit erroneously, that a spark had rekindled between us. So when John Scott had called her up, looking for something to do in Tokyo, had she invited him to climb Fuji with the sole intent of making me jealous? Had she kept silent about their history, knowing I would inevitably find out? Had she, in fact, gotten in touch with *him*, not the other way around?

Talk about some sick twisted shit.

Was Mel really capable of that?

And what the hell was that pseudo threat of breaking up all about? No way she could be serious. It was a bluff, a phase. After all, it wasn't as though she'd caught Shelly and me in bed together. That might have been a cause for something as drastic as breaking up. This was just a couple text messages, a misunderstanding.

Well, screw it, I thought. If Mel wanted to prance around with John Scott to make me jealous, fine. If she wanted to threaten breaking up to make a point, fine. I wasn't going to get sucked into these stupid games.

In the distance I caught a flash of Nina's yellow jacket among the green foliage. She saw me and waved. I waved back. She came over and sat on the rock Mel had been sitting on. Her face was flushed and she was breathing hard, from anger or exertion I wasn't sure.

"Ben is gone," she said, shaking her head. "Did you hear?"

"Was he in your tent when you went to sleep last night?"

"Yes, he was there. He wanted to talk, talk, talk, about nothing. I was tired. I told him this. He got restless and left the tent. I went to sleep."

"What time was that?"

"An hour after you left me. Why, Ethan?"

"I thought I heard someone walking around outside the tents last night."

"So?"

"So nothing. I'm just trying to piece things together."

"Who was it?"

"If not Ben, I'm guessing someone who needed to relieve themselves."

"Relieve?"

"Go pee."

"Oh. You know what I am worried about? I am worried Ben got lost."

"He must have gone pretty far," I admitted. "I mean, if he can't hear you calling his name."

"Yes, that, or he could not find his way back and just went to sleep somewhere. Do you think he is sleeping right now?"

"Could be," I said. It was a better alternative than lying in one of those lava craters with a cracked skull. "I'm guessing you've tried ringing him?"

"I do not have a phone."

"Why not?"

"I have one at home, but I did not bring it with me. It is too expensive to use when you travel."

"So you don't have Ben's number?"

"He does not have a phone either."

"So what do you want to do?"

"I want to find him, of course."

"Maybe he went to the parking lot?"

She frowned. "The parking lot?"

"If the forest was tripping him out, he might have wanted to get clear of it, get in the open."

"Without telling me?"

"Maybe. I don't know."

"No, I think he is lost," she said firmly. "We must wait for him to come back."

"And what if he doesn't come back?"

"He will. He is probably just sleeping. You will see."

BACK at the camp Mel was already dismantling our tent. Neil was still reading his book, while Tomo had dozed off. John Scott was sitting up on the patch of ground where he'd slept, smoking a cigarette. I had to resist the urge to say something to him about Mel and him. It would be a sign of weakness, a concession I saw him as a threat. He'd likely get off on that; it would feed his alpha male complex.

"How late were you up last night?" I asked him instead.

"Late."

"Did you see Ben around?"

"Nope. What's going on?"

"He is missing," Nina said, placing her hands on her hips. It was a confrontational pose, almost as if she were blaming John Scott.

I was liking her more and more by the minute.

"He's fine," John Scott said.

"You think so?" she said with an edge.

"Yeah."

"You know, it is your fault he is missing. You could at least pretend to be concerned."

"I'm not his babysitter. If he can't handle—"

"Oh, just shut your mouth." Nina turned to the others. "He does not have a phone, so we cannot contact him. I am going to wait here until he returns. You may all do what you wish."

"I still want to go check out that body," John Scott said. "Tomo was too chicken shit to do it last night."

"I was too drunk," Tomo said without opening his eyes.

"What about now?"

"Yeah, man, let's do it."

"Neil?" John Scott asked.

"I'll live vicariously through your description."

I didn't feel I was in a position to speak for Mel right then, so I simply looked at her. She continued to dismantle the tent in silence.

"Mel?" I said.

"Yes?"

"Stay or leave?"

"Of course we'll stay until Ben returns," she said. "We can't leave Nina here by herself."

17

AFTER we finished dismantling the tents and packing our stuff, we sat in a circle for breakfast, which was leftovers from the previous night's dinner. Given everyone's slim pickings, we decided to pool the food together, then divide it up amongst all of us. In total we had a bag of grapes, some nuts, dried fruit, a browning banana, and two packages of instant noodles, only we no longer had any water in which to boil them. I created seven portions, setting aside Ben's. Neil, however, said he wasn't hungry, so we divvied his up as well.

"Too bad you left your food at the ant site," John Scott said to me.

"We'll pick it up on the way back."

"If the ants didn't eat it all."

They wouldn't have. I hadn't left anything open; it had all been packaged. Still, I didn't bother telling John Scott this.

I couldn't stop picturing the fucker and my girlfriend in bed together.

While we were eating, Neil disappeared into the forest, returning five minutes later.

"You just shit, man?" Tomo said.

"You're bloody vulgar, aren't you?" Neil replied, turning red.

"You have..." He made a farting noise.

"Come on, Tomo," I said. "We're eating."

"How you say? Diareema?"

"The shits," John Scott said.

"My stomach is upset, yes," Neil said.

"Told you that fish smelled nasty, dude."

"It wasn't the fish. Kaori wouldn't have given me bad fish."

"Yeah, you right," Tomo said. "Probably the bottled water."

Neil scowled. Color had risen to his cheeks again, this time in irritation rather than embarrassment. He was about to snap.

"So what's the plan?" I said, changing topics. "Should we start looking for Ben?"

"What's the point?" John Scott said. "If he can't hear us shouting from here, then he's too far away for us to find regardless."

"He might be injured," I said.

"If he was, and within a potential search parameter, he would still be able hear us."

"Not if he's unconscious." I glanced at Nina, then at each of the others, making sure I had their attention. "He was gone when we woke up, which means he left sometime during the night or early morning. He might have slipped and hit his head on a rock...or fallen into one of those big craters."

"Whoa, slow down," John Scott said. "If we start wandering around aimlessly, we're likely going to get lost ourselves."

"We won't go far," I told him, getting pissed off he was arguing with me. "But we have to do something."

"When?" Nina asked.

"Now. There's no point putting it off."

"And what if we don't find him?" Mel asked.

I looked at Nina. It was her call.

"Then we wait here," she said. "If he does not return by lunchtime, then we head back to the parking lot."

John Scott shook his head. Everyone else, however, seemed okay with the plan.

I said, "I think we should search in pairs. How about John Scott and Tomo, Nina and Neil, Mel and me?"

"I'll go with Neil," Mel said pointedly.

I looked at her. She looked away.

I shrugged. "Okay. Mel and Neil. Nina and me."

"I think Tomo and me will follow the string to the body," John Scott said, standing. "Who knows? Maybe Ben wanted to go back and see it for some reason."

"Why would he want to do that?" I said. "It's what tripped him out in the first place."

"Maybe once he sobered up he wanted to see what all the fuss was about."

I didn't want to concede to the prick, especially when I knew he only wanted to visit the body to assuage his own curiosity, but he had a valid point. Ben might have returned there.

We got to our feet, paired up, and began spreading out.

NINA and I went in the opposite direction she had gone earlier. We walked mostly in silence, focusing on searching for signs of Ben's passage. Then, suddenly, she tripped on a rock, stumbling forward. I grabbed her by the waist, preventing her from toppling over.

"You okay?" I said.

"Yes, thank you. I was not paying attention."

We began walking again.

I said, "I'm sure Ben's okay."

"I am sure too."

"Even if we don't find him, the police will put together a search party. They'll find him. This isn't Yellowstone Park."

"Where the bear Yogi lives?"

"That's Jellystone."

"You know," she said, "I feel bad—"

"He'll be fine—"

"No, you do not understand." She frowned. "You see, I think he loves me."

I looked at her. "That's a bad thing?"

"I do not love him back."

"Oh."

"I know, I know. That is not nice thing for me to say, especially with him missing, but it is true. It is why I feel bad, because I am thinking like this, now, when I should be worried for him."

I didn't say anything.

"You know," Nina went on, "I was not sure I wanted him to come with me to Japan. But he did. He insisted. I thought why not. Better than being alone. But maybe I was wrong. I like being alone."

"Where are you going next?"

"After Japan? The United States, your country."

"You've never been?"

"No."

"You should visit Wisconsin."

"That is where you are from?"

"Yes—no. It's where I'm from, yes, but you don't need to visit. I was joking. There's not much to do there."

"It is peaceful?"

"Quiet."

"Ah, that is what I am looking for! Remember, I told you I am searching for a place to meditate. You should come with me, Ethan. We will live together."

I looked at her again. She was brutally blunt.

"So what do you think?" she pressed.

I shook my head. I didn't know what else to do.

"Do not be shy," she said.

"I'm not shy. You're just—I don't know."

"I am what?"

"Is Ben going to the US too?" I asked.

"He cannot."

"Why not?"

"He has not completed his service in the military. We both finished our three years around the same time, but he has to do an extra nine months because he is an officer."

"You were in the military too?"

"Yes, in Israel, both men and woman have to serve."

"That's nuts."

"We are a small country, in a part of the world where not many other countries like us. We do what we can to survive. Women have served in the military since before the Palestine War."

"What did you do—your role or whatever?"

"I was part of the Border Guard."

"Like the Border Patrol in the US?"

"Do they protect against terrorists?"

"More like illegal immigrants."

"Then I do not think they are similar."

"Have you ever shot anyone?"

"No, but I am trained to use machine guns, grenades, mortars, anything. So do not mess with me, Ethan."

"And you have a mean karate chop."

"That is right."

I tried picturing Nina in military uniform with a machine gun, and for some reason the image came easily. Perhaps it was her headstrong personality—

Mel screamed.

The sound iced the marrow in my bones because it wasn't a scream of surprise or alarm.

It was one of pure horror.

"Come on!" I shouted at Nina, already running, my heart drumming inside my chest.

Mel and Neil were not far away, and I reached them quickly. Through the trees I saw them standing side by side, their backs to me.

Abruptly the forest took on a surreal quality, because ahead, past them, I glimpsed what they were staring at.

When I reached Mel, I spun her away from the grisly sight, pulling her against my chest, shushing her softly, telling her that everything was going to be all right, which, of course, was the farthest thing from the truth.

18

AS I stood there holding onto Mel, facing Ben, I felt as though I had fallen down the rabbit's hole—either that or I had been whacked in the face with a stupid stick—and it was with a detached clinical eye that I studied the husk of what had once been the go-happy Israeli.

He was suspended several feet in the air above the ground, which led me to believe he had climbed the tall pine tree from which he was hanging, stood on one of the lower branches, tied the rope above his head to a higher branch, and stepped to his death.

His head seemed too large, at least larger than I remembered it, in comparison to the rest of his body. Then I realized his head wasn't too big at all; his neck was too thin, too elongated. The rope was knotted snug beneath his jawline, pulled impossibly high and tight by gravity and his own body weight, crushing the soft tissue in his throat, providing the illusion that his neck had been stretched.

His eyes were closed, his mouth a gaping orifice, from which his tongue protruded, swelled thick, a blood-purple color. I couldn't be sure given the distance between us, but it appeared as though his face was covered with small red blotches, almost as if he had developed a bad case of the measles, and it took me a moment to realize these were likely the result of burst capillaries that had bled into his skin.

In the still forest his body drooped bonelessly, resembling

a puppet at rest, except there were no strings or rods connected to a puppeteer's hands, only the rope, the horrible rope, stretched taut and groaning softly as it struggled with the weight of the burden it bore.

Ben was wearing the same clothes as he had the day before, though his jumper was unzipped, revealing a T-shirt with the words "Meat is Murder—Tasty, Tasty Murder"—a joke that seemed terribly wrong right then. The inside legs of his jeans were damp and colored brown, an indication he'd urinated and defecated on himself.

This last detail made me think of a documentary on capital punishment I had once seen. The program had dedicated a considerable amount of time to hangings, given that they remained a legal method of judicial execution in sixty or so countries, including in some parts of the United States. From what I recalled, the goal in an ideal hanging was to break the subject's neck and sever the spine. Brain death would then take a couple minutes to occur while complete death could take up to twenty minutes—yet the subject would lose consciousness almost instantly and not experience any of it. On the other hand, if the distance of the drop through the trapdoor was miscalculated, and not enough torque was created to break the subject's neck, he or she would either die of decapitation if the drop was too long or strangulation if the drop was too short.

I couldn't help but wonder now what happened to Ben. Had he died quickly—or had he dangled from the tree branch for a protracted period of time, kicking and twitching in a gruesome, extended fashion?

The vacuum I'd been in while all these thoughts plowed through my mind abruptly burst. Once again I became aware of Mel hugging me, mumbling something over and over. My first guess was "I can't feel;" then, more likely, "This can't be real."

Behind me vegetation thrashed, and a moment later Nina burst past us, making a strange moaning sound. When she came to Ben's body, she stopped, as if couldn't bring herself to touch it. That moaning became a whimper, higher pitched but just as awful.

John Scott and Tomo appeared. John Scott paused for a moment, swore to himself, then scrambled up the tree. He tugged furiously at the anchor end of the rope, but couldn't get it undone.

Seeing him take charge kicked me into gear.

Maybe Ben was still alive.

It seemed impossible, but…

I released Mel and went to Ben. I wrapped my arms around his waist and lifted, so the pressure from the noose was off his throat. His body was as stiff as a mannequin's. The stench of his feces almost made me puke. It smelled worse than shit—blood-and-guts rancid—almost as if he had discharged his internal organs into the seat of his pants.

"Get my knife!" I shouted, then recalled I had forgotten it back at the crevice. "Get a rock! Something!"

Tomo and Neil dashed away in different directions. John Scott continued to work at the knot. I remained where I was, elevating Ben. He seemed incredibly light, though I imagined that was due to the adrenaline coursing me. In fact, my thinking thus far seemed to be remarkably clear.

"He's already dead!" Mel blurted. "He's dead!"

Nina dropped to her knees and stared up at Ben, her arms outstretched. It was a strangely religious pose, almost as if she were praying to him.

"He's already dead!" Mel wailed.

I knew this was true—it was as obvious as day—but I continued to hold out hope, however illogical.

John Scott shouted triumphantly from above me, and suddenly Ben was free. I tried to lower him gracefully to the ground, but ended up dropping him like a board.

I knelt beside him and pressed my fingers to his neck, waited, then lowered my ear to his chest.

I looked at Nina and shook my head.

19

THE pandemonium passed. We calmed down somewhat, although everyone's nerves remained frayed and raw. Consciously or subconsciously, I wasn't sure which, we'd moved as a group a dozen feet away from Ben's body and kept our backs to it. He wasn't very long dead, but death was still death. No one wanted anything to do with it.

Mel and Nina gravitated toward each other and hugged. Nina cried softly while Mel stroked her hair. Tomo stared at the ground, Jay Gatsby cap in one hand, scratching his messy hair with the other, as if he couldn't figure out what happened. Neil was nowhere in sight; I wasn't sure where he'd gone. John Scott had lit a smoke and was pacing, his face a mask of concentration. He was likely thinking about the repercussions that Ben's death would have on him. As he should be; he was in some serious trouble.

After five minutes of this bizarre game of theater—nothing seemed real right then, more like a staged play, we the actors—I felt obliged to say something, though it wasn't very inspired.

"I'm sorry, Nina, I—" I shook my head, the rest of what I was going to say faltering on the tip of my tongue.

"I cannot believe he would do this!" she blurted, wiping tears from her eyes and shaking her head. "He was happy. Why would he do this?"

I waited for John Scott to say something. When he didn't, I fixed him with an expectant stare.

"What?" he said. Challenge in his voice.

"Why do you think Ben did this?"

"How the fuck am I supposed to know?"

"Are you serious…? Are you *serious*?" I might have kept my cool if the recalcitrant asshole had shown any signs of compunction. He didn't. Zero.

"Don't tell me you're going to blame this on the mushrooms?"

"He was tripping out all night," I said. "He took off into the forest on his own. Then he kills himself. What other explanation is there?"

"Nobody hangs themselves while on mushrooms."

"Apparently they do!"

"It wasn't the 'shrooms," he said defiantly.

"So what happened? He decided to give suicide a whirl? See what it felt like?"

John Scott's brow beetled over storming eyes. He balled his hands into fists, as if he were about to take a swing at me.

I wanted him to.

"You're going to lay this on me?" he snarled. "You're really going to try to lay this on me?"

I was too appalled to answer him. I looked at Tomo. "You have to call the police."

"And say what?" he asked. He was eyeing John Scott apprehensively.

"Tell them our friend is dead. They need to get out here."

"How they find us?"

It was true, I realized. We'd have to meet them in the parking lot.

John Scott said, "We tell the cops that Ben picked the mushrooms on his own."

Nina blinked, as if coming out of her stupor. "*Stom ta'peh!*" she spat. "*You* picked them."

"What does it matter? Why do any of us need to get involved in this? There's nothing that can be changed."

"You did this to him! You take responsibility!"

"I didn't do a fucking thing!" He jabbed a finger in Ben's direction. "*He* was the one who fucking hanged himself."

"I will tell the police I saw you pick them. I will tell them I saw you give them to him. He did not even want them. But you told him it was okay. That is manslaughter."

John Scott took an aggressive step toward Nina. I moved between them and shoved him hard. He lost his footing and fell on his ass. I had little time to enjoy the surprised look on his face because he rolled forward quickly onto his knees and sprang at me. His head rammed my gut, knocking the breath from my lungs. Before I could recover he dragged me to the ground. I couldn't shake him as he drove elbows into my face. Then one of the wild haymakers I was throwing connected with his jaw and he tumbled off me. I jumped on top of him and raised my fist. His eyes were unfocused, his jaw slack. I wanted to hit him so bad—for sleeping with Mel, for giving Ben the mushrooms, for threatening Nina—but I couldn't bring myself to do it.

I planted my hand on his head and pushed off, shoving his face into the ground.

Everyone was looking at me. No one seemed to know what to say.

"He was going to hit Nina," I said.

"The fuck I was," John Scott mumbled.

"You're bleeding, Ethan." Mel pressed her fingertips to a spot near my right temple.

I winced and jerked away. "I'm okay."

"You're bleeding."

"I'm fine."

John Scott pushed himself unsteadily to his feet. He glared at me. For a moment I thought he was going to continue the fight. Instead he turned to Nina and said, "It's my word against yours. You tell the cops I gave Ben the mushrooms, I'll tell them you gave them to him."

Nina threw her arms in the air. "Everyone here knows it was you!"

He must have tasted the blood leaking from his lip because he drew the heel of his hand across the cut. "Who was with me?" he said. "Just you and Tomo. And Tomo's not going to say anything, right dude?"

"Leave me out," Tomo said, holding up his hands.

"You have admitted you gave them to him!" Nina exploded.

"Bullshit!" He leveled a stare at Tomo, then Mel, then me. He returned to Mel, his best ally. "Mel?"

She wouldn't look at him. "What?"

"Did I say I gave him the mushrooms?"

She closed her eyes and shook her head. I couldn't tell if she was siding with him or if she was simply in denial that any of this was happening.

"Mel?" he repeated.

"Lord!" She spun away. I rested my hand on her shoulder, telling her not to listen to him.

"Don't you guys fucking peg this on me!" John Scott roared. "Tomo!" He opened his hands in a gesture of clemency. "Tomo?"

"I don't know, man. I don't know."

"You killed him!" Nina shrieked. She leapt at John Scott, pounding his chest with her small fists. He raised his arms in a half-assed attempt to block the blows. It was such a pathetic sight—such a humbling sight—I finally found pity for him.

I moved to pull Nina away. She didn't come easy. I had to lift her off her feet. She continued to swing her arms and kick madly. When I set her down, she glared at me, fury in her eyes, then collapsed on the spot. She pulled her legs to her chest, rested her forehead on her knees, and began to cry again.

Aside from Nina, the rest of us were sullenly quiet. John Scott gave me a brief glance and an even briefer nod, which pissed me off.

"Listen," I said, deciding that we needed to put blame aside for now. "This isn't helping any. We need to figure out what to do."

"We have to get out of here," Mel said. "We have to get out of here right now."

"I meant with Ben's body. Do we leave it here or take it with us?"

"We cannot leave it here," Nina said sharply.

"But how do we carry it?"

"We can make a litter," John Scott suggested.

Mel folded her arms across her chest. "Won't we be, I don't know, contaminating the scene?" she said.

"We've already taken him down," I said. "I can't see how moving him will hurt. We'll bring the police back here later."

Mel's lips tightened and her eyes hardened, as if she were just realizing the scope of this, the fallout. Getting Ben out of the forest was just the beginning. There would be interviews, statements, possible detainment until the facts were sorted out, perhaps a trial, all of it happening in a foreign language, in a foreign country.

"Oh God," she mumbled. "Oh God."

And that about summed it up.

20

ACCORDING to John Scott we needed two tent poles and two jackets to make a litter. You turn the jackets inside out and zip them up, leaving the sleeves on the inside. Next you tear out the shoulders, slip the poles through the holes you made, through the sleeves, and out the bottom, one jacket after the other, like a skewer through a kebab.

I handed him my jacket. It was chilly out, but I knew I would warm up quickly once we started moving.

"Okay," he said, "we need one more."

"All right." I looked at him expectantly.

"Dude, you can't tear a hole through this leather without a knife."

"I'm sure I could."

"You can take mine." Nina slipped off her jacket. She only had on a thin T-shirt beneath.

"You're going to get cold," I told her.

"I brought a sweater with me."

"Use mine," Mel said.

"No, Mel, keep it," I said. "We're using John Scott's."

"I told you—"

"Bullshit! I'll rip the shoulders."

"What's your problem?"

"What's the deal with you and that jacket?"

"What are you talking about?"

"That leather fucking jacket." I reached for a lapel.

"Get your dickskinners off me." He swatted my hand away.

"Give me it!" I said, grabbing the front and tugging.

He punched me in the face. My knees went weak. Still, as I went down I managed to grab an inside pocket and heard a loud tear.

I landed hard on my tailbone. The impact cleared the stars from my vision, and to my satisfaction John Scott was holding the jacket open, staring with incredulity at the huge swath of lining I'd torn nearly free.

"Told you," I said, though my jaw was numb, the words blubbery.

"You fuck stick," he sneered.

He might have come after me, but Tomo, Mel, and Nina held him back.

I spat the blood out of my mouth and saw a tooth exit as well.

MEL tended to my injury while John Scott got to work on the litter. He ended up using my jacket and Ben's, considering Ben would no longer need his. Tomo and Nina kept to themselves. Neil went to the trees to take another shit.

"What is it with you and his jacket?" Mel said as she dabbed the blood away from my split lip. Her hands were shaky, her complexion pale.

"It wasn't his jacket. It was the fact he'd let you and Nina sacrifice yours before he would his."

"You mentioned something about his jacket yesterday."

"Whatever. It's him. Not his jacket."

"You're upset over Ben. Your anger spilled over to John."

"I'm okay."

"You're in denial."

"Denial that Ben's dead?"

"Yes."

I shrugged. I didn't think I was. But I wanted to get off the topic; I didn't like Mel playing shrink. Given how visibly rattled she was over Ben's death, she was the last person who should be dishing out post-traumatic advice.

"Okay," she said with a final rub to get the last of the blood from my chin. "That's the best I can do. Just bite on this until it stops bleeding." She gave me the T-shirt she'd been using.

"Thanks."

"Now I want you to do something for me."

"What?"

"Apologize to John Scott."

I was incredulous. "For what?"

"Ripping his jacket."

"Are you kidding?"

"We don't need this right now, hon. We need to put everything behind us. We all need to be on the same team."

"He punched me."

"You started it."

"Jesus, how old are we?"

"Exactly, Ethan."

"Tell him to apologize to me."

"Will you accept it if he does?"

I hesitated.

"Good," she said.

JOHN Scott sauntered over to me just before we were ready to leave. "Hey, Ethos," he said, "sorry for punching your face in."

I glanced past him to Mel. She silently urged me on.

"Sorry about ripping your jacket." I paused. "Looks like you'll probably have to get it relined. Expensive."

"Won't be as expensive as fixing your tooth."

My tongue probed the spot where my left incisor had been. "Yeah, well."

"So we cool?"

"Yeah, cool."

"Shake," Mel told us.

John Scott stuck his hand out. I shook. He used a rock-hard

grip, as I knew he would, holding my hand for longer than comfortable, squeezing tighter and tighter, as I also knew he would.

Then he let go.

Best friends again.

JOHN Scott and I returned to Ben's body and set the litter down on the ground.

"Take his shoulders," he told me. "I'll take his legs."

"Wait. What about the rope?" The ligature still encircled Ben's neck.

"What about it?"

"Shouldn't we take it off him?"

"I don't think we should mess with it. We'll put the rest on his chest—"

"Hey," I said in a sudden epiphany. "Where the hell did he get the rope from?"

"It's the string."

"The string?"

"That we followed in."

I realized he was right. The string was a thick twine, made with woven coir fiber, easily strong enough to support a person's weight.

"Tomo and I couldn't find it when we went looking for the body."

"It's gone? All of it?"

John Scott nodded.

"It was hundreds of feet long. Where's the rest of it?"

"Maybe some of it's still lying around. We didn't have time to look. Now let's do this. On the count of three."

We lifted Ben off the ground, stepped sideways, and set him on the litter. Then we piled the string on top of him and covered him with his sleeping bag. We carried him back to camp, John Scott at the front, facing forward, me at the back. Tomo, Mel, and Nina were waiting for us, their backpacks on.

Neil, however, was slumped against a tree, holding his belly.

I told John Scott to set the litter down, then I went over to Neil and crouched next to him. "Neil? You okay?"

"Hurts like a son of a whore."

"Can you walk?"

"Don't know. Help me up."

I pulled him to his feet. He swayed, then lurched off into the trees. He doubled over, placing a hand against a tree trunk for balance. A moment later he vomited. I saw the first bit of brownish sick gush from his mouth and turned quickly away. He vomited again and again. I could do nothing to block out the wet, splashing sounds or the putrid stench, which made my own stomach queasy.

He returned, wobbly, but looking a little better.

"We're leaving now," I told him. "Can you make it?"

"I don't have a choice, do I?"

"You can wait here. We're going to bring the police back."

He shook his head and reached for his backpack.

"Leave it," I said. "We'll get it later."

"No, mate..."

"No one's going to touch it."

He reached for it again.

"I'll take it," I told him, since I no longer had mine to carry. I slipped it onto my back. "You just focus on walking."

I returned to where John Scott was waiting for me. We lifted the litter again—it was heavier than I'd hoped it would be—and led the way to where the string had once been.

"Hey!" Mel said, sounding panicked. "Where's the string?"

I explained.

"He took it?" She was incredulous. "But how will we find our way out?"

"We know the general direction. We'll come to the red ribbon eventually."

"What if we get lost?"

"We won't."

"You don't know that for sure—"

"Mel, there's no other option."

I pushed forward, shunting John Scott with the litter, and we began to walk.

IT was impossible not to think of Ben, of course. I had only known him for a very short time, less than twenty-four hours, but his sudden death made me feel as if we were much closer. It bonded us in some way. And it left an ache inside me. He'd been so young, so full of alacrity and life. I recalled the way he'd greeted us outside the train station. Open, friendly, displaying none of the automatic suspicion most people harbor toward strangers. Kissing Tomo in the parking lot. How excited he'd been upon discovering the Nike shoe and the painted arrows, like a kid on Christmas morning. The way he'd affectionately talked about his parents and grandparents. It was almost surreal to glance down now and see his body in front of me, covered by the sleeping bag, inert, something that would soon begin to atrophy and rot. It didn't seem right.

My mind skipped to his relationship with Nina. At first I'd assumed the two of them had been together for a long time. They came across that way. The familiar touches, the knowing looks, the conversations in Hebrew, which no one else could understand. Not to mention the fact they simply seemed good as a couple. Then came the first revelation that he and Nina had only met last month in Thailand, and the second, that the attraction between them was not as mutual as it appeared.

Hearing the latter had admittedly given me a thrill. Nina was available. I could get with her if I wanted, or it was likely I could get with her, given the way she'd been flirting with me. This was pure fantasy. Despite the Shelly/John Scott fiascos, Mel and I were near perfect together, I would never cheat on her. Still, it was nonetheless an ego boost to know I *could* get with Nina if the circumstances were different. It made me feel attractive and vital.

Not anymore.

In fact, I wished Nina had never revealed any of her Ben woes to me. Because now I not only felt guilty about coveting a dead guy's girlfriend, but my memory of them had become tainted. I would have preferred to remember Ben and Nina as happy and in love, not Ben foolishly courting someone who would not or could not reciprocate his sentiments.

I flexed my fingers around the tent poles. We'd been walking for twenty minutes. The blisters on my right hand stung, and I guessed they had ruptured. But I wasn't going to stop for a rest; there'd be time enough for that when we reached the ribbon.

I began to think in the here and now, particularly what was going to happen when we got out of Aokigahara and rang the police. They would meet us in the parking lot. We would be questioned—no, interrogated. The police in Japan were extra thorough when it came to the petty crimes often associated with foreigners. This never made sense to me, especially given the blind eye they turn toward the yakuza, which performs all kinds of illegal activities on an epic scale.

I'd been arrested in the country before, or at least detained, so I knew what I was talking about. After a night out with a friend, I caught the last train heading to my side of the city—or I thought I had—because it ended its service at what appeared to me to be an arbitrarily chosen station miles and miles from where I wanted to be.

I began walking in the direction I thought my place was, and along the way I came upon an unlocked bicycle propped against a utility pole. I hopped on it, telling myself I would return it the next day. The bike only had one speed, but the streets were flat, and soon I was zipping right along—straight into a dragnet. I would later learn that the police often erected these traffic stops specifically to curb the number of bicycles borrowed by one-way joyriders like me, which, not so surprising, is a common occurrence in a city with ten million bikes that all look alike and are rarely locked up.

The officer asked me if the bicycle was mine. I told him it was. He checked the registration sticker. This was something else I didn't know then. It was compulsory for cyclists to register their bikes and attach a sticker to the frame. The officer called in the number on his radio. My ride turned out to belong to a woman named Kimiko Kashiwa. He asked me if I was Kimiko Kashiwa. I told him, no, I wasn't.

The police station was a big white building where everyone spoke Japanese to me. One cop eventually attempted English. It was good enough that I could guess at his questions. What is your name? Where did you get the bike? Why did you take it? Where do you live? Where do you work? Then he got into the weird questions. How much money do you earn? What do your parents do? Where did you grow up? What school did you go to? When they ran out of irrelevant things to ask, they made me sit in an uncomfortable seat for the next five hours, though I could see no purpose to this. Finally, after filling out a bunch of forms I couldn't read, having to redo several pages because my penmanship went outside the provided boxes, they set me free with an ominous-sounding warning I didn't fully understand.

Given how serious they had reacted to the theft of a crappy fifty-dollar bike, I could hardly imagine how they would treat a case involving a questionable death.

I had done my research after this late-night encounter, to determine whether I'd been illegally detained, and learned there's no habeas corpus in Japan. The police can hold you for up to twenty-three days without charging you with a crime and without allowing you access to legal counsel or counselor assistance.

I flexed my fingers again. Now it wasn't just my right hand that was hurting. My biceps and shoulders had started to ache. How long had we been walking for? Thirty minutes? Longer? How far was it to the red ribbon? No more than forty minutes. Which meant another ten minutes before we could rest.

I continued to stare ahead at John Scott's back. I wondered

if he was tiring as well. He had to be. He wasn't Superman, though he might like to believe he was. Strangely, as much as I disliked him, I felt bad for him. Because he, of course, had the most to be anxious about. The rest of us had done nothing worse than trespass, if even that. He had given Ben the mushrooms, had taken them himself, which could be proven with a urine test. And drugs, even soft drugs, were a big no-no in Japan. Paul McCartney had once been locked up here for nine days, the Wings tour cancelled, because he had been caught with marijuana at Narita Airport. The Stones had struggled for years to enter the country because the band members had previous drug convictions. And then there were all the stories you heard about concerning friends of friends. One off the top of my head involved a Brit who was arrested for smoking a joint in his own home. Ten cops searched his apartment and found some cannabis seeds in a box and a few grams of pot in the freezer. He was sentenced to eighteen months in prison.

And this was just for possession. If John Scott was convicted of supplying a controlled substance and involuntary manslaughter, he could be looking at a long, long time behind bars.

He might be an American soldier, but his crime was committed off-base. There was nothing Uncle Sam could do for him if he was already in Japanese custody.

Finally I could continue no further. I was about to tell John Scott to hold up, but he beat me to it, calling for me to set down the litter.

I did so quickly and wrung out my arms, which felt like overcooked noodles. Mel, Tomo, Nina, and especially Neil all seemed grateful for the break.

"So where is it?" Mel said, brushing back the hair that had fallen in front of her face. "Where's the ribbon?"

"That's why I stopped," John Scott said. "I think we're lost."

21

"WE can't be lost," I said, surprised that he would make such a fear-mongering statement. "We just haven't reached the ribbon yet."

John Scott shook his head. "We've been walking for forty-five minutes. The walk in was only thirty."

"It was longer than that."

"I kept track." He tapped his wristwatch. "Thirty, thirty-five, tops."

"We're carrying Ben. We're not walking as fast."

"We're keeping the same pace, dude. Now listen to me. We should have come to the ribbon at least ten minutes ago. We haven't."

Mel frowned. "So we've been going in the wrong direction?"

"We strayed somehow."

"No way," I said. "The ribbon continued for hundreds of feet in both directions from where it intersected the string. There's no way we strayed around it."

"Then we've gotten totally turned about."

I glanced about at the forest, a sinking feeling in my gut.

"I think him right," Tomo said. "We walk too long."

"I knew this was a bad idea," Mel said.

"Knew what?" I asked, well aware her comment was directed at me. I'd been the one who'd confidently stated we wouldn't get lost.

"Heading off without the string to follow."

"What should we have done, Mel?"

"Does anyone have a compass?" she asked.

"They don't work here," Tomo said. "The rock fuck them."

"The rock what?" John Scott said.

"The rock. The iron. Fucks them. It true."

"Bullshit."

"Did anyone bring a compass anyway?" I asked. When no one replied, I added: "So what does it matter?"

"Maybe Ben took it," Mel said.

I looked at her. "The ribbon?"

"Maybe."

"That's really unlikely, Mel," John Scott said.

"Well, he took the string, didn't he?"

"Because he needed it to, you know."

"Where is the rest of it?" Nina asked.

We all turned to her. She'd been quiet until now. Her face was expressionless, her eyes unreadable. She seemed small, fragile, under the weight of her backpack.

"Ben did not need a kilometer of string to hang himself," she went on. "So what did he do with the rest of it?"

"He must have tossed it away somewhere," John Scott said.

"Why would he reel in so much string? Why not cut off what he needed and leave the rest where it was?"

"Who knows? He was fucked up."

Neil, I noticed, was shuffling off into the trees. The others watched him go too. A moment later we heard him retching.

"He needs water," Mel said.

I glanced up and could make out dark patches of storm clouds between breaks in the canopy. I wanted to tell her that it might rain, that we could collect rainwater, but I didn't. The need to resort to such a measure would be an admission we were not leaving the forest anytime soon.

"So what we do?" Tomo asked.

"We have to find our way out of here," I said.

"No kidding," John Scott said.

"What do you suggest?" I said. "If we keep walking, and we're going in the wrong direction, then we're screwed. We'll get more lost."

"We will stay here," Nina said, slipping off her backpack. "We will call the police."

Mel said, "How will they find us if we don't even know where we are?"

"They can track the phone's signal," John Scott said.

"They can do that? Track a mobile phone?"

I was skeptical as well.

John Scott nodded sagely. "Sure. Why not?"

"So we just wait here for them?"

"Do you have a better idea?"

He was right, I decided. "Okay, Tomo. Can you call them?"

"What I say?"

"Tell them someone is dead and someone is very sick. Tell them we're lost in Aokigahara Jukai. We need them to come find us."

Tomo dumped his backpack on the ground and began fussing through it. He started with the top pouch, then moved on to the main pocket. Soon all his clothes and comic books were scattered around him on the ground. He patted down his jacket and pants. "Shit, man," he said. "Where my phone?"

John Scott dug through his rucksack, looking for his, while I checked Mel's pack, where I had stuck mine the night before.

They were both missing.

"This is ridiculous," I said. "There's no way we've all lost our phones."

"I dropped mine in the crevice," Mel reminded me.

"But where are Tomo's, John Scott's, and mine?"

John Scott looked pissed. "Seriously, if someone is playing a joke, you got us. Now where the hell are they?"

"Would Ben have taken them?" Mel asked.

"Why would he do that?" Nina said.

"He was tripping," John Scott said. "Maybe he thought they

were teleportation devices that could beam him home. The fucker!"

"Ben did not take them," Nina said firmly. "He was tripping, yes. But he was not crazy."

"He took the goddamn string, didn't he?"

"Should we go back?" I suggested.

Mel looked at me. "To the camp?"

"He might have stashed them somewhere."

John Scott was shaking his head. "We don't even know which way the camp is anymore."

We stood there silently, all perplexed faces. Would Ben really have taken our phones? I wondered. It seemed so unlikely.

I felt Nina's eyes on me. I met them and immediately knew what she was thinking. The swinging crucifixes, the apparition-like blur in the photograph, the mysterious phone call. I contemplated the possibility that something supernatural was going on, I *believed* it for a moment—but only for a moment. Ghosts didn't exist. There was no such thing as a haunted forest. I shook my head. She turned away from me.

I lifted Ben's backpack off the litter and went through it. "What the...?" I said, holding up a copy of *The Complete Manuel of Suicide*.

"That's the book that was at that woman's gravesite!" Mel exclaimed. "Why would Ben have a copy—" She caught herself. "That's hers, isn't it? He took it."

She was right. It was old and weatherworn, the same condition Yumi's had been in.

"Did you know he had this?" I asked Nina.

"I—no." She shook her head. "No, I had no idea."

"Why would he take it?" John Scott said.

"For souvenir?" Tomo suggested.

"Tell them what you told me," I said to Nina. "Last night, in the woods. Tell them why Ben wanted to come to Suicide Forest."

She appeared uncomfortable.

"Spill it," John Scott said.

"Ben," she said reluctantly, "he knew someone who killed themselves. He has been obsessed with suicide ever since."

Silence.

Then John Scott: "See—it *wasn't* the mushrooms. He was planning suicide all along." He wasn't so much having a revelation as stating a fact for our benefit. That Ben's death was a premeditated suicide got him off the hook. Goodbye manslaughter charge, thank you very much.

"That is not true," Nina hissed.

"Sure it is," John Scott continued triumphantly. "He was obsessed with suicide. You said so yourself. Everyone here heard you."

She was seething. "You are a pig."

"Whatever. I just want answers. Also, this proves Ben took the phones."

"How does it do that?"

"He's a thief."

"He is *not* a thief. Do not call him that."

"The book was in his bag. It didn't belong to him. That sounds like a thief to me."

Neil emerged from the trees, interrupting the argument. He sensed the animosity in the air and said, "Sorry. I can't control it." He sank to the ground, holding his stomach, grimacing. "I don't think I can go any farther."

"Can I check your bag for your phone?" I asked him.

"Why?"

"We need it."

He withdrew his phone from that pouch he kept on his belt, which had been hidden by his jacket. My exclamation of elation was lost in everybody else's.

Neil frowned at us, confused.

"We need to call the police so they can come get us," I said simply.

I took the phone—it was a basic flip model from DoCoMo—and glanced at the tiny monochrome display. There were two reception bars and one battery bar.

"It's almost out of battery," I said and passed it to Tomo. "Call the police, quickly."

He punched in the three-digit number and a moment later was speaking Japanese to someone. After a couple minutes he turned to us and said, "They want call back."

John Scott was outraged. "Why?"

"She need talk someone else."

"Well, tell her to go get him! Now!"

Tomo relayed the message. He shook his head. "He's not there. She need call the guy."

"Tomo," I said evenly, "tell her the phone's battery is almost dead. Tell her we can't wait."

He spoke to the dispatcher again for several minutes.

I paced, furious with the police, cursing, probably unfairly, their ineptitude.

"How much battery is left, Tomo?" I asked, interrupting him midsentence.

He checked. "Empty square."

"Tell them to hurry up!" John Scott bellowed. "Where is this guy? The fucking moon?"

Tomo spoke for another two minutes, his voice rising in frustration.

Then he hung up.

"Well?" I said, knowing it was going to be bad news.

"They call phone company first, then us. Phone company trace."

"How long is that going to take?"

"Don't know. They call back."

John Scott scoffed. "What good is that going to do if the phone is dead?"

"I try, man."

"So what should we do?" Mel asked.

"What can we do?" John Scott said. "Hope they call back before the phone dies."

"Turn it off," I said promptly.

Tomo frowned. "Huh?"

"Turn the phone off. Save the battery. We'll call *them* in a few hours. They should have things sorted by then and be standing by to get the trace going quickly."

Tomo looked at the others.

"It might not come back on," John Scott said.

"That's a risk we have to take," I said.

He weighed that, shrugged. "This is your call, Ethos."

I glared at him. He was willing to go along with my suggestion, but if it didn't work out, he was making sure the onus would be squarely on me while he remained blame-free for being too chicken shit to make a decision.

"Do it, Tomo," I said.

He powered off the phone.

22

OUR situation had gone to hell remarkably quickly, I mused as I sat on my own, away from the others. Ben had hanged himself, we were lost, and Neil was getting sicker by the minute. My thoughts were bunting around inside my head, and I tried to slow them down, sort them out. There was nothing we could do for Ben, so I pushed him to the backburner. Deciding to remain where we were was probably a smart move. The last thing we wanted was to get more disorientated. It was a two-hour-plus hike to the parking lot, which put us in a very remote spot. Hopefully the police would be able to triangulate our position and come get us. If not, they knew we were here, we were lost, and we had one dead and one sick. They would coordinate a search party. In the meantime we would have to sit tight and try to find a water source.

Which led to the most pressing concern. Neil. I'd had food poisoning once when I was eight years old. My parents had been away for the weekend. Gary had been tasked with looking after me and making my meals. The first evening he cooked chicken burgers on the barbeque on the back deck. The chicken breast was mushy inside and unappealing. Gary, only thirteen then, told me to add more onions and other toppings to it, which I did, masking the unpleasant taste. The next morning—God, the abdominal cramps. I was positive an alien was growing inside me, ready to burst forth from my gut. I spent the entire day in bed, making regular visits to the bathroom, never knowing what end stuff was going to come out. Eventually I became too weak to make the trips and plopped down in front of the toilet. Gary remained with me the entire time, bringing me glass after glass of water so I could rehydrate. If it hadn't been for him, I don't know what would have happened in a worst-case scenario. I'd heard of fit and healthy people dying from food poisoning, even when they had access to water and medicine. Really, it came down to the toxicity of the poisoning.

So how toxic was the virus or bacteria inside Neil? Would he be able to wait out another day or two if it came to that?

I glanced over at him. He was lying on his back, his hands on his stomach, his knees pointing toward the sky. He appeared almost peaceful. I thought he might be asleep until he convulsed suddenly, crying out gruffly, as if someone had struck his abdomen with a golf club.

The others either ignored him or eyed him helplessly.

What could we do?

I concentrated on the mystery of the missing phones. I tried putting myself in Ben's frame of mind. Seeing the body, in the stage of decomposition it had been in, had obviously flipped a switch inside him. I know how easily that can occur while you're on magic mushrooms. It happened to me once during college. After eating a chocolate brownie laced with three grams of mushrooms, I was having one of the best times of my life, experiencing enlightenment after enlightenment, or what I'd thought were enlightenments.

Then the bad trip kicked in.

While floating around my dorm room, I called a girl named Amy I had met at a pub-crawl the day before. She lived off-campus at her parents' home. When her mother told me Amy was out, I asked if she had already gone to the party I was planning on attending later, some toga thing at a frat house. Her mother said no, she was at a friend's, and what was this party anyway? Although it was an innocuous question, I freaked, believing I'd gotten Amy in trouble. I hung up on her mother and soon found myself pacing up and down my residence's corridors. In my warped thinking I was convinced Amy must have lied to her mother about the party, told her she was going to her friend's for the evening, and I had blown the whole subterfuge wide open. Amy would come home tomorrow to her screaming parents, and she would blame it all on me. The more I thought about this, the more I convinced myself of the severity of the problem. Soon it was a full-scale disaster in my mind. Amy would be grounded for weeks. She'd tell me to go to hell, then blabber to everyone what I'd done. People would think I was an asshole and begin avoiding me. My freshman year would be ruined.

This was all nonsensical, of course, but you don't think or act rationally on mushrooms. Less than an hour into my trip I was so fucked up I couldn't speak with anybody and ended up outside, wandering the perimeter of the woods that lined the campus. I was wired, unable to sleep, and wanted nothing more than to be sober again. The anxiety and paranoia got so bad I began brainstorming nonlethal ways to knock myself out. And it all started from something as simple as a phone call (which, I learned the following day from Amy herself, was no big deal at all; Amy's mother had simply been making conversation).

So was this what happened to Ben, only on a more devastating scale? Had the mushrooms turned against him, his trip compounding so much he decided the only way to end it was to hang himself? After all, who knew the potency of the mushrooms out here, or how much he'd eaten. They wouldn't have been dried and sliced into slivers and placed in a baggie. He could have unknowingly taken a self-destructive dose.

Anger at John Scott's stupidity rose in me again, but I forced it aside.

The phones.

Why would Ben take them? Was he so delusional he'd thought we were his enemy? Had he convinced himself we'd killed the man with the pen in his front pocket? Had he hidden the string and the phones so we would be doomed to perish in Aokigahara with him?

This didn't sit right with me. I felt as if I were forcing an explanation to fit the conclusion I'd already drawn.

I approached the enigma from a dozen different angles, but after another thirty minutes of no progress I began to re-examine what I had seen in Nina's eyes and had summarily dismissed earlier: the paranormal.

I've never believed in ghosts and the like because the idea of spirits trapped between this world and the next seemed too hokey pokey to me, religious propaganda, more the stuff of Hollywood and TV programs than real life.

But what if there was a more scientific explanation?

I thought back to something I'd read in an old dog-eared *Popular Science* magazine I'd thumbed through at a Barcelona hostel a few days before my foolish attempt to cross the Camino del Ray. The article in question was titled: "The Science Behind Unseen Phenomena." Citing string theory and quantum physics and other stuff I was unable to recall in detail now, the author argued that there existed not one but billions of universes, forming a kind of cosmic foam in which there were an infinite number of dimensions and timelines. When one of those timelines or dimensions overlapped ours, it was possible for us to catch an electromagnetic glimpse of someone or something existing on a different plane.

I suppose I preferred this to trapped spirits because it was based on science and not blind faith. The problem, of course, was that said science was unproven. Not to mention the whole concept, although neat in a metaphysical way, still sounded iffy, almost like a cheap magic trick, something that would go over great at a party when everyone was drunk, but which would undoubtedly be derided and deconstructed on closer reflection the next morning.

Then I recalled what a Chinese girl named Bingbing Wong who lived in my guesthouse had once told me. One evening we had gotten onto the topic of ghosts, and she admitted that as a child she'd often heard footsteps outside her room in the middle of the night. She had always been too scared to check if anyone was there, but her dog would sit by the door and growl until the footsteps stopped. Years later she learned from her parents that the original owner had built the home for his fiancée as a wedding gift, but she died before the wedding, and he later hanged himself from the attic fan.

Bings was one of the smartest and most rational people I knew, so I wasn't surprised when she justified this story by saying that certain rocks and minerals within the earth, or even large bodies of water above- or belowground, were conductive to storing the residual energy left behind when someone died, and this energy could play back for years, decades, or even centuries. This was why most ghosts didn't seem to possess an intelligence, personality, or mass, and why their actions were always the same; they were the three-dimensional equivalent of old TV programs playing over the air long after the actors in them had died.

Thinking over Bings' argument now, I began to get carried away as I wondered whether the iron deposits in the solidified magma underlying Aokigahara Jukai could constitute a geological formation conductive to storing and replaying the images of the dead who had killed themselves here—until I realized what I was overlooking.

If ghosts were mere recordings imprinted upon the environment, without intelligence and mass, and thus had no way to interact with our world, how did you explain the swinging crucifixes or the missing phones?

I sat there, frowning, as I tried to envision other possibilities that would explain the existence of ghosts. This had become a game for me, a way to pass the time. But I could come up with nothing more. I had played devil's advocate with myself and lost. Ghosts didn't exist, and I couldn't convince myself otherwise. I had been right all along. Ghost sightings were nothing but psychological phenomena or, as I'd told

Nina, projections: you see what you want or expect to see. The grieving widow sees her dead husband because she needs the comfort of knowing he is all right and happy in the afterlife. Her mind allows her to hallucinate to help her cope with the stress of the loss.

I guess if you wanted to get crazy—and this whole train of thought had been crazy, so why the hell not—you could take this idea of projecting farther and argue that sightings were not just hallucinations but real physical manifestations, created either by your subconscious or someone else's. Psychokinetic energy or whatever it's called. And why not? Science has yet to fully understand the powers of the human mind. How much of it did the common person use? Ten percent? Fifteen? There was so much about it that we didn't know that it was certainly possible it was capable of producing manifestations and noises.

Which brought me back to the beginning of my ruminations and the only possible culprit for the missing phones: Ben. He'd been delusional, paranoid, and for reasons we may never know he took them, hid them, then killed himself.

I shook my head slightly, not liking the uncertain, cheating feeling that persisted in my gut—then I became aware of the forest around me once again. It had darkened as the day faded to dusk, swelling with hidden malevolence and dread.

I got up and joined the others, eager to call the police back.

NINA and Mel sat next to one another, holding hands, staring mutely at the ground before them. John Scott had taken off his leather jacket and was doing pushups. I'd like to think he was being a pompous meathead, but exercise was likely his way of dispelling nervous energy. I knew I could have done with a good jog had a track been handy. Tomo was twenty feet away from everyone, crouched next to Neil, looking helpless as Neil lay curled in a fetal position, arms clamped around his stomach, rocking back and forth, moaning.

My stomach had been growling for the past couple hours, and I considered divvying up Ben's uneaten breakfast ration, but I decided to save it—just in case.

"Are you ready to call the police again, Tomo?" I asked him.

"Hell, yeah," he said, coming over.

Suddenly he was the center of attention, everyone crowding around him. He pressed the phone's power button. The DoCoMo logo appeared with a cute musical jig.

Although the tension among us was palpable, no one produced a celebratory reaction. Eyes remained fixed on the display. We were far from home free yet.

Tomo dialed the police and stuck the phone to his ear. A voice answered. It sounded small and mechanical. Tomo spoke quickly. He began nodding, giving us the thumbs-up.

Then he jerked the phone away from his ear, as if it had bitten him.

The display was black.

"Oh shit!" he said.

Everyone was speaking:

"It's dead!"

"It can't be dead."

"Try again!"

Tomo attempted to power it up to no avail.

I turned away, kicking at pine needles.

"I told you, Ethos," John Scott said. "I told you we shouldn't turn it off. Now we're as fucked as a soup sandwich."

I whirled on him. 'The hell you did!"

"This is your fault—"

I lunged at him, but he ducked behind Tomo, out of my reach.

Suddenly Mel was in front of me, yelling at me to stop.

"No more!" she said. "Not again! Cool it you two!"

I made a last-ditch attempt to grab John Scott, then gave up.

The fucker had a smirk on his face.

"Lying prick," I said.

"Go suck balls—"

"Enough!" It was Mel again, her voice like a knife. "Will you two grow up and stop bickering. We have more serious matters to deal with here, don't you think?"

She was right, of course. I stepped away from her, considered a feint-dash to reach John Scott, but decided he wasn't worth it.

"We have to get out of here," she said more softly. "We have to figure out a way out of here."

"I think that way," Tomo said, pointing past me.

"It's that way," John Scott said, jutting his chin in a different direction.

I had no idea anymore and didn't speculate.

Nina said, "Maybe the police were able to trace the call?"

"After five seconds?" I said.

"Maybe."

"I doubt it."

"How do you know?"

"I don't."

"So we wait?" Tomo asked.

Nina nodded. "Yes. That is what we should do."

I agreed. "Even if they weren't able to trace the call," I said, "they know we're here. They'll organize a search party."

"But Aokigahara too big," Tomo said. "How they find us?"

"They have the video of us entering the forest," I said. "They'll know we at least went up that path. They'll suspect we followed the arrows left or right. It can't be that hard for them to track us down."

"What about Neil?" Mel said.

We all glanced at him. His eyes were closed. I thought he might have been sleeping until I saw the tight lines around his eyes and mouth.

Not sleeping. In pain.

"He can't walk anyway," John Scott said. "Best let him rest."

"So when will they come?" Nina asked. "The search party? Tonight?"

I shook my head. "There's only a couple hours of light left. By the time they got anything organized it would be dark. I'm guessing they start the search first thing tomorrow morning."

"I can't spend another night in this forest," Mel said, folding her arms across her chest. "No way. There's... I think there's..."

"What?" John Scott said.

"There's something out there."

"Something?" I said.

"I don't know," she said, clearly uncomfortable.

"Ghosts," Nina stated.

"You gotta be fucking kidding?" John Scott said.

"Then what happened to our phones?"

"Ben—" I began.

"That is not true," Nina said sharply. "And you know it."

John Scott guffawed. "Have you girls lost it?"

"This isn't funny, John," Mel said.

"You've watched too many horror movies."

"Our phones are gone. The red ribbon is gone—"

"We don't know it's gone."

"Why would Ben take everything?" she plowed on. "It doesn't make sense."

"Why would a *ghost*?"

"Because it doesn't want us to leave."

"Right," John Scott said, grinning. "Hey, maybe Ben didn't kill himself. Maybe the ghost possessed him and made him to do."

The silence that followed was charged with thoughtful consideration. I could almost see Mel and Nina nodding mentally.

"For fuck's sake," John Scott said. "Tomo, are you buying this?"

"Killer ghost?"

"Yeah."

"No way, man."

"Ethos?"

"I'm not ruling anything out," I said, mainly because I

191

didn't want John Scott to think I was on his side.

"But you want to stay here overnight?"

"It's better than wandering aimlessly. We need to conserve our energy." I shrugged, getting impatient with all this talk of the supernatural. "Look, it's only one more night. If you're worried something is out there, Mel, then John Scott, Tomo, and I will take turns keeping watch. There are six of us. We'll be fine."

I could see in Mel's eyes what she was thinking but what she undoubtedly felt silly speaking out loud: six people, or six hundred people, it made no difference against a ghost.

"There's still light," she said. "You keep saying we might go the wrong way. But if we go the *right* way, then we could be out of here before nightfall."

"What do you want to do?" I asked her. "Vote on this?"

She bit her lower lip in frustration. She knew she was outnumbered.

John Scott stuck up his hand. "I say we should stay put."

Tomo raised his hand. Then, after a moment, Nina raised hers as well.

Mel looked at me, angry and pleading at the same time.

"It doesn't matter how I vote," I told her. "It's already three to one."

"What about Neil?"

"He can't vote."

"Why not?" she demanded.

"He can barely walk."

"He'll want to leave. I know he will. He needs help."

"Whoa, hold on," John Scott said. "Ethos, just vote."

"I'm sorry, Mel," I said. "I think we should stay."

She glared at me, tears glistening in her eyes, then turned away.

23

SHADOWS emerged from their daytime sanctuaries, perverting the trees more than they already were, turning them into looming monsters out of a sadistic fairytale. Grays became charcoals, and charcoals, blacks. Then night was upon us like a thief, swiftly and silently. If anyone tells you they're not afraid of the dark, that's because they have never spent a night in Aokigahara Jukai. It doesn't matter how brave you think you are, there is something so deranged and wrong about this forest that it worms its way into the deepest closets of your mind and awakens your most primitive fears.

Not wanting to get caught out again without the reassurance of a fire, we'd spent the last of the daylight erecting our tents and collecting more than enough firewood to last us until morning. Now we sat in a circle around three-foot-tall flames, everything the same as the evening before—except for the fact we didn't have any food or water, and one of us was dead.

The group mentality was bad. Nobody spoke. Nobody did much of anything. We sat and waited, either for the police to miraculously show, or for sleep to whisk us to morning. I wanted to say something, to break the suffocating silence, but there was nothing to say.

My stomach was sour with an unpleasant mix of anxiety and hunger. My mouth was dry, my head and body ached, and I was growing lightheaded as well.

I glanced at Neil. He remained a good fifteen feet away from the rest of us at his stubborn insistence. When he wasn't curled in a fetal position rocking back and forth, he was either vomiting or shitting. He could barely muster the strength to lug himself to his feet, and he never got farther than a dozen yards or so from camp before performing these bodily functions. His constant moaning and toilet trips began to grate on my nerves. I knew he couldn't help himself, but I was irritable and in a somber frame of mind, and it seemed almost disrespectful to Ben's memory that Neil would go and get food poisoning now out of all times and places.

It wasn't just me who was irrationally unsympathetic. In the flickering firelight I caught everyone shoot Neil a vexed look at one point or another.

Feeling guilty for harboring these thoughts, I went over to check on him again. He was on his side, turned away from me. His face was sheathed in perspiration. His shirt was likely drenched as well, though I couldn't see it. His sleeping bag covered his body, cinched tightly around his neck. He looked like a caterpillar wrapped in a cocoon, with only its head poking free.

"Hey, Neil," I said, crouching beside him. "It's Ethan."

He didn't respond, let alone acknowledge my voice. I touched his forehead gently with the back of my hand. He was burning up.

"How you doing over here?" It was a stupid question. But what else was there to say? *Is your will up to date, old buddy? Any last words you want me to pass on to Kaori?*

I didn't think Neil was in mortal danger. He'd been sick for close to a day already. The symptoms should lessen overnight. If not, the police would be here tomorrow. They would get him to a hospital.

And if the symptoms don't lessen? I asked myself. *And if the police don't come? What then? I'll tell ya. Neil really will be in mortal danger. He'll die right here, in this forest, wasted and putrid, probably from organ failure, but, hey, anything is possible, maybe he'll suffer a stroke...or decide he was a goner anyway and take his own life. This was sure the place to do something like that.*

He mumbled something.

"What's that, Neil?" I asked, bending close to him.

"Wadda." The word was dry, papery.

"We don't have any. We finished it this morning."

His response was to squeeze his eyes shut tighter.

I stared at him helplessly. How long could you last without water? Three days? That sounded about right. Three days under normal circumstances, though after two you would be pretty wretched. So how about when you had a raging fever and were sweating and pissing and shitting every last drop of liquid out of you? Half that time? Less?

If only it would rain, I thought wistfully, we could string up the tents between the trees to act as large nylon buckets. We would have enough water to bathe in. But the tantalizingly low and pregnant storm clouds remained impossibly distant. Who knew how long they would retain their precious load for, or if they would blow over completely.

I tried to recall movies I'd seen in which the main characters were stranded somewhere without water. A couple vague images materialized in my mind's eye. One was of a guy wrapping his shins in old rags, then stomping through tall grass to catch dew. Another guy—or maybe it was the same one— made a belowground still. The mechanics of this took me a few seconds to puzzle out, but I thought I got it. You dig a bowl-shaped hole about three feet across and two feet deep. You make a sump and place a container in it. You cover the hole with plastic and set a rock in the center so it hangs about a foot or so directly over the container to form an inverted cone. The moisture from the ground reacts with heat from the sun to produce condensation on the plastic, which runs down the sill and drips into the container.

It was a good concept in theory, but would it work? Unfortunately, we wouldn't be able to test it out until morning. And even then we would need a clear day and an open glade where the sunlight could penetrate the overstory to the forest floor.

Urine? I wondered desperately. Could he drink urine?

Although it was mostly water, it was also laced with all the toxic electrolytes your body expelled. These would contribute to dehydration, which meant you couldn't sustain yourself on it for long. But would it serve as a quick fix?

I simply didn't know.

"Help me," Neil rasped.

"What do you need?" I asked quickly.

"Bathroom."

I slipped my arms beneath his armpits and hiked him to his feet. I was right; his shirt was saturated with salty sweat stains. He wobbled unsteadily, teetering back and forth. I heard John Scott calling to me, asking if I needed help. But the offer came too late as Neil and I were already lumbering into the trees. For one awful moment Neil lurched over, dry-retching, while I waited expectantly for him to puke all over my trainers. Nothing came out thankfully, and we continued onward. When we reached a thick tree he let go of me and fumbled with the button on his pants. I moved away several paces, facing camp. I could see the glow of the fire, but that was all.

Neil shat. The sound was like a faucet fully throttled. I pulled my T-shirt up over my nose.

"Neil?" I said, after a break in activity on his part. "You okay?"

"Wait."

Ten seconds later there was a gaseous noise, then another, then nothing.

"Neil?"

"What?"

"You ready?"

"No."

I waited another two minutes. The thin cotton stretched over my nose was hardly a gas mask, and I could taste the foul stench in the back of my throat. This almost made me lose my breakfast, but I bit back the gag reflex.

Then I heard something, or I thought I did, a rustle of vegetation, somewhere ahead of me. I strained my ears—and heard a crack.

A twig snapping?

I stared into the darkness, but there were no other noises.

I glanced over my shoulder. Neil was crouching, his pants around his ankles, his head resting on his forearms, which were folded across his fish-belly white knees. His penis dangled below him like a pale slug.

Was he sleeping?

"Neil?"

"Gimme a sec."

Thirty seconds or so later I heard him rising, pulling his pants up. I turned around just in time to see him keel over and vomit stringy, watery black gunk. He wiped his mouth with the back of his hand, then shuffled toward me. I led him back to where he'd been resting. He collapsed on the spot, the last of his strength used up.

I draped his sleeping bag over his body, up to his chin, and hoped to hell the worst of his sickness had passed.

I glimpsed Mel through the door flap of our tent. She was lying on her side, reading a book with one of the flashlights. I was about to tell her to turn it off, tell her we needed to save the batteries, but I was too exhausted for another confrontation.

"How's Neil?" John Scott asked me. He was sitting cross-legged, smoking a Marlboro. I had an almost irresistible desire to bum one from him right then.

"Bad," I said, eyeing the cigarette.

"He want anything?"

"Water."

"We shouldn't have drank it all."

I waited for him to blame me for whatever reason. Instead he tossed a chunk of dirt at the fire.

Tomo's eyes were closed. I didn't know if he was sleeping

or thinking. I remained standing. If I sat, I would likely have to keep speaking to John Scott.

I scanned the trees and saw Nina some distance away, sitting at the base of a fir, at the periphery of the glow cast by the fire. She raised a hand in a half wave. I took this as an invitation to join her even if it wasn't and went over.

"He is very sick," she stated. She was staring past me, toward Neil. "Will he be okay during the night?"

"I don't know," I admitted.

"What can we do?"

"Nothing."

She made a grim face.

I sat beside her. "You don't have another joint, do you?"

She shook her head.

Probably for the best, I thought. I would have liked a few tokes to relax and to dose my cigarette craving, but I didn't know how introspective or philosophical I wanted to get right then.

"How are you doing?" I asked her.

She shrugged.

"Ben—he was a good guy." I winced inwardly at how lame that sounded.

"It is okay," Nina said.

"What is?"

"You do not have to say anything."

I nodded, relieved I didn't have to wax bullshit. If I'd known Ben better, I would have told Nina a story about him, a heartfelt memory we could both smile at. But I didn't even know his last name, let alone something nostalgic, and I was content to leave it at "He was a good guy."

"He wanted to be an actor," Nina said. "Can you believe that? An actor?"

I didn't say anything.

"He was smart," she went on. "There were so many things he could be, yes? A doctor. A lawyer. An entrepreneur. But he wanted to be an actor—a famous actor." She wiped a tear that had crept into her eye. "And you know what? He might have made it. That is the thing. Everyone told him it was an impossible dream. But how is it impossible if other people achieve that same dream? Because they do. You see them on the TV, in the movies. So some people reach those dreams. Ben, he might have been one of those people. He was so likeable. He had so much passion. He could do many impersonations. Woody Allen. He could do him. Many others."

"Had he acted in anything?" I asked.

"No, nothing."

"A commercial? A school production?"

"Not that he told me. He was scared of performing in front of people."

I raised my eyebrows. "But he wanted to be an actor!"

"What a stupid guy, yes?"

After an uncertain pause, I chuckled self-consciously. It felt good. For a brief moment I saw Ben full of his boyish optimism. This was how I would like to remember him. Not blue and bloated and hanging from a rope.

I heard John Scott and Tomo talking and glanced over at them. Tomo was passing John Scott one of his manga comics. Nina picked up a small stick beside her and drove it into the ground. This wasn't anything dramatic. Just a quick, hard jab, which she repeated three times.

"He did not kill himself," she said suddenly.

"Nina, we've talked about—"

"You saw the photograph."

I thought about it again: the ghostly shape superimposed over the fire, the hard edges that outlined it. The vague formation of a face.

"It was a dirty lens," I said, "a distortion."

"That affected only one picture?"

"You're believing what you want to believe."

"Projecting," she said tightly.

"Yes."

"Ethan, open your mind! Just because you cannot see something does not mean it does not exist. Millions of people believe in ghosts. Are you to say they are all misled?"

"Yes."

"You are a fool then."

"Millions of people believe in a god. That doesn't mean one exists."

"Ah," she said.

"Ah what?"

"Are you Christian?"

"I was baptized. But, no, I'm not religious."

"That is what I thought, and that is your problem."

"What is?"

"You do not believe in anything. You have no faith in anything. You are a forever skeptic. I am arguing against a brick wall."

"With a wall."

She made a face. "Do you wish to continue in Hebrew?"

"Against a wall is fine."

"So what do you think happens when we die, Ethan?"

"Nothing."

"That is very depressing, yes?"

"I guess. But saying I believe in something isn't going to change how I feel."

"Well, I believe, Ethan. I believe in a god and an afterlife. Because we are here. We exist and have purpose. Something is responsible for that. And just because you do not know what happens next does not mean there is nothing."

I didn't say anything, I wasn't going to start preaching, and my lack of response seemed to anger her. She shook her head and exhaled loudly.

"*Ben would not kill himself*," she said. "He was happy. He wanted to be an actor. You do not have such a dream one day and then kill yourself the next."

"I agree with you there."

"Well?"

"He was on drugs."

"That is a stupid excuse."

"No, it's not. They mess with your mind. They make you do things."

"Not Ben," she insisted stubbornly.

"Nina, you said Ben was obsessed with suicide. Maybe you didn't know the entire picture. Maybe John Scott was right and Ben was a bit suicidal himself. Some people...you can never tell. If he was, and he took drugs..."

Nina began fiddling with the stick and wouldn't look me in the eyes. "There is something I have to tell you," she said. "I have not been honest with you."

I frowned. "What about?"

"Ben was not obsessed with suicide. It was not his idea to come to Suicide Forest."

"But you said his friend—"

"His friend did not commit suicide. She attempted to. She took a sharp knife from the kitchen, ran a hot bath, climbed in the tub, and slit both her wrists."

"What—who found her?"

"The Chinese woman whose house she had been staying in. She called the police. Doctors saved her life."

I blinked as understanding registered. I looked at Nina's wrists. They were hidden by the sleeves of her yellow rain jacket.

Smiling sadly, she rolled up the cuffs, then the pink sweatbands she wore around each wrist, revealing a series of white, ragged scars. The cuts appeared to have been made recently.

"Jesus, Nina, why—" I stopped myself. "He raped you."

"I did not karate chop him in the throat. I did not escape him. He raped me in that alleyway, and then he got in his taxi and drove away."

"I'm—I'm so sorry. God, Nina—I'm sorry."

She nodded silently.

"So..." I said, believing I had to say something, "it was your idea to come to Suicide Forest?"

She nodded again.

"And it was you who took that book about suicide from the gravesite?"

"We kept our food in my backpack. I did not want the book near our food. So I put it in Ben's."

"Does—did Ben know? I mean, your wrists..."

"No, I never told him about the rape or the suicide attempt."

"He never saw those scars?"

"I never showed him. You know, Ethan, Ben and I—we were more friends than partners. We never had sex. We slept in the same bed, we kissed sometimes, but we never had sex. Do you believe that? He tried one night in Thailand, but I made it clear I did not want to. He did not try anymore. As I told you before, I think he loved me. Or he was in love with the idea of loving me. He was very romantic like that. He would have done anything I asked." She set the stick aside. "Do you think I am crazy, Ethan? Do you think less of me now?"

"No, not at all," I said honestly.

"Good. Because I care what you think of me."

She leaned close and kissed me on the mouth. Her lips were soft, and they lingered for a long moment. I was so surprised I didn't move—or pull away.

Then she got up and went to her tent.

24

I tried not to read too much into the kiss. Nina was under duress, emotionally distraught. She was appreciative she could talk to me. That was all. Believing there to be something more between us would be baseless—and dangerous. So instead I focused on her confession. I was amazed she had tried to kill herself, and I told myself I shouldn't be. Just because she was young, intelligent, and beautiful didn't exclude her from being suicidal. Most people who knew me would never suspect I had once contemplated suicide. It was a sickness, a disease that could affect anyone, anytime.

Nevertheless, her admission that Ben hadn't been obsessed with suicide didn't change my mind regarding what caused his death, didn't make me jump on the ghost bandwagon with her. Whether Nina wanted to believe it or not, Ben had taken his own life, and the drugs were responsible. It was the only terrestrial and thus logical explanation.

I stood and returned to the campfire where John Scott and Tomo were silently reading their comic books. Nina had zipped the door flap of her tent tight while Mel, still inside our tent, had turned off the flashlight and was either lying awake in the dark or sleeping. Maybe I was feeling guilty about the kiss, but I no longer gave a damn about Mel and John Scott's sketchy relationship, no longer cared what he was doing here. All I wanted was to slip under the crappy emergency blanket next to her, pull her against me, and tell her I was sorry—sorry for everything. For bringing her to this forest, for not being straightforward with the Shelly situation, for siding with the others and voting not to leave. This last point bothered me the most. She was my girlfriend, my future fiancée, my future wife. She was scared and, old-fashioned or not, it was my job to take care of her. I could see why she was pissed off. In her eyes I had betrayed her.

Still, what could I have done differently? Packed our bags and tried to forge our way out of Aokigahara an hour or two before dark? I hadn't thought it was a good idea then, and I still didn't now. Survival 101: if you get lost, remain at ground zero until rescuers find you. Statistically, the heroes who wander off to search for help are more likely to get caught out by the climate or geography and die from exposure.

There was a guy I knew in college who punched his ticket just that way. His name was Craig "Stag" VanOrd. He was six foot two, a rugby player with spikey blond hair and pale gray eyes, and probably the most popular student in our year. He was the guy you talked to if you wanted to know where the party was that night. The guy you talked to if you wanted to score pot, mushrooms, ecstasy, blow, whatever popped your button. He wasn't a dealer. He didn't make money selling the stuff. He didn't need money; his parents were loaded. He simply knew who had what and got it for you. He wasn't stupid though. He didn't do this for anyone. You had to be a friend, or at least a close friend of one of his friends.

I wasn't certain why he was nicknamed Stag, but I imagined it had to do with the fact he had his way with women. Rumor had it, to kick off Frosh Week, he was one of the guys responsible for hanging twenty-foot banners on the freeway overpasses near the college which read: "THANK YOU FATHERS FOR YOUR DAUGHTERS!" Stag must have burned through two dozen of those daughters between the time school began in September and when he died in February. This number always amazed me because the girls he wooed back to his room would be well aware of his reputation. Even more, they likely knew most of the other girls he slept with. Nevertheless, he not only pulled it off, but did so with panache, somehow remaining on good terms with all his one-night stands, so much so they never said a bad word about him behind his back.

Needless to say I was astounded when Shelly—my ex, Shelly—told me she had slept with him. My first question was whether she had been tested for STDs. She thought I was joking, which I was not, and told me breezily that she got tested every year. My second question—and this felt odd to admit because Stag had been in a grave for three years at that point—was whether he was any good in bed or not. Shelly smirked and did some mysterious shrug of her shoulders. I left it at that, deciding I didn't want to know.

To celebrate Valentine's Day, Stag took his latest girl, Jenny Walton, to his parents' cabin in the Pocono Mountains, a three-hour drive east in Pennsylvania. They squeezed the trip into a long weekend and were driving back late Monday night when Stag lost control of his Jeep and shot off the road down a fifty-foot rocky embankment (rumor was that Jenny had been giving him head at the time). Although Jenny was beat up badly in the accident, Stag came away from it without a scratch. You would think the guy had been blessed at birth by the angel Gabriel himself to lead a charmed existence...if you didn't know what happened next.

It was twenty below zero in the mountains. The Jeep's engine was demolished in the crash, which meant Stag and Jenny couldn't run the heater to stay warm. Moreover, it was late, the road they'd skidded off was little used to begin with, and the embankment was too steep to climb, so Stag decided to head down the mountain on foot to find help.

Jenny was discovered three hours later by a Fedex driver who'd noticed the missing stretch of cable-and-post guardrail. It took the police another two hours before they could rig together a lift to hoist her back up to the road. She had frostbite on her toes and fingers and had broken two ribs and her collarbone. Stag wasn't discovered until midafternoon the following day. His tracks led to a frozen river fifteen miles away, which he'd followed for another six miles. Paradoxically, he had taken off most of his clothes, a common side effect of hypothermia, before he made a burrow in the snow, where he had spent his last hours alive on earth.

So, yes, I told myself now. We'd made the right decision. Staying put had been the smart move. Mel might be mad with me, but she would see. She would thank me tomorrow.

I noticed the paper cups in their hands for the first time. Confusedly I wondered where John Scott and Tomo had found water, and why they were drinking it when a quick glance at Neil told me he had none. Then I saw the Suntory whiskey bottle propped against a tree root.

"What the fuck are you two doing?" I said.

John Scott knocked back whatever was left in his cup. "Didn't think Neil would mind if we raided his bottle, given his condition."

"Have you thought about *your* conditions tomorrow?"

"I can hold my own, dude."

"It's a diuretic," I said.

"Die what?" Tomo asked.

"It makes you piss," John Scott said.

"Ah," Tomo said.

"Yeah, ah, Tomo," I said. "We're in the middle of a forest with no water."

"Police go here tomorrow."

"We hope. But what if they can't find us?"

"Don't get melodramatic on us," John Scott said.

"It's possible."

He shrugged. "If they can't find us, and it doesn't rain, we die in a few days anyway." As if to prove he subscribed to this brand of fatalism—or, perhaps more likely, to rub his defiance in my face—he grabbed the bottle and filled his cup. He sipped from it this time, returning his attention to the comic.

"You want some?" Tomo asked me.

"No, Tomo. And I think you should stop drinking."

"Yeah, okay, no more. This last one. You want manga?"

"No."

"Big titties."

"No."

"They there. In my bag."

I watched the two of them for a few moments, reading and drinking, as if they were at a lazy slumber party. One word came to mind: *idiots*.

Since I had nowhere else to go, and felt foolish standing there lording over them, I sat down and flexed my right hand. The blisters had indeed ruptured, though the rawness of the pain had diminished and wasn't very noticeable anymore. Aside from the crackle and pop of the fire the night was unsurprisingly quiet. Even Neil remained silent. It seemed his cramps had finally subsided and he had fallen asleep.

Smoke billowed from the burning wood, the musky smell tempting my hunger. I imagined myself cooking a sausage over the flames, blackening the skin, sizzling the fat. The image was so powerful I began to salivate. My eyes flicked hungrily to the bottle of whiskey, which was half full. A cup of rye might not be food, but it would suppress my appetite. It would also take the edge off my nerves, let me forget about Ben for a little, the ordeal awaiting us tomorrow. A cup, maybe even two. It wouldn't hurt. Probably let me fall asleep a little easier as well...

"How are we going to organize this watch?" I asked, to distract myself.

"You're not serious, are you, dude?" John Scott said.

"It can't hurt."

"Don't be a tool." He lowered his voice. "There are no fucking ghosts out there."

"Maybe not. But someone's got to keep an eye on Neil—and Ben."

"Ben?"

"Make sure no animals come around or whatever."

"Oh shit," Tomo said, pulling his eyes from his comic.

"All right then." John Scott shrugged. "I'll take the first watch."

"Which begins when?"

"Now."

"Screw that."

"What?"

It was a little past eight o'clock. If John Scott took the first watch, and began it now, he'd be done around eleven—or about the time he'd likely choose to go to sleep regardless.

"The first shift will start at ten," I said. "Each will last two hours. That will take us to four, which isn't that long before the sun rises."

"So what?" John Scott said. "You want the first shift?"

"We'll draw sticks. Longest gets first choice."

I scavenged a small branch from the woodpile and broke it into three unequal segments. I turned away while I aligned the tops of the pieces so they were even with one another. John Scott might be an adult, but I didn't trust the guy not to cop a look. I turned back and held forth my hand.

Tomo chose first, then John Scott. We compared our selections. Tomo had the longest. I had the shortest.

"I want first," Tomo said.

"First shift?" I said.

"Yeah."

"I'll take balls to two," John Scott said.

I nodded. "All right, Tomo, you wake John Scott up at midnight then."

"You know it."

He finished the whiskey in his cup, then tossed it in the fire.

"Hey!" I said. "We only have a few cups, Tomo. We might need them to catch rain."

"Dude," John Scott said reproachfully.

"What?"

"Stop being such a drama queen. We're fine, okay? We're not on a deserted island."

"Do you know how big this forest is?"

"So what? Worst comes to worst we'll climb a tree, locate Fuji, and follow the yellow brick road all the way home."

"Hope you're good at climbing."

He harrumphed and went back to his comic.

"You guys, you know you remind me?" Tomo said. "Married guys. Fight, fight, fight. And me, I'm kid, right? I gotta listen. You scar me forever."

"They teach you that in psych school?" I said.

"You know it."

"Is this some new catch phrase?"

"You know it."

Tomo had taken his hat off. His hair was sticking up all over the place, his elfish sideburns daggered in front of his ears. Bags had formed beneath his eyes while stubble had started to sprout on his upper lip and chin. Looking at him now, I thought of a suspect in an interrogation room. An outward face of calm but inside scared shitless. Like John Scott, he seemed confident we would be found tomorrow, so he wasn't worried about dying out here. I imagined his fear was born more from what he believed would happen after the police arrived. He was supposed to start a residency at some hospital in Shibuya-ku soon. What would happen to him if it was revealed he had been camping in Aokigahara with a bunch of foreigners, one of whom committed suicide? This was not the sound judgment you expected a psychiatrist to uphold. If our expedition made the papers, his entire career could be in jeopardy before it even took off.

"Hey, man," Tomo said to John Scott. "You have ciggy?"

"You smoke?"

"Like after sex only. But now I want."

John Scott took a butt from the pack, tossed it to Tomo, then knocked another out for himself. He lit Tomo's with his bolt-action lighter, then his own. He shifted so he was on his back, his head on his rucksack, looking up at the canopy, blowing smoke from his mouth in a blue swirl. He had been panicky immediately after we'd discovered Ben's body, when he'd realized how badly the fallout could affect him, but ever since he had kept his cool together. Right now he could have been chilling in a bar with not a care in the world. He either had a very good poker face or a total lack of empathy. The latter made me wonder if he had ever killed anybody.

If he'd participated in the invasion of Iraq, the possibility was fairly high. He might have killed a good number of people. Surely he would have experienced death in one form or another.

"You been to Iraq?" I asked him.

"For vacation?"

Yeah, for fucking vacation. Why did I bother?

"One tour," he said a few moments later.

"How was it?"

"Paradise." He ashed out his cigarette, immediately lit another. "And, yeah, I've killed people."

I looked at him.

"That's what you wanted to know, isn't it? It's what everyone wants to know."

Tomo asked, "How many?"

"Two."

"You shoot?"

"My unit was on patrol. A roadside bomb took out the lead Humvee. It was an ambush. We came under a shitload of gunfire. I shot back."

"You kill every fucker?"

"There were too many. We called in backup. A Blackhawk arrived five hundred yards away. We ran for it, shooting at anything that moved."

"Were you scared?" I asked. I wasn't pushing buttons; I was genuinely interested.

"You don't have time to be scared," he said simply.

"When was this?"

"Few months ago." He patted his left leg. "Took a round above the knee. It's why I'm sitting on my ass in Japan now." Then he sat up straight and looked at both Tomo and me. He appeared simultaneously pensive and grave. "If I get fingered for giving Ben the mushrooms," he said in a low, serious voice to match his expression, "I'll probably end up in prison here."

The conversation's abrupt change of direction threw me off guard.

"It was stupid, I know that," he went on. "I wish I could take it back. But I can't. And Ben's *gone*. Don't fuck me over here."

"What we say doesn't matter," I said. "Nina's the one you have to talk to."

"I will. Tomorrow. But she'll be easier to convince if you guys are already on board. Tomo? What do you say, buddy?"

Tomo hesitated. "Yeah, okay...I don't know nothing."

John Scott looked at me.

He was right: giving Ben mushrooms out here was stupid. But it was a temporary lack of judgment. Did he deserve to spend the next seven or eight years in a Japanese prison for that?

"Dude?"

I shrugged noncommittally.

John Scott nodded. Apparently that was good enough for him.

I didn't turn around, but I knew they were following me, the way you know things in dreams. I was back in grade five. The guys behind me were in junior high. The ringleader's name was Hubert Kelly. He lived one street over from mine, which meant more often than not we saw each other on the way home from our respective schools. Aside from this all I knew about him was that he supposedly carried around a pair of brass knuckles—and he liked to pick on younger kids.

For more than a year I had dreaded walking home, never knowing if I was going to get ambushed or not. It came down to a matter of who was walking in front of whom. If Douche-bag Kelly was ahead of me, I kept my distance and was relatively safe. Sometimes he would glance back, see me, and stop. I would stop too, never taking my eyes off him, until he grew bored and continued on. If I was ahead of him, however, it was a different story. I got pretty good in those days at checking over my shoulder. Yet I was a kid still, I was prone to daydreaming, and I often wouldn't know Kelly was coming until I heard his shoes slapping the pavement behind me. He might have been a lot older than me, but he was fat and slow. If I had a good enough head start, I could outrun him. And even when he got lucky and caught me, I would often escape the encounter with only a few bruises because he had nobody else to prove anything to. It was when he came after me with his two friends which I dreaded most. They were both slim and fast and when I had my head in the clouds they caught me eight out of ten times. And they were vicious. They'd sit on me and slap my face and rip my clothes. A few times when I talked back they would wallop me hard enough to draw blood.

In the dream I finally turned around and my heart polevaulted up my throat when I found them right behind me. I didn't know how they got so close without me hearing them —another dream anomaly—but they did. I yelped and tried to take off, but Kelly grabbed my hair and shoved me to the ground. Then the three of them pinned me down and began shoving snow in my mouth and down my jacket.

I squirmed and yelled but couldn't buck them off me.

"One of these nights we're gonna come for your parents too, Childs," Kelly spat in my ear. "We're gonna come in the night and tie them up and hack them to pieces. Then we're gonna do the same to you, snotnose, cut you up—"

Kelly was suddenly yanked off me. I looked up to see Gary looming above us. Forget that it was three against one. Forget that they were all roughly Gary's height. Forget that Hubert Kelly had been carrying a branch the size of a golf club which he could use effectively as a weapon. Forget all of that because

Gary certainly didn't care about any of it. He challenged each of them to take a swing at him, telling them whoever did would be going home with a lot less teeth. Kelly and his cronies started away, cussing and promising future pummelings, the way bullies do to save face. Gary was having none of that either. He chased after them. The two quick ones got away, but Gary caught fatso Hubert Kelly easily enough. He threw him onto the ground, stepped on his head with one booted foot, and slipped a noose around his neck.

"Don't!" Kelly screamed. "I'll tell my parents!"

Gary tossed the other end of the rope up and over a tree branch and tugged it, lurching Kelly to his feet, then off his feet, so they kicked frantically at air.

"Gare! Stop!" I shouted.

But it wasn't Gary anymore. It was John Scott.

"Shut up, Ethos!" he said. "You agreed to this. You said you wouldn't talk. So shut up or we're both going to prison, you hear me?"

Kelly's pig-eyes were bulging now. Red blood vessels webbed the whites. He opened his fat mouth and let out a glassy, terrifying wail—

I came awake, disorientated, wondering for a moment why I was so cold and stiff. Then I smelled the crisp, brittle air. Camping? Camping with Gary? We'd done that several times, just the two of us, up in the Porcupine Mountains. But no—Gary was dead. I had been dreaming about him again. Something about the bullies who used to chase me. Gary had beat them up in the dream, just like he had in real life that afternoon in November—

"What the fuck was that?" I heard someone say.

I sat up and saw John Scott crouched next to the dying fire.

Everything came back with a sickening punch of dread.

Suicide Forest. Ben. Dead.

"What was what?" I asked, my head foggy.

The zipper to Nina's tent whipped downward. She stuck her head through the door flaps. "Did you hear that?" she de-

manded. Her eyes were wide, her face pale, almost lumines-
cent in the darkness.

I sat straighter. What had I missed? What was going on?

"Hear what?" I asked.

"*Shhh*," John Scott hissed.

Mel appeared beside me, making me jump. "Someone
screamed," she whispered.

I thought immediately of my dream, of Hubert Kelly opening his mouth and letting loose that spine-chilling wail.

"Who?" I said, getting worked up.

"A woman," Mel said. "I think it was a woman—"

"*Quiet!*" John Scott hissed again.

We waited and listened. Tomo remained fast asleep.

After a minute I said, "Are you sure—"

A banshee scream rose from the forest, high-pitched and
savage, cutting me off midsentence. It climbed higher and
higher, thinning to a bloodcurdling moan. Then it ended as
abruptly as it began.

"Holy fucking shit," I said, looking wildly at the others.

"It is them," Nina whispered. "It is *them*."

"Shut the fuck up, Nina," John Scott snapped.

"Then what is it? *What is it?*"

"It's a bird," I said without thinking.

"That was *not* a bird, Ethan."

"Maybe a wildcat," John Scott said. "Maybe in heat."

Mel was as stiff as a corpse beside me. Her hand gripped
mine painfully. "What do we do?" she said so softly I barely
heard her.

"Nothing," John Scott said. "We stay here, by the fire—"

The scream ripped through the night once again, a short,
feminine burst of mindless agony and terror. It shattered into
what might have been mad laughter. The hair on the back of
my neck stood up in hackles. I felt a crazy urge to run, to get
the hell out of there. But we were in the middle of nowhere.
Stranded. Helpless.

Mel began tugging her hand. I realized I was crushing it in

mine. I released my grip and found my palm slick with something—blood. Her nails had dug into my flesh.

"Oh my God," she said. "Oh my God. *Ohmigod.*"

Nina ducked back inside her tent.

"Calm down everyone," John Scott stated, authority in his voice. "It's probably...it's just someone who came here to kill themselves."

"Why's she screaming?" Mel asked hoarsely. "What's *happening* to her?"

"Maybe she screwed up," John Scott said.

"Screwed up?" I said.

"Killing herself."

"If you have a noose around your neck, you're not screaming like that."

"Maybe she didn't hang herself. Maybe, like you said earlier, she blew half her face off."

"Did you hear a gunshot?"

"Something then!" John Scott barked. "You get the point."

Nina emerged from her tent. She had her backpack on. We stared at her.

"We have to leave," she told us in a hollow, monotonous voice.

"We can't leave, Nina," I said. "There's nowhere to go."

"They are out there!"

"No, they aren't, Nina," I said. "John Scott is right. It's just some woman who botched her suicide. Maybe she took pills, or poison, and she's reacting badly, causing her pain—"

Nina yelled something in Hebrew at us, then marched off into the trees.

"Nina!" I sprang to my feet and ran after her. I caught her quickly and positioned myself in front of her. She tried to push past me. I grabbed her by the shoulders. "Nina, stop! You can't leave."

"I am not staying here!"

"It's just a woman."

"You know that is not true."

"It's just a woman."

"Let go of me!"

"You'll get lost."

She tried to shake my hands from her shoulders. I held her firm.

She took a deep breath, composing herself. "Ethan," she said with a frosty confidence, "move out of my way right now. You cannot hold me against my will."

"Where are you going to go?"

"Away from here!"

"Where?" I gestured violently at the dark trees. "In there? By yourself?" Doubt flickered in her eyes, and I pressed on. "You're no safer out there than right here."

"I cannot stay here."

"Just until morning. It's only a few hours until dawn. You don't have to go to sleep. You can stay awake by the fire. We'll all stay awake. It's only a few hours."

"No," she said, and tried to shake my hands off her again, though she wasn't trying very hard this time.

I let her go. "Come back to the fire, Nina. It's safe there."

Although her eyes glistened with terror, with each passing second I could see the panic that had gripped her begin to loosen its hold.

Losing some inner debate, she wrapped her arms around me and mumbled something into my chest. We remained like that for a good minute until she released me.

We returned to camp. Nina zippered herself inside her tent without a word to anyone. I sat back down. The next few minutes seemed slow and blurred and dreamlike, like I was underwater. I kept expecting to hear the scream again, but it never came. Amazingly Tomo remained asleep. Neil hadn't stirred either.

Sobs from Nina's tent broke the silence. They grew louder, more miserable. John Scott stared at her tent, his face unreadable. Mel rubbed her eyes, and I realized she was crying as well.

"Go back to sleep," I told her quietly.

"Was it really just a woman?"

"Yeah."

"It wasn't...?"

"Positive. Now go back to sleep."

"Come in the tent with me."

"I can't. It will be my watch soon."

"I'll stay up with you."

"Go back to sleep. The sooner you do, the sooner it will be morning."

That apparently was too tempting for her to pass up. She kissed me on the cheek and returned to the tent, leaving the door flaps open.

Nina's sobs became muffled, then stopped altogether. John Scott shifted his gaze past her tent, to the forest, in the direction the screams had come from. I wanted to talk with him, toss some more theories back and forth. But Nina and Mel would hear us. This wasn't the time.

I lay back down, my head on Mel's backpack, and glanced at my wristwatch. One hour until my shift. I closed my eyes, hoping for sleep, knowing it would be an impossibility, but trying nonetheless. I saw a woman flopping around on the ground, limbs spasming, body convulsing, a pale-faced *yūrei* floating forlornly through the trees, head thrown back, mouth gaping open in an obtuse hole, a dozen other scenarios to explain what we'd heard, and then I shut off and was thinking no more.

25

EVENTUALLY I gave in to my discomfort and awoke during the early morning between dark and dawn. My eyes cracked open, but I didn't move. The night's cold had penetrated deep into my bones. The ground had been like concrete, and I had tossed and turned constantly. Pressure had built in my bladder until it was a sharp pain, but I had refused to get up to relieve myself, knowing if I did I would remain awake until morning.

The world was an ethereal bruised-gray. Through the curdling mist I could see the vague outlines of the craggy branches netted together overhead. I pushed myself up onto my elbows. The fire had died down to a smokeless bed of red embers. John Scott lay next to it, snoring, bloated from the clothes he had layered beneath his leather jacket. Tomo's spot was empty. I assumed he had retired inside his tent. Smart guy. I should have returned to mine. I could have climbed under the emergency blanket and pressed myself against Mel, sharing our body heat.

For a moment I wondered why I hadn't done that, why I was out here, then I remembered we had agreed to take watch. Tomo, John Scott, then me. But why hadn't John Scott woken me? Had he fallen asleep? I looked at him again. Probably.

I got to my feet, hating the cotton taste in my mouth and the icy feel of my clothes against my skin. God, I hoped it wasn't overcast today. I would give anything to see a bright blue sky and golden sun.

Now that I was up and moving, the pressure in my bladder intensified tenfold to a kidney-stone level of pain. I moved toward the trees—and caught sight of Ben. He was exactly how we'd left him, on the litter, beneath his sleeping bag. His body was still under the eerie control of rigor, twisted at the waist, knees bent. I assumed it had another day or two before decomposition set in and it began to relax.

Thinking about this I felt oddly indifferent. *Just another dead person.* It was how I'd felt following Weasel's death, and Stag's death. Shock when I first heard the news, an empty, queasy feeling all day—but then, the next morning, nothing. Either I was one cold-hearted son of a bitch, or the human brain had a remarkable ability to cope with death—at least, the death of little-known acquaintances.

Despite my pincushion bladder I detoured from my path so I could check on Neil quickly. I knelt beside him, and for a horrible moment I thought he was dead. He looked like a corpse. His face was gaunt and white and smudged with dirt. There were flecks of dried sick on his skin and chin which I wanted to brush away but couldn't bring myself to touch. Nevertheless, when I leaned close—getting a whiff of his sickly, putrid stench—I heard him breathing. It was faint and phlegmy, as if there was too much fluid in it.

I let him rest and walked two dozen yards away into the forest, careful to avoid the patches of vomit or feces that seemed to be everywhere, as strategically placed as landmines.

I stopped near a maple tree, unzipped, and aimed at a helpless shrub. Steam rose from the arc of urine. Afterward I surveyed the pre-dawn forest. The fog drifted languidly between the trees, almost like some amorphous, sentient life form, sniffing out its prey.

No chirruping insects or cheerful morning birdcall greeted the new day, only that deep and expectant silence I had become uneasily familiar with.

The mist parted and I saw someone standing fifteen feet away from me.

I likely would have cried out if my chest hadn't abruptly locked up. This knee-jerk reaction passed in a flash, however, replaced with a magical kind of awe as I realized what I was staring at was not a person but a deer.

It stood statue-still, staring directly at me. Its eyes were a liquid black, timeless, and if you didn't know better it would have been easy to believe they held some sort of secret, ancient wisdom. The scuffed ears were alert, like two small satellite dishes, nestled at the base of a majestic set of velvety antlers. The licorice-black nose glistened, the nostrils flaring noiselessly. It was more compact and dainty-legged than a North American stag and sported white spots along the mahogany pelt. The fluffy tail twitched once.

We stared at each other for a long time. I had an almost irresistible urge to move forward, to get closer to it, though I knew it would bound away if I tried. Instead I raised my hands slowly, showing I was unarmed. Its nose tested the air.

"Hey there," I said. "It's okay. I'm not going to hurt you."

A billow of fog drifted between us, thick and gray, and when it dispersed the stag was gone. I scanned the crooked trees, astounded that the deer could depart so silently—as silent as a ghost, a voice suggested from an ignored corner of my mind—and I had to convince myself I had really seen it.

For several long minutes I refused to move, unwilling to let go of the experience. It had been unlike anything I would have anticipated. During those few seconds our eyes connected, a transcendent peacefulness had settled over me, fuelled by an intoxicating sense of freedom, as if I could shed my civility and do anything I wanted in a world where there were no worries, no decisions to make, no consequences of actions, no concept of past or future.

I had been completely in the moment, blissfully, ignorantly alive.

BACK at camp everyone was still sleeping, so I sat down quietly, did my best to ignore my hunger and thirst, and played over the ghastly screams of the previous night. Now, with darkness marching a hasty retreat, what we'd heard seemed more perplexing than terrifying, a mystery to be solved rather than a superstition to be feared.

Had John Scott been right? Had the screams come from a woman who had botched her suicide? I figured most people who couldn't stomach hanging themselves would opt for washing a handful of Valium down their throat with a bottle of booze. This, of course, would not elicit the screams we had heard. But if Woman X didn't have access to such pills, she might have tried something more creative and dangerous such as, say, drain cleaner, or rat poison. If she didn't consume enough of either to kill herself quickly, she very well could have suffered a slow, agonized death as her internal organs were eaten away. I could almost see her slumped against a tree stump, her gums and nose bleeding, her body thrashing, the tendons in her neck bunching like cables as she belted out those horrible wails.

While waiting for the others to wake I kept myself occupied with a half dozen other gruesome scenarios, one of which had Woman X slitting her wrists while unknowingly disturbing a colony of fire ants, just as I had done, only she lacked the strength to brush them off or move away.

Gradually the eddying mist thinned and evaporated altogether, revealing the empty, lifeless forest in all its green glory. My wish did not come true. The sky did not clear but remained swollen with the dirty clouds keeping at bay direct sunlight. This meant there was no need to attempt a belowground still—which I don't think I would have dug even had the sun been out in full force for the same reason I hadn't bothered to collect dew on rags tied around my shins or piss in a bottle.

I was cold, thirsty, hungry, and spent. I no longer had the energy or desire to entertain worst-case scenarios. I wanted this nightmare trip to be over with; or, more accurately, I wouldn't accept that it could go on any longer. The police were coming. They would be here in a few hours. Noon at the latest. I no longer gave a damn about the potential statements and interrogations. All I wanted was to be in a heated room with a hot plate of food and a coffee before me.

And if for whatever reason the police failed to show, we would leave here on our own. I didn't care if I had to carry Neil on my bloody back all afternoon. One way or another, we were leaving Aokigahara today.

JOHN Scott was the first to wake. He stirred, opened his eyes, but like me earlier, he didn't move. He saw me watching him and closed his eyes again.

"You didn't wake me last night," I said.

He grunted.

"Why didn't you wake me for my shift?"

"Fell asleep," he mumbled.

Mel must have heard us talking because a few moments later there was a rustling from within our tent and she emerged. Her hair was a tousled blonde mess, and she appeared younger, more vulnerable with most of her makeup now smudged off her face. She glanced at the remnants of the fire and frowned slightly, as if she had expected to see a kettle seated in the embers, the water boiling for a cup of morning tea. She shifted her gaze to me, then John Scott, then me again. "What time is it?" she asked tiredly.

"Half past six."

"When will the police be here?"

"Probably not for a few hours."

She shivered, hugging herself, then turned back toward the tent, as if she had decided to return to bed.

"Come with me," I said, standing. "We'll find some more

wood for the fire. The exercise will warm you up."

We spent the next thirty minutes or so scouring the surrounding area for tinder and deadwood, then built a fire. I stood so close to the licking flames they scorched my bare skin, though I didn't move. The heat rejuvenated my spirit and made me forget temporarily about Ben's body and Neil's sickness and my empty stomach.

Nina stuck her head through the door flaps of her tent and surveyed the camp. She reminded me of a prairie dog peeking out of its burrow, wary of a circling hawk. When we made eye contact, she looked quickly away. I couldn't decide whether she was embarrassed about her attempted escape from the forest the night before or whether she was mad at me for stopping her.

John Scott poked a stick at the fire. Sparks exploded. I had to jump backward to avoid getting hit.

"Did we finish all the food?" Mel asked. She was sitting on the ground, her knees pulled to her chest, looking miserable.

I said, "There's still Ben's ration from yesterday's breakfast. It's not much."

"Break it out, dude," John Scott said. "What have you been hoarding it for?"

"I haven't been hoarding it," I said. "I've been holding on to it until we really needed it."

I withdrew the ration from Mel's backpack. I had sealed it in a plastic Ziploc baggie that one of the sandwiches had been in. She set six paper plates on the ground. I divided the food into six even portions: a tablespoon of nuts, half a tablespoon of dried fruit, a thin slice of browning banana, and a small pile of dried ramen noodles.

The sight of it made my stomach growl noisily.

"What about the grapes?" John Scott asked, eyeing the eleven grapes I hadn't doled out.

"I think Neil should have them," I said. "He needs the liquid."

"You think Neil can eat?"

"It's up to him to decide, not us."

John Scott shrugged. Mel and Nina nodded.

"Okay, Mel," I said. "Choose."

She took the portion closest to her. Nina took hers, then John Scott. He tossed the nuts and fruit into his mouth, chewed quickly, then inhaled the noodles from his hand. He finished everything in under ten seconds. Mel, Nina, and I ate our portions more slowly. I deposited the nuts in my mouth a few at a time, savoring the crunch and texture. I sucked on the sweet squares of mandarin, apricot, and apple until I could tease myself no more and swallowed. The banana was mushy but delicious nonetheless. I consumed the noodles like John Scott had, all at once, crunching them between my teeth until they were a paste, surprised at how good something so plain could taste.

John Scott watched us silently, most likely regretting wolfing his food back so quickly. He reminded me of a dog hanging around the table for scraps.

I told Mel to wake Tomo and give him his portion, then I brought Neil's to him. If he'd looked bad when I woke, he looked doubly so now in the budding morning light. His eye sockets were shadowed, his cheeks cadaverous, his mouth slack. He seemed somehow shrunken, like a mummy.

"Hey, buddy," I said. "You up?"

He opened his eyes. They were rheumy and distant and unfocused.

"I have some food for you. You hungry?"

He said something, but it was so quiet I could barely hear.

I lowered my head. "What was that?"

"...wadda..."

"We don't have any. But the police are going to be here soon. They'll have water."

He closed his eyes.

"Do you want food?"

A barely perceptible shake of the head.

"Have a grape. They have water in them."

No reply.

"Neil?"

"...no..."

"Here."

I pressed a grape against his mouth. His lips parted and the grape disappeared inside.

"Chew, Neil. You have to chew."

He worked his jaws slowly. A rill of juice spilled out of his mouth.

"Swallow now. Okay? Swallow—"

He coughed, rolled laboriously to his side, then vomited, though the only thing that exited his mouth was the butchered purple grape. He continued to dry retch. The sound was abrasive and dusty and strained.

I remained at his side, frustrated at my inability to assist him in any way.

John Scott shouted Tomo's name. I glanced over my shoulder, confused. John Scott was turning in a circle, surveying the forest.

"Tomo!" he called again.

Neil flopped onto his back and closed his eyes. Tears streaked his pale face.

"I'll be back," I told him, then returned to the campfire. "What's going on?"

"Tomo's gone Elvis," John Scott said.

"What?"

"He's missing," Mel said. "He's not in his tent."

The words hit me like a sledgehammer to the chest. I looked at his tent. The door was now unzipped, the inside empty except for his sleeping bag and backpack.

"He's fine," I said automatically. "Probably woke early and did some exploring." But even as I said this I doubted my sincerity. I had been up for nearly an hour now, almost since first light. Where would Tomo have been for all that time?

"Tomo?" I shouted.

The only reply was the echo of my own voice.

"This is seriously fucked up," John Scott said.

"He's fine," I repeated, unable to come up with anything else, even as panic built inside my chest. I kept thinking, *Not Tomo. Come on. Give me a fucking break. Not Tomo.*

Mel said, "Where would he go? *Why* would he go somewhere?"

"Maybe he's looking for the ribbon," I said.

"Without telling anyone?" Mel shook her head. "That's not like him."

"Well, where do *you* think he went?"

She didn't answer. She didn't need to. I saw it in her eyes.

"He didn't hang himself."

"Ben—"

"Ben was on drugs!" I said.

"All right, everyone calm down," John Scott said. "We'll go look right now. He's around here somewhere. He has to be around here somewhere."

Ten minutes later we found him.

26

I spotted red thirty yards away from me. It was the same rich crimson as the vertical stripes on Tomo's motorcycle jacket, and I likely would have missed it if it didn't contrast so strongly with the surrounding verdant foliage. At first I told myself it was my imagination. I was projecting. I had been expecting to find Tomo's body hanging from a tree, I had morbidly convinced myself of this when he failed to respond to our repeated calls, so here I was, my mind playing tricks, confusing a cluster of wild berries for racing stripes. But that didn't stop me from charging forward, bending and snapping branches out of my way.

It had been no act of the imagination. It was Tomo. His back was to me, his body suspended in the air by his Louis Vuitton scarf.

I smashed the final branches away from my face and pulled up three feet short of him. I attempted no heroic rescue this time. I had known Ben was dead when we saw his dangling body, of course I had known, but I gave into false hope and tried to save him. Not again. I had come to expect the horrors that Aokigahara had on offer, and to believe in their authenticity.

Tomo's hair was, as always, even in death, fashionably unkempt. The biker-style collar on his sheep-leather jacket was upturned, how The Fonz sometimes wore his in *Happy Days*. I'd been with Tomo when he'd bought the jacket in a retro shop in Kitchijoji. I'd told him not to get it because I didn't like the oversized, in-your-face American eagle embossed on the back, which I was staring at now. Above it were the words LIVE TO RIDE and below it RIDE TO LIVE. Derek and I had nicknamed Tomo "Easy Rider" for a few weeks, though this didn't stick because Tomo either missed or ignored the sarcasm, which made the teasing redundant.

His left Converse All-Stars had fallen off his foot, revealing his foot in a bright yellow sock. The blue canvas shoe rested on the ground below him, eerily reminiscent of the lone Nike we came across on our way into the forest.

People say your life flashes before your eyes when you're on the cusp of death. I believe this to be possible because I experienced a similar phenomenon right then, only the kaleidoscope of images were not of me but of Tomo. I thought of the first time Derek and I met him drinking the tallboy at Shinagawa station, and he greeted us with a ridiculous sounding "G'day mate!" taught to him, we learned later, by an Aussie friend. I thought of his twenty-second birthday party which, for reasons known only to him, he decided to hold at a club in which all the patrons were sweaty, dancing Nigerians and young hip hop girls who were into sweaty, dancing Nigerians. Tomo and his Japanese friends fit in well enough, but Derek and I stood out in a bad way and almost got beaten up for being white. I thought about the *yakitori* restaurant in Shimokitazawa that he had taken me to where, to his grand amusement, I unknowingly filled up on pig's heart, liver, tongue, and uterus.

In this brief moment when time seemed to have ground to a halt, I thought of a dozen other occasions I'd shared with Tomo, but one stood out above the others. The day I spent with him and his younger sister and the way he had so patiently and expertly dealt with her autistic episodes. It reminded me of his future, or, more precisely, of his lack of future. He would never begin his residency at the hospital. He would never become a psychiatrist, never start his own practice, never help anyone with their problems. Never get married or have kids. Never travel overseas. Never have grandchildren. *Never, never, never, never.* He would never do any of those things again nor a thousand others. He was dead. The end. Game over. Gone.

I touched a hand to his shoulder. His body turned slowly toward me, rotating, like a side of beef on a butcher's hook. His eyes were open and blank. His skin, like Ben's had been, was pale and patchy with burst capillaries. To my horror, a beetle scuttled out of his parted lips and up his face.

This has to be a dream, I told myself. *I'm dreaming. No way this is real. It can't be.*

Mel, who I realized was standing beside me, didn't move, didn't cry, didn't speak, didn't react at all. I think I might have been waiting for her to scream, and if she did that, I probably would have screamed too. But she didn't. She was likely in shock. I was likely in shock as well. Then she broke her paralysis and gripped me in a fierce hug, burying her face in my shoulder.

God almighty, life could be an awful mess sometimes.

I was still holding Mel when John Scott and Nina arrived. John Scott went immediately to the scarf and hacked through it with a sharp rock he'd been carrying. The ready-to-use rock surprised me, making me wonder if he had been expecting to find Tomo hanging from a tree branch. The scarf snapped with a sharp rip and Tomo collapsed inelegantly to the ground. This was perhaps the most horrible sight yet: seeing my friend crumple the way he crumpled. It reinforced the idea he was no more, nothing but a torso and limbs, raw meat, not unlike the nose-to-tail cuts of pork you find in the supermarket's frozen section.

I released Mel and knelt beside Tomo, straightening him out, providing him whatever dignity I could. I drew my fingers over his eyes, closing his eyelids. I had only seen this done in movies and on TV before, and it was something I never wished to do again. Then, in the next instant, I was consumed with a scorching rage. I was going to find out who did this, and I was going to make them pay.

I stood, my hands balled into fists. Mel touched my shoulder. I flinched away.

"Who did this?" I demanded. "Who the fuck did this?"

No one answered, and I realized I was likely scaring them.

I took a deep breath, stepped backward to gain space, held up my hands. "Tomo didn't kill himself," I said quietly.

"Neither did Ben," Nina said.

I glared at her. She stared back, defiant. I was about to remind her that Ben had been on drugs, Tomo hadn't been, there was a difference—when I realized how senseless that would sound. Two suicides in less than twenty-four hours. Of course there was a connection. Their deaths were linked as inseparably as blood and bone.

"Okay," I said.

Nina bit her lower lip, which had begun to tremble. I was confused, wondering how she could have misinterpreted "okay"—unless she was simply relieved. For the past day she had been the outsider, on her own. No one would believe what she had inherently known—and she must have inherently known Ben hadn't killed himself, just as I inherently knew Tomo didn't kill himself.

What assholes we had been to her.

"So who did it?" John Scott asked. "Who killed them? We're out here by ourselves."

"We don't know that," I said.

"You've seen someone?"

"Someone killed Ben, and someone killed Tomo. That means there's someone out here."

Nina was staring at me. I knew what she was thinking.

"No," I said.

"Why not, Ethan? Why will you not—"

"Because there are no such things as fucking ghosts!"

"How could someone make him hang himself? We would have heard him shouting. We would have heard a struggle—"

"Check," Mel said.

"What?" I said.

"Nina's right. Tomo couldn't have been hanged without a struggle. Check."

I looked at Tomo's body. Mel dropped to her knees. She cupped Tomo's head in her hands, turned it from side to side. She parted his hair, bit by bit, how chimpanzees groom their offspring for lice and other parasites.

"See!" she said suddenly, excitedly. "See!"

I knelt beside her and saw a blood-crusted contusion.

NINA ran back toward camp. I wasn't sure what she had planned—I suspected, but I wasn't sure—so I chased her down. She went directly to Ben's body.

"Nina!" I said. "Wait—"

She tugged the sleeping bag back and recoiled, spinning around, her cheeks blown out. Her head bobbed back and forth like a regurgitating pelican, then she vomited onto the ground. When she finished, she immediately covered her nose with the crook of her arm.

I pulled my shirt up over my lower face and joined her next to Ben. The stench coming off him was as nauseous as garbage left out in the sun for a week. His face was yellowish now, the blood having drained from it to settle and pool in the lowest portion of his body. His tongue still protruded from his mouth, though it had darkened further to an eggplant purple. His neck was covered with red abrasions and contusions.

Using her free hand, Nina began parting his hair for signs of blunt-force trauma. Her fingers focused on a spot near the back of his skull. She leaned closer. I did too.

The bump was nearly identical in size and location to Tomo's.

27

I pulled the sleeping bag back over Ben's corpse and stood on suddenly rubbery legs. I took Nina's hand and led her to Mel and John Scott, who were emerging from the trees opposite us.

"Ben has the same injury as Tomo," I said.

"So...someone killed them?" Mel said dubiously. "Both of them? How?"

"He obviously hit them on the back of the heads with something," John Scott said.

"But *why*?"

"Because whoever it is, he has fucking problems, that's why."

I was staring at John Scott, my mind sluggish, still struggling to come to terms with what was going on—and that's when pieces clicked into place. How indifferent John Scott had been to Ben's death, only concerned about diverting the blame from himself. How little Suicide Forest had seemed to bother him thus far. How he'd been carrying the rock to cut Tomo down—as if he'd known we were going to find him strung up.

"Why did you have a rock?" I asked him.

He frowned at me. "What?"

"When we went looking for Tomo. You were carrying a rock. You used it to cut him down. You knew he was dead."

"What are you talking about?"

I stepped toward him. "You *knew*."

"Ethos, I think you better cool down."

"You killed them, didn't you?"

"Have you fucking lost it?"

I swung at him. He dodged the blow and landed an upper-cut beneath my jaw. But I didn't go down and used my height and weight advantage to pull him into a headlock. He pummeled my body with short jabs, and somehow the headlock became a front facelock/reverse headlock. I lost my balance and dropped to my rear, keeping my hold around his neck, driving his head into the ground.

Mel and Nina, both yelling, tried to pull us apart. I was almost crazy enough to go after them too—almost, but not quite.

I released John Scott, bringing my knees to my chest, ready to kick out at him if he tried anything. He rocked back on his ass and spat dirt from his mouth.

"What the fuck, dude?" he said, wiping at his lips.

Mel stared at me. "Ethan, what is wrong with you?"

"He killed Ben and Tomo," I said.

"Why would I want to kill them?" John Scott barked.

"Why are you here? Why did you come on this trip?"

He flicked a hand. "Mel invited me."

"I know about you two. Yeah, I know about your past. You fucked her in college. Are you still fucking her?"

"You're mad, Ethos."

"Ethan, please," Mel said.

I shoved myself to my feet and whirled on her.

"Are you?" I demanded. "Are you still fucking?"

"No, *we are not*! Okay?"

I backed away from them. I didn't believe her. I didn't trust anyone.

I bumped into Nina.

"Ethan—" she began, touching my arm.

I wrenched free. "Did you and Ben know John Scott from before too?"

Nina frowned. "From before? From before when, Ethan? Before we met you randomly at the train station?"

"Was it random?"

John Scott whistled, like I was crazy.

"Shut up," I told him. "I'll break your fucking face. I swear I will."

"You're upset about Tomo, Ethan," Mel said. "We all are. But you have to get a hold of yourself. You're not making any sense."

"You three always stuck together," I said to Nina. "You, Ben, and John Scott. You did mushrooms together. You're telling me you've never, ever met before this weekend?"

"That is exactly what I am telling you, Ethan. And I did not do mushrooms."

"You're lying."

"Ethan, think back! You first approached Ben and me. You did. No one else."

I shook my head in frustration, because I knew she was right. Still, I couldn't let this go. John Scott had something to do with all of this. I ran my hand through my hair and paced back and forth.

"Who killed Tomo then?" I said, glaring at each of them. "We're in the middle of nowhere. Who the fuck killed him?"

No one had an answer to that.

I stalked off deeper into the forest. I didn't want to be around anybody right then. Mel, however, came running after me, telling me I shouldn't be on my own. I tried to ignore her, but she latched onto my arm.

"Let go of me, Mel," I said dangerously, and for the first time ever I contemplated using my strength against her.

"I know you're mad at John," she said, almost tripping over her words to get them out, "and you're mad at me, but you shouldn't be. John and me—I lied. We never slept together."

"What are you talking about?"

"We never slept together. I made that all up."

"Bullshit."

"It's true, Ethan. I swear to you. I'm so sorry."

"You made it up?" I frowned, confused. "Why?"

"Shelly—she really bothers me, Ethan. She's so pretty. You had those pictures of her on your computer, then she calls you on your birthday. Then the messages. Then her calling you *here*—I don't know. I had almost put her behind me, but that was too much. I couldn't deal with it. I was so mad at you. I knew you didn't like John. So I made up...that stuff about us. And, well, it all seems so stupid now, doesn't it?"

"So why's he here then?" I said. "Why did you invite him?"

"I told you the truth before. We're just old friends. He called, wanted something to do. I mentioned we were going to Fuji and suggested he come. That's it."

"Jesus, Mel," I said, at a loss for words. I wasn't sure if I was more angry at her for the deception, or relieved there was nothing going on between her and John Scott.

"I'm sorry," she said. "Really, I am. It was stupid. And—and I love you, Ethan. I love you so much. I would never, ever..."

The wall I'd thrown up finally crumbled. I pulled her against me, kissing her on the top of the head.

"I love you too, Mel," I whispered.

BACK at the campfire, with a cooler head than before, I acknowledged the conclusion that everyone else had already accepted. Somebody was in Suicide Forest with us, stalking us, somebody we didn't know anything about. He was the predator in the dark. The bogeyman in the closet. The cancer in your cells. A threat you knew little about, couldn't see, couldn't predict—and thus against which you could do little to defend yourself. Understanding this, Aokigahara now seemed not only ominous but sinister. It had become a co-conspirator in Ben and Tomo's deaths, both holding us captive and concealing a murderer.

Mel, who was sitting next to me, holding my hand, said, "Where are the police? What's taking them so long? We need to get out of here right now."

"It's only a bit past eight," I told her. "They're likely just getting to the parking lot."

"How long's it going to take them to find us?"

"I don't know, Mel."

"Maybe they do not come," Nina said.

"Why wouldn't they come?" Mel said. "We called them, right? They know we're here. They have to come. Don't they, Ethan? They have to come?"

"They should be coming," I said.

"But what if they do not?" Nina pressed. "We cannot remain here any longer. Your friend is very sick. We must go."

"She's right," John Scott said. "We can't spend another night here."

"What if the police arrive after we've left?" Mel said. "What if we can't find our way out of here on our own?"

"Yesterday you were all for leaving."

"And you were all for staying. That was then. This is now."

"We'll wait until noon," I stated decisively. "That will give the police another couple of hours to reach us. If they don't show for whatever reason, then we'll still have four or five hours of light to find our way out of here. Anyone have a problem with that?"

No one did.

JOHN Scott and I discussed making a second litter, but elected to wait first to see what the police brought with them. Instead we used Ben's litter to transport Tomo back to camp. The sight of the two bodies lying next to each other reminded me of how developing countries would line up bodies side by side on a hospital floor for identification by family members after some disaster, such as a tsunami or collapsed building. It was impersonal, indecorous, and hit home the fragility of human life. You could win a hundred-million-dollar Powerball jackpot one day, then drive your brand-new Ferrari headfirst into an oncoming Mac truck the next. Death isn't picky, doesn't play favorites. It doesn't care in which country you were born or how much money you had amassed in your brief existence or how happy you are. It's supremely patient and rightly so, for it knows you can't escape its reach. One day you too would be lying on that hospital floor or on a stainless-steel gurney in a morgue.

It had already won. It would always win. In other words, we were born to lose.

I rubbed my eyes with my fingers. I was bumming myself out with these depressing thoughts, but I couldn't help it. Tomo's death had dragged me down to a low I had only experienced after Gary died—a low I'd told myself I would never allow myself to sink to again.

John Scott went into army mode and began fashioning spears for us. He dismantled Tomo's tent, placed the aluminum support poles flat on the ground, scavenged a rock the size of a five-pin bowling ball, and hammered the ends into sharp points. He gave one to each of us. I hefted mine in my hand. It was roughly three feet long, hollow, and light. I thought you might be able to impale a fish with it, maybe even a squirrel, but I didn't say anything. John Scott seemed proud of his handiwork, and the girls seemed reassured to be holding weapons.

Armed and on guard, we huddled morosely around the fire and waited for the police to arrive. Mel chewed her fingernails, something I had only seen her do on a few occasions when she was either stressed or excited. Nina sat quietly, saying nothing. John Scott smoked his cigarettes and said inane things every so often like, "I wonder if Tomo got a look at the asshole's face?" or, "If see this fucker, I'm going to drive this pole through his heart."

I kept to myself, trying to recreate what happened to Tomo exactly. Sometime in the early morning, after we'd heard those chilling screams, he must have wandered into the trees to relieve himself. The assailant, who I'll call John Doe, snuck up behind him and struck him on the back of the head with a blunt object. There was no reason for Tomo to venture the one hundred yards or so to where we found his body, so John Doe must have carried him this distance. Tomo, however, was the height of an average adult Japanese male, which meant John Doe was likely abnormally large and strong because it would be extremely difficult for someone to carry their own body weight that far in the dark. In fact, he'd probably have to be about my size.

This gave me pause. In the four or so years I've been in Japan I had only encountered one Japanese taller than me—and the guy was an anomaly, likely suffering from gigantism, standing well in the seven-foot range. I suspect he worked nearby my school because I often saw him during the morning rush out of the train station to the surrounding office buildings. On a few occasions I noticed him walking—though "lurching" would be a more accurate description of his gait—next to a four-foot-nothing guy who had a condition which caused him to drag his left foot along the ground. This pairing of extremes seemed too coincidental to be happenchance, and I always wondered if they were friends by default of being outcasts.

Anyway, the point was that the percentile of Japanese men of the physical stature to haul Tomo away like a sack of flour would be very small. So could John Doe belong to a different nationality then? I doubted it. The prospect of a murderous six-foot-four Dane or Russian hanging out in Aokigahara seemed ludicrous.

My eyes fell on Neil, and I wondered why he had been spared. After all, he would have been the easiest target. He was already incapacitated and isolated from the rest of us. So why hadn't John Doe gone after him? Because he was no threat?

Was John Doe saving the weakest for last?

"You guys were supposed to be keeping watch," Mel said abruptly. "You said you were going to take turns keeping watch."

"We did," I said, knowing where this was leading.

"So this happened on Tomo's shift?"

"No," I said. "It happened on mine."

"And you saw nothing?"

"I was asleep."

"You fell asleep?"

"I was never woken up."

"Who was supposed to wake you up?"

I didn't say anything, because I didn't blame John Scott. I wanted to, but it wouldn't be fair. It was me, not him, who had volunteered his service. He didn't believe in ghosts, just as I didn't. How foolish would he have felt, sitting up in the cold while everyone else was asleep, watching the trees for an imaginary enemy. After an uneventful thirty minutes, I likely would have dozed off as well.

Nina and Mel, however, were not so forgiving. They glared at John Scott with ice picks in their eyes.

Nina said, "Why did you not wake Ethan up?"

John Scott shrugged. "I fell asleep."

"God! You are so—"

"I suppose you're going to pin this one on me too?"

"This isn't about you!" Mel jumped in. "Tomo *died*. He's *dead*. Do you get that? How hard is it to stay awake for a couple hours?"

"I didn't see you offering to keep watch."

"I wouldn't have fallen sleep."

"Whatever."

"Don't 'whatever' me."

"Whatever."

"Gosh, John, you're such a dick sometimes."

Finally, I thought, something about John Scott that Mel and I could agree upon.

"YOU said that woman had screwed up killing herself," Nina

said to John Scott. "But what if you were wrong? What if she was murdered just like Ben and Tomo?"

"No way," he said immediately.

Another half hour had passed. It was now 9:24 a.m. The daylight was a little brighter, the air a little warmer. But the sun still refused to show itself, the sky the same unrelenting gray.

"Why not?" Nina challenged.

"Those screams had been far away. I'd say over a mile, maybe two. How would he have made his way back here in the dark?"

"We had a fire. He could see that."

"Not from a distance. He would be walking blind."

"He could do it," Nina persisted.

John Scott shrugged. "Okay. Fine. Maybe," he conceded. "But let's look at the facts. He killed Ben two nights ago. Which meant he had been here, nearby. Which meant at some point between then and early this morning he would have to have gone wandering around the forest, searching for another potential victim, stumbling randomly upon the woman, killing her, then coming all the way back here and killing Tomo in the span of, what, a couple hours? It seems like a hell of a lot of work to do in one night."

"Why us?" Mel said. "Why stalk us?"

"Because we're different," I said.

"Huh?"

"We're foreigners. Maybe he wanted a change."

"A change from what?"

"Japanese victims."

"You think this isn't the first time he's done this?"

"People who kill for no reason," I said, "they're sick. They have issues. They can't control their desires. So imagine that was you. Would you go around Tokyo, hunting for victims, where there was a good possibility you could get caught? Or would you go somewhere with a constant supply of victims—and where they were expecting to be found dead? No foul play suspected, no investigation. You get away every time."

"You think he's a serial killer?" Mel said, aghast.

"Shit, maybe you're right," John Scott said. "The guy wouldn't care if his targets were going to kill themselves anyway. He just wants the thrill of taking their lives. Maybe— maybe he was even watching the parking lot. He chooses who he wants, then follows them into the forest."

"This is crazy," Mel said.

"Or maybe," John Scott went on, "he was one of the suicide guys himself. He comes out here to hang himself, decides he doesn't want to do it, but he's still pissed off at society or whatever so he takes it out on others who come here."

"Regardless of who he is," I said, seeing that the discussion was upsetting Mel and Nina, "he's a coward who only attacks at night, and we're going to be long gone from here by then."

THE following two hours inched by with painful slowness. I spent much of it preoccupying myself with the Chicago Blackhawks, who hadn't won the Stanley Cup since 1961, but who I'd watched religiously as a kid growing up. When I was eleven, my father surprised Gary and me with tickets to a game against the Montreal Canadians. This was way back in '88 when the Blackhawks still played in Chicago Stadium, aka "The Madhouse on Madison." I'd spent almost as much time gawking at the triple-tiered seating filled with rambunctious fans as I did the players on the ice, and I've never forgotten the aged smell of stale beer and sweat that permeated the old arena, or the roar of the crowd which seemed to shake the building when the Blackhawks scored, or the circusy music the pipe organ belted out between whistles.

Eventually I got up to check on Neil, swooning lightheadedly when I stood.

"Hey, Neil," I said. "You feeling better?"

He tried to wet his lips, but had no saliva to do this with. "Tomo?" he said in a dry whisper.

JEREMY BATES

"Do you need anything?" I asked him, avoiding the question.

"Tomo?" The word was thick and cumbersome, as if his tongue was engorged, and sounded like "Dhomo."

I shook my head.

"Wha'appen?"

"The police are going to be here soon. Probably an hour or so. We're getting ready to leave. Do you need to go to the bathroom before?"

He nodded, and I helped him to his feet. He baby-stepped into the forest, hunched over, his head down. He might no longer be puking and moaning, but his condition was serious bordering on critical.

He stopped by a tree and undid his pants with clumsy fingers. We hadn't ventured far from camp, but I nonetheless felt exposed and vulnerable. I remained vigilant, scanning the shadows, paranoid John Doe was going to burst from the vegetation and attack us at any second. I silently urged Neil to hurry up. Finally I heard a short splash, then he was re-buttoning his pants. He hadn't defecated yet today, and I wondered if that was because he had nothing left inside him, or because he was constipated, a result of dehydration.

I led him back to his sleeping bag, pulled it up to his chin, and returned to the campfire.

"How is he?" Mel asked me.

"If you checked on him once in a while," I snapped, "you would know."

"I have checked," she said defensively. "Several times. But I just can't stand seeing him how he is." She lowered her voice. "He looks like he's already half dead."

"Yeah, I—sorry," I mumbled, scratching my hand through my hair, which was itchy and oily. The headache that had begun the night before was now a steady, thumping pulse, impossible to ignore. It wasn't helping my mood any. "He's weak from the food poisoning," I added more sociably. "But the bug has passed. He'll get his color back with some water and food."

"Maybe Kaori has called the police as well?"

"Kaori?" I frowned, unable to place the name.

"His wife."

"Yeah, right." But I still had no idea what Mel was talking about. Why would Kaori call the police? Suddenly I was finding it hard to think straight.

"If this trip went according to plan," Mel explained, "we would have been back down Mt. Fuji yesterday afternoon. Kaori would have been expecting a call from Neil. You know how he is. Like clockwork with things. So if he didn't call her yesterday, she might have gotten worried. When he didn't call today, she might have been worried enough to call the police. Then they'd know for sure we were in serious trouble."

I nodded, but that was all I offered. Because whether Kaori had called the police or not really didn't matter. They had one more hour to arrive.

After that, we were on our own.

AT a quarter to noon I think we had all given up hope of a deus ex machina to save the day, and I said, "We should leave."

No one agreed vocally, but no one disagreed either.

"Is Neil able to walk?" Mel asked.

"No."

Nina frowned. "How will we carry three people?"

"We need to make a second litter."

"Yes, but there are *three* people—"

"We can't take Ben, Nina. I'm sorry."

There was a vacuous silence.

"We cannot leave Ben here!" Nina exploded.

"There are only four of us," I said. "Two per litter."

"We will put Ben and Tomo together then," she declared.

"That's going to be too heavy to carry."

"You and John Scott can do it."

"For a short distance maybe. But we don't know where we are. We're going to be walking for hours. We need to move at a fast pace, make the most of our time."

"Then we will all carry one corner."

"Nina…"

"We cannot leave Ben's body here!"

"We'll leave a trail or something. The police will be able to come back for him. I'll come with them."

"I will not leave his body for that—that person out here."

"He's not interested in the bodies, Nina. He hanged them for us to find. He'll likely be following us."

"Animals. What if they—"

"Have you seen any animals? I haven't. None in two days." I was omitting the deer, of course, but we were talking about carnivores.

"Why Ben? Why not Tomo?"

I saw the accusation in her eyes: *Because he is your friend.*

I said, "Ben's been dead for a day longer. He's…decomposing. He smells."

"Ben is smaller, lighter."

"They're about the same size."

"This is not fair!"

"Do you want to vote—"

"Oh shut up! Just shut up!"

She turned around and began to cry.

JOHN Scott and I crafted the second litter using Tomo's and John Scott's jackets. Surprisingly John Scott had surrendered his without a word, tearing holes in the shoulders with one of his homemade spears.

He saw me watching him and said, "What?"

I shook my head and said, "Nothing."

When we finished we placed Tomo's body on one litter, covering it with his sleeping bag, and Neil on the other. Neil didn't question us or protest.

John Scott and I had discussed digging a temporary grave for Ben, but the topsoil was only a thin membrane over the solidified magma, no more than a foot deep where we hacked away at it with rocks. We also decided to leave the tents behind to lighten our loads. We needed to conserve as much energy as possible.

"Mel, you and Nina will carry Tomo," I said. "John Scott and I will carry Neil."

"Which way should we go?" Mel asked.

I glanced at John Scott. "You still want to climb that tree?"

I thought he would tell me to fuck a monkey or something else creatively undesirable, but he nodded and said, "Which one?"

"You're going to climb a tree?" Mel said.

"It's too overcast to get a read on the sun," he said. "But if I climb a tree, I'll be able to see Fuji, which is, what, east of here?"

"Yup," I said.

Mel craned her neck and looked up at the towering trees. "I don't think that's a good idea," she said skeptically.

"I'm a good climber," John Scott assured her. "So which one?"

"The tallest," I said.

28

AFTER several minutes of searching we decided on a species of fir. It wasn't the tallest tree around, contrary to what I'd suggested John Scott attempt, but unlike some larger cedar, the crown reached nearly to the ground, which meant we could climb it without ropes and spikes—which of course we didn't have. Also, the branches stemmed horizontally from the trunk and were arranged in flattened sprays, making them perfect for climbing. I guessed it cleared the canopy at about one hundred feet and topped off at one hundred twenty. The shape wasn't conical, like the firs back home in Wisconsin, but more irregular, the leading shoots drooping downward as if laden with invisible weights.

"You ready?" I asked John Scott.

He nodded. "Give me a lift."

I made a stirrup by interlocking the fingers of my hands and heaved him upward. He grabbed the lowest branch and started kicking, trying to swing his legs over the branch. One of his feet struck me in the head. I cursed and watched as he continued squirming in the manner of a recently birthed tadpole. He hooked his left leg on the branch, and for a moment it appeared as though he would be able to pull himself up. But his leg slipped and lost purchase. He hung for a moment, refusing to concede, before letting go and dropping to the ground.

All in all it had been a spectacularly uncoordinated display of athleticism.

"Are we sure about this?" Mel said.

John Scott ignored her. "Give me another lift," he said to me.

We repeated the process, though this time he hoisted himself up with greater finesse.

"Be careful," Mel cautioned.

John Scott started to climb. Several of the lower branches appeared dead, or barely alive, due to the deprivation of sunlight at their lowly level. He avoided these, opting for the ones sprouting the needle-like leaves. The branches grew close together, both aiding and hindering his ascent. It made it easy for him to find hand- and footholds, but it also made for tight quarters.

Nina, Mel, and I stood with our necks craned, watching his progress. I didn't know about the others, but I was filled with both excitement and dread. If John Scott could reach the top, we could figure out which way was which and get the hell out of this prison. However, if he fell— well, he was already fifty feet up, which was high enough to be fatal.

"He was right," Mel said from beside me. "He is a good climber." Her hands were steepled over her mouth.

"Yeah," I replied absently.

"He's going to make it."

"I think so."

Up and up he went, getting closer to the canopy, though his progress had slowed considerably. He was likely running out of solid branches that could support his weight.

"Can you see anything?" I shouted.

A pause. "Not yet!"

"Make sure the branches aren't rotten!"

He didn't answer.

I could barely see him now except for flashes of his white pullover. I think he had stopped moving.

"Are you there?" Mel shouted.

"Not yet!"

"What's wrong?"

"Branches are thin!"

"Maybe you should come back down?"

"Little farther!"

There was movement again—then a tremendous crack, like a starter gun going off. A huge commotion followed, branches shaking and snapping as if the tree was suddenly full of riotous monkeys.

He's falling! Oh my fucking Lord, he's falling!

Mel and Nina screamed in unison, short, high-intensity bursts of alarm.

John Scott didn't plummet straight to the ground. It was a staggered descent, like a pachinko ball teeter-tottering through the maze of pins. He would drop five or ten feet until he hit a large branch, flip one way or the other, drop farther, hit another branch, on and on.

He didn't utter a sound, and I had no idea whether he was conscious or not. All I could see were his limbs flip-flopping every which way.

Then, miraculously, he came to a rest twenty feet up.

"John!" Mel cried. "John!"

He didn't reply.

"John!"

"Give me a boost," I said quickly. "I'll get him."

Mel didn't seem to hear me. She was staring up, her eyes bulging in her pallid face. Her hands were no longer steepled but covering her mouth, the way a child does when he or she accidently blurts a swear word in front of Mom or Dad.

"John!"

"…yeah…" It was weak, more a groan than a word.

Alive. "Can you move?" I called.

"…no…"

"Hold on! I'm coming up." I turned to Mel. "I need a—"

There was another whack-snap as whatever perch John Scott had landed on gave out. The ride began all over again, though this time it was much quicker. One moment he was twenty feet up, the next he plummeted through the final few branches. He hit the hard ground with the dead, heavy sound a medicine ball makes when it strikes the floor of the gym.

I heard him blurt "oomph!" as the last of the air was knocked from his lungs at the same time I heard something much worse: the sharp, wet snick of a bone fracturing.

Then John Scott began to scream.

HIS face and arms were covered with multiple cuts. His pullover was torn in a half-dozen places, red blooming beneath. He looked as though he had been dragged through a thorny bramble, and I suppose in a sense he had, albeit a gigantic, vertical one.

His left leg—the one he'd had so much trouble hooking over that first branch—was folded in upon itself. It was bent at such an impossible angle I thought his knee must have popped out of its socket. Yet that couldn't be the case, for below the knee there was a strange protrusion several inches tall pressing tautly against the denim of his loose jeans. I knew what must be causing the alien bulge, and my stomach roiled nauseously.

"Oh gosh!" Mel shrieked. "Look at his leg!"

I barely heard her because John Scott was still screaming, half in pain, half, I think, in dismay as the extent of his injury dawned on him.

I wanted to help him but was paralyzed by my inability to decide what needed to be done. This was no schoolyard gash you got when you tripped during a five-on-five match of hoops, which the doctor could sew up with a few stitches.

His leg was snapped in fucking half.

I turned to Mel and Nina, wanting someone else to take charge. Mel was pointing a crooked finger at John Scott's leg while hopping up and down on the spot, looking for all the world like Beetlemania had just gripped her forty years late. Nina was facing away, maybe wanting to puke again and discovering she was all puked out.

I ran to the camp, my legs moving at a faster speed than my thoughts. All I knew was that I needed something to make a tourniquet. I stopped at the extinguished fire, hesitated only a moment, then ran to Neil's tent. I undid one of the guy ropes and ran back to where John Scott lay writhing in pain on the ground.

At least's he's moving, I thought. *It could have been worse. He's not paralyzed.*

I brushed past Mel and dropped beside John Scott. He had stopped screaming with an apparently Herculean effort. His mouth was stretched into a trembling grimace. A vein pulsed in his forehead.

"I'm going to make a tourniquet," I told him, looping the string around his thigh.

"No!" he hissed.

"I have to stop the bleeding—"

"You make a fucking tourniquet, you'll kill my leg. It'll have to be amputated."

I hesitated. "What do you want us to do?"

"My pants. Take them off."

"Why—?"

"You have to reset the bone!"

My stomach dropped as his words hit home. He was right. We were going to have to somehow shove the fractured shinbone back into the flesh.

I undid the laces of his Doc Martins and tugged the shoes off one after the other.

"Mel!" I said. "Help me!"

I fumbled his belt open, unbuttoned his jeans, and unzipped the zipper.

Mel appeared on the other side of him.

"We're going to pull his pants off," I said. "Slowly."

She nodded and together we hitched his pants down over his thighs, stopping when they bunched above the knees. We grabbed the cuffs and slid the pant legs over his feet.

I did my best to tent the denim as it moved over the exposed shinbone, but there wasn't enough free material and it dragged. I expected John Scott to howl in pain, but he remained resolutely silent except for the ragged, snorting breaths coming through his nose.

Then the pants were off.

"Oh..." Mel said, and that single word was full of horror and disgust.

The injury was something straight out of a film studio's special effects department, because the sight was so grotesque it couldn't be real, the waxy skin nothing but silicone rubber, the red mush of exposed flesh red-dyed foam.

John Scott's tibia protruded a good four inches from the lipless tear it had made in his skin, bright white, like some colossal, prehistoric tooth. Stringy bits of tendon and ligament clung to the bone while blood pooled in the bed of flesh where it was supposed to be, overflowing down his leg in crisscrossing rivulets. His left sock was soaked red.

John Scott had propped himself on his elbows so he could see. I expected him to be big-eyed and slack-jawed with shock and disgust. Instead his face was a steely mask of ferocious determination, and right then I had a newfound respect for the guy. I don't know how I would have reacted in his situation, but I was sure I wouldn't have managed his level of composure.

"Now what do I do?" I asked him.

"You gotta push the bone back in."

"Just push it?"

"Do it!"

I didn't think you could simply shove a bone back into its fleshy housing. You had to create some sort of traction, stretching the limb taut, so the broken halves of bone didn't overlap each other.

"Nina?" I said over my shoulder. "Nina?"

"Yes?" she said.

"Go get me a clean shirt, any shirt, and the bottle of whiskey. It should be by the fire somewhere."

I heard her hurry off.

"Mel," I said, "get behind John Scott, behind his head."

"Why?"

"Hurry!"

She crouched behind John Scott's head and began telling him he was doing good, he was going to be all right. Nina returned and handed me a pink tee and the bottle of whiskey.

"Okay, listen to me, Mel," I said. "Grab John Scott under his arms, and when I say go, you pull him toward you."

"Why?"

"Just do it!"

She grabbed John Scott beneath the arms. I pressed my knee firmly on his left foot, pinning it in place.

"Okay—go!"

Mel pulled. John Scott cried out. She stopped.

"Keep pulling!" I said.

"He's hurting!"

"You gotta keep pulling. Now—pull!"

She pulled. John Scott bit back the pain this time. When his left leg had stretched as far as the intact muscles would allow, I wrapped my hand in the pink shirt, placed it on top of the shinbone, and shoved the shinbone back into place. John Scott screamed. The bone slid home surprisingly easily.

"Last thing," I said, uncapping the whiskey quickly to keep up the momentum we had created. "This is going to sting. Ready?"

John Scott opened his eyes and looked at his leg mutedly. There was still a huge red weeping gash, but at least there was no bone sticking out.

He nodded.

I poured the alcohol over the wound, using everything that remained in the bottle. John Scott convulsed. A moan escaped his clenched jaws. I wrapped the bloodied shirt around the wound, pressed a tent pole against his lower leg, and fastened the impromptu splint in place with the guy rope.

John Scott flopped onto his back. He was breathing heavily

and dripping with perspiration, but I thought he would be all right.

Part of me was thrilled by our accomplishment, but another part told me not to celebrate prematurely, because successful operation or not, John Scott wasn't going to be doing any walking for a while—which put a major crimp in our exit strategy.

29

RATHER than attempt to move John Scott back to camp, we brought Neil to our new location at the base of the fir so we could keep an eye on him. Then Mel and Nina got busy tending to John Scott's variety of superficial wounds, which were mostly on his face, arms, and torso. Since there was no water or whiskey to clean the cuts with, they mostly applied pressure with yet another T-shirt to stop the bleeding. Bruises invisible before now started to appear all over his body. His right biceps and shoulder had turned a yellowish-brown, while a large purplish area had appeared on his right thigh, where his Calvin Klein boxer shorts ended. I kept an eye on his left leg below the fracture, making sure it didn't become numb, cold, or pale, which might indicate a severed nerve or blood vessel. So far so good, it seemed, as I could distinguish nothing but a slight discoloration and puffiness.

He was damn lucky, I thought, to have fallen from the height he had and survived with only a broken leg, as bad as the break was. Nevertheless, he was far from home free. The risk of infection was possible during any open fracture, especially one that occurred in the wild where there were no proper disinfectants or antibiotics. Moreover, he might be bleeding internally which we were not aware of. Best case scenario then: doctors drive a metal rod down the marrow canal of his tibia and he sets off airport alarms for the rest of his life. Middle case, he gets gangrene and loses the leg. Worst case, he goes into hemorrhagic shock and suffers either brain damage or death.

The bottom line was that we had to get John Scott and Neil to a hospital, pronto. Unfortunately, unless the cavalry hadn't totally bungled things up and were still coming to rescue us, the possibility we get to a hospital any time soon seemed extremely unlikely.

My stomach growled hungrily. It obviously didn't care about anything except getting fed. I swallowed, which was becoming increasingly uncomfortable. The headache continued to throb, only now it would flare up if I moved my head too fast. Although it was still morning, I wanted to close my eyes and drift off into sleep, to get away from all this, but that was not an option.

Mel came over and joined me beneath the pine tree where I had retreated to so I could think about our next move without distractions.

"Hey," she said.

"Hey," I said.

"What are you doing over here?"

"Nothing."

"Do you mind if I sit here with you?"

I shook my head, and she snuggled against me.

"John Scott is doing...okay."

"Good," I said.

"You saved his leg."

"I did what he told me to do."

"It might have gotten infected."

"It still might."

We went quiet.

She said, "I want to go home, Ethan."

"Me too, Mel. Me too." I wrapped an arm around her—and felt something press into my side. I glanced down. "What's in your pocket?" I asked.

She sat up straight again. "My pocket? It's—nothing."

"Mel?"

She was staring at an invisible spot on the ground ahead of her, as if by not acknowledging me I would forget about her. An ostrich with its head stuck in the ground had a better chance of being more inconspicuous.

"Show me," I said, my mind already three steps ahead, trying to guess what she could be hiding. My first suspicion was a phone—but that made no sense.

"It's nothing," she repeated.

"Then show me."

"No."

"I'm not letting you leave until I see what it is."

"Jeez, Ethan! You don't own me."

"You're starting to worry me, Mel. What is it?"

"It's nothing! It's just—it's food. Okay?"

She unzipped her pocket angrily and removed from it a rectangular yellow box. It was a CalorieMate Block, a flavored energy-supplement snack you could find in any Japanese convenience store. I'd tried one years ago solely because they were featured in the *Metal Gear Solid* video game series. The main character, Snake, eats them to keep his stamina up. Made almost entirely of sugar and fat, they likely do boost your stamina, though they taste like dry shortbread.

"Where did you get that?" My tone wasn't accusing...but almost.

"It was in one of the small pockets in my backpack."

"How long have you had it for?"

"I bought it at the Mini Stop."

That wasn't what I meant. "Why didn't you share it with everyone at breakfast?"

"I didn't know I had it then."

"So how long have you known about it?"

"What does it matter, Ethan?"

"It matters because the rest of us have been starving, Mel, that's why."

"No one's been *starving*. People can go weeks without

food."

Maybe it was her insolent tone, or her refusal to fess up to what she'd done, but I snapped. "Neil's *dying*, Mel," I said. "He's thrown up or shit out everything inside him. He doesn't have the strength to stand on his own. Weeks without food? He's not going to last another night. And you've had food the entire time?"

She accomplished the feat of paling and blushing at the same time, her face draining of color except for rosy patches on her cheeks. "I—I just found it this morning, after breakfast."

I took the box from her and shook out the contents. Two of four bar-shaped cookies emerged.

"Were they good?" I asked.

"You can't judge me, Ethan," she said quietly. "You have no right to judge me."

"I'm not judging you," I lied.

"I was so hungry," she said. "I found it this morning, and I was so hungry. I just took a little bit. I was going to share it with everyone, but it tasted so good. And—and I put it back. I was saving it in case someone really needed it."

"Neil needed it," I said.

"Will you stop with Neil! Look at him—he can't eat anything. He'll throw it up again. Then it goes to waste. Like you said, he might not even...he might not even survive."

I stared openly at her. Was I really hearing this? This wasn't the Mel I knew. She had a heart of gold. She always put others first. And now she was hoarding a vital resource and willing to throw Neil to the wolves to appease her hunger?

"Don't look at me like that," she said, and her voice warbled, as if she was on the verge of tears. "Don't do that. It's not my fault. I was hungry. And it was *mine*."

"Enjoy the rest," I said.

"Fuck you, Ethan! You can't judge me. You have no right." The tears began to spill. "You would have done the same thing. If it was yours, you would have done the same thing."

I didn't say anything. I wanted her to go.

"I'm the smallest," she went on. "Everyone's bigger than me. You have more fat reserves—"

"Shut up, Mel. Okay? Just shut up."

She glared at me, biting her lower lip.

"Do you want some?" she asked.

I looked away from her.

"I'll divvy it up now."

"Do what you want."

She took the remaining two cookies from my hand and broke them into four even pieces. "Look—for you, Nina, John Scott, and Neil. I won't have any more."

I stared at the brown chocolate-flavored pieces in her hand.

I said, "Give mine to Neil."

"Don't be—"

"You heard me."

"Right—because you're Mr. Noble." She shoved away from me. "Fuck you, Ethan. Fuck you. I hope you starve."

I watched Mel return to the others and dole out the CalorieMate. I couldn't hear what she was saying—I was a good fifty feet away—but I imagined she was telling them where she'd gotten it from. Then she went to Neil and tried to feed him. Despite what I'd told her about Neil needing food, I didn't think the cookie would do him any good. It would dry his mouth out more than it already was. And even if he somehow swallowed it, he would, as Mel pointed out, likely vomit it up again. Nevertheless, I had been angry at her deception. I had wanted to hurt her.

I rubbed my eyes. *What was happening to me?* It was just a goddamn cookie. We had much more important things to deal with.

I went back to contemplating our next move, and the dilemma that we now had more bodies to evacuate than capable hands to transport them. Because even if we left Ben and Tomo behind, Mel, Nina, and me couldn't carry both John

Scott and Neil. Which meant we remained where we were for yet another night, or we left one of them behind. Staying put, I believed, was out of the question. It had been nearly thirty-six hours since any of us had anything apart from whiskey to drink. Neil, if he survived the night, would be in critical condition. The rest of us would be weak and sluggish. So we had to act, and we had to act now rather than later, while we still had our energy and were thinking clearly. That meant leaving here. But who did we take? Neil or John Scott? Both needed medical attention immediately, so the question became, who needed it *more*?

I heard a snapping sound from somewhere behind me and spun around.

I searched the trees, half expecting to be confronted by a crazy man barreling down on me, but all I saw was green and green and more green.

Deciding what I'd heard had been a falling acorn or pine-cone, I returned my attention to the dilemma at hand.

Neil or John Scott?

It was 2:37 p.m.

I told Mel and Nina I needed help with something back at camp and led them away from John Scott and Neil. When we were out of hearing distance, I stopped and said, "We can't waste any more time. We have to leave now if we're going to have any hope of getting out of the forest by nightfall."

"The three of us can't carry both John and Neil," Mel said. She was stone-faced, and I couldn't tell if she was still bitter because of the way I'd treated her, though I suspected she was.

"That's the problem," I agreed. "And it leaves us with only one option." I hesitated. "We leave one of them behind."

She blinked. "Leave one behind?" She lowered her voice. "There's no way we're leaving anyone behind."

"Yes, I agree," Nina said. "We cannot."

"What other choice do we have?" I said. "Keep waiting

for the police? We have to seriously consider the possibility they're not coming, at least not today. You want to stay another night in this forest with some crazy killer out there?"

Mel chewed her lower lip. Nina pulled compulsively at a lock of her hair.

"It's not right," Mel said softly.

I held up my hands. "If you have any better suggestions, I'm open for them, please."

"One of us can go," she said. "You, me, or Nina. It'll be faster, just one person—"

"I've thought of that. But there's no way I'm letting you or Nina, or even both of you, run off on your own with this guy in the forest. Nor am I leaving you two behind."

"So you won't leave us, but you'll leave Neil or John?"

"What the fuck do you want me to do, Mel?" I said, the last of my patience gone. "I wouldn't leave anyone behind if it could be helped, but it can't. Now, if we get lucky, and get out of here quickly, we could be back within a matter of hours."

"And if we're not lucky? If we get lost?"

"They will die," Nina stated. "At least Neil will. He is already dying."

"Exactly," I said. "Neil's dying. Whether we stay here, doing nothing, or we attempt to leave and get lost, he's a goner. Our only hope is we *don't* get lost. We get out of here. We bring help back."

"How do we find the way back here?" Nina asked.

"We'll make a trail. Two of us will carry the litter, the third will leave a trail of branches or something."

"How do we decide which way to go?" Mel said.

"I'm going to climb the tree," I said.

"*You* will?"

"It's the only way."

"You're scared of heights!"

"Mel, unless you want to climb the fucking tree, then quit it, because there are no other options—"

A loud noise cut me off midsentence. Nina sprang straight

to her feet while Mel and I made it into half crouches—a freeze frame of three people about to run for their lives.

"What the hell was that?" I whispered. It had sounded like someone banging a baseball bat against the trunk of a tree.

No one replied.

I grabbed my spear, which was beside me.

Knock-knock-knock.

I started toward the banging, wondering what I was doing. My spear seemed absurdly insubstantial. What if the guy had a pistol or machete or crossbow—

KNOCK-KNOCK.

I stopped in my tracks and almost melted with relief.

Twenty feet up the trunk of a nearby cypress was a bright green woodpecker. Its gray head swiveled toward me, revealing a red mustache and yellow bill. The head ticked this way and that, then returned its attention to the hole it was excavating.

Knock-knock-knock.

I pointed and said, "It's just a woodpecker." I wanted to laugh, but my nerves were too jacked up.

"I will kill it!" Nina said, stepping out from behind the tree where she had hid. "It almost gave me a heart attack."

Mel picked up a small branch and threw it, though it came nowhere close to the bird. "So there *is* life in here," she said.

"I saw a deer too," I admitted.

"When?"

"This morning, right after I woke up."

"Why didn't you tell us?"

"You were still sleeping. Then we realized Tomo was missing..." I shrugged. The deer didn't matter. "Anyway, look, it's already three o'clock. We're running out of time. We have to get going."

"We cannot abandon someone!" Nina said stubbornly.

"Christ, Nina, are you listening? There is no choice! If we stay here, Neil's going to die, then John Scott, then us. Yeah, us too. You think you feel bad now? Imagine how you'll feel this time tomorrow without any water? That's if we don't find you hanging somewhere in the morning."

She blanched. I shook my head.

"I'm sorry, Nina. But every second we waste debating this is a second less daylight we have. Okay? So the question isn't whether we stay or not. We *are* leaving. The question is: who do we take with us?"

"I suppose you want to leave John then?" Mel said.

"I think Neil's condition is more critical."

"You don't want to take John because you don't like him."

"My personal feelings have absolutely nothing to do with any of this right now."

"I want to take John then."

"Now you're choosing based on emotion."

"I am not."

"Then tell me why we should take John Scott over Neil?"

"John's in pain. Neil's not. And we don't know how bad John's leg is. It's still bleeding. If his blood pressure drops too much he can pass out or go into cardiac arrest."

"Nina?" I said.

"I will not choose."

"Stop fucking around, Nina! John Scott or Neil?"

Her eyes brimmed with tears, and I didn't think she would answer. Then, very softly, she said, "John Scott. I think we should take John Scott."

"Why?" I asked.

"He's younger," she said simply.

I wanted to argue with them, tell them they were making a mistake, they were risking Neil's life, but we had to leave. The choice had been made.

I went to explain to Neil what we were doing while Mel explained to John Scott. Neil's skin was papery, his mouth slightly open. He made that wet, phlegmy sound with each brittle breath.

"Hey, Neil. It's Ethan. Can you hear me?"

He didn't respond.

"Neil. You hear me?"

He opened his eyes, stared vacantly at me for a moment, then closed them again.

"Listen," I said. "John Scott's had an accident. He fell from a tree. His leg is pretty bad. Anyway, we're going to take him out of here right now so he can get some help. But then we're going to come straight back for you. Do you hear me? We're coming straight back."

He didn't respond.

"It might get dark," I went on. "But you'll be fine. Just stay beneath your sleeping bag. And don't go anywhere. This is the most important thing. Don't go anywhere at all, otherwise we might not be able to find you."

I didn't think Neil had the strength to go even a dozen feet in any given direction, but I wanted to make sure he stayed put if he experienced a miraculous recovery while we were gone.

"Neil? You hear me?"

He didn't respond.

I found his hand beneath the sleeping bag and gave it a squeeze. "I'll see you soon."

I got up and went over to the others. Mel seemed to be arguing with John Scott.

"What's going on?" I asked.

"John's not thinking clearly,' Mel said. "He wants us to take Neil."

I looked at John Scott in utter surprise.

"He's worse off than me," he said, his voice firm. "I can manage on my own for a night."

"Don't be a fool, John," Mel said. "You'll bleed to death if you don't—"

"Then you better stop dicking around and get a move on."

"We're not going to—"

"You heard me."

"John—"

"*This is my choice!*" he snapped, and that ferocious determination was back in his face. "My fucking choice. Okay, Mel? Mine. Not yours. End of discussion."

For a moment Mel seemed about to defy John Scott's altruistic assertion of free will, but the blaze in his eyes—a cocktail of intensity and pain and resolution—made her reconsider.

"Yo, Ethos?" he said, turning those feverish eyes on me.

"Yeah?" I said.

"You really going to climb that tree?"

"Yeah."

He nodded in what might have been approval. "Don't fuck up."

30

WE stood at the bottom of the fir John Scott had attempted to climb, looking up, way up. He fell from it, yes, but it was still the best candidate around. This time Nina made the stirrup with her hands, and with Mel pushing me up by my rear, I was able to surmount the lowest branch on my first attempt.

I raised myself into a semi-stance, holding onto nearby branches to brace myself. The trunk was a foot from my face. It was thick and scaly with deep furrows and scarred with resin blisters. These emitted a sharp, spicy odor that mixed with the rosemary aroma from the matte-green needle leaves.

I began to climb.

From the ground looking up the branches had appeared to grow evenly from the trunk in a ring-like fashion. But it quickly became apparent they were produced in a series of whorls, spiraling upward. I might be a big guy, but like John Scott I was fairly agile and able to bend in and out of the branches to progress at a decent pace. My hands quickly became sticky with resin while several small twines protruding from the branches like nails punctured my flesh, drawing blood. I noticed all kinds of gnarls, knots, holes, and other imperfections in the bark that had been invisible from far away, and for whatever reason these made me think of the old red oak I used to climb as a kid back in Wisconsin. I had spent hours at a time in the oak, collecting acorns to use as weapons against imaginary intruders, peeling back bark to watch the metallic blue and green shield bugs go about their business, or just gazing at the panoramic view of my family's fifty acres and the Victorian farmhouse on the horizon, all gingerbread, turrets, gables, and shingles.

Before I knew it I had ascended at least forty feet through the forest understory. I wasn't sure because I refused to look down. In fact, I didn't look up either. I focused only on the branches within my immediate vicinity, making sure to carefully spread my weight among four separate ones at any given time, pushing with my legs rather than pulling with my arms to save strength and energy. It helped, I found, to visualize Spider-Man climbing a glass building, left hand/right foot, right hand/left foot, over and over.

Up until this point I'd felt relatively safe. The branches were solid, and they cradled me within their embrace. Yet once I approached sixty feet or so they began to thin out in both volume and thickness—and my fear of heights kicked in. I suddenly second-guessed what I was doing. This was not natural. I was not a fucking monkey. And even though I wasn't looking down, I nonetheless was hit by an extreme wave of vertigo. This created the sensation of spinning, throwing my balance off.

Abruptly terrified I was going to fall, I hugged the trunk of the tree with both arms and waited for the symptoms to pass.

"Ethan?" Mel shouted, her voice small and concerned. "Are you okay?"

"Yeah!" I called back. My chest was so tight I barely got the word out, and even had I wanted to elaborate I wouldn't have been able to.

For a good minute I remained frozen in place. My heart was pounding, I was breathing too fast, and all I could think was: *I'm stuck. Fuck going any farther. I can't get back down. I'm stuck up here.*

I tried to tell myself this was all in my head. I'd gotten this far without problems. I could keep going. But this failed to psych me up. The vice-like grip of fear had paralyzed every inch of my body and wouldn't let go.

"Ethan?" Mel shouted. "What's wrong?"

I opened my mouth but my tongue felt thick and I couldn't respond.

"Ethan!"

"Resting!" I managed.

My breathing continued much too fast. I felt a numbness in my lips. I figured this was because my cheek was pressed hard against the trunk, then I realized the tingling was also in my hands and feet.

Was I hyperventilating?

What if I fainted?

I closed my eyes and tried to forget where I was. I told myself I was in the red oak on the farm, only ten feet up, no biggie, I could jump down if I wanted. I thought of the warm summer afternoon when I had spent hours in the tree flipping through the May 1987 issue of *Playboy* magazine I'd discovered hidden away at the bottom of Gary's box of baseball cards. I had been looking for a Kenny Griffey Jr. rookie card to trade with my friend Danny Spalding, who said he would give me one of his GI Joes for it, but instead of Kenny Griffey Jr. I found Vanna White staring up at me. This was the first time I had seen nude photographs of a woman—and a famous one at that—and I tore free a half-naked picture of Vanna White sitting at a window, hid it in the metal tackle box in which I kept all my other favorite stuff, and returned the magazine to the bottom of the box of baseball cards before dinner.

Gary realized the picture was missing a week later, but he couldn't tell our parents on me unless he wanted to admit his pubescent fascination with naked women. Instead he strolled into my room one evening and in his affable way told me he knew I had the picture and wanted it back. When I denied taking it, he wrestled me to the carpeted floor and put me in the Million Dollar Dream, a submission move Ted DiBiase had used on the Macho Man Randy Savage in Wrestlemania IV's main event. But when I wouldn't submit he got creative and began pulling my hair out one strand at a time while telling me it wouldn't grow back and I'd go bald—

"Ethan!" It was Mel again. "Come down right now! You're scaring me!"

I blinked, remembering where I was.

"Why aren't you moving?"

Jesus bleeding Christ, *move*! I told myself.

I released the trunk and gripped a branch above my head with my left hand. I felt around with my right foot for a new purchase, found one twenty inches higher than the last, and eased myself upward, my stomach brushing the rough trunk.

I continued in this fashion for another ten feet, then fifteen, then twenty-five. Mel and Nina encouraged me from below. I barely heard them. Their voices seemed a million miles away right then. I had one thought on my mind only.

Climb.

As I progressed the branches became thinner still, so much so they bent beneath my weight. This freaked me out, but I had come too far to turn around: I was almost above the canopy.

To my left, a broken branch was intertwined with a live one. The end where it had snapped off was pulpy and jagged. This would be the branch John Scott had broken. I saw him falling, toppling ass over tits on an express trip to the ground...and I pressed onward and upward.

Soon I came to the severed limb. It jutted two dozen inches from the trunk. Moving as deliberately as a mime feigning slow motion, I inched up another ten feet. The crown of the fir had begun to narrow into a conical shape, and the branches had reduced in density enough I could finally see through them—and the view took my breath away. An emerald landscape stretched away to the horizon. Honda had said Jukai translated to "Sea of Trees," and now I knew why—

The branch beneath my left foot gave way with a sickening crack. My foot plummeted. I kicked wildly until it landed on another branch.

Mel and Nina were yelling at me. I wanted to tell them to shut up, but my heart was pounding out of control, and I had no breath.

Mt. Fuji, I noticed, was not ahead of me. I turned my head slowly to the left, afraid that even the simplest shift of weight could send me to my grave. Not there. I rotated it to the right. Nadda.

Behind me?

Wrapping my arms around the trunk—it had narrowed to the circumference of a utility pole—I turned and saw Fuji directly behind me. It seemed to be impossibly far away, one of those distance shots you see on postcards.

Nevertheless, that didn't matter. All we needed to know was the direction, because then we could figure the way back to the parking lot.

I marked the direction of the mountain with a couple of nearby pines, so even if I got disorientated on the way down I would know the correct way we had to travel.

I was about to begin my descent when I noticed, perhaps two miles away, three at the most, a curlicue of gray smoke trickling up through the canopy.

31

THE climb down was just as harrowing as the climb up had been, only with each branch I passed I was comforted by the thought I was getting closer to the ground.

I remained facing the trunk the entire way, and soon I was back to sixty feet, then forty, then twenty. Then, thank God, I stood on the lowest branch, a paltry ten feet from the ground. Nina and Mel were directly below while John Scott was a few feet away, where he had crash landed, laying with his head on his rucksack, watching me.

"I am never, ever letting you do that again!" Mel said. "I was scared half to death."

"Piece of cake," I said, sitting on the branch, dangling my feet.

"Did you see Fuji?"

"That way." I pointed toward one of the large pines I had made a mental note of.

"Excellent, Ethan!" Nina exclaimed.

I shoved my butt off the branch, hung by my hands for a few seconds, then dropped to the ground. My legs, overcome from the exertion I had put them through, and still a little weak with fear, gave out completely. I collapsed to my knees, then keeled over and lay on my side, inhaling the smell of rotten leaves, never so glad to feel solid earth beneath me.

"So if Fuji is that way," Mel said, computing to herself, "then the parking lot is…" She turned on the spot and pointed. "That way."

"Hold on," I said, and sat up. "I saw something else."

Mel and Nina frowned down at me. John Scott propped himself up on his elbows.

"Smoke," I said. "Nearby. Maybe a couple miles away."

"Smoke?" Nina said. "Like a forest fire?"

I shook my head. "Like a campfire."

"Where?" Mel said quickly.

I indicated the opposite direction of Fuji.

"Who do you think—" She cut herself off.

"It could just be hikers," I said.

"Hikers aren't stupid enough to hike in this forest."

"We did."

"We were stupid."

"Someone who…" John Scott started, then stopped. It was obvious speaking had become an effort for him. "Someone who came here…to commit suicide."

"What does it matter who it is?" Nina said. "We are not going that way, yes?"

"I'm wondering if we should go check," I said.

Mel looked at me like I was crazy. "We have our own problems right now, Ethan. We don't have time to go try talking someone else out of suicide."

"He might have a phone."

Silence.

"We can keep it powered on until the police track it this time," I added. "It will be a lot faster than us walking out and walking back in. Not to mention we don't have to leave anyone behind. John Scott will remain here with Neil. We'll bring the phone back and stick together."

"What if whoever it is doesn't have a phone?" Mel said.

"Everyone in Japan has a phone. Someone coming out here, whether it's a hiker or a suicide, will have brought theirs in case they got lost or changed their mind about killing themselves. And if it's the guy who killed Ben and Tomo, well—he has our phones, right?"

Mel said, "You're just going to ask him, 'Hey, can we get our phones back to call the cops on you for killing our friends?'"

"We overpower him and take them. There will be three of us. We have the spears. And he won't be expecting us."

"What if he has a gun?" Nina said.

"Guns are illegal in Japan and pretty much impossible to get. Besides, if he did have one, he could have simply stormed our camp and shot us all. Instead he's been hiding out until night and sneaking up on us one by one. That tells me he likely doesn't have any weapon at all."

"Do it," John Scott grunted.

Mel and Nina exchanged glances, equal parts desperation and fortitude.

"*Do it*," John Scott repeated.

"Okay," Mel said grudgingly.

"Okay," Nina said a moment later.

NINA and Mel gave John Scott a peck on the cheek, and Mel promised him we'd be back soon. I didn't want to shake his hand, knowing it would be awkward, but I didn't think I should leave without saying anything, so I told him to hang tough, which sounded fatuous and condescending, though that was not my intent.

Then we started off, unaware that this would be a one-way trip from which none of us would be returning.

32

DESPITE Ben and Tomo decaying beneath their sleeping bags, despite Neil holding onto life by a thread and John Scott facing the possibility of amputation and internal hemorrhaging, despite the fact we were still trapped in the most terrifying place I have ever been, despite all of the darkness that had stolen into our lives—invited, if you believe we'd brought it upon ourselves—a tiny kernel of hope burned inside me. We were moving. Finally, we were moving. We had been at the campsite for forty-eight hours. Forty-eight hours in any one spot can make you go stir crazy. Add a lack of food and water and everything that had happened and it can make you go asylum crazy. I was exhausted, ill-tempered, dehydrated, jumpy, and scared witless. One more night doing nothing except thinking about death and dying and a lurking killer likely would have pushed me over the edge. So moving was good. It gave me hope. We had a plan. We were going to get through this. We were almost at the end.

The little light that penetrated the canopy was an otherworldly bluish-gray. It permeated the understory unevenly, creating a disconcerting mismatch of floating shadows and emerald foliage. I wasn't sure if it was my imagination, but the trees seemed even more dense and overcrowded here than they had been anywhere earlier, many growing so close together we would often have to turn sideways to slip between them. There were also more herbaceous plants, ferns, and shrubs, which we could do nothing about but raise our arms and plow straight through.

The farther we went the more anarchic the scenery became. We passed beneath a vine as thick as my leg that at one point in the past had looped itself around a tree several times, only now the tree had died and decayed, leaving the vine suspended in the air like a giant spring. One medium-sized pine, defying the rules of nature, had grown in the form of a horseshoe, almost as if it had decided it did not like the world it found itself in and tried to return to the safe haven belowground. So much deadfall was strewn around the base and the doubled over crown you couldn't tell where the tree began or ended.

Every minute or two we would stop, scavenge a couple dead branches, and place an X-shaped marker on the ground so we would be able to find our way back again.

The feeling of isolation, of traversing some forbidden corner of the globe, was so extreme I was caught off guard when we came across yet another ribbon. It was blue and intersected our path at a ninety-degree angle. We expressed mild surprise at seeing it, but otherwise forged on. We had a mission to complete. There was no longer time for melancholic reflections.

My thoughts turned to the encounter that awaited us. It was going to be more complicated than I had initially assumed, because it would be impossible to know from a distance whether the person at the campfire was a harmless hiker, a suicide, or the killer himself. This meant we couldn't simply sneak up and whack him on the head while he was sleeping. We'd have to first confront him, which was not ideal. Killer or not, he might panic and flee. And if he didn't, and he wasn't wearing a T-shirt that read "The Aokigahara Murderer," how were we supposed to determine his guilt or innocence? If he was uncooperative and refused to lend us his phone, or said he didn't have one, did we forcibly search him and his belongings—even if he was an innocent person?

Yes, I thought. *That's exactly what we'll do.* This was an emergency, martial law declared, fuck civil rights.

By five o'clock the sun had begun to set behind the veil of clouds, and what little light the forest allowed quickly faded to darkness. I guessed we had traveled two miles already—two miles in one hour. It wouldn't win any races, but it was acceptable given the obstacle-laden terrain. Still, if my calculations were even somewhat accurate, this left us with possibly one more mile to go. This worried me, because soon we would be walking blind. What if we had strayed off course? What if the campfire had been put out? What then? We would no longer have a beacon to home in on. We would have to turn back and return to John Scott and Neil with nothing to show for our efforts except a wasted few hours.

I banished these thoughts. We had made our decision, we had to stand by it, and we would succeed.

We had to succeed.

I picked up a large stick, then a second smaller one. I knelt and placed another X on the ground. Then I turned around and waited for Nina and Mel to catch up. They trudged up to me, panting.

"We can't be too far away now," I said.

"How much longer do you think?" Mel asked.

"Less than a mile. It will likely be dark before we reach the campfire. But that will work to our advantage. We'll be more difficult to detect while the fire will be easier to see."

"I am so thirsty," Nina said.

"There might be water there," I said. "But listen, we're going to have to keep quiet from here on in. Try to tread lightly. Sound carries."

"So we just sneak up on him?" Mel asked.

"When we get close enough to see his setup, we'll make the call. If he's sitting at his fire, we might have to wait until he returns to his tent so we can corner him there."

"How will we know if he's the killer?"

"Hopefully we'll be able to tell."

"That's it? That's the plan?" Mel said doubtfully.

"We'll question him. Read it on his face."

"He might be a good actor."

"If he's just some regular guy, he would have no reason not to lend us a phone."

"And if he refuses?"

"Then it's probably the killer, and I'll search him. You two just make sure he doesn't make a break for it. Got it?"

They nodded tentatively, and we continued on. The shadows lengthened and thickened, layer upon layer, playing tricks with my eyes again. Then, in the span of minutes, the shadows bled together into an undivided stretch of night. I could barely see a few feet in front of me. I didn't want to turn on the flashlight for fear of giving away our approach, but we didn't have a choice.

I took it from my pocket and flicked it on.

Even with the light the dense vegetation kept us moving at a snail's pace, but I refused the impulse to press recklessly ahead. Our footsteps already seemed extra loud in the darkness, and I once more cautioned Mel and Nina to try to make less noise.

Suddenly Nina said, "What's that? Over there."

I swung the beam back to where it had been a moment before.

"See it?"

"See what?" I said quietly.

She pointed. After a moment I thought I could make out flowers marking what appeared to be another gravesite. It was perhaps twenty feet away.

"It doesn't matter," I told her. "We need to keep going."

"Wait—I think there's a bottle," Mel said. "What if it contains water?"

The temptation was too great to pass up and we detoured —but not before placing another marker. We weren't taking any chances with wandering off target.

It turned out Mel was right: there was a bottle. Unfortunately it was filled not with water but shōchū. Alongside the dried and long-dead flowers was a silver-framed photograph of a young couple in their mid-thirties. They were both wearing eyeglasses, both smiling, both seemingly in love and happy about their futures together.

There were no scattered personal belongings, and I assumed what had once littered the ground had been cleaned up by the surviving spouse in the picture. He or she must have asked whoever discovered the body to guide them back so they could leave the memorial, just as family members and friends leave roadside crosses, handwritten signs, or personal mementos to commemorate the site where a loved one perished in a car accident.

Then again, I thought somberly, maybe it was a double suicide.

I took the shōchū and stuck it in my pocket, explaining that we could use it to sterilize John Scott's wounds later.

We made our way back to the path—but couldn't find the marker.

I was sure I was standing on the spot where I had placed it.

"Where's the cross?" I said.

Mel and Nina studied the ground in confusion.

"I don't see it," Mel said.

"It couldn't just disappear," I said.

"Are you sure you placed one here?"

"One hundred percent."

From somewhere in the darkness a branch cracked.

"Did you hear that?" Mel whispered.

I nodded, realized she couldn't see me, and said, "Yeah." I swung the flashlight in the direction of the noise. There was nothing there.

"What was it?" Nina said.

"Just an animal," I told them. "Come on."

We continued onward, but I was suddenly feeling extremely vulnerable. What if we were not the hunters, as we imagined we were, but still the hunted? What if the killer had been watching us the entire time we climbed the tree? What if he'd slaughtered Neil and John Scott after we'd left and now had come for us?

Stop it, I told myself. *Stop jumping to conclusions. It's just some nocturnal rodent, a wood mouse or—*

Another crack.

I froze. So did Mel and Nina.

Then Nina said in a skeletal hiss: "That was a footstep."

"No, it wasn't," I told her.

"Yes, it was!"

My heart was pounding, the hand holding the flashlight sweating.

Get a grip, Ethan. Get a grip. There are three of us. We have spears. We can take the fucker down. Nothing's changed. We're still in control.

I directed the flashlight's white beam toward where the noise had originated.

Nothing but ghostly trees.

"Told you," I said.

"Shhh," Mel said.

A loud crack-snap on the other side of us.

I spun around, jerking the beam with me. The light danced in and out of the trees, almost giving the branches and leaves the illusion of movement.

Nina screamed.

"*What?*" I said. "What is it?"

Nina continued to scream.

I had no idea what was going on, but I was filled with crazed terror. *Something* was happening. Something bad.

What had Nina seen?

"Nina!" I said. "Quiet!"

She clamped her mouth closed.

"What is it?" Mel asked. "What did you see?"

Nina merely stared at the trees, unresponsive. *Scared to death* came to mind.

Was she about to keel over in cardiac arrest?

Was she injured?

I turned the light on her, half expecting to see a bloody arrow protruding from her chest. She appeared physically okay.

"There!" Mel hissed, pointing into the darkness.

I aimed the flashlight. "Where?"

"I saw something move—there!"

I followed her finger, sweeping the flashlight back and forth with quick, jumpy movements. "What was it, Mel? What did you see?"

"I don't know!"

Movement behind us. We all whirled around.

Mel inhaled sharply. Nina croaked. I couldn't breathe.

I felt as if I had stepped into a waking nightmare, a world where the impossible was possible. Whatever inner barrier my adult mind had erected to separate reality from fantasy vanished in a heartbeat, and through it flooded a knowledge so dark and cold and inconceivable it left me numb and full of a funereal bleakness.

Illuminated in the white light was a pale, androgynous face peeking out from behind a tree trunk, the onyx-black eyes staring at us with fiendish indifference. Long black hair fell past the shoulders and blended with the night. The thin mouth curled into a smile.

Mel screamed. Nina screamed. I screamed.

This is what it's like to go crazy, I was thinking, only it wasn't me thinking this, couldn't be, because the voice was far too calm to belong to me. *This is how it happens, all at once. Don't worry. It doesn't hurt. It will be over soon enough.*

I could almost feel my sanity tearing away from my body, fleeing from this horror even when I couldn't move.

—you're right, it doesn't hurt, doesn't hurt at all—

I took a step forward. I had to. I was sinking into oblivion and I had to move or I was lost. We were no longer screaming, I realized. My ears were ringing, and now I was thinking, *Why are we just standing here? We have to run, get away, before it gets one of us!*

I took another step, impossibly slow, my leg as heavy as concrete—

Nina yelped.

I spun toward her just in time to see her vanish into the thick vegetation. She didn't run. She was dragged or carried away. It happened so fast all I glimpsed was a flash of gray and then—nothing. She was gone.

"Nina!" I shouted.

The only reply was the rustle of the foliage as she was taken deeper into the forest.

"*What was that?*" Mel blurted from beside me, her voice cracking on *that*. "What happened to Nina? *What was that?* Is she *dead*?"

"I don't know," I whispered.

"It was a ghost!"

Was it? I wondered. Could it have been—?

No. Whatever it was had shape and substance.

I *heard* it.

So it was real. It was a person. It had to be.

"Ethan..." Mel moaned. She had turned away from me. I turned too—it seemed incredibly difficult to do even that—and played the flashlight beam amongst the wraithlike trees. I couldn't see anything, but I heard more movement. The whoosh of leaves, the rustle of saplings. The noises seemed to be coming from all around us.

Then I spotted a gray-clad form. It slipped from one tree trunk to the next incredibly fast. As I tried to follow its movement, I caught a glimpse of another, and another, each visible for only a moment before melting back into the blackness.

There were several of them out there.

And they had us surrounded.

"What do you want?" I said in a loud, challenging voice as I turned in a tight circle, searching the trees. Mel was glued to my back, moving with me.

"My foressssttttt," a gravelly voice floated from the dark.

I stiffened. *Was that the same voice I heard on my phone two nights ago?* I was sure it was. But how could these people have gotten my number? Could they have somehow retrieved Mel's phone from the crevice? My number would have been at the top of the call log list. So had they been following us even then? Had they been watching Nina and me smoke the joint?

Had they watched me answer the phone?

"You in my forrrreesssssstttttt."

Closer? Farther?

I couldn't tell.

"We're leaving," I said. "Okay? We're leaving."

"You in my foresssstttt. You dieeeeeeeee."

Finally I spied the speaker. He was perhaps twenty feet away. A spectral figure standing tall between two trees. In his hand a blade glinted sharply.

Mel, presumably seeing this too, tugged me so hard I almost fell over backward.

"Run," I instructed her under my breath. "Don't stop."

"What are you going to do?"

"I'll be right behind you—now go!"

I heard her take off. I remained facing the speaker, wanting to give her a head start.

Then I turned and fled as well.

I only made it two-dozen feet before an icy pain spread throughout my back. I staggered to my knees, regained my feet clumsily, and continued forward, all the while reaching over my shoulder for the dagger I knew was stuck in my back.

My fingers touched the handle. It was below my left shoulder bone. The blade had gone straight through Mel's backpack, which had likely protected me somewhat. I gripped the handle tightly and yanked hard. I grunted and almost blacked out, but the jolt lasted for only a moment.

I knew I couldn't keep running. If I did, I would get another dagger in the back. I whirled about, holding the bloody weapon high in front of me.

Three pursuers were directly behind me. They appeared almost identical to one another. Gray robes, black eyes, black hair falling in tangles around ephemeral faces. I was shocked to discover they were young, teenagers only, though they were lean and muscular and didn't appear to have an ounce of fat shared between them.

They stopped now, as if we were playing a life-or-death game of Red Light Green Light.

Then, without a word, they began spreading out, slinking silently from tree to tree, apparently intent on flanking me. I shone the flashlight from one to the other, following their progress, not wanting them to get out of my direct field of vision.

"Stop!" I shouted, needing to buy some time.

Amazingly they did.

"Do you speak English?"

They stared at me, their pale faces almost glowing in the harsh beam of the flashlight. They didn't seem fazed in the least that I was bigger than them, or that I was holding a bloody dagger in my hand and had several spears poking from my backpack, within quick reach.

I didn't blame them either. It was three against one. I was injured and weak from hunger and thirst.

"English?" I said. "You spoke it before. Can you understand me?"

They began moving again.

"Stop!"

They didn't obey this time.

I swung the beam back and forth. They were fanning out too quickly. I would be surrounded in seconds.

I aimed the light directly in the eyes of the tallest one, then launched the dagger at him. The blade deflected off his shoulder and spun away into the night.

Nevertheless, the blow knocked him down, and the other two moved to his aide.

I shuffled backward, never taking my eyes off them, and

only when I'd put several trees between us did I feel safe enough to turn around.

In the distance Mel began screaming.

33

THE flashlight beam bobbed madly ahead of me. Branches raked my face. I didn't care or feel any pain, not even the wound in my back.

Mel continued to scream, and I tried not to think what was happening to her.

I don't know how long I ran for, or how far I'd gone. This would require some sort of analytical reasoning, numbers, mathematics. And none of that existed right then. I was too jacked up, too in the moment.

I had never before experienced the desperation that drove me right then. If a sheer-sided canyon appeared directly before me, I probably would have plunged right off it, for in control now was one overriding directive: FIND MEL! And below this, repeating over and over like the tickertape at the bottom of a Breaking News report: *There're more of them, she's going to die, there're more of them, she's going to die...*

I could almost accept my death. I could see me falling, the teenagers catching up, smashing my skull in, the blackness that would ferry me away. This I could almost accept in a detached, nihilistic way because I have seen myself grow old, I have contemplated my own mortality, and I have come to understand that one day I'm going to die. But I've never envisioned Mel's mortality or death. Never, not once. I've always seen her as she is now: youthful, beautiful, full of life. She couldn't die. It was unfathomable.

How was this happening?

I realized I was praying, praying I found Mel, praying she was okay, praying we got out of this, got away. I didn't know what I was praying to, didn't care, but I was praying to something bigger than me.

Then, all at once, I came upon a scene from hell. A writhing mass of gray robes and hands and feet piled high in a football scrimmage—and Mel's legs sticking out from the bottom, kicking at nothing.

One of the attackers reared up with a large rock in his hand and raised it over his head. For a moment bodies parted and I glimpsed Mel's face, stormy eyed and terrified.

"Stop!" I roared without slowing, running straight at the throng, consumed with an insane rage. I was going to destroy them, every last one of them, I was going to beat them to puddles of blood, or I was going to die trying.

But they dispersed before I could reach them, escaping effortlessly into the trees, leaving Mel curled into a protective ball on the ground, still kicking at nothing.

I scooped her into my arms. She screamed and hit me.

"Mel!" I shouted. "It's me!"

She stared at me, deer-like.

I carried her in an arbitrary direction until she regained her wits and could move on her own. We ran. Arms swinging, legs bounding uncoordinatedly, we were staggering parodies of two kids being chased by the biggest, meanest dog on the block.

Soon we were both panting for breath, lurching as if moving through snow or shallow water, but we didn't stop. Because even though we had gotten away, I didn't think it was over. Those teens would regroup. They would come after us again. They would—

In the distance I saw a glow flickering in and out between the trees.

The campfire?

"Look!" Mel cried ecstatically.

"I see it!" I said.

We redoubled our efforts.

34

I had been wrong all along. There was no campfire awaiting us. No tent. No hiker, no suicide guy, no killer. For ahead of us was an old, roughly built cabin with a wood exterior. My eyes took in everything at once—the weathered bench out front, the chopping block with an ax lodged into the top surface, the saw leaning against a neatly stacked woodpile—then we were clambering up the front stoop. Mel reached the door first and began pounding her fist against it, shouting for whoever was inside to open up. I was about to try the handle when the door swung open.

A clean-shaven man in his fifties appeared. He was wearing beige khaki pants, a brown leather belt, and a mustard-colored button-down shirt. He raised bushy white eyebrows in surprise and said something in Japanese, a question, I think.

I shoved Mel past him, then I followed, slamming the door closed behind us.

THE interior of the cabin was a spartan affair and smelled faintly of wax and creosote and soot. Aside from a scuffed table and two chairs, the only other furnishing was a wood cooking stove. Basic foodstuff, mostly instant noodles and canned goods, were visible in an open-faced cupboard. A pot and pan and dishes rested on a short counter, while a broom and dustpan hung on the wall. There was no sink, which implied no running water. Nor were there any electric lights or wall sockets. The light that had guided us here had been provided by the crackling blaze in the stone fireplace to our left and several large candles the size of cookie jars.

I went immediately to the lone window and looked out. I could see little aside from the floating red reflections made by the candle flames.

The man had a look of astonishment on his face. He'd likely never entertained company here before, let along two crazed foreigners acting as if they had just seen the devil himself.

"Do you speak English?" I asked him. I wiped a shaking hand across my lips, which were velvet dry. My chest was still so tight it hurt to breathe, and I couldn't stop glancing at the door and window.

Mel slumped into one of the chairs and cradled her head in her hands and stared mutely at the table.

"English?" I repeated harshly. "Do you speak English?"

He blinked. "Yes—no. *Skoshi*." He pinched his forefinger and thumb together. His posture was stooped, and I couldn't decide if he was cowering or permanently bowing.

"There are—there are some people in the forest. They attacked us."

"People?" he repeated.

"Kids!" Mel cried, still staring at a spot on the table.

"Kids?"

"An entire group of them," I said. "Pale faces, long black hair. They attacked us. Our friend is still out there. She's badly hurt. We need your phone. Do you have a phone?"

"Phone?"

"A phone! We need to call the police."

"Police?"

What the fuck was wrong with the guy? I grabbed him by his shirt and shouted, "*Where is your damn phone?*"

"Phone? No phone."

I stared at him in disbelief, then realized I had no idea why he was out here, in this cabin. I released him, stepped back, studied his clothes. I couldn't tell whether it was some sort of uniform or not. "Are you a forest ranger?"

"Ranger, *hai*." He attempted an uncertain smile.

"How do you keep in touch?"

He looked at me blankly.

"Talk? Base? Other rangers? Talk?"

He shook his head.

I glanced around the room. There was a door opposite the wood stove. I went to it, threw it open. A bedroom. Next to a twin bed, on a small table, was a handheld two-way radio.

I felt as if I'd just fallen in love.

"Hey!" I said. "You! Come here."

Both he and Mel came over.

"A walkie-talkie!" Mel exclaimed.

I gripped the man's arm and pointed to the radio. "You call help. Okay?"

"Help, *hai*."

"Tell them my friends are dead."

"Friends?"

"*Tomodachi*, dead." I drew a hand across my throat. "You call. Okay?" I made a phone with my pinky and thumb. "You call. Get help."

"Me call."

"You don't understand a fucking word I'm saying, do you?"

He looked at me blankly.

Cursing, I crossed the room to the radio, deciding I was going have to call the base station myself and hope to hell whoever answered could do more than parrot everything I said.

The ranger followed me and took my arm just as I picked up the radio. He shook his head. "I call," he said. "Help. Okay?"

"Yes, yes, yes!" I shoved the radio at him. "Call."

He twisted a knob, depressed the push-to-talk button, and said something in Japanese. He released the button and waited. There was a burst of static, then someone replied.

Mel squawked with joy.

The ranger and the dispatcher spoke back and forth for less than a minute. I listened closely, trying and failing to identify certain words that might give me some clue as to what they were saying. Finally he set the radio back down on the table.

He nodded. "Help, okay."

"How long?" Mel asked quickly.

"Long?"

I tapped my wristwatch. "Time. How long? Help?"

He held up one finger.

"One hour?" I said.

"One hour, *hai*."

"How will they get here so fast?" Mel asked. "Is there a road? Ask him if there's a road."

I pulled open the top drawer in the table and discovered a small stenographer's notepad and a sharpened pencil. I drew a quick map of the area, including Mt. Fuji, the town of Kawaguchiko, Lake Saiko, Aokigahara Jukai, and our position, which I marked with an X.

It took a few minutes of prodding and clarification, but eventually I determined that the cabin was accessible by a dual combination of access road and hiking trail.

Mel and I embraced, almost sinking into one another, while the ranger watched us with a perplexed expression.

35

"YOU can't go back," Mel said to me. "What if they're still out there?"

We were seated at the table near the warmth of the fireplace. The ranger had left to fetch us water, which I assumed he drew from a nearby well. I cautioned him not to go outside, but he insisted, and I relented. This was his forest after all. While he was gone, Mel had found a first aid kit in the cupboard and had cleaned and bandaged the puncture in my back. Although it hurt, it was not as deep as I'd feared.

"We can't leave John Scott and Neil," I said.

"The police will go get them."

"What if they can't find them?"

"They can follow the crosses we left just as well as you can. And maybe they'll have dogs. It's going to be a big rescue party, right?"

"We don't know who's coming."

"But the rangers would have called the police, who already know we're missing. They'll send everyone they have."

"I hope so."

She frowned. "Well?"

"What?"

"Why wouldn't they send everyone they have?"

"I never said they wouldn't."

"You don't sound convinced."

"I am, I'm sorry, I am. I was just thinking."

"About?"

"How this has to be a dream or something. I keep expecting I'm going to wake up at any moment, and we'll be back at the campfire, and Tomo will be there, and Ben, and John Scott and Neil will be fine."

"It's not a dream."

"I know."

The fire crackled and sparked.

"Who *are* they, Ethan?" Mel said. "Why are they doing this? They're just...how old were they?"

"The ones I saw? Seventeen. Eighteen. I couldn't tell. Which means there're adults around too."

She blanched. "You think so?"

"Has to be. There's no way teenagers are living out here by themselves."

"Maybe they're feral kids?"

Feral kids?

A vague tickling feeling bubbled inside me.

"You know," she added, "like those kids you read about who are raised by wolves or bears or some kind of animal."

That tickling was in my chest now, sneaking up my throat —it was Mel's expression as much as the subject matter that was causing it; she looked so serious, so stone cold sober, while she talked about kids being reared by animals—then the tickle exploded from my mouth in a burst of laughter that I couldn't control.

"Ethan, stop it," Mel said. "Stop it."

I couldn't reply; I was in fits.

"Ethan, you're scaring me!"

I shook my head. My eyes watered.

"Ethan!"

I held up a hand.

"Ethan!"

"I'm...fine," I managed, getting hold of myself.

"What's so funny?" She was not pleased.

I breathed deeply and steadily.

"What's wrong with you?" she pressed.

"I'm okay."

"Talk to me."

I looked at her and said, "Are we...?"

"Are we what?"

"Crazy?" I wiped my eyes. "Are we going crazy, Mel?"

"You're certainly acting like it."

"Are we?"

"No, we're not. Absolutely not. Besides, we both couldn't be crazy. Only one of us could be. If this was all in my head, then you would be in my head too. You'd be a figment of my imagination."

"I'm not a figment," I said, biting back more zany laughter.

"I'm not either."

"Then I suppose we're not crazy."

We were silent for a stretch.

"You know what I don't get?" I said. "Why they're playing with us. Why hang Ben and Tomo? Why not simply leave their bodies where they'd killed them?"

"Maybe they're trying to scare us."

"But why?"

"Maybe to scare us out of the forest."

"Murder two people to prevent them from camping in their forest? There has to be another reason."

"Maybe it's how they get their kicks. Maybe they're part of a suicide cult or something—"

A loud knock on the front door caused us to jump.

I got up and padded cautiously across the room.

"Hiroshi?" I said, using the name the ranger had told us before he left.

"*Hai!*"

I unlocked and opened the door.

Hiroshi entered, carrying a plastic bucket of water. He filled two glasses. Mel and I drank them quickly, refilled them, and drank more. I've read that when you're suffering from dehydration or heatstroke you're supposed to drink slowly and moderately to avoid throwing up or becoming sick, but right then I couldn't help myself. The water was an elixir.

Finally, when we had our fill, Mel and I set our glasses aside. We grinned stupidly at one another, our chins dripping wet, two kids who had just received a forbidden treat and had enjoyed the heck out of it.

For the first time in what seemed like ages I was starting to feel almost human again—and then my phone rang.

36

I stared at Mel, my puzzlement reflected in her eyes. I was suddenly terrified that she was a figment of my imagination after all, that I really was crazy, because this was impossible, there was no way my phone could be ringing.

But Slash kept on fingerpicking and Axl kept on singing.

"That's your ringtone!" Mel exclaimed.

The ceramic plate Hiroshi had been holding dropped to the floor and shattered into a dozen shards. He looked like a man who'd just cut off his own hand—and that's when it all came together.

"You!" I said, pointing at him.

He moved quickly, darting for the door. I tackled him from behind and dragged him to his knees, slipping my arms around his chest so I had him in a bear hug. He jerked and twisted, but I held him in place.

"Ethan!" Mel said. "It's him!"

"Get something to tie him up!"

"There's nothing here! What should I use?"

Hiroshi flung his head back, his skull striking my nose. I went woozy and tasted blood. Hiroshi sprang to his feet, lurched for the door. I grabbed his left foot and tugged hard. His hand slipped off the doorknob, and he dropped to his stomach with a wild, frustrated screech. I scrambled onto his back, pinning him down with my weight.

"Get the phone, Mel!" I said. "Answer it."

She ran to the other room, disappeared from my view, and after a moment shouted, "It's locked! There's a chest or something in here. It's locked."

I pressed Hiroshi's face against the floor, one hand on his temple, above his ear, one on his cheek. He was breathing quickly and with effort, his lips puckered into a fish mouth.

"Where's the key?" I demanded.

He blurted a sound that may or may not have been a word.

"Key! Where's the key?"

He scowled defiantly.

The phone stopped ringing.

Mel reappeared. "I couldn't get it."

"Come here," I told her.

She approached cautiously.

"Reach under him and undo his belt."

"To tie him up?"

"Yeah, do it."

I rocked forward onto my knees, so my weight was off his back and fully on his shoulders. Mel tried to slip her hands beneath him.

She said, "He's pressing his stomach against the floor."

"You can't get your hands under?"

"Hold on. Ow—no! He's crushing them."

I lifted Hiroshi's head by the hair, then slammed it down. "Don't," I told him. "Don't."

"*Kono yaroou.*" *You shit*—or something along those lines.

"Can you get it, Mel?"

"I'm trying..."

I slid an arm under and around Hiroshi's neck and twisted him onto his side, locking my legs around his waist. He tried to reverse headbutt me again. I flexed my biceps, squeezing his throat tighter. My face was in his hair, which smelled faintly of wet dog and apples.

Mel crouched in front of us. He kneed her in the thigh.

"Watch his legs!" I said.

She fumbled with the belt buckle and said, "Got it!" She

grabbed one end, stood, and pulled the length of leather free. I heard at least one belt loop tear, then she was holding it in front of her, at arm's length, as if it were a dead snake she had proudly killed.

I yanked Hiroshi to his feet, keeping him locked in a choke-hold, walked him to a chair, and shoved him into it.

"Tie his wrists, Mel," I said.

She crouched next to us and grabbed one of his arms. He yanked it free.

"Stop it or I'll snap your neck," I hissed, applying more pressure to his throat.

On the second attempt Mel was able to pull both his arms behind the back of the chair and secure them with the belt.

"Is it tight?" I asked her.

"I think so."

I released Hiroshi, ready to tackle him again if he tried to take off. He didn't.

I examined Mel's handiwork. The belt was wrapped around his wrists so tightly the edges of leather bit into his skin. If we left him unattended, he would be able to work himself free. But with both of us present he wasn't going anywhere.

"Good job," I said.

Mel nodded, wary, keeping her eyes on Hiroshi, as if he could still pounce at any moment.

I crouched in front of him. "Where is the key for that chest?"

He sniffed.

I slapped him across the face. "Where's the key?"

He raised his eyes. They glittered darkly, insolently.

I stood. "Watch him," I told Mel, and crossed the room.

"Wait! Where are you going?"

"I'll be right back."

I unlocked the front door, opened it, scanned the night. I dashed to the cutting block, yanked the ax free, and returned inside, locking the door again.

Mel's eyes widened at the sight of the ax, but she didn't say anything as I walked past her and Hiroshi and entered the bedroom. I grabbed the chest by an end handle and dragged it into the main room, where I examined the locking mechanism. It was polished brass and attached flush to the wood with an old-fashioned keyhole in the center. I gripped the ax like you do a baseball bat and swung it horizontally, striking the lock plate. Sparks flew and wood splintered. I repeated this three more times until the lock dangled brokenly.

I set the ax aside and lifted the lid of the chest. Inside were at least fifty wallets of all shapes and sizes, mostly men's, black and brown, though there were larger female ones as well. None were new, and most were fat with bank cards and IDs and yen notes. Sprinkled among these were dozens of shiny wristwatches, a smorgasbord of multicolored cell phones, wedding bands, a couple glittering diamond rings, and several pieces of other jewelry such as gold and silver necklaces and jewel-encrusted broaches.

I was trying to make sense of what I was seeing—I think I did understand, but my mind was overloaded and sluggish and struggling with the eureka! moment—when Mel said, "He loots the bodies."

"Damn, you're right," I said. "He's a fucking grave robber."

"He took our phones while we were searching for Ben."

"But did he *kill* Ben?" I shouted at him: "*Did you kill our friends?*"

He only stared at the fire.

Mel touched my arm. "What about the teens?"

The teens. The goddamn teens. "What's going on?" I blurted. "What the hell is going on, Mel?"

"We'll find out soon. The police—"

"Shit!" I reached inside the chest and grabbed my cell phone. On the display, under missed calls, was Derek's number.

I called it.

Derek answered on the second ring. "Childs!"

"Listen to me, Derek," I said, "and listen closely."

I summarized everything that had happened, beginning with our arrival at the base of Mt. Fuji and meeting Ben and Nina and ending with finding my cell phone in the ranger/grave robber's cabin. At first Derek thought I was having him on and kept interrupting, but soon he fell silent and listened without saying a word.

"Jesus Christ, man!" Derek said when I'd finished. "This is—I don't know what to say. What do you want me to do?"

"Is Sumiko with you?"

"She's right here. We were about to grab something to eat."

"Get her to call the police. Tell them they need to bring medicine for Neil and antibiotics and painkillers for the other guy. Then tell them to call me and trace my number and get out here."

"She's going to call them right now. This better be no joke, Childs."

"It's not. Call me back after you talk to them."

"We'll call you back right away."

We disconnected.

"YOU think he was tricking us?" Mel said, nodding at Hiroshi. "When he was on the walkie-talkie, you think he was talking about the weather or something?"

"I don't know. Maybe. I don't know what his connection is with everything that's been going on. He could be a simple thief, or he could be… I don't know."

Hiroshi said something quietly.

I turned to him. "What's that?" I said.

He began to chuckle to himself.

"Motherfucker," I said, and walked purposely toward him.

"What are you doing?" Mel asked me, alarmed.

"Getting some answers." I crouched in front of Hiroshi and grabbed the front of his shirt with both hands. "Who's out there?" I demanded. "Who are those kids who killed our friends?"

His lips parted in a thin smile.

"The police are coming. I'm going to tell them everything. I'm going to tell them *you* killed my friends if you don't tell me who's out there."

He spat in my face.

I yanked him toward me, causing the chair to topple forward. His knees struck the floor first, then his forehead. He cried out.

I kicked him in the gut. Mel told me to stop, but I ignored her. I kicked him again, harder, then swung him and the chair back into an upright position.

"Ethan, enough," Mel pleaded. "You're going to get in trouble."

I whirled on her. "Tomo's dead, Mel! And this guy knows something. Fuck trouble!"

I tore at the laces of Hiroshi's left boot, whipped the boot off, then retrieved the ax.

Mel went into a total fit. "Ethan, don't! Don't do this, think, please, Ethan, don't do this."

I stepped on Hiroshi's big toe to prevent him from moving his foot.

He was no longer chuckling or smiling.

I choked the ax so I was gripping the haft a few inches below the head. I raised it and said, "Who's out there?"

He tried kicking me with his free foot.

"Who's out there?"

He muttered something.

I swiveled the ax in my hand so the blade faced the ceiling and swung the head like a hammer. The flattened butt crushed his little toe and every bone in it.

A scream exploded from his mouth. His eyes were manic, tearing up, his nostrils flaring, perspiration popping out all over his face.

I raised the ax again, the blade facing downward this time.

"Tell me!"

Nothing.

I swung. The blade sliced through flesh and bone and cartilage cleanly, severing his ruined toe. He wailed and thrashed against his restraints as blood pooled onto the floor.

"Stop it, Ethan!" Mel shrieked. "He doesn't understand!"

"I can do this all night," I told him, ignoring her. "One, two —"

"Okay!" he said. "Okay!"

I lowered the ax, but only reluctantly.

37

"**Y**OU know history? You know Japanese history?" Hiroshi asked me after he had pulled himself together and we had plugged his toe-stump with a dishtowel.

I stared at him in amazement. Although his cadence was choppy and almost Yoda-like without the backward syntax, he spoke with a slight British accent, indicating he had likely lived overseas at some point.

In other words, he had played us as suckers.

"No?" he added impertinently. "Nothing?"

I grabbed him by the hair and jerked. "Talk!"

He tried to pull his head away, but I held firm.

"Long time ago," he said, his eyes boring into me, "many Japanese do *ubasute*."

I recognized the word—and then recalled that Honda had mentioned it back out front the train station. I said, "Families would abandon those who couldn't feed themselves."

He raised his white eyebrows. "Maybe you not dumb, huh?"

I jerked again.

"Okay—I talk!" He worked his mouth, as if to generate saliva. "Most Japanese, they stop *ubasute* one hundred, two hundred years ago. Most stop. Not all. After last war, it very difficult for Japanese. Very difficult. Many suffer. One family, they don't have food for children, so they bring them to Jukai, tell them go play. Then they leave them to die." He smacked his lips. "I'm thirsty. I talk. You get me water."

"You watch him," Mel said. "I'll get it."

She went to the counter, filled a glass from the plastic bucket, and handed it to me. I tipped it against Hiroshi's mouth, half expecting him to make a sudden move. He swallowed, then turned his head away. Water spilled down his chin and onto his shirt.

"My hands hurt," he said. "You untie?"

"I don't think so,' I said.

"Where I go?"

"Have you lived overseas?"

"You like my English?"

I didn't reply.

"You English teacher, huh?" He nodded. "Yes, yes. Why else you come my country? I have many English teacher friend from my *eikaiwa*. I don't talk them now. Not anymore. That long time ago. Sometimes I miss them. Very lonely here. Very lonely."

I released his hair. "Tell me about the children," I said.

He licked his lips, but didn't say anything.

I slapped him across the face.

He scowled at me.

I slapped him harder.

"Ethan—" Mel said.

"Stay out of this!"

I brought my hand up.

"The family leave girl and boy in Jukai," Hiroshi said, his voice croaky. "The girl, she die. The boy, he survive. He catch animals, eat berries. He smart boy. When he strong again, he leave forest, go his village. He thinks his parents forget him is accident. He thinks they happy when he comes home. They not happy. They still no food. They tell him go away. They don't want. But he don't go. He stays near village, in forest. He steals chickens, vegetables. And he sees girl. Very beautiful girl. She's farmer man daughter. One day, she disappears. Nobody knows what happen—only me."

"He brought her back here?" I said. "To Aokigahara?"

"This cabin, it built 19-7-3. I work here. My job, find the bodies. One time I find man. Maybe thirty. Maybe. I think he come here to suicide. I try to talk, but he don't talk. He run away. I look for him, for his body, for one year. But I don't find. He find me. He knows where my cabin. He lives here twenty year, maybe more. He knows forest very good."

"What did he want with you?"

"He bring me woman. She's dying. She made baby, but something wrong. Baby died, and she...she so much blood. I help her. Give medicine. Many days I help her. And I talk to man. His name Akira. He tells me everything. He tells me his parents leave him here, leave sister here. The woman he brings me, she's farmer man daughter. He took her. He stole her. They make many babies before this one, but babies don't live. They kill them. They don't have food to give them."

I looked at Mel, who was watching Hiroshi with disgusted fascination. I turned back. "What happened to his wife?" I asked. "Did she survive?"

"She die. I can't help. She bleed so much. Akira, he go away. I don't see him ten years. Maybe more. Then he comes back. He comes winter. Very bad winter. He has pneu—pneuma."

"Pneumonia."

"He has that. I give him medicine. He gets better. Then, two days later, three days, he comes back. He gives me so many gifts. Like that." He nodded to the chest. "Jewelry. Wallets. But no phones. No phones then."

"He took them off the bodies of the suicides."

"So good idea, huh? I give him rice and sugar and salt. He's very happy, very happy, and we continue to trade. Every month he gives me jewelry, money, I give him food, clothes. Finally he has good life. So he makes children. He has eight now. Only boys. No girls. He kills girls."

"The kids we saw in the forest," I stated.

"Yes, you meet already. I know."

I rose to my feet slowly, shaking my head, dumbfounded at Hiroshi's tale. A gypsy and his crew of ragtag children. That's who's been terrorizing us. I turned to Mel, to see her reaction, and found her frowning.

"You said his wife died," she said. "So who—?" The color drained from her face. "Oh no."

"He catches them before they suicide," he told her. "Then he keeps them prisoner. Sometimes you hear them scream. You hear last night? She scream so loud."

Hiroshi's narrative—my longing for answers—had held me captive until now. But suddenly it was all too much. I thought of Ben and Tomo and all the shit we had gone through, and I had to resist the urge to pick up the ax again. I said, "And our other friends? Why did he kill them?"

"He wants women. He tells me yesterday, when he gives me phones, he tells me he sees beautiful women. Very beautiful." Hiroshi smirked at Mel. "He calls you White Mother. You should be honor. He's very excited."

"So Nina…?" Mel said. "She's not dead?"

"Don't you listen? He don't kill. He wants baby. He wants her baby, and he wants your baby."

She blanched.

"Yes, yes, he comes for you," Hiroshi said, "he comes for you right now."

38

"**D**ON'T listen to him, Mel," I said. "He couldn't know that. He's lying."

"Lie?" Hiroshi seemed insulted. "His children already outside cabin. I talk them when I get water. They send message to father."

Mel said, "What if he's telling the truth?"

I shook my head. "It doesn't matter. This Akira guy, he's an old man. Has to be sixty now. I can handle him."

"You think?" Hiroshi chuckled humorlessly.

"I took you out easily enough, didn't I?"

"He and children like animal. They kill you so easy."

My phone rang, making me start, even though I had been expecting the call. I answered it immediately.

"We called the police," Derek said without preamble. "Apparently they already sent a team out there looking for you?"

"We called them yesterday with Neil's phone before it died, but they never reached us."

"Well, they said there's only one ranger cabin in the forest you're in, so they know where you are. They're going to send the team out again now."

"Tell Sumiko to call them back and tell them we need them here as soon as possible."

"I'm sure they're coming—"

"The people after us, they might be outside the cabin right

now."

"What? Christ! Okay, yeah, yeah, shit, I'll get Sumiko to call them back right now. Stay inside and hold on."

We hung up.

"The police know where we are," I told Mel. "They're coming right now."

"How long will they be?"

"Not long—"

"Ethan!" she yelped, pointing at the front door.

I spun around, but saw nothing out of the ordinary.

"What, Mel? What is it?"

"The doorknob! It was moving back and forth. Someone's trying to get in!"

39

I hefted the ax and went to the door and double-checked the lock. It was secure. I peeked out the window and saw a low, dark shape dash between the trees before moving beyond my field of view.

I swore, pressing my back to the wall.

"You still think me lie?" Hiroshi said.

"Tell them to go away."

"Why I do that?"

"Because if you let them attack us, you're going to be in big trouble."

"I already big trouble."

"No, you're not—"

"You tell your friend about me. Then Sumiko, she tells police about me."

"We can work this out."

"Why you think I explain you Akira? Because pain? Because you hit me?" He shook his head. "No, I already in big trouble."

I stalked over to him and shoved the head of the ax against his chest. "Tell them to leave us alone, otherwise I'll kill you right now."

"You learn nothing in Jukai?"

"What are you talking about?"

"Suicide! Death! You learn nothing? You don't afraid death. Death no problem, death exit. Life, that you scared. Life is monster. Life, there so much pain. You want kill me? Do it! I die with honor."

A loud bang shook the front door.

Mel yelled, stumbling backward into the wall. She slid down it like Jell-O, wrapped her arms around her knees.

"It's okay, Mel," I said, trying to parlay an absurd casualness. "They can't get in—"

Bang!

"Call them off!" I shouted at Hiroshi.

BANG!

"Call them—"

A heavy tree branch crashed through the window behind me, sending glass everywhere. I spun, swinging the ax blindly.

The blade whistled through the air and lodged with a heavy thunk into the empty window frame.

More glass shattered, from another part of the cabin. *The bedroom!* I'd forgotten about the window in the bedroom.

As I tried to jig the ax free I sensed something hurtling toward me. It struck me in the head. I staggered but remained on my feet. My hand instinctively went to the injury and came away wet with blood.

I stumbled to the center of the room.

"Stay down, Mel!" I told her.

There was more banging at the door. But the lock was holding.

I moved past Hiroshi. The bedroom door was on my right. I shoved it open. A kid was crouched on the windowsill, half in the room.

He glowered at me from behind long hair that had fallen in front of his face.

I clenched the haft of the ax with both hands and rushed him.

He sprang back outside into the night. I stuck my head through the broken window pane, inhaling the brisk air. It was all but pitch black, and I couldn't see where he'd gone.

I turned around just as another kid with a long horse face leapt at me from the bed, swinging a dagger. I parried to the left and smashed the flat of the ax head against the back of his skull. He landed in a heap at my feet.

A third kid was already coming around the bed toward me, dagger raised. He and the one on the floor must have been concealed behind the door when I entered the room a few seconds ago.

I pointed the ax at him, keeping him at bay.

He drew back his lips in a grimace, revealing several missing teeth, and hurled the dagger. I twisted sideways, to create the narrowest possible target. The blade sank into my triceps. I yelled, dropping the ax. The kid barreled into me, driving me into the wall, trapping my arms to my sides.

I was amazed by his strength. He was a tightly coiled ball of muscle, and I couldn't shove him aside no matter how much I struggled. He was snorting and grunting and reeked of sour body odor.

From the other room Mel screamed.

I bit the kid's ear, tugging at it as if it were a tough piece of beef, tasting blood. He shrieked and loosened his hold. I broke free and seized him around his throat with both hands, at the same time driving him toward the window. I shoved his head through the open space, so his back was on the sill, and leaned forward with all my weight. His hands scraped at me. I gave him a final thrust. He dropped the five feet to the ground below and landed hard. He hollered something savage and guttural at me, then crab-crawled away.

Mel screamed again.

With fading strength I plucked the dagger from my arm, seized Horseface by the collar of his yukata, and dragged him into the main room.

I registered the scene in a split second: Mel against the wall where I'd left her, her eyes locked on the largest kid yet, who just now hopped from the front windowsill to the floor. One hand was pressed against his shoulder. He must have been the one I'd struck with the dagger earlier. In his other hand he held a long stick. I noticed he had a black sash tied around his robes, while Horseface and Toothless had gray ones.

Was this arbitrary? I wondered. Or was he some sort of black-belt karate expert? That seemed a ridiculous conclusion, but karate was a Japanese tradition. And what else did you do with your time growing up in a forest? Martial arts seemed like a reasonable pursuit.

"Mel," I grunted, "get over here."

"Ethan!" she cried, seeing me for the first time. She dashed past Hiroshi, who was writhing in his chair, trying to free himself, and ducked behind me.

I hauled semi-unconscious Horseface to his feet and held him against my chest. I pressed the blade of the dagger to his throat.

"Get out of here!" I told Blackbelt. "Or I'll kill him."

He stared at me but didn't move.

"Leave!"

Still, he didn't move.

Horseface groaned, then wriggled in my hold. He was coming around.

Blackbelt took a step forward.

"Stop! Now!"

Another step.

I plunged the dagger into Horseface's thigh. He howled and thrashed. I shoved the blade back against his throat.

"I'll kill him! I'll slit his throat!"

Blackbelt stopped, then backed up slowly.

"Keep going," I said, "keep going—"

Mel shouted a warning.

I reeled around and saw a much older man with a topknot moving quickly toward us. He tossed Mel against the wall as if she weighed nothing and in the same movement bashed me in the head with the pommel of the sword he was holding.

The world bucked, then I was falling, spinning into darkness.

40

I opened my eyes. A burst of jagged pain ripped through my head. I noticed two people. They seemed to be swimming, shape-shifting, blending into one another. Gradually, however, they focused. One was Akira. He was holding a samurai sword close to his chest, the tip pointed toward the ceiling. Directly in front of him Hiroshi sat on the floor, cross-legged, staring at a middle distance. He unbuttoned his shirt, tugging the tails from his pants, revealing his nearly hairless chest and stomach. He picked up a dagger from a plate before him, holding it by a portion of cloth wrapped around the blade.

He plunged it into his abdomen.

Even as I fought to stay conscious, I tried to make sense of what I was seeing. *Seppuku*, or *hara-kiri*, was originally practiced by the samurai class in feudal Japan, an honorable way to die by disembowelment if they'd shamed themselves or failed their masters or wanted to avoid falling into enemy hands.

So was this Hiroshi's punishment for letting himself get captured by me, his way to avoid prosecution by the police?

I recalled what he'd said earlier, gibberish about dying with honor.

He drew the cut across his belly, left to right, then down in a diagonal, forming a bleeding 7. He started to slice left to right again, in what would create a Z, but he faltered. His hands were shaking badly, his face was screwed up in agony, and he didn't seem able to complete the cut.

Blood gushed from the wound as he keeled forward—

Akira brought down his sword across the back of Hiroshi's neck, ending his suffering by decapitation.

No, I realized—*near* decapitation, for he'd left a slight band of flesh between the head and body, so Hiroshi's head hung against his chest, as if embraced in his hands.

Akira walked around the lifeless body and crouched next to me. His face and neck were leathery, almost scaly, and wind-creased. His mouth was a severe, unimpressed line, pulled down at the corners. His eyes were thin and black and widely set. They stared at me with imperial indifference, as if I were a lowly peasant, scum of the earth, meaningless to him.

He drew the blade of his sword along my shirt, cleaning the blood from it.

Then he stood and went to the fireplace, pierced a burning log with the blade, and set it on the table, where the flames immediately began to feed off the cotton tablecloth.

Without another look in my direction, he left through the front door.

I faded back into the depths of darkness.

THE Harvest Fair at the Wisconsin State Fairground was an annual event held during the last weekend of September. Gary and I had gone every year as kids, stuffing our faces with cotton candy and caramel apples and running from one activity to the next. My favorite had always been the fishing pond, where you had a rod with a magnetic hook to pick up prizes floating in the plastic tub.

Now, however, it was nighttime and the fairground was empty as Gary and I made our way down Main Street.

"I always loved this place," Gary said as we passed a scattering of abandoned kiddie tractors and bales of hay.

"Me too," I said. "We got our pumpkins here for Halloween."

"Right over there, bud," he said, pointing to a sprawling

pumpkin patch. He waded into it, picked out a pumpkin, and returned to me. "Not bad, hey?"

The pumpkin was a deep orange, evenly ribbed, and perfectly round. Gary always had a knack for finding the best specimens to carve into jack-o-lanterns. I tended to go for the biggest ones I could find, which were often yellowish, the skin bumpy and indented.

"It's perfect, Gare," I said.

He nodded, though he seemed melancholy. "I was looking forward to taking Lisa here when she got older. You think Cher will take her?"

"I don't know. They're in Chicago now."

"With that new guy, right?"

I nodded.

He sighed. "I should never have done it."

I looked at him. "Done what, Gare?"

"Stopped to help the punk who shot me. Or I should have just given him my wallet. If I had, I'd still be around. I'd be able to take Lisa to the fair. One decision, bud, that's all it takes, one decision, and everything can change."

"I wish you'd just given him your wallet too."

"But you never know. That's the catch. You never know what that decision is going to lead to. Hell, how could you have known what you were getting yourself into?"

"You mean Suicide Forest?"

"There's something I need you to do, bud."

"Sure, Gare. What is it? I'll do anything for you."

"I need you to wake up."

"Wake up?"

"If you don't wake up, you're going to die. Can't you feel the fire?"

Although the night surrounding us was quiet and black, it was filled with a pulsating heat I hadn't noticed moments before.

"Yeah, I can feel it," I said.

"You have to get out."

"I don't know if I can."

"You have to. You have to help Mel."

Mel! "Is she in the fire too?" I asked urgently.

We arrived at the intersection with Grandstand Avenue.

Gary patted me on the shoulder and said, "I gotta go, bud." He started toward the field that stretched away before us.

"Gare! Wait!"

"Remember what you have to do."

"I'll come with you!"

"Save Mel..."

"I can't! I don't know how!"

But then he was gone.

Suddenly the fairground burst into flames all around me, the heat became a furnace, sucking all the oxygen out of the air—

I opened my eyes again. It was hot, so hot, and smoky, the smoke filling my nose with its acrid stench. I could barely see, but I could hear the fire, licking and whooshing. I coughed and sucked back dry, sauna-like air.

I was lying on my back. I tried to roll onto my side and succeeded on the second attempt. Everything came back then.

Hiroshi committing *hara-kiri.*

Akira setting the cabin on fire.

Where was Mel?

Smoke was everywhere, white and thick, everywhere except for down here, a foot or two off the floor. *Stop, drop, and roll,* I remembered one of my elementary school teachers telling my class during a fire drill. It wasn't bullshit after all.

Then I heard someone calling Mel's name, then my own. I crawled in a clumsy circle, searching for Mel, my eyes stinging, watering.

I bumped something heavy and round. It was Hiroshi's head. The band of skin that had connected it to his body had either torn or melted.

His eyes stared up at me, dull and unseeing.

I banged it away and collapsed forward in a coughing fit.

I'm going to die, I was thinking, *I'm not going to be able to help Mel, I'm going to burn to death in this cabin—*

Someone began dragging me.

They had me by the back of my shirt collar, so the neck line strangled me. I tried turning my head, to see who it was, but I couldn't seem to do that.

The heat vanished. A cool blackness washed over me. I thought I had died, this was death and it wasn't so bad, before realizing I was outside.

Whoever had rescued me dropped to the ground and began coughing up a lung. I was coughing just as hard, my throat stripped raw.

When this finally ended, which for a while I didn't believe it would, I extended an arm. A hand gripped mine. The person was talking to me, shaking me.

My vision focused, and I saw John Scott looming over me.

"Where is she, dude? Where's Mel? Is she in there?"

I opened my mouth, but broke into another coughing fit.

He lurched to his feet with the aid of some makeshift crutch and limped back into the burning cabin.

41

I was getting to my knees when John Scott stumbled drunkenly through the front door of the cabin. He made it only a few steps before collapsing to the ground.

I swayed lightheadedly over to him, grabbed him by the arms, and pulled him farther into the trees, out of danger.

I started back toward the cabin, but he gripped my leg.

"She's not in there," he rasped.

"There's a bedroom—"

"I checked. Everywhere. She's not there."

I stared at the cabin. Smoke billowed out of the broken window and open door. Behind that, thinly veiled, pulsed an orange furnace.

Then, dramatically, flames shot up the door frame, outlining it like a lion tamer's fiery hoop.

It would be suicide to go back inside. And I was pretty sure John Scott was right. Mel wasn't in there. She had been taken. She was with Nina now.

John Scott sat up, coughing into his hand. Soot covered his face, leaving only his eyeballs untouched.

"She's alive," I told him.

He wiped his forearm across his mouth, streaking the ash. "Where?"

"I don't know." I slumped to the ground. "He took her."

"Who took her?"

"Akira."

"Fuck, Ethos, talk some sense!" The outburst set off a paroxysm of more body-wracking coughs.

"The guy who killed Tomo and Ben," I said when he'd caught his breath.

John Scott hawked and spat. "I saw a body in the cabin."

"That's not him."

I explained everything as succinctly as I could.

"Fuck me," he said. Then: "We have to find them."

But he didn't say anything more. He understood as well as I did.

They were long gone.

MY eyebrows had been singed away, as well as the hair on my arms. The skin beneath the soot was pink and pig-smooth. It continued to hurt to breathe, making me wonder if I had some sort of pulmonary swelling. My head throbbed from where I was struck with what I believe must have been a thrown rock, but it was nothing to the pain in my back and arm, both of which were bleeding freely. Nevertheless, I inventoried all of this with distracted interest. I couldn't stop thinking about Mel: where she was right now, what she might be going through, both physically and emotionally.

When some of my strength returned, I searched for the well Hiroshi had drawn water from. I found it not far behind the burning cabin. I rotated a crude wooden crank to retrieve a bucketful of water. My thirst had been slated earlier, but now it was back, as brutal as ever. I drank greedily, then raised another bucketful, untied the rope from the metal handle, and carried it to John Scott.

I prayed the police would bring dogs with them, like Mel had suggested they might. Because that was our only hope of finding Mel and Nina, wasn't it? I could lead the police back to our camp. They could help Neil, and I could give the dogs an article of Mel's clothing, the sweater she'd been sleeping in, or her underwear. She hadn't showered for two days. Her trail would be strong.

"Hey," I said to John Scott.

We were sitting side by side, staring at the blazing cabin.

"Yeah?" he said.

"Thanks."

"Yeah?"

"You saved my life."

"My mistake."

"I'm serious."

"I am too. I was searching for Mel."

I looked at him. A smile ghosted his lips, though it didn't reach his eyes, which were distant.

"You still saved me."

"You would have done the same."

Would I have? I wondered. I hoped I would have.

"How did you find us?" I asked.

"I heard you guys shouting and screaming and shit. Mostly Mel and Nina, but I think I heard you too."

I could barely recall the ambush in the forest. It was as if I had been so focused on the immediate threats I'd ignored all the details, or hadn't had the time to store them properly.

"You can walk okay with that?" I nodded at the forked branch-cum-crutch near his feet.

"Not easily."

"You followed the crosses we left?"

"Until they stopped."

"That's when we ran."

"I was lost for a bit, but Mel started screaming again. I ended up here."

A support beam collapsed inside the burning cabin, causing a large portion of the roof to fold in upon itself with a thunderous crack.

I remembered the shōchū in my pocket. I withdrew it, uncapped it, and took a long belt. I passed it to John Scott. "For your leg—and the pain."

He accepted the bottle and downed a large mouthful.

He said, "Mel told me about you, you know."

"Yeah?"

"Your brother. He was shot."

I didn't reply.

"That sucks." A pause. "My older bro died too."

I looked at him.

"Both him and his wife. Did Mel tell you that?"

I shook my head.

"They were walking down a street in Charlotte. We grew up in Raleigh, but he moved there for work. They were downtown. It was a windy day. A wall blew over and killed them."

"A wall?"

He took another swig of the booze. "A fucking shitty brick thing along a footpath. There were cracks in the bottom of it. It just blew over. Crushed them."

"I'm sorry."

"It happened eight years ago. He was a lot older than me. Still, it changes you. It makes you...hesitant."

I frowned. "What do you mean?"

"At least for a while anyway."

"What do you mean 'hesitant?'"

"About life. The choices you make."

"What kind of choices?"

"Life choices. The big ones."

"I don't think so."

"Because you haven't made any yet."

"What the fuck are you talking about?"

"Mel's a good girl. You two are good together."

I didn't say anything.

"Don't let her get away," he said.

"I'm not planning on it," I said tightly.

"That's the thing, dude. You're not planning anything. You've been together for, what, four years? Why haven't you proposed to her?"

"I'm not ready."

"Do you love her?"

Was I really talking to John Scott about this?

"Do you, dude?"

"Yeah, I do."

"Just because you lost your bro doesn't mean you're going to lose Mel."

"I don't think that."

"Yeah, you do. I know. I've been there. Some people, after losing someone, they become scared of being alone. They get clingy, settle down, try to hold onto everything in their life. Others, like you, like me, we're the opposite. We become scared of getting close. We get indifferent toward life. We push people away. We figure we can't get hurt again if there's no one else close to lose."

I've heard all this pop psychology before, but hearing it again now, after everything I'd been through in this forest, with Mel potentially lost from me forever, I realized how true it was.

I've been pushing Mel away, or at least a life with her away. I've been so focused on the future, so scared of what might or might not happen, I've failed to live in the present and appreciate what I had now—

A distant scream rose into the night.

I sprang to my feet.

"That was Nina!" John Scott exclaimed. He pointed past me. "That way!"

It's the direction I'd thought as well. I snatched the spear and flashlight he'd brought with him off the ground.

John Scott struggled to his feet.

"Stay here," I told him. "Wait for the police."

"Fuck no!"

"You can't walk!"

"I'm not missing this."

I didn't have time to stick around debating with him. I started away.

"Ethos! Wait!" he said, conceding to the reality of the situation. "Take this." He held forth his rucksack. Three tent poles protruded from the top of the main pocket. "I've already hammered the ends into points."

I slung the bag over my shoulder.

"Thanks...John," I said.

"Stay frosty, dude. And kick some fucking ass."

42

FORGING a path with the flashlight, I picked my way through the multitude of trees as fast as I could, dodging branches and roots and volcanic rocks. I knew Mel wouldn't have gone with Akira willingly. So had he carried her away kicking and screaming? Or had he knocked her out cold, which seemed to be his modus operandi? John Scott had said he'd heard her screaming, but had that been while I was interrogating Hiroshi, or later, while I was unconscious? I almost hoped she had been knocked out, because at least that meant she would be relatively safe for the time being. Akira wouldn't rape her in that state, would he? Not to mention she would be spared the knowledge of being kidnapped and held captive deep within Suicide Forest by a gang of savages.

Nina, unfortunately, hadn't been so lucky. I was positive that had been her macabre scream ten minutes or so ago. So what had happened? Had Akira begun to violate her? But if that was the case, why had there only been one scream? Wouldn't she keep screaming and screaming and screaming until it was over—and maybe long after that as well?

TWENTY minutes now. My lungs and throat, already tender from smoke inhalation, felt seared, while my legs, my thighs specifically, burned with exertion. I had drifted into some kind of auto-pilot. One foot in front of the other, exhale on

323

every third step, bat away branches, repeat. I tried not to think about how much farther I had to go, or whether I was still heading in the correct direction. This would only lead to second-guessing, hesitation, and ultimately inaction. The only option was to run and keep running. Run until I caught up to Mel and Nina, run regardless of the pain, run, run, run.

HOW long? How long had it been now? I had no idea. I was beyond exhaustion. The air was acid, my legs deadweights, my feet dragging. I stumbled forward zombie-like, on the verge of defeat. I should have waited for the police, should have done this properly, now I was lost, unable to help—

The ground vanished beneath me. For one or two impossibly long seconds I sailed through the air, my mind anticipating the inevitable collision with whatever lay beneath me —then impact. The pain was excruciating. It felt as if someone had swung a frying pan at my face. Stars burst across my vision. Blood gushed into my mouth, far more than when Hiroshi had struck me. I remained on my chest, stupefied by what had happened, coughing, spitting out blood, though my mouth kept filling up with it, thick and syrupy.

The blackness around me was overwhelming. I blinked, thinking my eyes were closed. They were open. I must have dropped the flashlight in the fall, jarring the batteries loose, or breaking the bulb.

I tried to push myself into a sitting position and groaned. Something was wrong with my left arm or shoulder, I couldn't tell which. That side of my body throbbed, everywhere and nowhere specific. I tested my other arm. It worked. I brought my hand to my face. It was tender and pulsing. My fingers came away coated with slimy blood. I explored my mouth, my numb and sausage-sized lips. Then I became aware of my breathing. It was too loud and…large. In fact, it sounded as if it was originating outside my body—

My breath hitched in my throat. I held it there. The other

breathing continued, coarse and close.

It's not mine.

I lurched to my feet, my good hand swatting the rocky wall behind me, preventing me from falling back over. I staggered blindly along the wall of what must have been one of those massive craters. When I came to a spot where I could climb, I scrambled frantically up the jagged shelf of rock, slicing my good hand and both knees and not caring. I kept expecting something to grab my ankle and not let go.

Then I was pulling myself up and over the crater's lip. I glanced into the opening and made out a large black shape next to where I'd landed.

It's a deer, I thought, sagging with relief. *Just a deer, lying on its side.*

Perhaps I had startled it, and it had bounded into the hole. Or perhaps it had fallen in by itself and had been there for a while.

It grunted.

I stumbled away from the lip of the crevice and slumped against the trunk of a tree. I examined my left arm. I hadn't broken it, as I'd feared. In fact, most of the feeling had returned. Nevertheless, that was the extent of my good news. My body was a wreck. I was operating on willpower alone, and now that was all but gone—because my pursuit had become hopeless.

I no longer had any clue in which direction I had been heading.

I began to sink into despair. I could feel myself giving up, my mind shutting off. Maybe I'd just lie down, close my eyes, and...go away. No more pain, no more suffering. Mel was gone, who was I kidding, she was gone, and I was never going to find her—

A second scream tore through the night.

I snapped my head upright. I was on my knees.

Why was I on my knees?

The scream resumed, part-terror, part-pleading, part-anger.

And originating from somewhere close by.

I stumbled away from the tree—straight into a huge spider web. It was thick and sticky. I wiped hysterically at the silky strands, bumbling through more and more webs, unable to avoid them in the black night.

While brushing the latest one away—*where had they all come from? Was this real? Have I finally lost it?*—my hand stroked something on the back of my neck. I grabbed it without thinking, knowing it was a spider before I glimpsed it.

It was huge and plump and hairy. I flicked it away in utter revulsion.

TWO minutes later, once more questioning my sanity, whether I'd really heard the scream at all, I saw the glow of a distant fire.

43

I approached as silently as possible. I was electric with fear. Not fear of Akira or his devilish brood but fear of what I might find. I could all too easily imagine Nina or Mel hanging from a knobby tree branch by a string or ribbon, their bodies as limp as ragdolls, swinging in a nonexistent wind.

I forced the hellish images aside and concentrated on the fire ahead. I could only see the black silhouette of one person tending it. I didn't know what to make of this.

Where was everyone else?

I paused behind a tree. I had lost the tent pole I had been carrying when I fell into the crater, and now I reached back over my head and extracted a new one from John Scott's ruck-sack, leaving me with two backups. I tested the point. It was sharp. Still, I felt foolish and vulnerable. Hiroshi had been right: Akira was one hardcore son of a bitch. And his sons were no pushovers either. These would have been challenging odds had I been healthy and rested. In my present condition they were so overwhelming no bookie in Vegas would have bet on me.

I peeked around the tree. The solitary figure hadn't moved. I stole forward again.

Three long branches, I noticed, stood teepee-like over the fire, suspending a cooking pot above the heat. The person stirred the contents with a stick. He wore a tattered white robe with straight seams and wide sleeves.

This was wrong. Every fiber of my being told me this. I'd heard Nina scream. It had come from right around here. So where was she? And Mel? And Akira? And who was this lone person? He appeared too small and frail to be Akira. One of the kids then? But why was he by himself?

I tripped on something and blundered forward. When I regained my balance, I froze. The person was staring in my direction.

It was a female. She had to be about forty.

The firelight didn't reach me, so she couldn't see me. However, she had heard me and knew I was there. I tensed, ready to charge if she attempted to raise an alarm. But she didn't do anything except stare—seemingly right at me—and I began to think that perhaps she could see me after all.

I raised my hands, a redundant gesture because I was in fact armed, and approached. After ten paces the shadows began to peel away from me. I moved into the jittery light.

The woman would definitely be able to see me now, though she didn't react to my appearance—

She had no eyes. Where they should have been was only ragged scar tissue.

I came to an abrupt halt, horror and pity warring within me. I lowered my hands.

"*Sumimasen,*" I said quietly. "*Gomen nasai.*" *Excuse me, sorry.* It didn't make any sense, but I had to say something.

She didn't reply.

"*Eigo o hanashimasu ka?*" *Do you speak English?*

Nothing.

I glanced behind me, suddenly positive she was a diversion so someone could sneak up on me. No one was there. When I turned back, she was bent over the pot, stirring again.

"Akira?" I said.

She raised her head.

"Akira?" I repeated, more insistent.

She pointed to the right. I followed her finger and noticed for the first time another crater similar to the one I had fallen into, only this one was much smaller, less than ten feet across, and a perfect circle.

Was this a trap after all? Was Akira hiding there, preparing to attack?

Holding the spear above my shoulder like a javelin, I crept toward the hole.

I stared in amazement. It wasn't an isolated crater. It was more like the entrance to a ground-level cave, as a tunnel appeared to continue beyond the skylight into blackness.

Did Akira and his children *live* down there?

I glanced back at the woman, pieces of the puzzle clicking into place. She would be one of Akira's captives, a poor soul who came to Aokigahara to find death but instead found rape, mutilation, and slavery. It appeared Akira had broken her to the extent she had become a zombie, capable of no real autonomous thought or action, existing solely to mother his children and serve him.

The fate he had planned for Nina and Mel.

A frantic urgency filled me. I started down the breakdown of boulders and small rocks that created a ramp connecting the forest floor and the crater floor. At the bottom I squinted ahead into the mouth of the cave—and saw a soft orange light perhaps fifty feet ahead.

They did live down here. They lived underground like rodents.

I stepped into the cave. The air turned cool and damp and stale. I couldn't see my hands in front of me. I raised one over my head. My fingers brushed the ceiling of molten rock that had crusted over the original lava channel to form this conduit. It was ropey, the texture irregular.

I felt my way forward with my feet, straining my ears but hearing nothing.

This was madness, I thought. I was burrowing beneath the skin of Aokigahara into its very veins with no game plan in mind, no clear idea of what awaited me.

I was gripped, I suppose, by the same type of do-or-die mentality that soldiers experience when ordered to storm the enemy. There's simply no alternative.

The light ahead drew me closer, growing brighter and brighter, until I realized it was coming up through another hole.

I heard voices—faint and echoing, either excited or angry.

I dropped to my knees, peered over the lip of the window in the floor, and found myself staring into a drained magma chamber. It was easily the size of a movie theater, the rock walls spectacularly colorful, likely something to do with oxidation.

Several of Akira's kids were huddled together on the rock-strewn floor, playing a Gameboy. This, like the lantern next to them, would have been scavenged off suicides, or, more likely, acquired in a trade with Hiroshi.

The Russian folk music of *Tetris* played beneath their quick, guttural exclamations.

I didn't see Mel or Nina anywhere, nor Akira or the remaining boys. I could, however, make out the mouth of another tunnel.

I clenched my jaw. How far did this this subterranean world extend for? It could be labyrinthine in its complexity, extending for miles and miles with any number of lava tubes and fissures and caverns. And how could I get past the kids without them raising an alarm and bringing everyone to me? The only way down was to descend the talus deposit that extended away from the window at a steep angle. However, they would surely see me coming. My one advantage, the element of surprise, would be forfeited.

I moved away from the hole—and wondered if I could stage an ambush outside. I'd initially believed the zombie woman would bring the food she was cooking inside. But she was likely too weak, the pot too big, to do that. She could make several trips, but it made more sense that everyone would return outside to eat. And if this was true, and I could surprise and kill Akira instantly, then there would only be the kids to deal with, of which no more than three were old enough to constitute serious threats. It would be a difficult contest to win but not impossible. Not to mention if they did overwhelm me, and I had to retreat, I wouldn't be trapped down here with nowhere to go.

Decided, I started back.

44

THE blind woman didn't look away from the earthenware pot when I emerged from the crater. I glanced around the clearing, deciding how I was going to stage the ambush. Given that I would be vastly outnumbered, close combat was not ideal. Unfortunately, the spears were too light to use as effective projectiles. Instead I scrounged several chunks of rock the size of baseballs, which I could launch from a short distance. I slipped off John Scott's rucksack and was about to toss the rocks inside the main pocket alongside the two extra spears when I paused. There was something in the bottom of the bag. I stuck my hand in and pulled out a number of rubbery, stringy items which turned out to be the psychedelic mushroom John Scott had picked. The caps were a light brown color, the gills dark.

What the fuck had the guy been thinking? I wondered. *There were enough here to have made all seven of us see Jesus—*

Stung with an idea, I dumped the mushrooms onto the ground, then searched the pocket for any I had missed. I discovered another two handfuls and added them to the pile before me. Easily two hundred grams, maybe three hundred. I've heard mushrooms lose ninety percent of their weight when dried, the state in which most were distributed and sold, which meant I was in possession of anywhere between twenty to thirty street grams.

I tossed all of them back into the rucksack and began tearing them into pieces so they would not be so recognizable. Then I carried the bag to the fire. The woman heard me approach and stopped stirring.

"Hey there," I said quietly, amiably. "My name's Ethan. What are you cooking there?" I peeked into the pot. A variety of vegetables bobbed in a boiling yellowish broth: sweet potatoes and carrots and cabbage, as well as what looked to be strips of *daikon*, a giant white radish. "Looks good, smells good. What's your name...?"

As I continued to speak nonsense I slipped the 'shrooms into the stew, then backed away, watching the woman to see how or if she would react. She began stirring again.

Faint with anticipation, telling myself this was going to work, this *had* to work, I made my way deeper into the trees, laying up where I would not be discovered but where I still had a view of the party that was about to commence.

TEN minutes later the three eldest kids—Blackbelt, Horseface, and Toothless—emerged not from the cave but from the forest. They moved so silently I didn't notice them until they stepped into the firelight, all long black hair and gray yukatas. Horseface was limping badly, no doubt because of the stab wound in his thigh.

At first I was irrationally convinced they had been hunting for me—irrationally because they would have believed I'd died in the fire. Then I noticed that Blackbelt and Toothless were carrying dead rabbits. They clearly had better than average night vision, but I didn't think they could catch rabbits in the dark, which meant they would be returning from checking previously set snares.

Blackbelt and Toothless went to the zombie woman, while Horseface disappeared into the cave. I tensed. Would she tell them about me? Reveal I had tampered with the food?

They ignored her, withdrew their daggers, set the rabbits on a large flat rock, and chopped off their feet, tails, and heads.

Then they skinned, gutted, and jointed what was left, tossing everything except the intestines into the pot.

Shoving the zombie woman aside, they assumed stirring duty.

They didn't say much to one another, but when they did it was more grunts and snorts than words. Moreover, their postures were hunched, their body language loutish. No polite bows or nods but only violent thrusts of their chins or arms.

I thought again about what Mel had called them—feral children—and I realized how right she had been. However, these were no noble savages; they were brutal, beastly, lacking most of the social skills acquired in enculturation.

This made it easier for me to view them as less than human—and eased my reservations about the slaughter I had planned.

HORSEFACE emerged from the cave carrying a large wooden chest. He set this down next to the fire and opened it. The remaining boys spilled out of the crater moments later, pushing and shoving each other all the way to the fire, where they formed a jostling, noisy line that extended away from the chest.

Akira appeared last, rising from the earth like some battle-hardened, sour-faced samurai from centuries past. His yukata, like Blackbelt's, was secured with a black sash.

He paused at the top of the breakdown of rubble and shouted something into the skylight. I noticed he gripped three yellow ribbons in his hand. He tugged these sharply. Nina lumbered into view, followed by Mel and some Japanese woman in her twenties. All three of them were dressed identical to the zombie woman in shapeless white robes. The ribbons were secured around each of their necks, like dog leashes.

A blistering, indignant rage rose within me, and it took every ounce of my willpower not to rush forward and drive a spear through the fucker's throat.

Akira tied his end of the ribbons to a tree branch, then barked an order. The Japanese woman sat obediently, but Mel and Nina didn't clue in quickly enough. He walloped Nina across the face, then backhanded Mel, knocking them both to the ground.

I gritted my teeth and held my position.

Akira went to the fire. Horseface took a ceramic bowl and a pair of wooden chopsticks from the chest and passed them to him. Akira spent some time bent over the pot. I held my breath, convinced he had noticed the mushrooms. But when he went to sit down without incident, I realized he had likely only been choosing the choicest pieces of stew. Blackbelt served himself next, followed by Toothless, Horseface, then the rest.

They ate like animals, all of them, tipping the bowls to their mouths and using the chopsticks to slurp back the stew as fast as they could, smacking their lips, liquid spilling down their chins.

Akira and the older boys finished first and went back for seconds, then thirds. I silently urged them on.

When Akira was sated, he grunted something, and Horseface tossed a few raw vegetables in front of the zombie woman and some more in front of Mel, Nina, and the other captive. The two Japanese women ate slowly, indifferently, while Nina and Mel showed no interest in the food, even though they would have been starving.

Then the scene morphed into a surreal Saturday night with *The Brady Bunch* as everyone settled down like one big happy family. Akira sipped from a bottle of what was likely some sort of liquor and smoked a pungent pipe, both of which had been inside the chest. Blackbelt and Horseface huddled next to one another, playing the Gameboy, while Toothless pored over a manga comic. The others organized themselves into teams and played a game that involved kicking a rubber ball.

I watched and waited.

ROUGHLY ten minutes later the kids playing ball began to lose focus in their game as their trip kicked in. One after the other they stopped chasing the ball and stumbled about aimlessly, struggling with what would no doubt be intense head-and body-buzzes. Soon most of them plopped to the ground, spaced out. The biggest stared in my direction, slack-jawed, as if he'd just stuck a paperclip in an electrical socket and got the zap of a lifetime. Then he began plucking at his yukata, either trying to figure out what it was or why he was wearing something other than his skin. He bent over and puked.

Oblivious to what was happening around him, Akira stared at the bottle in his hands, apparently engaged in his own warped version of time, space, and reality. Blackbelt and Horseface remained insanely focused on the Gameboy. The music of the game they played was now the only sound to disturb the night. Toothless set aside the manga and wandered unsteadily to a tree to relieve himself. Afterward he pressed his hands against the trunk's bark hesitantly, wonderingly, as if he thought it might be moving or melting or, what the fuck, maybe even breathing. Eventually he turned around and sank to his butt. His eyes were wide and scared, his breathing exaggerated, as if he'd forgotten how to breathe and was trying to consciously replicate the action.

Akira stood suddenly and shuffled in a circle, shaking one hand, clearly struggling with some thought or idea. Then he went to the zombie woman. He shouted at her. She shook her head. He slapped her, and when she didn't respond, he slapped her harder. She bellowed something, the words butchered and unrecognizable, and pointed toward the trees where I had first emerged. Akira kept shouting and beating her. I wondered why she was holding out, why she wasn't giving me up—and then I realized that perhaps, in an ironic twist, he had cut out her tongue as well as her eyes.

Giving up on her, Akira stumbled toward Mel and Nina and

the Japanese woman. He untied Mel's ribbon from the tree branch and dragged her roughly into the firelight. She writhed and wailed. He slammed her face-first into the ground, tugged up her robe, and mounted her, using his knee to pry apart her legs.

BLACKBELT and Horseface were so stoned and fixated on the Gameboy they didn't notice me as I reared up behind them. Holding one of the spears tightly in both hands, I shoveled it into the back of Blackbelt, believing he was the more lethal of the two. It tore through his flesh with little resistance and burst out of his chest, wet with blood. Horseface stared at it in mute surprise. Then he looked back at me just as I thrust a second spear into his side, above his hip and beneath his ribcage. It hit a bone and came to an abrupt halt. He leapt to his feet, howling, spinning in pirouettes, batting at the spear hanging out of his side. I yanked it free, then drove it through his upper chest.

For a moment I felt pity and revulsion, then I heard John Scott's voice in my head saying: *Tangos down, motherfucker.*

And he was right.

Two down.

My head pulsing with a blood-rage, painting everything red, I charged Toothless, who was trying to push himself to his feet. I didn't waste my last spear on him. Instead I smothered his mouth with my hand and hammered his head backward into the tree trunk. It bounced off the wood with a hefty thud. I repeated this several more times until the back of his skull cracked like the shell of a hard-boiled egg.

I stumbled away from him and spun toward Akira. He was crouched above Mel, a dagger suddenly in his hand. His black eyes shone with a wild, primal fury as he spat gibberish at me.

I took a cautious step toward him, the spear held before me.

He continued to yell. White spittle flecked his lips like

frost rime.

I took another step.

Mel tried to scramble away on her knees. Akira grabbed her by the hair and yanked her against his body, using her as a shield.

"Ethan!" she shrieked.

"Let her go!" I roared.

Akira spat more gibberish.

It was bedlam, everyone speaking at once.

"Let her go!"

"Ethan!"

Akira again.

"Let her go!"

"Help me!"

Akira began back-pedaling, dragging Mel with him. He was trying to retreat deeper into the trees. There was no way I was letting Mel out of my sight, but as soon as I made a move to follow he screamed manically and shoved the knife harder against Mel's neck, the blade depressing the skin and tilting her chin skyward.

I halted and watched helplessly as they slipped farther into the shadows. I felt like I was going to explode. I couldn't let Akira take Mel, but what options did I have? Akira was a lunatic—a lunatic tripping out on mushrooms. He wouldn't hesitate to slit Mel's throat from ear to ear.

"Ethan!" Mel pleaded, her eyes glistening with tears.

I decided to risk a full-on charge. I couldn't lose Mel again. Couldn't bear the thought of her being held captive on her own in this forest, being raped over and over by Akira, her tongue and eyes gouged out.

Death was better than that.

"Ethan!" Mel screamed—and there was something different in her voice this time. More alarm than fear.

Arms grappled me around the neck, crushing my throat. They were slick with blood, and I couldn't pry them loose. As I grasped them with my hands, fighting to breathe, Akira and

Mel faded into the darkness of the forest.

I went berserk, twisting and bucking, and managed to rotate my body enough to see who was behind me.

It was Blackbelt. The spear I'd impaled him with was smeared red with blood and protruded a foot from his chest.

He thrust a hand in my face, his fingers digging into my eyes.

I shook my head, breaking the eye gouge. He went for them again. I bit his hand, sinking my teeth into the meaty part below the thumb.

Bone crunched. Hot, salty blood gushed into my mouth.

Blackbelt released the chokehold. I jerked around. His yukata was soaked black around the spear, his complexion ashen. Yet somehow he continued to defy death and reached for me.

I clutched the jutting spear with both hands and wrenched it sideways. He screamed and slumped to his knees. I worked the spear back and forth several times, widening the tear, causing as much damage to his internal organs as I could. A geyser of blood burst from his mouth, splashing me on the neck and chest. His body convulsed. Then he fell forward onto to his front, his left side twitching.

I glanced at Horseface and Toothless, to make sure there were no more surprises. Horseface was curled into a fetal position, unmoving, while Toothless remained sprawled at the base of the tree trunk, also unmoving. The younger ones were either ignoring what was going on or staring at me with dull expressions.

I became aware of Nina yelling at me to help her as she worked frantically at the knot tied around her neck.

I went to her, teetering slightly, and hacked through the ribbon with the tip of the spear. She threw her arms around me and squeezed tight.

"He raped me," she repeated over and over.

I tried pushing apart, but she wouldn't let go.

"Nina, stop it!" I said. "We have to help Mel!"

She released me and blinked, her eyes vacant. She was in shock, and I didn't think she knew what I was talking about.

"Stay here," I told her, then ran in the direction Akira and Mel had gone. My eyes had adapted adequately to the dark, and I was moving at a good clip, ducking branches and dodging tree trunks. I was raising a cacophony of noise, but there was nothing I could do about that. Akira had spent his life in this forest. He hunted in it. He would likely hear me coming even if I tiptoed.

From somewhere ahead and to the left Mel shouted my name.

I changed course, bowling branches out of my way.

"Mel!" I said.

"Ethan!"

I corrected my course again and fifty feet later emerged in a small grove silvered in moonlight. I was so focused on the undergrowth, watching where I stepped, I didn't see the foot until it smacked me on the shoulder.

I whirled around, thinking Akira had thrown it at me—a severed foot—but then it swung back toward me.

My eyes followed it up the bare leg, up the naked, withered torso, all the way to the head. Aside from the long black hair, which seemed impervious to putrefaction, the face was little more than a skull sheathed in patches of blistered and peeling skin.

Even after everything I'd witnessed in Suicide Forest, the sight of this latest atrocity jarred me. I bumbled away from it —right into a second pair of feet. They belonged to another woman, also naked, though she hadn't been dead for as long. Meat and fat insulated her bones and filled her plump, drooping breasts. Her pubic hair was a scraggly bush. The hair on her head was shoulder length, framing a face that once might have been considered pretty. Her eyes were half open, showing only whites.

I barreled past her, revolted to be touching her corpse, and saw another woman hanging from a tree ahead of me, and beyond that, another.

They were all around me.

There must have been a dozen or more. They were all female, all naked, all suspended five or six feet off the ground. They ran the gamut of decay, some little more than skeletons, others looking remarkably lifelike.

Akira's ex-baby makers.

"Mel!" I shouted, hearing hysteria in my voice.

Nothing.

"Mel!"

"Eth—"

She was cut off mid-word. There was a commotion. Then Akira stepped out from behind a large tree, holding her against him.

Before I could decide what to do, Mel jabbed her hand over her shoulder. I think she was holding a stick. Whatever it was it hurt Akira enough he bellowed in pain and released her. She fell to all fours and crawled away from him.

I rushed forward, spear extended.

He braced himself, dagger raised.

The spear torpedoed through his gut, all the way up to where my hands gripped the shaft. He swung the dagger in a downward arc, driving the blade into my back. He yanked it free with a kissing sound and tried to bring it down again.

I clutched his wrist. Like his sons, he was incredibly powerful, even impaled as he was, and we shuffled back and forth in a deadly waltz, neither able to gain an advantage.

Then Mel was beside me. She was trying to pry Akira's fingers free from the dagger's handle.

"The spear!" I grunted. "Get it!"

She seized the shaft and tugged it free. Akira howled and his strength faltered. I tore the weapon from his hand and plunged it into his chest.

He toppled backward and landed flat on his back.

He stared up at us, his face perspiring, his eyes bristling with rage.

I took the spear from Mel and tried to shove it in his mouth. He clenched his teeth shut. I stepped on his throat, causing him to gasp, then slipped the point neatly between his lips.

"How many people have you killed?" I demanded.

He made a rasping, choking sound.

"How many have you raped?"

He gurgled.

"Rot in hell, you piece of shit—"

"No!"

Mel and I swiveled on the spot. It was Nina. She made her way through the hanging graveyard, pushing the corpses out of her way with disconcerting indifference. She stopped in front of Akira, a reclaimed dagger clenched in her hand.

Without a word she crouched between Akira's spread legs and tore his yukata open.

He guessed what was about to happen, and for the first time fear registered on his face. He tried to roll away.

Mel and I secured his shoulders, fixing him to the ground.

Then Nina began cutting, removing his genitals.

I've never heard a man scream the way Akira screamed then. He sounded as if his soul was being torn from his body. He didn't stop even when Nina shoved his manhood in his mouth.

45

WE used the ribbons that had once bound Nina, Mel, and the Japanese woman to secure the five surviving children. This proved an easy task as they were all in a catatonic state, which I guess wasn't surprising given the amount of mushrooms they had consumed, and what they had seen while tripping out. The zombie woman had disappeared, and we didn't bother looking for her. The Japanese captive's name was Oshima Mano. She spoke basic English and admitted she had come to Aokigahara to kill herself one week ago, but she was abducted during the night and taken here, where she said Akira had already raped her four times. At this point she broke down crying because she was sure she was now pregnant with his child.

Mel and Nina and I huddled side by side throughout the night, falling in and out of sleep. By first light one of the surviving boys—the one who had been first to throw up—was responsive enough that Oshima could communicate with him. We asked him if he knew where Hiroshi's cabin was, which he did, and whether he could take us there, which he could.

The walk took twenty-five minutes. Nothing remained of the cabin except for charred ruins. To our great relief a police officer was there to greet us. He cleaned and patched up the wound in my back with supplies from a first-aid kit, then radioed the officers searching for us. When they returned, most went with the boy to Akira's camp, while two escorted us on a fifteen-minute hike to where several police cars were parked at the end of the access road Hiroshi had told us about. They drove us to Yaminashi Red Cross Hospital, located on the outskirts of Kawaguchiko. Mel, Nina, Oshima, and I were taken to separate rooms, where we were looked over by doctors, then questioned incessantly by the police. I repeated my story to several different detectives and, later, to men I believed worked for one of Japan's intelligence agencies. I was told John Scott and Neil had been airlifted to a hospital in Tokyo. John Scott wasn't going to lose his leg, but Neil remained in critical condition.

When I was finally left alone, I fell asleep and woke in the middle of the night with a scream lodged in my throat, terrified by a nightmare I couldn't recall.

As I lay awake in the dark hospital room, I was bombarded by memories of Ben and Tomo and all the horrors of the last two days.

I closed my eyes against these graphic images, but I couldn't sleep or forget, and for the second time in my life I heard the degenerate whispers of escape that suicide promised.

EPILOGUE

WINTER in the Napa Valley was nothing like it was in Wisconsin, but on some days it could get downright cold. Today was one of those days. A wind battered the windows of the study, some of the stronger gusts rattling the entire frame. The sky was gray and overcast. It would be Christmas in a few days, though without snow on the ground it didn't feel like the iconic holiday. This didn't bother me. I had become used to snowless Christmases during my time in Tokyo.

It was 7:45 p.m. I was seated in an armchair in the study of Mel's mother's house, watching an animal documentary on the small television set. My mind, however, was wandering, as it often did these days, and unsurprisingly I found myself thinking about Japan and Aokigahara Jukai.

Following our deliverance from the forest, Mel, Nina, and I had remained in police custody for close to two weeks. We had not been lauded by the Japanese authorities for putting an end to the reign of one of the worst serial killers in Japan's history. Instead we were threatened with criminal charges, the detectives interviewing us suggesting we had established control of the situation before killing Akira, thus it was no longer self-defense/justifiable homicide, and we had gone beyond the definition of "reasonable force" when we did what we did to him. I'm not sure how long they would have held us for, or whether they would have actually prosecuted us or not, but we never had to find out thanks to my parents. When I was finally allowed to call them, they relayed our story to a regional TV network. Immediately after it was broadcast it was picked up by the national news. Amid a firestorm of international attention, the police, or the politicians pulling their strings, decided to save face and released us.

Mel, Nina, and I boarded the first flights we could to LA, Tel Aviv, and New York City respectively. After spending a few weeks at the farm with my parents—decompressing, I guess you could say—I took a Greyhound bus from Madison to San Francisco, then a shuttle van to a popular winery in St. Helena, where Mel picked me up.

Mel's mother's house was a couple miles outside the town on five acres of rolling hills. Initially I enjoyed the peace and quiet the location offered. I spent the cool sunny days mowing the grass, repainting the guesthouse, weeding the gardens, fixing roofs and fences, you name it. But as I always knew would happen, I inevitably became cagey with cabin fever. This was exacerbated by the fact I found myself unemployable. When the local high school began advertising teaching positions in the newspaper for the new school term, Mel and I applied and were turned down a week later. No explanations were given, though the ads continued to run for another two months.

I wasn't completely surprised. Although the media had labeled Mel and me heroes upon our return to the States (we had been bombarded with requests for television and radio interviews, all of which we turned down), we were not the kind of heroes who had rescued a family from a burning building; we were the kind who'd committed ghastly atrocities in the name of injustice and survival.

In other words, not the type that parents—especially those in a small, close-knit community—wanted around their children. In fact, most of the townspeople shared this attitude. You'd think Mel and I had contracted leprosy the way some of them treated us when we went to the supermarket or the cinema or a restaurant.

I began pestering Mel daily about moving to LA or somewhere else where we could fade into anonymity and find work, but I stopped after her mother had the accident. One day she had been cleaning the basement and had sprayed a chemical disinfectant too close to the ancient oil furnace. Part of it blew up, causing third-degree burns on much of her body and rendering her bed-bound.

The amazing spirit and resilience Mel had displayed in the aftermath of Suicide Forest immediately left her. It was as if the accident had been the final straw, one nudge too many. She became depressed and rarely did more than sleep or clean or sit with her mother. Even the unexpected news that she had fallen pregnant didn't snap her out of her downward spiral. Both John Scott and I had tried to convince her to see somebody, to get help, but so far she has stubbornly refused.

Speaking of John Scott, we kept in touch regularly, and he was now a good friend of mine. Following his release from the hospital in Tokyo, he was redeployed from Okinawa to Fort Bragg in his home state of North Carolina, where he recently made sergeant—and where he was dating a waitress from the Hooters restaurant chain. He was still on my back about proposing to Mel, something I was now more than ready to do…as soon as I found work and could afford a ring.

And the others? Neil recovered from the food poisoning and remained in Japan, where the Japanese public had raised him onto an almost god-like pedestal. The last I'd heard his mug was starring in print advertisements of all sorts, and he was doing commercials for BOSS coffee, alongside Tommy Lee Jones. Nina moved in with her parents and was back in school studying fashion. In a recent email she asked me how "my girl-friend" was doing and mentioned she still wanted to visit the US sometime. I told her if she ever made it to the Napa Valley to come say hi. I doubted she ever would, and that was probably for the best.

There was a knock at the door.

I turned and saw Mel standing at the threshold. She wore

gray track pants and an extra-large T-shirt to cover her extended belly.

"Hey," I said, smiling. "What's up?"

"Nothing much." She returned the smile, but it didn't reach her eyes.

"Want to watch some TV?"

"What is it?"

"A NatGeo thing on cheetahs."

"No, thanks. I have to do the dinner dishes." She hesitated. "I—I felt him kick."

I was immediately on my feet. "Really?"

"Earlier this afternoon. Just once."

I went to her, putting my hand on her belly. It was strange, I had reflected numerous times since she'd become pregnant, how quickly events could change your priorities. A year ago the last thing I had wanted was a kid. Now the idea of raising a baby filled me with excitement and purpose.

"You see any more jobs?" she asked.

I shook my head. "There's that bartending thing in Oakville. But they told me I need a certificate or something to serve alcohol."

"Why don't you take the course?"

"I might. But I'm waiting to hear from the construction company in Rutherford first."

"We don't have any money, Ethan. And when the baby comes—"

"I know, Mel," I said gently. "I know. I'm looking every day. I'll find something soon. It's just that there's not much around here—"

"Oh shoot!" she said suddenly. "I forgot to give Mom her medication earlier. She's going to wake up in pain."

She retreated down the hallway. I watched her go. Then I went back to the armchair and continued watching the animal documentary.

I was just getting back into the narrative when Mel screamed.

I ran to Mel's mother's bedroom, from where Mel continued to scream. Stepping through the door was like stepping into the past, and I came to an abrupt halt, as if I had collided with a wall. Mel's mother had tied an orange extension cord around her neck and hanged herself from an exposed beam in the cathedral ceiling. Her head was cocked to one side, her neck purple and swollen, her pajama bottoms soiled.

"Oh fuck no," I breathed.

My attempts to comfort Mel were to no avail, so I ran to the kitchen and called the police. While I spoke to the dispatcher, I heard myself telling her that I didn't know why Mel's mother had hanged herself, but that wasn't true. Your boyfriend murdered by your ex. Your daughter labeled a villain by the town in which you'd lived your entire life. Your face and body disfigured almost beyond recognition by third-degree burns.

Sure I knew why she'd hanged herself.

Nevertheless, I didn't feel pity for her; I felt compounding anger.

Why did she have to choose this way to do it—knowing what her daughter had gone through?

I hung up the phone and ran back to the bedroom. Mel had stopped screaming and was now sitting on the edge of the bed. Her hands were resting on her lap. In them she cradled a matte-black .44 caliber pistol. It was her mother's. She'd bought it years ago, fearing her ex-husband might somehow break out of prison and come after her.

"Mel," I said, starting slowly forward, "set the gun down."

She raised the barrel to her right temple.

I stopped. "Mel…"

"I'm sorry, Ethan."

"Don't do this, Mel, don't do this, think about what you're doing."

"It's never going to end, is it?" she said softly, wistfully.

She cocked the hammer.

"Mel!" I said. "Don't—the baby! Mel, the baby. You do this, you kill the baby. Please don't do this. Don't kill the baby."

She frowned.

"It will be all right. I promise you. It will be okay. Think of the baby."

Tears welled in her eyes, then overflowed, pouring down her cheeks. She lowered the pistol. I crossed the space between us quickly and removed the weapon from her hand. I returned it to the top drawer of the dresser, then led her to the living room, where I pulled her against me.

As sobs shook her body my mind ran at a ferocious pace. I thought about the words she'd spoken—*it's never going to end, is it?*—and told myself she was wrong. We would put Aokigahara Jukai behind us once and for all. As tragic as her mother's death was, it meant we were no longer tied to St. Helena. We would move somewhere else. We would get jobs. Both of us. Good jobs. We would start over. I'd done that before, I'd do that again, only this time with Mel at my side. We would start over together, and everything would turn out okay.

I rocked Mel and stroked her hair and listened as the sirens approached.

Made in the USA
Columbia, SC
20 May 2020